The Hampstead Mystery

By
John R. Watson & Arthur J. Rees
1916

Double 9
BOOKS

The Hampstead Mystery
by John R. Watson & Arthur J. Rees

ISBN: 978-93-57275-35-4

Published by

DOUBLE 9 BOOKS

2/13-B, Ansari Road
Daryaganj, New Delhi – 110002
info@double9books.com
www.double9books.com
Tel. 011-40042856

ABOUT THE AUTHOR

Australian author Arthur John Rees (1872-1942) was born in Australia. He was a Melbourne native who briefly worked for the Melbourne Age before switching to the New Zealand Herald. He probably traveled to England when he was in his early 20s. In the preface to Great Short Fiction of Detection, Mystery, and Horror, 1928, Dorothy Sayers attests to his skill as a writer of crime-mystery stories. Two of his pieces were included in a detective story anthology published in the United States. His writings have been translated into German and French, respectively. On January 9, 1878, Watson was born in South Carolina. When John was 13 years old, his drunken father, Pickens Butler Watson, abandoned the family to live with two Indian women, a crime he never forgot. John Watson was given that name by his mother, Emma Kesiah Watson (née Roe), a devout woman who upheld the restrictions against drinking, smoking, and dancing. She did so in the hopes that it would assist her son be called to preach the Gospel. Watson's mother sold their farm in an effort to escape poverty and moved Watson to Greenville, South Carolina to give him a better chance at success.

CONTENTS

CHAPTER I

"Hallo! Is that Hampstead Police Station?"

"Yes. Who are you?"

"Detective-Inspector Chippenfield of Scotland Yard. Tell Inspector Seldon I want him, and be quick about it."

"Yes, sir. Hang on, sir. I'll put you through to him at once."

Detective-Inspector Chippenfield, of Scotland Yard, waited with the receiver held to his ear. While he waited he scrutinised keenly a sheet of paper which lay on the desk in front of him. It was a flimsy, faintly-ruled sheet from a cheap writing-pad, blotted and soiled, and covered with sprawling letters which had been roughly printed at irregular intervals as though to hide the identity of the writer. But the letters formed words, and the words read:

SIR HORACE FEWBANKS WAS MURDERED LAST NIGHT

WHO DID IT I DONT KNOW SO IT IS NO USE TRYING TO FIND OUT WHO I AM YOU WILL FIND HIS DEAD BODY IN THE LIBRARY AT RIVERSBROOK

HE WAS SHOT THOUGH THE HEART

"Hallo!"

"Is that you, Inspector Chippenfield?"

"Yes. That you, Seldon? Have you heard anything of a murder out your way?"

"Can't say that I have. Have you?"

"Yes. We have information that Sir Horace Fewbanks has been murdered—shot."

"Mr. Justice Fewbanks shot—murdered!" Inspector Seldon gave expression to his surprise in a long low whistle which travelled through the telephone. Then he added, after a moment's reflection, "There must be some mistake. He is away."

"Away where?"

"In Scotland. He went there for the Twelfth—when the shooting season opened."

"Are you sure of that?"

"Yes; he rang me up the day before he left to ask us to keep an eye on his house while he was away."

There was a pause at the Scotland Yard end of the telephone. Inspector Chippenfield was evidently thinking hard.

"We may have been hoaxed," he said at length. "But I have been ringing up his house and can get no answer. You had better send up a couple of men there at once—better still, go yourself. It is a matter which may require tactful handling. Let me know, and I'll come out immediately if there is anything wrong. Stay! How long will it take you to get up to the house?"

"Not more than fifteen minutes—in a taxi."

"Well, I'll ring you up at the house in half an hour. Should our information be correct see that everything is left exactly as you find it till I arrive."

Inspector Seldon hung up the receiver of his telephone, bundled up the papers scattered on his desk, closed it, and stepped out of his office into the next room.

"Anyone about?" he hurriedly asked the sergeant who was making entries in the charge-book.

"Yes, sir. I saw Flack here a moment ago."

"Get him at once and call a taxi. Scotland Yard's rung through to say they've received a report that Sir Horace Fewbanks has been murdered."

"Murdered?" echoed the sergeant in a tone of keen interest. "Who told Scotland Yard that?"

"I don't know. Who was on that beat last night?"

"Flack, sir. Was Sir Horace murdered in his own house? I thought he was in Scotland."

"So did I, but he may have returned—ah, here's the taxi."

Inspector Seldon had been waiting on the steps for the appearance of a cab from the rank round the corner in response to the shrill blast which the sergeant had blown on his whistle. The sergeant went to the door of the station leading into the yard and sharply called:

"Flack!"

In response a police-constable, without helmet or tunic, came running up the steps from the basement, which was used as a gymnasium.

"Seldon wants you. Get on your tunic as quick as you can. He is in a devil of a hurry."

Inspector Seldon was seated in the taxi-cab when Flack appeared. He had been impatiently drumming his fingers on the door of the cab.

"Jump in, man," he said angrily. "What has kept you all this time?"

Flack breathed stertorously to show that he had been running and was out of breath, but he made no reply to the official rebuke. Inspector Seldon turned to him and remarked severely:

"Why didn't you let me know that Sir Horace Fewbanks had returned from Scotland?"

Flack looked astonished.

"But he hasn't returned, sir," he said. "He's away for a month at least," he ventured to add.

"Who told you that?"

"The housemaid at Riversbrook—before he went away."

"H'm." The inspector's next question contained a moral rebuke rather than an official one. "You're a married man, Flack?"

"Yes, sir."

"So the housemaid told you he was going away for a month. Well, she ought to know. When did she tell you?"

"A week ago yesterday, sir. She told me that all the servants except the butler were going down to Dellmere the next day—that is Sir Horace's country place—and that Sir Horace was going to Scotland for the shooting and would put in some weeks at Dellmere after the shooting season was over."

"And are you sure he hasn't returned?"

"Quite, sir. I saw Hill, the butler, only yesterday morning, and he told me that his master was sure to be in Scotland for at least a month longer."

"It's very strange," muttered the inspector, half to himself. "It will be a deuced awkward situation to face if Scotland Yard has been hoaxed."

"Beg your pardon, sir, but is there anything wrong about Sir Horace?"

"Yes. Scotland Yard has received a report that he has been murdered."

Flack's surprise was so great that it lifted the lid of official humility which habitually covered his natural feelings.

"Murdered!" he exclaimed. "Sir Horace Fewbanks murdered? You don't say so!"

"But I do say so. I've just said so," retorted Inspector Seldon irritably. He was angry at the fact that the information, whether true or false, had gone direct to Scotland Yard instead of reaching him first.

"When was he murdered, sir?" asked Flack.

"Last night—when you were on that beat."

Flack paled at this remark.

"Last night, sir?" he cried.

"Don't repeat my words like a parrot," ejaculated the inspector peevishly. "Didn't you notice anything suspicious when you were along there?"

"No, sir. Was he murdered in his own house?"

"His dead body is supposed to be lying there now in the library," said Inspector Seldon. "How Scotland Yard got wind of it is more than I know. We ought to have heard of it before them. How many times did you go along there last night?"

"Twice, sir. About eleven o'clock, and then about three."

"And there was nothing suspicious—you saw no one?"

"I saw Mr. Roberts and his lady coming home from the theatre. But he lives at the other end of Tanton Gardens. And I saw the housemaid at Mr. Fielding's come out to the pillar-box. That was a few minutes after eleven. I didn't see anybody at all the second time."

"Nobody at the judge's place—no taxi, or anything like that?"

"No, sir."

The taxi-cab turned swiftly into the shady avenue of Tanton Gardens, where Sir Horace Fewbanks lived, and in a few moments pulled up outside of Riversbrook. The house stood a long way back from the road in its own grounds. Inspector Seldon and Flack passed rapidly through the grounds and reached the front door of the mansion. There was nobody about; the place seemed deserted, and the blinds were down on the ground-floor windows. Inspector Seldon knocked loudly at the front door with the big, old-fashioned brass knocker, and rang the bell. He listened intently for a response, but no sound followed except the sharp note of the electric bell as Flack rang it again while Inspector Seldon bent down with his ear at the keyhole. Then the inspector stepped back and regarded the house keenly for a moment or two.

"Put your finger on that bell and keep on ringing it, Flack," he said suddenly. "I see that some of the blinds are down, but there's one on the first floor which is partly up. It looks as though the house had been shut up and somebody had come back unexpectedly."

"Perhaps it's Hill, the butler," said Flack.

"If he's inside he ought to answer the bell. But keep on ringing while I knock again."

The heavy brass knocker again reverberated on the thick oak door, and Inspector Seldon placed his ear against the keyhole to ascertain if any sound was to be heard.

"Take your finger off that bell, Flack," he commanded. "I cannot hear whether anybody is coming or not." He remained in a listening attitude for half a minute and then plied the knocker again. Again he listened for footsteps within the house. "Ring again, Flack. Keep on ringing while I go round the house to see if there is any way I can get in. I may have to break a window. Don't move from here."

Inspector Seldon went quickly round the side of the house, trying the windows as he went. Towards the rear of the house, on the west side, he came across a curious abutment of masonry jutting out squarely from the wall. On the other side of this abutment, which gave the house something of an unfinished appearance, were three French windows close together. The blinds of these windows were closely drawn, but the inspector's keen eye detected that one of the catches had been broken, and there were marks of some instrument on the outside woodwork.

"This looks like business," he muttered.

He pulled open the window, and walked into the room. The light of an afternoon sun showed him that the apartment was a breakfast room, well and solidly furnished in an old-fashioned way, with most of the furniture in covers, as though the occupants of the house were away. The daylight penetrated to the door at the far end of the room. It was wide open, and revealed an empty passage. Inspector Seldon walked into the passage. The drawn blinds made the passage seem quite dark after the bright August sunshine outside, but he produced an electric torch, and by its light he saw that the passage ran into the main hall.

His footsteps echoed in the empty house. The electric bell rang continuously as Flack pressed it outside. Inspector Seldon walked along the passage to the hall, flashing his torch into each room he passed. He saw nothing, and went to the front door to admit Flack.

"That is enough of that noise, Flack," he said. "Come inside and help me search the house above. It's empty on this floor so far as I've been over it. If you find anything call me, and mind you do not touch anything. Where did you say the library was?"

"I don't know, sir."

"Well, look about you on the ground floor while I go upstairs. Call me if you hear anything."

Inspector Seldon mounted the stairs swiftly in order to continue his search.

The staircase was a wide one, with broad shallow steps, thickly carpeted, and a handsome carved mahogany baluster. The inspector, flashing his torch as he ran up, saw a small electric light niche in the wall before he reached the first landing. The catch of the light was underneath, and Inspector Seldon turned it on. The light revealed that the stairs swept round at that point to the landing of the first floor, which was screened from view by heavy velvet hangings, partly caught back by the bent arm of a marble figure of Diana, which faced downstairs, with its other arm upraised and about to launch a hunting spear. By this graceful device the curtains were drawn back sufficiently to give access to the corridor on the first floor.

Inspector Seldon looked closely at the figure and the hangings. Something strange about the former arrested his eye. It was standing awry on its pedestal—was, indeed, almost toppling over. He looked up and saw that one of the curtains supported by the arm hung loosely from one of the curtain rings. It was as though some violent hand had torn at the curtain in passing, almost dragging it from the pole and precipitating the figure down the stairs. Immediately beyond the landing, in the corridor, was a door on the right, flung wide open.

The inspector entered the room with the open door. It was a large room forming part of the front of the house—a lofty large room, partly lighted by the half-drawn blind of one of the windows. One side was lined with bookshelves. In the corner of the room farthest from the door, was a roll-top desk, which was open. In the centre of the room was a table, and a huddled up figure was lying beside it, in a dark pool of blood which had oozed into the carpet.

The inspector stepped quickly back to the landing.

"Flack!" he called, and unconsciously his voice dropped to a sharp whisper in the presence of death. "Flack, come here."

When Flack reached the door of the library he saw his chief kneeling beside the prostrate body of a dead man. The body lay clear of the table, near the foot of an arm-chair. Instinctively Flack walked on tiptoe to his chief.

"Is he dead, sir?" he asked.

"Cold and stiff," replied the inspector, in a hushed voice. "He's been dead for hours."

Flack noted that the body was fully dressed, and he saw a dark stain above the breast where the blood had welled forth and soaked the dead man's clothes and formed a pool on the carpet beside him.

Inspector Seldon opened the dead man's clothes. Over his heart he found the wound from which the blood had flowed.

"There it is, Flack," he said, touching the wound lightly with his finger. "It doesn't take a big wound to kill a man."

As he spoke the sharp ring of a telephone bell from downstairs reached them.

"That's Inspector Chippenfield," said Inspector Seldon, rising to his feet. "Stay here, Flack, till I go and speak to him."

CHAPTER II

"Six-thirty edition: High Court Judge murdered!"

It was not quite 5 p.m., but the enterprising section of the London evening newspapers had their 6.30 editions on sale in the streets. To such a pitch had the policy of giving the public what it wants been elevated that the halfpenny newspapers were able to give the people of London the news each afternoon a full ninety minutes before the edition was supposed to have left the press. The time of the edition was boldly printed in the top right-hand corner of each paper as a guarantee of enterprise if not of good faith. On practical enterprise of this kind does journalism forge ahead. Some people who have been bred up in a conservative atmosphere sneer at such journalistic enterprise. They affect to regard as unreliable the up-to-date news contained in newspapers which are unable to tell the truth about the hands of the clock.

From the cries of the news-boys and from the announcements on the newspaper bills which they displayed, it was assumed by those with a greedy appetite for sensations that a judge of the High Court had been murdered on the bench. Such an appetite easily swallowed the difficulty created by the fact that the Law Courts had been closed for the long vacation. In imagination they saw a dramatic scene in court—the disappointed demented desperate litigant suddenly drawing a revolver and with unerring aim shooting the judge through the brain before the deadly weapon could be wrenched from his hands. But though the sensation created by the murder of a judge of the High Court was destined to grow and to be fed by unexpected developments, the changing phases of which monopolised public attention throughout England on successive occasions, there was little in the evening papers to satisfy the appetite for sensation. In journalistic vernacular "they were late in getting on to it," and therefore their reference to the crime occupied only a few lines in the "stop press news," beneath some late horse-racing results.

The *Evening Courier*, which was first in the streets with the news, made its announcement of the crime in the following brief paragraph:

"The dead body of Sir Horace Fewbanks, the distinguished High Court judge, was found by the police at his home, Riversbrook in Tanton Gardens, Hampstead, to-day. Deceased had been shot through the heart. The police have no doubt that he was murdered."

But the morning papers of the following day did full justice to the sensation. It was the month of August when Parliament is "up," the Law Courts closed for the long vacation, and when everybody who is anybody is out of London for the summer holidays. News was scarce and the papers vied with one another in making the utmost of the murder of a High Court judge. Each of the morning papers sent out a man to Hampstead soon after the news of the crime reached their offices in the afternoon, and some of the more enterprising sent two or three men. Scotland Yard and Riversbrook were visited by a succession of pressmen representing the London dailies, the provincial press, and the news agencies.

The two points on which the newspaper accounts of the tragedy laid stress were the mysterious letter which had been sent to Scotland Yard stating that Sir Horace Fewbanks had been murdered, and the mystery surrounding the sudden return of Sir Horace from Scotland to his town house. On the first point there was room for much varied speculation. Why was information about the murder sent to Scotland Yard, and why was it sent in a disguised way? If the person who had sent this letter had no connection with the crime and was anxious to help the police, why had he not gone to Scotland Yard personally and told the detectives all he knew about the tragedy? If, on the other hand, he was implicated in the crime, why had he informed the police at all?

It would have been to his interest as an accomplice—even if he had been an unwilling accomplice—to leave the crime undiscovered as long as possible, so that he and those with whom he had been associated might make their escape to another country. But he had sent his letter to Scotland Yard within a few hours of the perpetration of the crime, and had not given the actual murderer time to get out of England. Was he not afraid of the vengeance the actual murderer would endeavour to exact for this disclosure which would enable the police to take measures to prevent his escape?

No light was thrown on the cause of the murdered man's sudden return from grouse-shooting in Scotland. The newspaper accounts, though they differed greatly in their statements, surmises, and suggestions concerning the tragedy, agreed on the point that Sir Horace had been a keen sportsman and was a very fine shot. In years past he had made a practice of spending the early part of the long vacation in Scotland, going there for the opening of the grouse season on the 12th of August. This year he had been one of a party of five who had rented Craigleith Hall in the Western Highlands, and after five days' shooting he had announced that he had to go to London on urgent business, but would return in the course of a week or less. It was suggested in some of the newspaper accounts that an explanation of the cause of his return might throw some light on the murder. Inquiries were being made at Craigleith Hall to ascertain the reason for his journey to London, or whether any telegram had been received by him previous to his departure.

The fact that one of the windows on the ground floor of Riversbrook had been found open was regarded as evidence that the murderer had broken into the house. Imprints of footsteps had been found in the ground outside the window, and the police had taken several casts of these; but whether the man who had broken into the house with the intention of committing burglary or murder was a matter on which speculation differed. If the murderer was a criminal who had broken into the house with the intention of committing a burglary, there could be no connection between the return of Sir Horace Fewbanks from Scotland and his murder. The burglary had probably been arranged in the belief that the house was empty, Sir Horace having sent the servants away to his country house in Dellmere a week before. But if the murderer was a burglar he had stolen nothing and had not even collected any articles for removal. The only thing that was known to be missing was the dead man's pocket-book, but there was nothing to prove that the murderer had stolen it. It was quite possible that it had been lost or mislaid by Sir Horace; it was even possible that it had been stolen from him in the train during his journey from Scotland.

It might be that while prowling through the rooms after breaking into the house, and before he had collected any goods for removal, the burglar had come unexpectedly on Sir Horace, and after shooting him had fled from the house. Only as a last resort to prevent capture did burglars commit murder. Had Sir Horace been shot while attempting to seize the intruder? The position in which the body was found did not support that theory. Two shots had been fired, the first of which had missed its victim, and entered the wall of the library. Evidently the murdered man had been hit by the second while attempting to leave the room. It was ingeniously suggested by the *Daily Record* that the murderer was a criminal who knew Sir Horace, and was known to him as a man who had been before him at Old Bailey. This would account for Sir Horace being ruthlessly shot down without having made any attempt to seize the intruder. The burglar would have felt on seeing Sir Horace in the room that he was identified, and that the only way of escaping ultimate arrest by the police was to kill the man who could put the police on his track. Mr. Justice Fewbanks had had the reputation of being a somewhat severe judge, and it was possible that some of the criminals who had been sentenced by him at Old Bailey entertained a grudge against him.

The question of when the murder was committed was regarded as important. Dr. Slingsby, of the Home Office, who had examined the body shortly after it was discovered by the police, was of opinion that death had taken place at least twelve hours before and probably longer than that. His opinion on this point lent support to the theory that the murder had been committed before midnight on Wednesday. It was the *Daily Record* that seized on the mystery contained in the facts that the body when discovered was fully clothed and that the electric lights were not turned on. If the murder was committed late at night how came it that there were no lights in the empty house when the police discovered the body? Had the murderer, after shooting his victim, turned out the lights so that on the following day no suspicion would be created as would be the case if anyone saw lights burning in the house in the day-time? If he had done so, he was a cool hand. But if the burglar was such a cool hand as to stop to turn out the lights after the murder why did he not also stop to collect some valuables? Was he afraid that in attempting to get rid of them to a "fence" or "drop" he would practically reveal himself as the murderer and so place himself in danger in case the police offered a reward for the apprehension of the author of the crime?

If Sir Horace had gone to bed before the murderer entered the house it would have been natural to expect no lights turned on. But he had returned unexpectedly; there were no servants in the house, and there was no bed ready for him. In any case, if he intended stopping in the empty house instead of going to a hotel he would have been wearing a sleeping suit when his body was discovered; or, at most, he would be only partially dressed if he had got up on hearing somebody moving about the house. But the body was fully dressed, even to collar and tie. It was absurd to suppose that the victim had been sitting in the darkness when the murderer appeared.

Another difficult problem Scotland Yard had to face was the discovery of the person who had sent them the news of the murder. How had Scotland Yard's anonymous correspondent learned about the murder, and what were his motives in informing the police in the way he had done? Was he connected with the crime? Had the murderer a companion with him when he broke into Riversbrook for the purpose of burglary? That seemed to be the most probable explanation. The second man had been horrified at the murder, and desired to disassociate himself from it so that he might escape the gallows. The only alternative was to suppose that the murderer had confessed his crime to some one, and that his confidant had lost no time in informing the police of the tragedy.

The newspaper accounts of the case threw some light on the private and domestic affairs of the victim. He was a widower with a grown-up daughter; his wife, a daughter of the late Sir James Goldsworthy, who changed his ancient family patronymic from Granville to Goldsworthy on inheriting the great fortune of an American kinsman, had died eight years before. Sir Horace's Hampstead household consisted of a housekeeper, butler, chauffeur, cook, housemaid, kitchenmaid and gardener. With the exception of the butler the servants had been sent the previous week to Sir Horace's country house in Dellmere, Sussex. It appeared that Miss Fewbanks spent most of her time at the country house and came up to London but rarely. She was at Dellmere when the murder was committed, and had been under the impression that her father was in Scotland. According to a report received from the police at Dellmere the first intimation that Miss Fewbanks had received of the tragic death of her father came from them. Naturally, she was prostrated with grief at the tragedy.

The butler who had been left behind in charge of Riversbrook was a man named Hill, but he was not in the house on the night of the tragedy. He was a married man, and his wife and child lived in Camden Town, where Mrs. Hill kept a confectionery shop. Hill's master had given him permission to live at home for three weeks while he was in Scotland. The house in Tanton Gardens had been locked up and most of the valuables had been sent to the bank for safe-keeping, but there were enough portable articles of value in the house to make a good haul for any burglar. Hill had instructions to visit the house three times a week for the purpose of seeing that everything was safe and in order. He had inspected the place on Wednesday morning, and everything was as it had been left when his master went to Scotland. Sir Horace Fewbanks had returned to London on Wednesday evening, reaching St. Pancras by the 6.30 train. Hill was unaware that his master was returning, and the first he learned of the murder was the brief announcement in the evening papers on Thursday.

CHAPTER III

Inspector Chippenfield, who had come into prominence in the newspapers as the man who had caught the gang who had stolen Lady Gladville's jewels—which included the most costly pearl necklace in the world—was placed in charge of the case. It was to his success in this famous case that he owed his promotion to Inspector. He had the assistance of his subordinate, Detective Rolfe. So generous were the newspaper references to the acumen of these two terrors of the criminal classes that it was to be assumed that anything which inadvertently escaped one of them would be pounced upon by the other.

On the morning after the discovery of the murdered man's body, the two officers made their way to Tanton Gardens from the Hampstead tube station. Inspector Chippenfield was a stout man of middle age, with a red face the colour of which seemed to be accentuated by the daily operation of removing every vestige of hair from it. He had prominent grey eyes with which he was accustomed to stare fiercely when he desired to impress a suspected person with what some of the newspapers had referred to as "his penetrating glance." His companion, Rolfe, was a tall well-built man in the early thirties. Like most men in a subordinate position, Rolfe had not a high opinion of the abilities of his immediate superiors. He was sure that he could fill the place of any one of them better than it was filled by its occupant. He believed that it was the policy of superiors to keep junior men back, to stand in their light, and to take all the credit for their work. He was confident that he was destined to make a name for himself in the detective world if only he were given the chance.

When Inspector Chippenfield had visited Riversbrook the previous afternoon, Rolfe had not been selected as his assistant. A careful inspection of the house and especially of the room in which the tragedy had been committed had been made by the inspector. He had then turned his attention to the garden and the grounds surrounding the house.

Whatever he had discovered and what theories he had formed were not disclosed to anyone, not even his assistant. He believed that the proper way to train a subordinate was to let him collect his own information and then test it for him. This method enabled him to profit by his subordinate's efforts and to display a superior knowledge when the other propounded a theory by which Inspector Chippenfield had also been misled.

When they arrived at the house in which the crime had been committed, they found a small crowd of people ranging from feeble old women to babies in arms, and including a large proportion of boys and girls of school age, collected outside the gates, staring intently through the bars towards the house, which was almost hidden by trees. The morbid crowd made way for the two officers and speculated on their mission. The general impression was that they were the representatives of a fashionable firm of undertakers and had come to measure the victim for his coffin. Inside the grounds the Scotland Yard officers encountered a police-constable who was on guard for the purpose of preventing inquisitive strangers penetrating to the house.

"Well, Flack," said Inspector Chippenfield in a tone in which geniality was slightly blended with official superiority. "How are you to-day?"

"I'm very well indeed, sir," replied the police-constable. He knew that the state of his health was not a matter of deep concern to the inspector, but such is the vanity of human nature that he was pleased at the inquiry. The fact that there was a murdered man in the house gave mournful emphasis to the transience of human life, and made Police-Constable Flack feel a glow of satisfaction in being very well indeed.

Inspector Chippenfield hesitated a moment as if in deep thought. The object of his hesitation was to give Flack an opportunity of imparting any information that had come to him while on guard. The inspector believed in encouraging people to impart information but regarded it as subversive of the respect due to him to appear to be in need of any. As Flack made no attempt to carry the conversation beyond the state of his health, Inspector Chippenfield came to the conclusion that he was an extremely dull policeman. He introduced Flack to Detective Rolfe and explained to the latter:

"Flack was on duty on the night of the murder but heard no shots. Probably he was a mile or so away. But in a way he discovered the crime. Didn't you, Flack? When we rang up Seldon he came up here and brought Flack with him. He'll be only too glad to tell you anything you want to know."

Rolfe took an official notebook from a breast pocket and proceeded to question the police-constable. The inspector made his way upstairs to the room in which the crime had been committed, for it was his system to seek inspiration in the scene of a crime.

Tanton Gardens, a short private street terminating in a cul-de-sac, was in a remote part of Hampstead. The daylight appearance of the street betokened wealth and exclusiveness. The roadway which ran between its broad white-gravelled footwalks was smoothly asphalted for motor tyres; the avenues of great chestnut trees which flanked the footpaths served the dual purpose of affording shade in summer and screening the houses of Tanton Gardens from view. But after nightfall Tanton Gardens was a lonely and gloomy place, lighted only by one lamp, which stood in the high road more to mark the entrance to the street than as a guide to traffic along it, for its rays barely penetrated beyond the first pair of chestnut trees.

The houses in Tanton Gardens were in keeping with the street: they indicated wealth and comfort. They were of solid exterior, of a size that suggested a fine roominess, and each house stood in its own grounds. Riversbrook was the last house at the blind end of the street, and its east windows looked out on a wood which sloped down to a valley, the street having originally been an incursion into a large private estate, of which the wood alone remained. On the other side a tangled nutwood coppice separated the judge's residence from its nearest neighbours, so the house was completely isolated. It stood well back in about four acres of ground, and only a glimpse of it could be seen from the street front because of a small plantation of ornamental trees, which grew in front of the house and hid it almost completely from view. When the carriage drive which wound through the plantation had been passed the house burst abruptly into view—a big, rambling building of uncompromising ugliness. Its architecture was remarkable. The impression which it conveyed was that the original builder had been prevented by lack of money from carrying out his original intention of erecting a fine symmetrical house. The first story was well enough—an imposing, massive, colonnaded front in the Greek style, with marble pillars supporting the entrance. But the two stories surmounting this failed lamentably to carry on the pretentious design. Viewed from the front, they looked as though the builder, after erecting the first story, had found himself in pecuniary straits, but, determined to finish his house somehow, had built two smaller stories on the solid edifice of the first. For the two second stories were not flush with the front of the house, but reared themselves from several feet behind, so that the occupants of the bedrooms on the first story could have used the intervening space as a balcony. Viewed from the rear, the architectural imperfections of the upper part of the house were in even stronger contrast with the ornamental first story. Apparently the impecunious builder, by the time he had reached the rear, had completely run out of funds, for on the third floor he had failed altogether to build in one small room, and had left the unfinished brickwork unplastered.

The large open space between the house and the fir plantation had once been laid out as an Italian garden at the cost of much time and money, but Sir Horace Fewbanks had lacked the taste or money to keep it up, and had allowed it to become a luxuriant wilderness, though the sloping parterres and the centre flowerbeds still retained traces of their former beauty. The small lake in the centre, spanned by a rustic hand-bridge, was still inhabited by a few specimens of the carp family—sole survivors of the numerous gold-fish with which the original designer of the garden had stocked the lake.

Sir Horace Fewbanks had rented Riversbrook as a town house for some years before his death, having acquired the lease cheaply from the previous possessor, a retired Indian civil servant, who had taken a dislike to the place because his wife had gone insane within its walls. Sir Horace had lived much in the house alone, though each London season his daughter spent a few weeks with him in order to preside over the few Society functions that her father felt it due to his position to give, and which generally took the form of solemn dinners to which he invited some of his brother judges, a few eminent barristers, a few political friends, and their wives. But rumour had whispered that the judge and his daughter had not got on too well together—that

Miss Fewbanks was a strange girl who did not care for Society or the Society functions which most girls of her age would have delighted in, but preferred to spend her time on her father's country estate, taking an interest in the villagers or walking the country-side with half a dozen dogs at her heels.

Rumour had not spared the dead judge's name. It was said of him that he was fond of ladies' society, and especially of ladies belonging to a type which he could not ask his daughter to meet; that he used to go out motoring, driving himself, after other people were in bed; and that strange scenes had taken place at Riversbrook. Flack had told his wife on several occasions that he had heard sounds of wild laughter and rowdy singing coming from Riversbrook as he passed along the street on his beat in the small hours of the morning. Several times in the early dawn Flack had seen two or three ladies in evening dress come down the carriage drive and enter a taxi-cab which had been summoned by telephone.

CHAPTER IV

W hen Rolfe had finished questioning Police-Constable Flack and joined his chief upstairs, the latter, who had been going through the private papers in the murdered man's desk in the hope of alighting on a clue to the crime, received him genially.

"Well," he said, "what do you think of Flack?"

Rolfe had obtained from the police-constable a straightforward story of what he had seen, and in this way had picked up some useful information about the crime which it would have taken a long time to extract from the inspector, but he was a sufficiently good detective to have learned that by disparaging the source of your information you add to your own reputation for acumen in drawing conclusions in regard to it. He nodded his head in a deprecating way and emitted a slight cough which was meant to express contempt.

"It looks very much like a case of burglary and murder," he said.

He was anxious to know what theory his superior officer had formed.

"And how do you fit in the letter advising us of the murder?" asked the inspector.

He produced the letter from his pocket-book and looked at it earnestly.

"There were two of them in it—one a savage ruffian who will stick at nothing, and the other a chicken-hearted specimen. They often work in pairs like that."

"So your theory is that one of the two shot him, and the other was so unnerved that he sent us the letter and put us on the track to save his own neck?"

"Something like that."

"It is not impossible," was the senior officer's comment. "Mind you, I don't say it is my theory. In fact, I am in no hurry to form one.

I believe in going carefully over the whole ground first, collecting all the clues and then selecting the right one."

Rolfe admitted that his chief's way of setting to work to solve a mystery was an ideal one, but he made the reservation that it was a difficult one to put into operation. He was convinced that the only way of finding the right clue was to follow up every one until it was proved to be a wrong one.

Inspector Chippenfield continued his study of the mysterious message which had been sent to Scotland Yard. It was written on a sheet of paper which had been taken from a writing pad of the kind sold for a few pence by all stationers. It was flimsy and blue-lined, and the message it contained was smudged and badly printed. But to the inspector's annoyance, there were no finger-prints on the paper. The finger-print expert at Scotland Yard had examined it under the microscope, but his search for finger-prints had been vain.

"Depend upon it, we'll hear from this chap again," said the inspector, tapping the sheet of paper with a finger. "I think I may go so far as to say that this fellow thinks suspicion will be directed to him and he wants to save his neck."

"It's a disguised hand," said Rolfe. "Of course he printed it in order not to give us a specimen of his handwriting. There are telltale things about a man's handwriting which give him away even when he tries to disguise it. But he's tried to disguise even his printing. Look how irregular the letters are—some slanting to the right and some to the left, and some are upright. Look at the two different kinds of 'U's.'"

"He's used two different kinds of pens," said Inspector Chippenfield. "Look at the difference in the thickness of the letters."

"The sooner he writes again the better," said Rolfe. "I am curious to know what he'll say next."

"My idea is to find out who he is and make him speak," said the inspector, "Speaking is quicker than writing. I could frighten more out of him in ten minutes than he would give away voluntarily in a month of Sundays."

Again Rolfe had to admit that his chief's plan to get at the truth was an ideal one.

"Have you any idea who he is?" he asked.

Inspector Chippenfield had brought his methods too near to perfection to make it possible for him to fall into an open trap.

"I won't be very long putting my hand on him," he said.

"But this thing has been in the papers," said Rolfe. "Don't you think the murderer will bolt out of the country when he knows his mate is prepared to turn King's evidence against him?"

"Ah," said Inspector Chippenfield, "I haven't adopted your theory."

"Then you think that the man who wrote this note knew of the murder but doesn't know who did it?"

"Now you are going too far," said Inspector Chippenfield.

The inspector was so wary about disclosing what was in his mind in regard to the letter that Rolfe, who disliked his chief very cordially, jumped to the conclusion that Inspector Chippenfield had no intelligible ideas concerning it.

"If it was burglars they took nothing as far as we can ascertain up to the present," said Inspector Chippenfield after a pause.

"They were surprised to find anyone in the house. And after the shot was fired they immediately bolted for fear the noise would attract attention."

"What knocks a hole in the burglar theory is the fact that Sir Horace was fully dressed when he was shot," said the inspector. "Burglars don't break into a house when there are lights about, especially after having been led to believe that the house was empty."

"So you think," said Rolfe, "that the window was forced after the murder with the object of misleading us."

"I haven't said so," replied the inspector. "All I am prepared to say is that even that was not impossible."

"It was forced from the outside," continued Rolfe. "I've seen the marks of a jemmy on the window-sill. If it was forced after the murder the murderer was a cool hand."

"You can take it from me," exclaimed Inspector Chippenfield with unexpected candour, "that he was a cool hand. We are going to have a bit of trouble in getting to the bottom of this, Rolfe."

"If anyone can get to the bottom of it, you can," said Rolfe, who believed with Voltaire that speech was given us in order to enable us to conceal our thoughts.

Inspector Chippenfield was so astonished at this handsome compliment that he began to think he had underrated Rolfe's powers of discernment. His tone of cold official superiority immediately thawed.

"There were two shots fired," he said, "but whether both were fired by the murderer I don't know yet. One of them may have been fired by Sir Horace. Just behind you in the wall is the mark of one of the bullets. I dug it out of the plaster yesterday and here it is." He produced from a waistcoat pocket a flattened bullet. "The other is inside him at present." He waved his hand in the direction of the room in which the corpse lay.

"Of course you cannot say yet whether both bullets are out of the same revolver?" said Rolfe.

"Can't tell till after the post-mortem," said the inspector. "And then all we can tell for certain is whether they are of the same pattern. They might be the same size, and yet be fired out of different revolvers of the same calibre."

"Well, it is no use theorising about what happened in this room until after the post-mortem," said Rolfe.

"You'd better give it some thought," suggested the inspector. "In the meantime I want you to interview the people in the neighbourhood and ascertain whether they heard any shots. They'll all say they did whether they heard them or not—you know how people persuade themselves into imagining things so as to get some sort of prominence in these crimes. But you can sift what they tell you and preserve the grain of truth. Try and get them to be accurate as to the time, as we want to fix the time of the crime as near as possible. Ask Flack to tell you something about the neighbours—he's been in this district fifteen years, and ought to know all about them. While you're away I'll go through these private papers. I want to find out why he came back from Scotland so suddenly. If we knew that the rest might be easy."

"I haven't seen the body yet," said Rolfe. "I'd like to look at it. Where is it?"

"I had it removed downstairs. You will find it in a big room on the left as you go down the hall. By the by, there is another matter, Rolfe. This glove was found in the room. It may be a clue, but it is more likely that it is one of Sir Horace's gloves and that he lost the other one on his way up from Scotland. It's a left-hand glove—men always lose the right-hand glove because they take it off so often. I've compared it with other gloves in Sir Horace's wardrobe, and I find it is the same size and much the same quality. But find out from Sir Horace's hosier if he sold it. Here's the address of the hosiers,—Bruden and Marshall, in the Strand."

Rolfe went slowly downstairs into the room in which the corpse lay, and closed the door behind him. It was a very large room, overlooking the garden on the right side of the house. Somebody had lowered the Venetian blinds as a conventional intimation to the outside world that the house was one of mourning, and the room was almost dark. For nearly a minute Rolfe stood in silence, his hand resting on the knob of the door he had closed behind him. Gradually the outline of the room and the objects within it began to reveal themselves in shadowy shape as his eyes became accustomed to the dim light. He had a growing impression of a big lofty room, with heavy furniture, and a huddled up figure lying on a couch at the end furthest from the window and deepest in shadow.

He stepped across to the window and gently raised one of the blinds. The light of an August sun penetrated through the screen of trees in front of the house and revealed the interior of the room more clearly. Rolfe was amazed at its size. From the window to the couch at the other end of the room, where the body lay, was nearly thirty feet. Glancing down the apartment, he noticed that it was really two rooms, divided in the middle by folding doors. These doors folded neatly into a slightly protruding ridge or arch almost opposite the door by which he had entered, and were screened from observation by heavy damask curtains, which drooped over the archway slightly into the room.

Evidently the deceased judge had been in the habit of using the divided rooms as a single apartment, for the heavier furniture in both halves of it was of the same pattern. The chairs and tables were of heavy, ponderous, mid-Victorian make, and they were matched by a number of old-fashioned mahogany sideboards and presses, arranged methodically at regular intervals on both sides of the room. Rolfe, as his eye took in these articles, wondered why Sir Horace Fewbanks had bought so many. One sideboard, a vast piece of furniture fully eight feet long, had a whisky decanter and siphon of soda water on it, as though Sir Horace had served himself with refreshments on his return to the house. The tops of the other sideboards were bare, and the presses, use in such a room Rolfe was at a loss to conjecture, were locked up. The antique sombre uniformity of the furniture as a whole was broken at odd intervals by several articles of bizarre modernity, including a few daring French prints, which struck an odd note of incongruity in such a room.

The murdered man had been laid on an old-fashioned sofa at the end of this double apartment which was furthest from the window. Rolfe walked slowly over the thick Turkey carpets and rugs with which the floor was covered, glanced at the sofa curiously, and then turned down the sheet from the dead man's face.

At the time of his death Sir Horace Fewbanks was 58 years of age, but since death the grey bristles had grown so rapidly through his clean-shaven face that he looked much older. The face showed none of the wonted placidity of death. The mouth was twisted in an ugly fashion, as though the murdered man had endeavoured to cry for help and had been attacked and killed while doing so. One of Sir Horace's arms—the right one—was thrust forward diagonally across his breast as if in self-defence, and the hand was tightly clenched. Rolfe, who had last seen His Honour presiding on the Bench in the full pomp and majesty of law, felt a chill strike his heart at the fell power of death which did not even respect the person of a High Court judge, and had stripped him of every vestige of human dignity in the pangs of a violent end. The face he had last seen on the Bench full of wisdom and austerity of the law was now distorted into a livid mask in which it was hard to trace any semblance of the features of the dead judge.

Rolfe's official alertness of mind in the face of a mysterious crime soon reasserted itself, however, and he shook off the feeling of sentiment and proceeded to make a closer examination of the dead body. As he turned down the sheet to examine the wound which had ended the judge's life, it slipped from his hand and fell on the floor, revealing that the judge had been laid on the couch just as he had been killed, fully clothed. He had been shot through the body near the heart, and a large patch of blood had welled from the wound and congealed in his shirt. One trouser leg was ruffled up, and had caught in the top of the boot.

The corpse presented a repellent spectacle, but Rolfe, who had seen unpleasant sights of various kinds in his career, bent over the body with keen interest, noting these details, with all his professional instincts aroused. For though Rolfe had not yet risen very high in the police force, he had many of the qualities which make the good detective—observation, sagacity, and some imagination. The extraordinary crime which he had been called upon to help unravel presented a baffling mystery which was likely to test the value of these qualities to the utmost.

Rolfe looked steadily at the corpse for some time, impressing a picture of it in every detail on his mental retina. Struck by an idea, he bent over and touched the patch of blood in the dead man's breast, then looked at his finger. There was no stain. The blood was quite congealed. Then he tried to unclench the judge's right hand, but it was rigid.

As Rolfe stood there gazing intently at the corpse, and trying to form some theory of the reason for the murder, certain old stories he had heard of Sir Horace Fewbanks's private life and character recurred to him. These rumours had not been much—a jocular hint or two among his fellows at Scotland Yard that His Honour had a weakness for a pretty face and in private life led a less decorous existence than a judge ought to do. Rolfe wondered how much or how little truth was contained in these stories. He glanced around the vast room. Certainly it was not the sort of apartment in which a High Court judge might be expected to do his entertaining, but Rolfe recalled that he had heard gossip to the effect that Sir Horace, because of his virtual estrangement from his daughter, did very little entertaining beyond an occasional bridge or supper party to his sporting friends, and rarely went into Society.

Rolfe began to scrutinise the articles of furniture in the room, wondering if there was anything about them which might reveal something of the habits of the dead man. He produced a small electric torch from his pocket, and with its light to guide him in the half-darkened room, he closely inspected each piece of furniture. Then, with the torch in his hand, he returned to the sofa and flashed it over the dead body. He started violently when the light, falling on the dead man's closed hand, revealed a tiny scrap of white. Eagerly he endeavoured to release the fragment from the tenacious clutch of the dead without tearing it, and eventually he managed to detach it. His heart bounded when he saw that it was a small torn piece of lace and muslin. He placed it in the palm of his left hand and examined it closely under the light of his torch. To him it looked to be part of a fashionable lady's dainty handkerchief. He was elated at his discovery and he wondered how Inspector Chippenfield had overlooked it. Then the explanation struck him. The small piece of lace and muslin had been effectually hidden in the dead man's clenched hand, and his efforts to open the hand had loosened it.

"Well, Rolfe," said Inspector Chippenfield, when his subordinate reappeared, "you've been long enough to have unearthed the criminal or revived the corpse. Have you discovered anything fresh?"

"Only this," replied Rolfe, displaying the piece of handkerchief.

The find startled Inspector Chippenfield out of his air of bantering superiority.

"Where did you get that?" he stammered, as he reached out eagerly for it.

"The dead man had it clenched in his right hand. I wondered if he had anything hidden in his hand when I saw it so tightly clenched. I tried to force open the fingers and that fell out."

Inspector Chippenfield was by no means pleased at his subordinate's discovery of what promised to be an important clue, especially after the clue had been missed by himself. But he congratulated Rolfe in a tone of fictitious heartiness.

"Well done, Rolfe!" he exclaimed. "You are coming on. Anyone can see that you've the makings of a good detective."

Rolfe could afford to ignore the sting contained in such faint praise.

"What do you make of it?" he asked.

"Looks as though there is a woman in it," said the inspector, who was still examining the scrap of lace and muslin.

"There can't be much doubt about that," replied Rolfe.

"We mustn't be in a hurry in jumping at conclusions," remarked the inspector.

"No, and we mustn't ignore obvious facts," said Rolfe.

"You think a woman murdered him?" asked the inspector.

"I think a woman was present when he was shot: whether she fired the shot there is nothing to show at present. There may have been a man with her. But there was a struggle just before the shot was fired and as Sir Horace fell he grasped at the hand in which she was holding her handkerchief. Or perhaps her handkerchief was torn in his dying struggles when she was leaning over him."

"You have overlooked the possibility of this having been placed in the dying man's hand to deceive us," said the inspector.

"If the intention was to mislead us it wouldn't have been placed where it might have been overlooked."

As the inspector had overlooked the presence of the scrap of handkerchief in the dead man's hand, he felt that he was not making much progress with the work of keeping his subordinate in his place.

"Well, it is a clue of a sort," he said. "The trouble is that we have too many clues. I wish we knew which is the right one. Anyway, it knocks over your theory of a burglary," he added in a tone of satisfaction.

"Yes," Rolfe admitted. "That goes by the board."

CHAPTER V

"What is your name?"

"James Hill, sir."

"That is an alias. What is your real name?" Inspector Chippenfield glared fiercely at the butler in order to impress upon him the fact that subterfuge was useless.

"Henry Field, sir," replied the man, after some hesitation.

Inspector Chippenfield opened the capacious pocketbook which he had placed before him on the desk when the butler had entered in response to his summons, and he took from it a photograph which he handed to the man he was interrogating.

"Is that your photograph?" he asked.

Police photographs taken in gaol for purposes of future identification are always far from flattering, and Henry Field, after looking at the photograph handed to him, hesitated a little before replying:

"Yes, sir."

"So, Henry Field, in November 1909 you were sentenced to three years for robbing your master, Lord Melhurst."

"Yes, sir."

"Let me see," said the inspector, as if calling on his memory to perform a reluctant task. "It was a diamond scarf-pin and a gold watch. Lord Melhurst had come home after a good day at Epsom and a late supper in town. Next morning he missed his scarf-pin and his watch. He thought he had been robbed at Epsom or in town. He was delightfully vague about what had happened to him after his glorious day at Epsom, but unfortunately for you the taxi-cab driver who drove him remembered seeing the pin on him when he got out of the cab. As you had waited up for him suspicion fell on you, and you were arrested and confessed. I think those are the facts, Field?"

"Yes, sir," said the distressed looking man who stood before him.

"I think I had the pleasure of putting you through," added the inspector.

The butler understood that in police slang "putting a man through" meant arresting him and putting him through the Criminal Court into gaol. He made the same reply:

"Yes, sir."

"I'm glad to see you bear me no ill-will for it," said Inspector Chippenfield. "You don't, do you?"

"No, sir."

"I never forget a face," pursued the officer, glancing up at the face of the man before him. "When I saw you yesterday I knew you again in a moment, and when I went back to the Yard I looked up your record."

The butler was doubtful whether any reply was called for, but after a pause, as an endorsement of the inspector's gift for remembering faces, he ventured on:

"Yes, sir."

"And how did you, an ex-convict, come to get into the service of one of His Majesty's judges?"

"He took me in," replied the butler.

"You mean that you took him in," replied the inspector, with a pleasant laugh at his own witticism.

"No, sir, I didn't take him in," declared the butler. He had not joined in the laugh at the inspector's joke.

"Get away with you," said Inspector Chippenfield. "You don't expect me to believe that you told him you were an ex-convict? You must have used forged references."

"No, sir. He knew I was a—" Hill hesitated at referring to himself as an ex-convict, though he had not shrunk from the description by Inspector Chippenfield. "He knew that I had been in trouble. In fact, sir, if you remember, I was tried before him."

"The devil you were!" exclaimed Inspector Chippenfield, in astonishment. "And he took you into his service after you had served your sentence. He must have been mad. How did you manage it?"

"After I came out I found it hard to get a place," said Hill, "and when Sir Horace's butler died I wrote to him and asked if he would give me a chance. I had a wife and child, sir, and they had a hard struggle while I was in prison. My wife had a shop, but she sold it to find money for my defence. Sir Horace told me to call on him, and after thinking it over he decided to engage me. He was a good master to me."

"And how did you repay him," exclaimed Inspector Chippenfield sternly, "by murdering him?"

The butler was startled by the suddenness of the accusation, as Inspector Chippenfield intended he should be.

"Me!" he exclaimed. "As sure as there is a God in Heaven I had nothing to do with it."

"That won't go down with me, Field," said the police officer, giving the wretched man another prolonged penetrating look.

"It's true; it's true!" he protested wildly. "I had nothing to do with it. I couldn't do a thing like that, sir. I couldn't kill a man if I wanted to—I haven't the nerve. But I knew I would be suspected," he added, in a tone of self-pity.

"Oh, you did?" replied Inspector Chippenfield. "And why was that?"

"Because of my past."

"Where were you on the date of the murder?"

"In the morning I came over here to look round as usual, and I found everything all right."

"You did that every day while Sir Horace was away?"

"Not every day, sir. Three times a week: Mondays, Wednesdays, and Fridays."

"Did you enter the house or just look round?"

"I always came inside."

"What for?"

"To make quite sure that everything was all right."

"And was everything all right the morning of the 18th?"

"Yes, sir."

"You are quite sure of that? You looked round carefully?"

"Well, sir, I just gave a glance round, for of course I didn't expect anything would be wrong."

Inspector Chippenfield fixed a steady glance on the butler to ascertain if he was conscious of the trap he had avoided.

"Did you look in this room?"

"Yes, sir. I made a point of looking in all the rooms."

"You are sure that Sir Horace's dead body was not lying here?" Inspector Chippenfield pointed beside the desk where the body had been found.

"Oh, no, sir. I'd have seen it if it had."

"There was no sign anywhere of his having returned from Scotland?"

"No, sir."

"You didn't know he was returning?"

"No, sir."

"What time did you leave the house?"

"It would be about a quarter past twelve, sir."

"And what did you do after that?"

"I went home and had my dinner. In the afternoon I took my little girl to the Zoo. I had promised her for a long time that I would take her to the Zoo."

"And what did you do after visiting the Zoo?"

"We went home for supper. After supper my wife took the little girl to the picture palace in Camden Road. It was quite a holiday, sir, for her."

"And what did you do while your wife and child were at the pictures?"

"I stayed at home and minded the shop. When they came home we all went to bed. My wife will tell you the same thing."

"I've no doubt she will," said the inspector drily. "Well, if you didn't murder Sir Horace yourself when did you first hear that he had been murdered?"

"I saw it in the papers yesterday evening."

"And you immediately came up here to see if it was true?"

"Yes, sir."

"And you were taken to the Hampstead Police Station to make a statement as to your movements on the day and night of the murder?"

"Yes, sir."

"And the story you have just told me about the Zoo and the pictures and the rest is virtually the same as the statement you made at the station?"

"Yes, sir."

"Do you know if Sir Horace kept a revolver?"

"I think he did, sir."

"Where did he keep it?"

"In the second drawer of his desk, sir."

"Well, it's gone," remarked Inspector Chippenfield without opening the drawer. "What sort of a revolver was it? Did you ever see it? How do you know he kept one?"

"Once or twice I saw something that looked like a revolver in that drawer while Sir Horace had it open. It was a small nickel revolver."

"Sir Horace always locked his desk?"

"Yes, sir."

"None of your keys will open it, of course?"

"No, sir. That is—I don't know, sir. I've never tried."

Inspector Chippenfield grunted slightly. That trap the butler had not seen until too late. But of course all servants went through their masters' private papers when they got the chance.

"Do you know if Sir Horace was in the habit of carrying a pocket-book?" he asked.

"Yes, sir; he was."

"What sort of a pocket-book?"

"A large Russian leather one with a gold clasp."

"Did he take it away with him when he went to Scotland? Did you see it about the house after he left?"

"No, sir. I think he took it with him. It would not be like him to forget it, or to leave it lying about."

"And what sort of a man was Sir Horace, Field?"

"A very good master, sir. He could be very stern when he was angry, but I got on very well with him."

"Quite so. Do you know if he had a weakness for the ladies?"

"Well, sir, I've heard people say he had."

"I want your own opinion; I don't want what other people said. You were with him for three years and kept a pretty close watch on him, I've no doubt."

"Speaking confidentially, I might say that I think he was," said Hill.

He glanced apprehensively behind him as if afraid of the dead man appearing at the door to rebuke him for presuming to speak ill of him.

"I thought as much," said the inspector. "Have you any idea why he came down from Scotland?"

"No, sir."

"Well, that will do for the present, Field. If I want you again I'll send for you."

"Thank you, sir. May I ask a question, sir?"

"What is it?"

"You don't really think I had anything to do with it, sir?"

"I'm not here, Field, to tell you what I think. This much I will say: If I find you have tried to deceive me in any way it will be a bad day for you."

"Yes, sir."

Grave, taciturn, watchful, secret and suave, with an appearance of tight-lipped reticence about him which a perpetual faint questioning look in his eyes denied, Hill looked an ideal man servant, who knew his station in life, and was able to uphold it with meek dignity. From the top of his trimly-cut grey crown to his neatly-shod silent feet he exuded deference and respectability. His impassive mask of a face was incapable—apart from the faint query note in the eyes—of betraying any of the feelings or emotions which ruffle the countenances of common humanity.

On the way downstairs, Hill saw Police-Constable Flack in conversation with a lady at the front door. The lady was well-known to the butler as Mrs. Holymead, the wife of a distinguished barrister, who had been one of his master's closest friends. She seemed glad to see the butler, for she greeted him with a remark that seemed to imply a kinship in sorrow.

"Isn't this a dreadful thing, Hill?" she said.

"It's terrible, madam," replied Hill respectfully.

Mrs. Holymead was extremely beautiful, but it was obvious that she was distressed at the tragedy, for her eyes were full of tears, and her olive-tinted face was pale. She was about thirty years of age; tall, slim, and graceful. Her beauty was of the Spanish type: straight-browed, lustrous-eyed, and vivid; a clear olive skin, and full, petulant, crimson lips. She was fashionably dressed in black, with a black hat.

"The policeman tells me that Miss Fewbanks has not come up from Dellmere yet," she continued.

"No, madam. We expect her to-morrow. I believe Miss Fewbanks has been too prostrated to come."

"Dreadful, dreadful," murmured Mrs. Holymead. "I feel I want to know all about it and yet I am afraid. It is all too terrible for words."

"It has been a terrible shock, madam," said Hill.

"Has the housekeeper come up, Hill?"

"No, madam. She will be up to-morrow with Miss Fewbanks."

"Well, is there nobody I can see?" asked Mrs. Holymead.

Police-Constable Flack was impressed by the spectacle of a beautiful fashionably-dressed lady in distress.

"The inspector in charge of the case is upstairs, madam," he suggested. "Perhaps you'd like to see him." It suddenly occurred to him that he had instructions not to allow any stranger into the house, and police instructions at such a time were of a nature which classed a friend of the family as a stranger. "Perhaps I'd better ask him first," he added, and he went upstairs with the feeling that he had laid himself open to severe official censure from Inspector Chippenfield.

He came downstairs with a smile on his face and the message that the inspector would be pleased to see Mrs. Holymead. In his brief interview with his superior he had contrived to convey the unofficial information that Mrs. Holymead was a fine-looking woman, and he had no doubt that Inspector Chippenfield's readiness to see her was due to the impression this information had made on his unofficial feelings.

Mrs. Holymead was conducted upstairs and announced by the butler. Inspector Chippenfield greeted her with a low bow of conscious inferiority, and anticipated Hill in placing a chair for her. His large red face went a deeper scarlet in colour as he looked at her.

"Flack tells me that you are a friend of the family, Mrs. Holymead. What is it that I can do for you? I need scarcely say, Mrs. Holymead, that your distinguished husband is well known to us all. I have had the pleasure of being cross-examined by him on several occasions. Anything you wish to know I'll be pleased to tell you, if it lies within my power."

"Thank you," said Mrs. Holymead.

She seemed to be slightly nervous in the presence of a member of the Scotland Yard police, in spite of his obvious humility in the company of a fashionable lady who belonged to a different social world from that in which police inspectors moved. It took Inspector Chippenfield some minutes to discover that the object of Mrs. Holymead's visit was to learn some of the details of the tragedy. As one who had known the murdered man for several years, and the wife of his intimate friend, she was overwhelmed by the awful tragedy. She endeavoured to explain that the crime was like a horrible dream which she could not get rid of. But in spite of the repugnance with which she contemplated the fact that a gentleman she had known so well had been shot down in his own house she felt a natural curiosity to know how the dreadful crime had been committed.

Inspector Chippenfield availed himself of the opportunity to do the honours of the occasion. He went over the details of the tragedy and pointed out where the body had been found. He showed her the bullet mark on the wall and the flattened bullet which had been extracted. Although from the mere habit of official caution he gave away no information which was not of a superficial and obvious kind, it was apparent he liked talking about the crime and his responsibilities as the officer who had been placed in charge of the investigations. He noted the interest with which Mrs. Holymead followed his words and he was satisfied that he had created a favourable impression on her. It was his desire to do the honours thoroughly which led him to remark after he had given her the main facts of the tragedy:

"I'm sorry I cannot take you to view the body. It is downstairs, but the fact is the Home Office doctors are in there making the post-mortem to extract the bullet."

Mrs. Holymead shuddered at this information. The fact that such gruesome work as a post-mortem examination was proceeding on the body of a man whom she had known so well brought on a fit of nausea. Her head fell back as if she was about to faint.

"Can I have a glass of water?" she whispered.

A fainting woman, if she is beautiful and fashionably dressed, will unnerve even a resourceful police official. Had she been one of the servants Inspector Chippenfield would have rung the bell for a glass of water to throw over her face, and meantime would have looked on calmly at such evidence of the weakness of sex. But in this case he dashed out of the room, ran downstairs, shouted for Hill, ordered him to find a glass, snatched the glass from him, filled it with water, and dashed upstairs again. His absence from the room totalled a little less than three minutes, and when he held the glass to the lady's lips he was out of breath with his exertions.

Mrs. Holymead took a sip of water, shuddered, took another sip, then heaved a sigh, and opened to the full extent her large dark eyes on the man bending over her, who felt amply repaid by such a glance. She thanked him prettily for his great kindness and took her departure, being conducted downstairs, and to her waiting motor-car at the gate, by Inspector Chippenfield. That officer went back to the house with a pleased smile on his features. But he would not have been so pleased with himself if he had known that his brief absence from the room of the tragedy for the purpose of obtaining a glass of water had been more than sufficient to enable the lady to run to the open desk of the murdered man, touch a spring which opened a secret receptacle at the back of it, extract a small bundle of papers, close the spring, and return to her chair to await in a fainting attitude the return of the chivalrous police officer.

Mrs. Holymead's return to her home in Princes Gate was awaited with feverish anxiety by one of the inmates. This was Mademoiselle Gabrielle Chiron, a French girl of about twenty-eight, who was a distant connection of Mrs. Holymead's by marriage. A cousin of Mrs. Holymead's had married Lucille Chiron, the younger sister of Gabrielle, two years ago. Mrs. Holymead on visiting the French provincial town where the marriage was celebrated, was attracted by Gabrielle. As the Chiron family were not wealthy they welcomed the friendship between Gabrielle and the beautiful American who had married one of the leading barristers in London, and finally Gabrielle went to live with Mrs. Holymead as a companion.

From the window of an upstairs room which commanded a view of the street, Gabrielle Chiron waited impatiently for the return of the motor-car in which Mrs. Holymead had driven to Riversbrook. When at length it turned the corner and came into view, she rushed downstairs to meet Mrs. Holymead. She opened the street door before the lady of the house could ring. Her gaze was fixed on a hand-bag which Mrs. Holymead carried—a comparatively big hand-bag which the lady had taken the precaution to purchase before driving out to Riversbrook.

The French girl's face lighted up with a smile as she saw by the shape of the bag that it was not empty.

"Have you got them?" she whispered.

"Yes," was the reply. "I followed out your plan—it worked without a hitch."

"Ah, I knew you would manage it," said the girl. "I would have gone, but it was best that you should go. These police agents do not like foreigners—they would be suspicious if I had gone."

"There was a big red-faced man in charge—Inspector Chippenfield, they called him," said Mrs. Holymead. "He was in the library as you said he would be—he was sitting there calmly as if he did not know what nerves were. He knew me as a friend of the family and was quite nice to me. I saw as soon as I went in that the desk was open— he had been examining Sir Horace's private papers. I asked him to tell me about the—about the tragedy. He piled horror on horror and then I pretended to faint. He ran down stairs for a glass of water, and that gave me time to open the secret drawer. They are here," she added, patting the hand-bag affectionately; "let us go upstairs and burn them."

CHAPTER VI

There was unpleasant news for Inspector Chippenfield when Miss Fewbanks arrived at Riversbrook accompanied by the housekeeper, Mrs. Hewson. In the first place, he learnt with considerable astonishment that it was Miss Fewbanks's intention to stay at the house until after the funeral, and for that purpose she had brought the housekeeper to keep her company in the lonely old place. Although they had taken up their quarters in the opposite wing of the rambling mansion to that in which the dead body lay, it seemed to Inspector Chippenfield—whose mind was very impressionable where the fair sex was concerned—that Miss Fewbanks must be a very peculiar girl to contemplate staying in the same house with the body of her murdered father for nearly a week. He was convinced that she must be a strong-minded young woman, and he did not like strong-minded young women. He preferred the weak and clinging type of the sex as more of a compliment to his own sturdy manliness.

His unfavourable impression of Miss Fewbanks was deepened when he saw her and heard what she had to tell him. The girl had come up from the country filled with horror at the crime which had deprived her of a father, and firmly determined to leave no stone unturned to bring the murderer to justice. It was true that she and her father had lived on terms of partial estrangement for some time past because of his manner of life, but all the girl's feelings of resentment against him had been swept away by the news of his dreadful death, and all she remembered now was that he was her father, and had been brutally murdered.

When she sent for Inspector Chippenfield she had visited the room in which lay the body of her father. It had been placed in a coffin which was resting on the undertaker's trestles in the bay embrasure of the big room with the folding doors. There was nothing in the appearance of the corpse to suggest that a crime had been committed, but it had been impossible for the undertaker's men to erase entirely the distortion of the features so that they might suggest the cold, calm dignity of a peaceful death. The ordeal of looking on the dead body of her father had nerved her to carry through resolutely the task of discovering the author of the crime.

She awaited the coming of the inspector in a small sitting-room, and when he entered she pointed quickly to a chair, but remained standing herself. In appearance Miss Fewbanks was a charming girl of the typical English type. She was of medium height, slight, but well-built, with fair hair and dark blue eyes, an imperious short upper lip and a determined chin, and the clear healthy complexion of a girl who has lived much out of doors. The inspector noted all these details; noted, too, that although her breast heaved with agitation she had herself well under control; her pretty head was erect, and one of her small hands was tightly clenched by her side.

"Have you found out—anything?" she asked the inspector as he entered.

The girl had chosen a vague word because she felt that there were many things which must come to light in unravelling the crime, but, from the police point of view of Inspector Chippenfield, the question whether he had found out anything was a stinging reflection on his ability.

"I consider it inadvisable to make any arrest at the present stage of my investigations," he said, with cold official dignity.

"Do you think you know who did it?" asked the girl.

"It is my business to find out," replied the inspector, in a voice that indicated confidence in his ability to perform the task.

The girl was too unsophisticated to follow the subtle workings of official pride. "The papers call it a mysterious crime. Do you think it is mysterious?"

"There are certainly some mysterious features about it," said the inspector. "But I do not regard them as insoluble. Nothing is insoluble," he added, in a sententious tone.

"If there are mysteries to be solved you ought to have help," said the young lady.

She glanced at Mrs. Hewson significantly, and then proceeded to explain to Inspector Chippenfield what she meant.

"I have asked Mr. Crewe, the celebrated detective, to assist you. Of course you know Mr. Crewe—everybody does. I know you are a very clever man at your profession, but in a thing of this kind two clever men are better than one. I hope you will not mind—there is no reflection whatever on your ability. In fact, I have the utmost confidence in you. But it is due to my father's memory to do all that is possible to get to the bottom of this dreadful crime. If money is needed it will be forthcoming. That applies to you no less than to Mr. Crewe. But I hope you will be able to carry out your investigations amicably together, and that you will be willing to assist one another. You will lose nothing by doing so. I trust you will place at Mr. Crewe's disposal all the facilities that are available to you as an officer of the police."

This statement was so clear that Inspector Chippenfield had no choice but to face the conclusion that Miss Fewbanks had more faith in the abilities of a private detective to unravel the mystery than she had in the resources of Scotland Yard. He would have liked to have told the young lady what he thought of her for interfering with his work, and he determined to avail himself of the right opportunity to do so if it came along. But the statement that money was not to be spared had a soothing influence on his feelings. Of course, officers of Scotland Yard were not allowed to take gratuities however substantial they might be, but there were material ways of expressing gratitude which were outside the regulations of the department.

"I shall be very pleased to give Mr. Crewe any assistance he wants," said Inspector Chippenfield, bowing stiffly.

It was seldom that he took a subordinate fully into his confidence, but after he left Miss Fewbanks he flung aside his official pride in order to discuss with Rolfe the enlistment of the services of Crewe. Rolfe was no less indignant than his chief at the intrusion of an outsider into their sphere. Crewe was an exponent of the deductive school of crime investigation, and had first achieved fame over the Abbindon case some years ago, when he had succeeded in restoring the kidnapped heir of the Abbindon estates after the police had failed to trace the missing child. In detective stories the attitude of members of Scotland Yard to the deductive expert is that of admiration based on conscious inferiority, but in real life the experts of Scotland Yard have the utmost contempt for the deductive experts and their methods. The disdainful pity of the deductive experts for the rule-of-thumb methods of the police is not to be compared with the vigorous scorn of the official detective for the rival who has not had the benefit of police training.

"Look here, Rolfe," said Inspector Chippenfield, "we mustn't let Crewe get ahead of us in this affair, or we'll never hear the last of it. It's scandalous of a man like Crewe, who has money of his own and could live like a gentleman, coming along and taking the bread out of our mouths by accepting fees and rewards for hunting after criminals. Of course I know they say he is lavish with his money and gives away more than he earns, but that's all bosh—he sticks it in his own pocket, right enough. One thing is certain: he gets paid whether he wins or loses; that is to say, he gets his fee in any case, but of course if he wins something will be added to his fee. In the meantime all you and I get is our salaries, and, as you know, the pay of an inspector isn't what it ought to be."

Rolfe assured his superior of his conviction that the pay at Scotland Yard ought to be higher for all ranks—especially the rank and file. He also declared that he was ready to do his best to thwart Crewe.

"That is the right spirit," commented Inspector Chippenfield approvingly. "Of course we'll tell him we're willing to help him all we can, and of course hell tell us we can depend on his help. But we know what his help will amount to. He'll keep back from us anything he finds out, and we'll do the same for him. But the point is, Rolfe, that you and I have to put all our brains into this and help one another. I'm not the man to despise help from a subordinate. If you have any ideas about this case, Rolfe, do not be afraid to speak out, I'll give them sympathetic consideration."

"I know you will," said Rolfe, who was by no means sure of the fact. "You can count on me."

"As you know, Rolfe, there have been cases in which men from the Yard haven't worked together as amicably as they ought to have done. It used to be said when I was one of the plain-clothes men that the man in charge got all the credit and the men under him did all the work. But as an inspector I can tell you that is very rarely the case. In my reports I believe in giving my junior credit for all he has done, and generally a bit more. It may be foolish of me, but that is my way. I never miss a chance of putting in a good word for the man under me."

"It would be better if they were all like that," said Rolfe.

"Well, it's a bargain, Rolfe," said Inspector Chippenfield. "You do your best on this job and you won't lose by it. I'll see to that. But in the meantime we don't want to put Crewe on the scent. Let us see how much we'll tell him and how much we won't."

"He'll want to see the letter sent to the Yard about the murder," said Rolfe. "The *Daily Recorder* published a facsimile of it this morning."

"Yes, I knew about that. Well, he can have it. But don't say anything to him about that lace you found in the dead man's hand — or at any rate not until you find out more about it. The glove he can have since it is pretty obvious that it belonged to Sir Horace. We'll spin Crewe a yarn that we are depending on it as a clue."

Crewe arrived during the afternoon to inspect the house and the room in which the crime had been committed. There was every appearance of cordiality in the way in which he greeted the police officials.

"Delighted to see you, Inspector," he said. "Who is working this case with you? Rolfe? Don't think we have met before, Rolfe, have we?"

Rolfe politely murmured something about not having had the pleasure of meeting Mr. Crewe, but of always having wanted to meet him, because of his fame.

"Very good of you," replied Crewe. "This is a very sad business. I understand there are some attractive points of mystery in the crime. I hope you haven't unravelled it yet before I have got a start. You fellows are so quick."

"Slow and sure is our motto," said Inspector Chippenfield, feeling certain that a sneer and not a compliment had been intended. "There is nothing to be gained in arresting the wrong man."

"That's a sound maxim for us all," said Crewe. "However, let's get to business. I rang up the Yard this morning and they told me you were in charge of the case and that I'd probably find you here. Can you let me have a look at the original of that letter which was sent to Scotland Yard informing you of the murder? There is a facsimile of it in the *Daily Recorder* this morning, and from all appearances there are some interesting conclusions to be drawn from it. But the original is the thing."

"Here you are," said the inspector, producing his pocket-book, taking out the paper, and handing it to Crewe. "What do you make of it?"

Crewe sat down, and placing the paper before him took a magnifying glass from his pocket. As he sat there, in his grey tweed suit, his hat pushed carelessly back from his forehead, he might have been mistaken for a young man of wealth with no serious business in life, for his clothes were of fashionable cut, and he wore them with an air of distinction. But a glance at his face would have dispelled the impression. The clear-cut, clean-shaven features riveted attention by reason of their strength and intelligence, and though the dark eyes were rather too dreamy for the face, the heavy lines of the lower jaw indicated the man of action and force of character. The thick neck and heavily-lipped firm mouth suggested tireless energy and abounding vitality.

"At least two people have had a hand in it," he said, after studying the paper for a few minutes.

"In the murder?" asked the inspector, who was astonished at a deduction which harmonised with a theory which had begun to take shape in his mind.

"In writing this," said Crewe, with his attention still fixed on the paper. "But of course you know that yourself."

"Of course," assented the inspector, who was surprised at the information, but was too experienced an official to show his feelings. "And both hands disguised."

"Disguised to the extent of being printed in written characters," continued Crewe. "It is so seldom that a person writes printed characters that any method in which they are written suggests disguise. The original intention of the two persona who wrote this extraordinary note was for each to write a single letter in turn. That system was carried as far as 'Sir Horace' or, perhaps, up to the 'B' in 'Fewbanks.' After that they became weary of changing places and one of them wrote alternate letters to the end, leaving blanks for the other to fill in. That much is to be gathered from the variations in the spaces between the letters—sometimes there was too much room for an intermediate letter, sometimes too little, so the letter had to be cramped. Here and there are dots made with the pen as the first of the two spelled out the words so as to know what letters to write and what to leave blank. Look at the differences in the letter 'U.' One of the writers makes it a firm downward and upward stroke; the other makes the letter fainter and adds another downward stroke, the letter being more like a small 'u' written larger than a capital letter. The differences in the two hands are so pronounced throughout the note that I am inclined to think that one of the writers was a woman."

"Exactly what I thought," said Inspector Chippenfield, looking hard at Crewe so that the latter should not question his good faith.

"Then there are sometimes slight differences in the alternate letters written by the same hand. Look at the 'T' in 'last' and the 'T' in 'night'—the marked variation in the length and angle of the cross stroke. It is evident that the writers were labouring under serious excitement when they wrote this."

Rolfe was so interested in Crewe's revelations that he stood beside the deductive expert and studied the paper afresh.

"And now, about finger-prints?" asked Crews.

"None," was the reply of the inspector, "We had it under the microscope at Scotland Yard."

"None?" exclaimed Crewe, in surprise. "Why adopt such precautions as wearing gloves to write a note giving away this startling secret?"

"Easy enough," replied Inspector Chippenfield. "The people who wrote the note either had little or nothing to do with the murder, but were afraid suspicion might be directed to them, or else they are the murderers and want to direct suspicion from themselves."

"And now for the bullets," said Crewe, "I understand two shots were fired."

"From two revolvers," said the inspector. "Here are both bullets. This one I picked out of the wall over there. You can see where I've broken away the plaster. This one—much the bigger one of the two—was the one that killed Sir Horace. The doctor handed it to me after the post-mortem."

"Did Sir Horace keep a revolver?"

"The butler says yes. But if he did it's gone."

Crewe stood up and examined the hole in the wall where Inspector Chippenfield had dug out the smaller bullet.

"Sir Horace made a bid for his life but missed. Of course, he had no time to take aim while there was a man on the other side of the room covering him, but in any case those fancy firearms cannot be depended upon to shoot straight."

"You think Sir Horace fired at his murderer—fired first?" asked Rolfe.

"This small bullet suggests one of those fancy silver-mounted weapons that are made to sell to wealthy people. Sir Horace was a bit of a sportsman, and knew something about game-shooting, but, I take it, he had no use for a revolver. I assume he kept one of those fancy weapons on hand thinking he would never have to use it, but that it would do to frighten a burglar if the occasion did arise."

"And when he was held up in this room by a man with a revolver he made a dash for his own revolver and got in the first shot?" suggested Rolfe, with the idea of outlining Crewe's theory of how the crime was committed.

"It is scarcely possible to reconstruct the crime to that extent," said Crewe with a smile. "But undoubtedly Sir Horace got in the first shot. If he fired after he was hit his bullet would have gone wild— would probably have struck the ceiling—whereas it landed there. Let us measure the height from the floor." He pulled a small spool out of a waistcoat pocket and drew out a tape measure. "A little high for the heart of an average man, and probably a foot wide of the mark."

"And what do you make of the disappearance of Sir Horace's revolver?" asked Rolfe, who seemed to his superior officer to be in danger of displaying some admiration for deductive methods.

"I'm no good at guess-work," replied Crewe, who felt that he had given enough information away.

"Well," said Rolfe, "here is a glove which was found in the room. The other one is missing. It might be a clue."

Crewe took the glove and examined it carefully. It was a left-hand glove made of reindeer-skin, and grey in colour. It bore evidence of having been in use, but it was still a smart-looking glove such as a man who took a pride in his appearance might wear.

"Burglars wear gloves nowadays," said Crewe, "but not this kind. The india-rubber glove with only the thumb separate is best for their work. They give freedom of action for the fingers and leave no finger-prints. Have you made inquiries whether this is one of Sir Horace's gloves?"

"Well, it is the same size as he wore—seven and a half," said Inspector Chippenfield. "The butler is the only servant here and he can't say for certain that it belonged to his master. I've been through Sir Horace's wardrobe and through the suit-case he brought from Scotland, but I can find no other pair exactly similar. Rolfe took it to Sir Horace's hosier, and he is practically certain that the glove is one of a pair he sold to Sir Horace."

"That should be conclusive," said Crewe thoughtfully.

"So I think," replied the inspector.

"Well, I'll take it with me, if you don't mind," said Crewe. "You can have it back whenever you want it. Let me have the address of Sir Horace's hosier—I'll give him a call."

"Take it by all means," said the inspector cordially, referring to the glove. And with a wink at Rolfe he added, "And when you are ready to fit it on the guilty hand I hope you will let us know."

CHAPTER VII

Crewe made a careful inspection of the house and the grounds. He took measurements of the impressions left on the sill of the window which had been forced and also of the foot-prints immediately beneath the window. He had a long conversation with Hill and questioned him regarding his movements on the night of the murder. He also asked about the other servants who were at Dellmere, and probed for information about Sir Horace's domestic life and his friends. As he was talking to Hill, Police-Constable Flack came up to them with a card in his hand. Hill looked at the card and exclaimed:

"Mr. Holymead? What does he want?"

"He asked if Miss Fewbanks was at home."

Hill took the card in to Miss Fewbanks, and on coming out went to the front door and escorted Mr. Holymead to his young mistress. Crewe, as was his habit, looked closely at Holymead. The eminent K.C. was a tall man, nearly six feet in height, with a large, resolute, strongly-marked face which, when framed in a wig, was suggestive of the dignity and severity of the law. In years he was about fifty, and in his figure there was a suggestion of that rotundity which overtakes the man who has given up physical exercise. He was correctly, if sombrely, dressed in dark clothes, and he wore a black tie—probably as a symbol of mourning for his friend. His gloves were a delicate grey.

Crewe sought out Hill again and questioned him closely about the relations which had existed between Sir Horace Fewbanks and Mr. Holymead, whose enormous practice brought him in an income three times as large as the dead judge's, and kept him constantly before the public. Hill was able to supply the detective with some interesting information regarding the visitor, and, in contrast to his manner when previously questioned at random by Crewe, concerning his young mistress's habits, seemed willing, if not actually anxious, to talk. He had heard from Sir Horace's housekeeper that his late master and Mr.

Holymead had been law students together, and after they were called to the Bar they used to spend their holidays together as long as they were single.

When they were married their wives became friends. Mrs. Holymead had died fourteen years ago, but Mrs. Fewbanks—Sir Horace had not been a baronet while his wife was alive—had lived some years longer. Mr. Holymead had married again. His second wife was a very beautiful young lady, if he might make so bold as to say so, who had come from America. The butler added deprecatingly that he had been told that both Sir Horace and Mr. Holymead had paid her some attention, and that she could have had either of them. She was different to English ladies, he added. She had more to say for herself, and laughed and talked with the gentlemen just as if she was one of themselves. Hill mentioned that she had been out to see Miss Fewbanks the previous day, but that Miss Fewbanks had not come up from Dellmere then, so she had seen Inspector Chippenfield instead.

While Crewe and the butler were talking a boy of about fourteen, with the shrewd face of a London arab, approached them with an air of mystery. He came down the hall with long cautious strides, and halted at each step as if he were stalking a band of Indians in a forest.

"Well, Joe, what is it?" asked Crewe, as he came to a halt in front of them.

"If you don't want me for half an hour, sir, I'd like to take a run up the street. There is a real good picture house just been opened." The boy spoke eagerly, with his bright eyes fixed on Crewe.

"I may want you any minute, Joe," replied Crewe. "Don't go away."

The boy nodded his head, and turned away. As he went down the hall again to the front door he gave an imitation of a man walking with extended arms across a plank spanning a chasm.

"Picture mad," commented Crewe, as he watched him.

"I didn't quite understand you, sir," replied the butler.

"Spends all his spare time in cinemas," said Crewe, "and when he is not there he is acting picture dramas. His ambition in life is to be a cinema actor."

Crewe engaged Police-Constable Flack in conversation while waiting for Mr. Holymead to take his departure. Flack had so little professional pride that he was pleased at meeting a gentleman who usurped the functions of a detective without having had any police training, and who could beat the best of the Scotland Yard men like shelling peas, as he confided to his wife that night. He was especially flattered at the interest Crewe seemed to display in his long connection with the police force, and also in his private affairs. The constable was explaining with parental vanity the precocious cleverness of his youngest child, a girl of two, when Holymead made his appearance, and he became aware that Mr. Crewe's interest in children was at an end.

"Look at that man," said Crewe, in a sharp imperative tone to the police-constable, as the K.C. was walking down the path of the Italian garden to the plantation. "You saw him come in?"

"Yes, sir."

"Do you see any difference?"

"No, sir; he's the same man," said Flack, with stolid certainty.

"Anything about him that is different?" continued Crewe.

Police-Constable Flack looked at Crewe in some bewilderment. He was not a deductive expert, and, as he told his wife afterwards, he did not know what the detective was "driving at." He took another long look at Holymead, who was then within a few yards of the plantation on his way to the gates, and remarked, in a hesitating tone, as though to justify his failure:

"Well, you see, sir, when he was coming in it was the front view I saw, now I can only see his back."

But before he had finished speaking Crewe had left him and was following the K.C. Holymead had gone into the house without a walking-stick, and had reappeared carrying one on his arm. Crewe admired the cool audacity which had prompted Holymead to go into a house where a murder had been committed to recover his stick under the very eyes of the police, and he immediately formed the conclusion that the K.C. had come to the house to recover the stick for some urgent reason possibly not unconnected with the crime. And it was apparent that Holymead was a shrewd judge of human nature, Crewe reflected, for he calculated that the rareness of the quality of observation, even in those who, like Flack, were supposed to keep their eyes open, would permit him to do so unnoticed.

As Crewe went down the path he beckoned to the boy Joe, who at the moment was acting the part of a comic dentist binding a recalcitrant patient to a chair, using an immense old-fashioned straight-backed chair which stood in the hall, for his stage setting. Joe overtook his master as he entered the ornamental plantation in front of the house, and Crewe quickly whispered his instructions, as the retreating figure of the K.C. threaded the wood towards the gates.

"When I catch up level with him, Joe, you are to run into him accidentally from behind, and knock his stick off his arm, so that it falls near me. I will pick it up and return it to him. I must handle the stick—you understand? Do not wait to see how he takes it when you bump into him—get off round the corner at once and wait for me."

Crewe quickened his pace to overtake the man in front of him. He gave no glance backward at the boy, for he knew his instructions would be carried out faithfully and intelligently. He allowed Holymead to reach the big open gates, and turn from the gravelled carriage drive into the private street. Then he hurried after him and drew level with Holymead. As he did so there was a sound of running footsteps from behind, and then a shout. Joe had cleverly tripped and fallen heavily between the two men, bringing down Holymead in his fall. The K.C.'s stick flew off his arm and bounded half a dozen yards away. Crewe stepped forward quickly, secured the stick, glanced quickly at the monogram engraved on it, and held it out to Holymead, who was brushing the dust off his clothes with vexatious remarks about the clumsiness and impudence of street boys. For a moment he seemed to hesitate about taking the stick.

"I believe this is yours," said Crewe politely.

"Ah—yes. Thank you," said the K.C., giving him a keen suspicious glance.

CHAPTER VIII

Crewe had well-furnished offices in Holborn but lived in a luxurious flat in Jermyn Street. Although he went to and fro between them daily, his personality was almost a dual one, though not consciously so; his passion for crime investigation was distinct—in outward seeming, at all events—from his polished West End life of wealthy ease. Grave, self-contained, and inscrutable, he slipped from one to the other with an effortless regularity, and the fashionable folk with whom he mixed in his leisured bachelor existence in the West End, apart from knowing him as the famous Crewe, had even less knowledge of the real man behind his suave exterior than the clients who visited his inquiry rooms in Holborn to confide in him their stories of suffering, shame, or crimes committed against them. His commissionaire and body-servant, Stork, had once, in a rare—almost unique—convivial moment, declared to the caretaker of the building that he knew no more about his master after ten years than he did the first day he entered his service. He was deep beyond all belief, was Stork's opinion, delivered with reluctant admiration.

Although Crewe did not allow the externals of his two existences to become involved, his chief interest in life was in his work. He had originally taken up detective work more as a relief from the boredom of his lot as a wealthy young man, leading an aimless, useless life with others of his class, than by deliberate choice of his vocation. His initial successes surprised him; then the work absorbed him and became his life's career. He had achieved some memorable successes and he had made a few failures, but the failures belonged to the earlier portion of his career, before he had learnt to trust thoroughly in his own great gifts of intuition and insight, and that uncanny imagination which sometimes carried him successfully through when all else failed.

Serious devotees of chess knew the name of Crewe in another capacity—as the name of a man who might have aspired to great deeds if he had but taken the game as his life's career. He had flashed across the chess horizon some years previously as a player of surpassing brilliance by defeating Turgieff, when the great Russian master had visited London and had played twelve simultaneous boards at the London Chess Club. Crewe was the only player of the twelve to win his game, and he did so by a masterly concealed ending in which he handled his pawns with consummate skill, proffering the sacrifice of a bishop with such art that Turgieff fell into the trap, and was mated in five subsequent moves. Crewe proved this was not merely a lucky win by defeating the young South American champion, Caranda, shortly afterwards, when the latter visited England and played a series of exhibition games in London on his way to Moscow, where he was engaged in the championship tourney. Once again it was masterly pawn play which brought Crewe a fine victory, and aged chess enthusiasts who followed every move of the game with trembling excitement, declared afterwards that Crewe's conception of this particular game had not been equalled since Morphy died.

They predicted a dazzling chess career for Crewe, but he disappointed their aged hearts by retiring suddenly from match chess, and they mourned him as one unworthy of his great chess gifts and the high hopes they had placed in him. But, as a matter of fact, Crewe's intellect was too vigorous and active to be satisfied with the triumphs of chess, and his disappearance from the chess world was contemporary with his entrance into detective work, which appealed to his imagination and found scope for his restless mental activity. But if detective work so absorbed him that he gave up match chess entirely, he still retained an interest in the science of chess, reserving problem play for his spare moments, and, when not immersed in the solution of a problem of human mystery, he would turn to the chessboard and seek solace and relaxation in the mysteries of an intricate "four-mover."

He had once said that there was a certain affinity between solving chess problems and the detection of crime mystery: once the key-move was found, the rest was comparatively easy. But he added with a sigh that a really perfect crime mystery was as rare as a perfect chess problem: human ingenuity was not sufficiently skilful, as a rule, to commit a crime or construct a chess problem with completely artistic concealment of the key-move, and for that reason most problems and crimes were far too easy of detection to absorb one's intellectual interests and attention.

It was the morning after Crewe's visit to Riversbrook, and the detective sat in his private office glancing through a note-book which contained a summary of the Hampstead mystery. Crewe was a painstaking detective as well as a brilliant one, and it was his custom to prepare several critical summaries of any important case on which he was engaged, writing and rewriting the facts and his comments, until he was satisfied that he had a perfect outline to work upon, with the details and clues of the crime in consecutive order and relation to one another. Experience had taught him that the time and labour this task involved were well-spent. If an unexpected development of the case altered the facts of the original summary Crewe prepared another one in the same painstaking way. The summaries, when done with, were methodically filed and indexed and stored in a strong room at the office for future reference, where he also kept full records of all the cases upon which he had been engaged, together with the weapons and articles that had figured in them: huge volumes of newspaper reports and clippings; photographs of criminals with their careers appended; and a host of other odds and ends of his detective investigations—the whole forming an interesting museum of crime and mystery which would have furnished a store of rich material for a fresh Newgate Calendar. It was an axiom of Crewe's that a detective never knew when some old scrap of information or some trifling article of some dead and forgotten crime might not afford a valuable clue. Expert criminals frequently repeated themselves, like people in lesser walks of life, and Crewe's "library and museum," as he called it, had sometimes furnished him with a simple hint for the solution of a mystery which had defied more subtle methods of analysis.

Crewe, after carefully reading his summary of the murder of Sir Horace Fewbanks, and making a few alterations in the text, drew from his pocket the glove which Inspector Chippenfield had handed him as a clue, took it to the window, and carefully examined it through a large magnifying glass. He was thus engrossed when the door was noiselessly opened, and Stork, the bodyguard, entered. Stork belied his name. He was short and fat, with a red mottled face; a model of discretion and imperturbability, who had served Crewe for ten years, and bade fair to serve him another ten, if he lived that long. In his heart of hearts he often wondered why a gentleman like Crewe should so far forget what was due to his birth and position as to have offices in Holborn—Holborn, of all parts of London! But the awe he felt for Crewe prevented his seeking information on the point from the only person who could give it to him, so he served him and puzzled over him in silence, his inward perturbation of spirits being made manifest occasionally by a puzzled glance at his master when the latter was not looking. It was nothing to Stork that his master was a famous detective; the problem to him was *why* he was a detective when he had no call to be one, having more money than any man—and let alone a single man—could spend in a lifetime.

Stork coughed slightly to attract Crewe's attention.

"If you please, sir," he said, "the boy has come."

While Crewe was busy with his magnifying glass Stork returned with the boy who had accompanied Crewe on his visit to Riversbrook on the previous day.

The boy, a thin white-faced, sharp-eyed London street urchin, seemed curiously out of place in the handsomely furnished office, with his legs tucked up under the carved rail of a fine old oak chair, and his big dark eyes fixed intently on Crewe's face. The tie between him and the detective was an unusual one. It dated back some twelve months, when Crewe, in the investigation of a peculiarly baffling crime, found it advisable to disguise himself and live temporarily in a crowded criminal quarter of Islington. The rooms he took were above a secondhand clothing shop kept by a drunken female named Leaver; a supposed widow who lived at the back of the shop with her two children, Lizzie, a bold-eyed girl of 17, who worked at a Clerkenwell clothing factory, and Joe, a typical Cockney boy of fourteen, who sold papers in the streets during the day and was fast qualifying for a thief at night when Crewe went to the place to live.

Crewe soon discovered, through overhearing a loud quarrel between his landlady and her daughter, that Mrs. Leaver's husband was alive, though dead to his wife for all practical purposes, inasmuch as he was serving a life's imprisonment for manslaughter. A fortnight after he had taken up his temporary quarters above the shop the woman was removed to the hospital suffering from the effects of a hard drinking bout, and died there. The girl disappeared, and the boy would have been turned out on the streets but for Crewe, who had taken a liking to him. Joe was self-reliant, alert, and precocious, like most London street boys, but in addition to these qualities he had a vein of imagination unusual in a lad of his upbringing and environment. He devoured the exciting feuilleton stories in the evening papers he vended, and spent his spare pennies at the cinema theatres in the vicinity of his poor home. His appreciation of the crude mysteries of the filmed detective drama amused the famous expert in the finer art of actual crime detection, until he discovered that the boy possessed natural gifts of intuition and observation, combined with penetration. Crewe grew interested in developing the boy's talent for detective work. When the lad's mother died Crewe decided to take him into his Holborn offices as messenger-boy. Crewe soon discovered that Joe had a useful gift for "shadowing" work, and his street training as a newspaper runner enabled him not only to follow a person through the thickest of London traffic, but to escape observation where a man might have been noticed and suspected.

"Well, Joe," said Crewe, as the boy entered on the heels of Stork, "I have a job for you this morning. I want you to find the glove corresponding to this one."

Crewe, having finished his examination of the glove, handed it to the boy, whose first act was to slip it on his left hand and move his fingers about to assure himself that they were in good working order in spite of being hidden. It was the first occasion on which Joe had worn a glove.

"It was found in the room in which Sir Horace Fewbanks was murdered," continued Crewe. "The other one was not there. The question I want to solve is, did it belong to Sir Horace, or to some one who visited him on the night he was murdered? The police think it belonged to Sir Horace because it is the same size as the gloves he wore, and because Sir Horace's hosier stocks the same kind—as does nearly every fashionable hosier in London. They think he lost the right-hand glove on his way up from Scotland. It will occur to you, Joe, though you don't wear gloves, that it is more common for men to lose the right-hand glove than the left-hand, because the right hand is used a great deal more than the left, and even men who would not be seen in the street without gloves find there are many things they cannot do with a gloved hand. For instance, to dive one's hand into one's trouser pocket where most men keep their loose change the glove has to be removed."

"Then the gentleman would take off his right glove when he paid for his taxi-cab from St. Pancras," said Joe, who was familiar through the accounts in the newspapers with the main details of the Fewbanks mystery.

"Right, Joe," said his master approvingly. "And in that case he dropped the glove between the taxi-cab outside his front gates and his room, and it would have been found. I have made inquiries and I am satisfied it was not found."

"He might have lost it when he was getting into the train at Scotland," suggested the lad. "He had to change trains at Glasgow — he might have lost it there."

"That is a rule-of-thumb deduction," said Crewe, with a kindly smile. "It is good enough for the police, for they have apparently adopted it, but it is not good enough for me. What you don't understand, Joe, is that an odd glove is of no value in the eyes of a man who wears gloves. He doesn't take it home as a memento of his carelessness in losing the other. He throws it away. Therefore if this is Sir Horace's glove he took it home because he was unaware that he had lost the other. He would put on his gloves before leaving the train at St. Pancras. And he would pull off the right-hand one—he was not left-handed—when the taxi-cab was nearing his home so as to be able to pay the fare. Therefore, if it is Sir Horace's glove the fellow to it was dropped in the taxi-cab, or dropped between the taxi-cab and the house. If the glove had been lost at the other end of the journey in Scotland Sir Horace would have flung this one out of the carriage window when he became aware of the loss. As I have told you no glove was found between the gate at Riversbrook and the room in which Sir Horace was murdered. I got from the police the number of the taxi-cab in which Sir Horace was driven from St. Pancras, and the driver tells me that no glove was left in his cab. So what have we to do next, Joe?"

"To find the missing glove? It's a tough job, ain't it, sir?"

"Yes and no," replied Crewe. "It is possible to make some reasonable safe deductions in regard to it. These would indicate what had happened to it, and knowing where to look, or, rather, in what circumstances we might expect to find it, we might throw a little light on it. In the first place, it might be assumed that if the glove did not belong to Sir Horace it belonged to some one who visited him on the night he returned unexpectedly from Scotland. That indicates that his visitor knew Sir Horace was returning; a most important point, for if he knew Sir Horace was returning he knew why he was returning — which no one else knows up to the present as far as I have been able to gather — and in all probability was responsible for his return, say, sent him a letter or a telegram which brought him to London. So we come to the possibility of an angry scene in the room in which Sir Horace's dead body was subsequently found. We have the possibility of the visitor leaving the house in a high state of excitement, hastily snatching up the hat and gloves he had taken off when he arrived, and in his excitement dropping unnoticed the right-hand glove on the floor."

"And leaving his gold-mounted stick behind him," said Joe, who was following his master's line of reasoning with keen interest.

"Right, Joe," said Crewe. "That was placed in the stand in the hall, and when the visitor left hurriedly was entirely forgotten. But at what stage did the visitor become conscious of the loss of his glove? Not until his excitement cooled down a little. How long he took to cool down depends upon the cause of his excitement and his temperament, things which, at present, we can only guess at. He would probably walk a long distance before he cooled down. Then he would resume his normal habits and among other things would put on his gloves — if he had them. He would find that he had lost one and that he had left his stick behind. He would know that the stick had been left behind in the hall, but he would not know the glove had been dropped in the house. The probabilities are that he would think he had dropped it while walking. But if he felt that he had dropped it in the house, and he had the best of all reasons for not wishing anyone to know that he had visited Sir Horace that night, he would destroy the remaining glove and our chance of tracing it would be gone. The fact that he had left his stick behind was a minor matter that he could easily account for if he had been a friend of Sir Horace who had been in the habit of visiting Riversbrook. If anything cropped up subsequently about the stick he could say that he had left it there before Sir Horace closed up his house and went to Scotland.

"But the problem of the glove is a different matter, Joe. There are three phases to it: first, if the visitor thought he had dropped it in the house and wanted to keep his visit there a profound secret from subsequent inquiry he would take home the remaining glove and destroy it—probably by burning it. Secondly, if he thought he had dropped it after leaving the house he would not feel that safety necessitated the destruction of the remaining one, but he would probably throw it away where it would not be likely to be found. In the third place, if he had no particular reason for wishing to hide the fact that he had visited Riversbrook he would throw it away anywhere when he became conscious that he had lost the other. He would throw it away merely because an odd glove is of no use to a man who wears gloves. The man who doesn't wear gloves would pick up an odd glove from the ground and think he had made a find. He would take it home to his wife and she would probably keep it for finger-stalls for the children."

Crewe put down his notes and got up from his chair. "Your job is this, Joe. Go to Riversbrook and make a careful search on both sides of the road for the missing glove. I do not think he threw it away—if he did throw it away—until he had walked some distance, but you mustn't act on that assumption. Look over the fences of the houses and into the hedges. Walk along in the direction of Hampstead Underground. Search the gutters and all the trees and hedges along the road. Take one side of the street to the Underground station and if you do not find the glove go back to Riversbrook along the other side. Make a thorough job of it, as it is most important that the glove should be found—if it is to be found."

After Joe had departed Crewe put on his hat and left his office for the Strand. His first call was at the shop of Bruden and Marshall, hosiers, in order to find out if any information was to be obtained there about the ownership of the glove. He was aware that the police had been there on the same mission, but his experience had often shown that valuable information was to be gathered after the police had been over the ground.

On introducing himself to the manager of the shop that gentleman displayed as much humble civility as he would have done towards a valued customer. He could not say anything about the ownership of the glove which Crewe had brought, and he could not even say if it had come from their shop. It was an excellent glove, the line being known in the trade as "first-choice reindeer." They stocked that particular kind of article at 10/6 the pair. They had the pleasure of having had the late Sir Horace Fewbanks on their books. He was quite an old account, if he might use the expression. He was one of their best customers, being a gentleman who was particular about his appearance and who would have nothing but the best in any line that he fancied. On the subject of Sir Horace's taste in hose the manager had much to say, and, in spite of Crewe's efforts to confine the conversation to gloves, the manager repeatedly dragged in socks. He did it so frequently that he became conscious his visitor was showing signs of annoyance, so he apologised, adding, with an inspiration, "After all, hose is really gloves for the feet."

Crewe ascertained that a large number of legal gentlemen were customers of Bruden and Marshall. He innocently suggested that the reason was because the shop was the nearest one of its kind to the Law Courts, but this explanation offended the shopman's pride. It was because they stocked high-class goods and gave good value in every way, combined with attention and civility and a desire to please, that they did such an excellent business with legal gentlemen. In refutation of the idea that proximity to the Courts was the direct reason of their having so many legal gentlemen among their customers the manager declared that they received orders from all parts of the world—India, Canada, Australia, and South Africa, to say nothing of American gentlemen who liked their hosiery to have the London hall-mark. Their orders from the Colonies came from gentlemen who found that these things in the Colonies were not what they had been used to, and so they sent their orders to Bruden and Marshall.

Crewe's interest was in the legal customers and he asked for the names of some. The manager ran through a list of names of judges, barristers and solicitors, but the name Crewe wanted to hear was not among them. He was compelled to include the name among half a dozen others he mentioned to the manager. He ascertained that Mr. Charles Holymead was a customer of the firm, but it was apparent from the manager's spiritless attitude towards Mr. Holymead that the famous K.C. was not a man who ran up a big bill with his hosier, or was very particular about what he wore. The world regarded some of the men of this type famous or distinguished, but in the hosier's mind they were all classed as commonplace. But the manager would not go so far as to say that Mr. Holymead would not buy such a glove as that which Crewe had brought in. He might and he might not, but, as a general rule, he did not pay more than 8/6 for his gloves.

Crewe took a taxi to Princes Gate in order to have a look at the house in which Holymead lived. It occurred to him that if Holymead was not particular about what he spent on his clothes he was extravagant about the amount he spent in house rent. Of course, a leading barrister earning a huge income could afford to live in a palatial residence in Princes Gate, but it was not the locality or residence that an economically-minded man would have chosen for his home. But Crewe had little doubt that the beautiful wife Holymead possessed was responsible for the choice of house and locality.

After looking at the house Crewe walked back to the cab-stand at Hyde Park Corner. He had arrived at the conclusion that it was necessary to settle beyond doubt whether the K.C. had visited Riversbrook the night Sir Horace had returned from Scotland. If the K.C. had done so, he was anxious to keep the visit secret, for not only had he not informed the police of his visit but he had kept it from Miss Fewbanks. Crewe had ascertained from Miss Fewbanks that Mr. Holymead when he had called at Riversbrook on a visit of condolence had not mentioned to her anything about having left his stick in the hall stand on a previous visit. On leaving Miss Fewbanks Mr. Holymead had gone up to the hall stand and taken both his hat and stick as if he had left them both there a few minutes before.

Crewe reasoned that if Holymead had gone out to see Sir Horace Fewbanks at Riversbrook and had desired to keep his visit a secret he would not have taken a cab at Hyde Park Corner to Hampstead, but would have travelled by underground railway or omnibus. In all probability the Tube had been used because of its speed being more in harmony with the feelings of a man impatient to get done with a subject so important that Sir Horace had been recalled from Scotland to deal with it. He would leave the Tube at Hampstead and take a taxi-cab. He would not be likely to go straight to Riversbrook in the taxi-cab, if he were anxious that his movements should not be traced subsequently. He would dismiss the taxi-cab at one of the hotels bordering on Hampstead Heath, for they were the resort of hundreds of visitors on summer nights, and his actions would thus easily escape notice. From the hotel he would walk across to Riversbrook. But the return journey would be made in a somewhat different way. If Holymead left Riversbrook in a state of excitement he would walk a long way without being conscious of the exertion. He would want to be alone with his own thoughts. Gradually he would cool down, and becoming conscious of his surroundings would make his way home. Again he would use the Tube, for it would be more difficult for his movements to be traced if he mixed with a crowd of travellers than if he took a cab to his home. It was impossible to say what station he got in at, for that would depend on how far he walked before he cooled down, but he would be sure to get out at Hyde Park Corner because that was the station nearest to his house. Allowing for a temperamental reaction during a train journey of about twenty minutes, he would feel depressed and weary and would probably take a taxi-cab outside Hyde Park station to his home. That was a thing he would often be in the habit of doing when returning late at night from the theatre or elsewhere, and therefore could be easily explained by him if the police happened to make inquiries as to his movements.

As Crewe anticipated, he had no difficulty in finding the driver of the taxi-cab in which Holymead had driven home on the night of Wednesday last. The K.C. frequently used cabs, and he was well-known to all the drivers on the rank. Crewe got into the cab he had used and ordered the man to drive him to his office, and there invited him upstairs. He adopted this course because he knew that the driver, who gave his name as Taylor, would be more likely to talk freely in an office where he could not be overheard than he would do on the cab-rank with his fellow-drivers crowding him, or in an hotel parlour where other people were present.

"Tell me exactly what happened when you drove Mr. Holymead home on Wednesday night," said Crewe. "Did you notice anything strange about him, or was his manner much the same as on other occasions that he used your cab?"

"Well, I don't see whether I should tell you whether he was or whether he wasn't," replied the taxi-cab driver, who was as surly as most of his class. "What's it to do with you, anyway? He's a regular customer of mine on the rank, and he's not one of your tuppenny tipsters, either. He's a gentleman. And if he got to know that I had been telling tales about him it would not do me any good."

"It would not," replied Crewe, with cordial acquiescence. "Therefore, Taylor, I give you my word of honour not to mention anything you tell me. Furthermore, I'll see that you don't lose by it now or at any other time. I cannot say more than that, but that's a great deal more than the police would say. Now, would you sooner tell me or tell the police? Here's a sovereign to start with, and if you have an interesting story to tell you'll have another one before you leave."

The appeal of money and the conviction that the police would use less considerate methods if Crewe passed him over to them abolished Taylor's scruples about discussing a fare, and it was in a much less surly tone that he responded:

"I didn't notice anything strange about him when he called me off the rank, but I did afterwards. First of all, I didn't drive him home. That is, I did drive him home, but he didn't go inside. When I drew up outside his house in Princes Gate, I looked around expecting to see him get out. As he didn't move I got down and opened the door. 'Aren't you getting out here, sir?' I said, in a soft voice. 'No,' he said. 'Drive on.' 'This is your house, sir,' I ventured to say. 'I'm not going in,' he replied, 'drive on.' I was surprised. I thought he was the worse for drink, and I'd never seen him that way before. But some gentlemen are so obstinate in liquor that you can't get them to do anything except the opposite of what you ask them. I thought I'd try and coax him. 'Better go inside, sir,' I said. 'You'll be better off in bed.' 'Do you think I am drunk?' he said sharply. You could have knocked me down with a feather. He was as sober as a judge, all in a moment. 'No, sir, I didn't,' I said. 'I wouldn't take the liberty,' I said. 'Then get back on your seat and drive me to the Hyde Park Hotel—no, I think I'll go to Verney's. But don't go there direct. Drive me round the Park first. I feel I want a breath of cool air.'"

"Go on," said Crewe, in a tone which indicated approval of Taylor's method of telling his story.

"Well, I turned the cab round and drove through the Park. But I was puzzled about him and looked back at him once or twice pretending that I was looking to see if a cab or car was coming up behind. And as we passed over the Serpentine Bridge I saw him throw something out of the window."

"A glove?" suggested Crewe quickly.

The driver looked at him in profound admiration.

"Well, if you don't beat all the detectives I've ever heard of."

"He tried to throw it in the water," continued Crewe, as if explaining the matter to himself rather than to his visitor. "Did you get it?"

"Hold on a bit," said Taylor, who had his own ideas of how to give value for the extra sovereign he hoped to obtain. "I couldn't see what it was he had thrown away, and, of course, I couldn't pull up to find out. I drove on, but I kept my eye on him, though I had my back to him. As we were driving back along the Broad Walk I had another look at him, and bless me if he wasn't crying—crying like a child. He had his hands up to his face and his head was shaking as if he was sobbing. I said to myself, 'He's barmy—he's gone off his rocker.' I thought to myself I ought to drive him to the police station, but I reckoned it was none of my business, after all, so I'll take him to Verney's and be done with it. So I drove to Verney's. He got out, and paid me, but I couldn't see that he had been crying, and he looked much as usual, so far as I could see. I thought to myself that perhaps, after all, he'd only had a queer turn; however, I said to myself I'd drive back to the bridge and see what he'd thrown out of the window. It *was* a glove, sure enough. It had fallen just below the railing. I looked about for the other one, but I couldn›t find it, so I suppose it must have fallen into the water."

"No, it didn't," said Crewe. "I have it here." He opened a drawer in his desk and produced a glove. "It was a right-hand glove you found. Just look at this one and see if it corresponds to the one you picked up."

Taylor looked at the glove.

"They're as like as two peas," he said.

"What did you do with the one you found?" inquired Crewe. "I hope you didn't throw it away?"

"I'm not a fool," retorted Taylor. "I've had odd gloves left in my cab before. I kept this one thinking that sooner or later somebody might leave another like it, and then I'd have a pair for nothing."

"Well, I'll buy it from you," said Crewe. "Have you anything more to tell me?"

"I went back to the rank and one of the chaps was curious that I'd been so long away, for he knew that Mr. Holymead's place isn't more than ten minutes' drive from the station. But he got nothing out of me. I know how to keep my mouth shut. You're the first man I've told what happened, and I hope you won't give me away."

"I've already promised you that," said Crewe, flipping another sovereign from his sovereign case and handing it to Taylor, "and I'll give you five shillings for the glove."

Taylor looked at him darkly.

"Five shillings isn't much for a glove like that," he said insolently. "What about my loss of time going home for it? I suppose you'll pay the taxi-fare for the run down from Hyde Park?"

"No, I won't," said Crewe cheerfully.

"Then I don't see why I should bring it for a paltry five shillings," said Taylor. "If you want the glove you'll have to pay for it."

"But I don't want the glove," said Crewe, who disliked being made the victim of extortion. "What made you think so? I'll sell you this one for five shillings. We may as well do a deal of some kind; it is no use each of us having one glove. What do you say, Taylor? Will you buy mine for five shillings, or shall I buy yours?"

Taylor smiled sourly.

"You're a deep one," he said. "Here's the other glove." He dipped his hand into the deep pocket of his driving coat and produced a glove. "I suppose you knew I'd have it on me. Five shillings, and it's yours."

"The pair are worth about five shillings to me," said Crewe as he paid over the money. "Do you remember what time it was when Mr. Holymead engaged you at Hyde Park?"

"Eleven o'clock."

"You are quite sure as to the time?"

"I heard one of the big clocks striking as he was getting into my cab."

Taylor took his departure, and Crewe, after wrapping up the left-hand glove which he had to return to Inspector Chippenfield, put the other one in his safe.

"We are getting on," he said in a pleased tone. "This means a trip to Scotland, but I'll wait until the inquest is over."

CHAPTER IX

At the inquest on the body of Sir Horace Fewbanks, which was held at the Hampstead Police Court, there was an odd mixture of classes in the crowd that thronged that portion of the court in which the public were allowed to congregate. The accounts of the crime which had been published in the press, and the atmosphere of mystery which enshrouded the violent death of one of the most prominent of His Majesty's judges, had stirred the public curiosity, and therefore, in spite of the fact that every one was supposed to be out of town in August, the attendance at the court included a sprinkling of ladies of the fashionable world, and their escorts.

Both branches of the legal profession were numerously represented. All of the victim's judicial colleagues were out of town, and though some of them intended as a mark of respect for the dead man to come up for the funeral, which was to take place two days later, they were too familiar with legal procedure to feel curiosity as to the working of the machinery at a preliminary inquiry into the crime. They were emphatic among their friends on the degeneracy of these days which rendered possible such an outrageous crime as the murder of a High Court judge. The fact that it was without precedent in the history of British law added to its enormity in the eyes of gentlemen who had been trained to worship precedent as the only safe guide through the shifting quicksands of life. They were insistent on the urgency of the murderer being arrested and handed over to Justice in the person of the hangman, for—as each asked himself—where was this sort of crime to end? In spite of the degeneracy of the times they were reluctant to believe in such a far-fetched supposition as the existence of a band of criminals who, in revenge for the judicial sentences imposed on members of their class, had sworn to exterminate the whole of His Majesty's judges; but, until the murderer was apprehended and the reason for the crime was discovered, it was impossible to say that the English judicature would not soon be called upon to supply other victims to criminal violence. The murder of a judge seemed to them a particularly atrocious crime, in the punishment of which the law might honourably sacrifice temporarily its well-earned reputation for delay.

The bar was represented chiefly by junior members. The senior members were able to make full use of the long vacation, spending it at health resorts or in the country, but the incomes of the young shoots of the great parasitical profession did not permit them to enjoy more than a brief holiday out of town. Of course it would never have done for them to admit even to each other that they could not afford to go away for an extended holiday, and therefore they told one another in bored tones that they had not been able to make up their minds where to go. The junior bar included old men, who, through lack of influence, want of energy, want of advertisement, want of ability, or some other deficiency, had never earned more than a few guineas at their profession, though they had spent year after year in chambers. They lived on scanty private means. Broken in spirit they had even ceased to attend the courts in order to study the methods and learn the tricks of successful counsel. But the murder of a High Court judge was a thing which stirred even their sluggish blood, and in the hope of some sensational development they had put on faded silk hats and shabby black suits and gone out to Hampstead to attend the inquest.

The interest of the junior bar in the crime was as personal as that of the members of the Judicial Bench, though it manifested itself in an entirely different direction. They speculated among themselves as to who would be appointed to the vacancy on the High Court Bench. A leading K.C. with a political pull would of course be selected by the Attorney-General, but there were several K.C.'s who possessed these qualifications, and therefore there was room for differences of opinion among the junior bar as to who would get the offer. The point on which they were all united was that vacancies of the High Court Bench were a good thing for the bar as a whole, for they removed leading K.C.'s, and the dispersion of their practice was like rain on parched ground. Metaphorically speaking, every one—including even the junior bar—had the chance of getting a shove up when a leading K.C. accepted a judicial appointment. Some of the more irreverent spirits among the junior bar, in drawing attention to the fact that Sir Horace Fewbanks had been one of the youngest members of the High

Court Bench, expressed the hope that the shock of his death would be felt by some of the extremely aged members of the bench who were too infirm in health to be able to stand many shocks.

The members of the junior bar chatted with the representatives of the lower branch of the profession who ranged from articled clerks whose young souls had not been entirely dried up by association with parchment, to hard old delvers in dusty documents who had lived so long in the legal atmosphere of quibbling, obstruction, and deceit, that they were as incapable of an honest impetuous act as of an illegal one. The gossip concerning the murdered judge in which the two branches of the profession joined had reference to his moral character in legal circles. There had always been gossip of the kind in his life-time. Sir Horace's judicial reputation was beyond reproach and he had known his law a great deal better than most of his judicial colleagues. Comparatively few of his decisions had been upset on appeal. But every one about the courts knew that he was susceptible to a pretty feminine face and a good figure.

Many were the conflicts that arose in court between bench and bar as the result of Mr. Justice Fewbanks's habit of protecting pretty witnesses from cross-examining questions which he regarded as outside the case. There was no suggestion that his judicial decisions were influenced by the good looks of ladies who were parties to the cases heard by him, but there were rumours that on occasions the relations between the judge and a pretty witness begun in court had ripened into something at which moral men might well shake their heads.

While the members of the legal profession struggled to obtain seats in the body of the court, an entirely different class of spectators struggled to get into the gallery. For the most part they were badly dressed men who needed a shave, but there were a few well-dressed men among them, and also a few ladies. Detective Rolfe took a professional interest in the occupants of the gallery. "What a collection of crooks," he whispered to Inspector Chippenfield. "A regular rogues' gallery. Look—there is 'Nosey George'; it is time he was in again. And behind him is that cunning old 'drop' Ikey Samuels—I wish we could get him. Look at the other end of the first row. Isn't that 'Sunny Jim'? I hardly knew him. He's grown a beard since he's been out. We'll soon have it off again for him. He's got the impudence to scowl at us. He'll lay for you one of these nights, Inspector."

The judicial duties of the murdered man had been concerned chiefly with civil cases at the Royal Courts of Justice, but when the criminal calendar had been heavy he had often presided at Number One Court at the Old Bailey. It was this fact which had given the criminal class a sort of personal interest in his murder and accounted for the presence of many well-known criminals who happened to be out of gaol at the time. The spectators in the gallery included men whom the murdered man had sentenced and men who had been fortunate enough to escape being sentenced by him owing to the vagaries of juries. There were pickpockets, sneak thieves, confidence men, burglars, and receivers among the occupants of the gallery, and many of them had brought with them the ladies who assisted them professionally or presided over their homes when they were not in gaol.

"Iwouldn'tbesurprisedifthemanwewantisamongthatbunch," said Rolfe to Inspector Chippenfield.

"You've a lot to learn about them, my boy," said his superior.

"There is Crewe up among them," continued Rolfe. "I wonder what he thinks he's after."

Inspector Chippenfield gave a glance in the direction of Crewe, but did not deign to give any sign of recognition. The fact that Crewe by his presence in the gallery seemed to entertain the idea that the murderer might be found among the occupants of that part of the court could not be as lightly dismissed as Rolfe's vague suggestion. It annoyed Inspector Chippenfield to think that Crewe might be nearer at the moment to the murderer than he himself was, even though that proximity was merely physical and unsupported by evidence or even by any theory. It would have been a great relief to him if he had known that Crewe's object in going to the gallery was not to mix with the criminal classes, but in order to keep a careful survey of what took place in the body of the court without making himself too prominent.

Mr. Holymead, K.C., arrived, and members of the junior bar deferentially made room for him. He shook hands with some of these gentlemen and also with Inspector Chippenfield, much to the gratification of that officer. Miss Fewbanks arrived in a taxi-cab a few minutes before the appointed hour of eleven. She was accompanied by Mrs. Holymead, and they were shown into a private room by Police-Constable Flack, who had received instructions from Inspector Chippenfield to be on the lookout for the murdered man's daughter.

Miss Fewbanks and Mrs. Holymead had been almost inseparable since the tragedy had been discovered. Immediately on the arrival of Miss Fewbanks from Dellmere, Mrs. Holymead had gone out to Riversbrook to condole with her, and to support her in her great sorrow. But the murdered man's daughter, who, on account of having lived apart from her father, had developed a self-reliant spirit, seemed to be less overcome by the horror of the tragedy than Mrs. Holymead was. It was with a feeling that there was something lacking in her own nature, that the girl realised that Mrs. Holymead's grief for the violent death of a man who had been her husband's dearest friend was greater than her own grief at the loss of a father.

One of the directions in which Mrs. Holymead's grief found expression was in a feverish desire to know all that was being done to discover the murderer. She displayed continuous interest in the investigations of the detectives engaged on the case, and she had implored Miss Fewbanks to let her know when any important discovery was made. She applauded the action of her young friend in engaging such a famous detective as Crewe, and declared that if anyone could unravel the mystery, Crewe would do it. She had been particularly anxious to hear through Miss Fewbanks what Crewe's impressions were, with regard to the tragedy.

The court was opened punctually, the coroner being Mr. Bodyman, a stout, clean-shaven, white-haired gentleman who had spent thirty years of his life in the stuffy atmosphere of police courts hearing police-court cases. Police-Inspector Seldon nodded in reply to the inquiring glance of the coroner, and the inquest was opened.

The first witness was Miss Fewbanks. She was dressed in deep black and was obviously a little unnerved. In a low tone she said she had identified the body as that of her father. She was staying at her father's country house in Dellmere, Sussex, when the crime was committed. She had no knowledge of anyone who was evilly disposed towards her father. He had never spoken to her of anyone who cherished a grudge against him.

Evidence relating to the circumstances in which the body was found was given by Police-Constable Flack. He described the position of the room in which the body was found, and the attitude in which the body was stretched. He was on duty in the neighbourhood of Tanton Gardens on the night of the murder, but saw no suspicious characters and heard no sounds.

The evidence of Hill was chiefly a repetition of what he had told Inspector Chippenfield as to his movements on the day of the crime, and his methods of inspecting the premises three times a week in accordance with his master's orders. He knew nothing about Sir Horace's sudden return from Scotland. His first knowledge of this was the account of the murder, which he read in the papers.

Inspector Chippenfield gave evidence for the purpose of producing the letter received at Scotland Yard announcing that Sir Horace Fewbanks had been murdered. The letter was passed up to the coroner for his inspection, and when he had examined it he sent it to the foreman of the jury. Then followed medical evidence, which showed that death was due to a bullet wound and could not have been self-inflicted.

The coroner, in his summing-up, dwelt upon the loss sustained by the Judiciary by the violent death of one of its most distinguished members, and the jury, after a retirement of a few minutes, brought in a verdict of wilful murder by some person or persons unknown.

As the occupants of the court filed out into the street, Crewe, who was watching Holymead, noticed the K.C. give a slight start when he saw Miss Fewbanks and his wife. Mr. Holymead went up to the ladies and shook hands with Miss Fewbanks, and to Crewe it seemed as if he was on the point of shaking hands with his wife, but he stopped himself awkwardly. He saw the ladies into their cab, and, raising his hat, went off. As Mr. Holymead had seen Miss Fewbanks in court when she gave evidence, it was obvious to Crewe that he could not have been surprised at meeting her outside. It was therefore the presence of his wife which had surprised him. That fact—if it were a fact—opened a limitless field of speculation to Crewe, but in spite of the possibility of error—a possibility which he frankly recognised—he was pleased with himself for having noticed the incident. To him it seemed to provide another link in the chain he was constructing. It harmonised with Taylor's story of Mr. Holymead's decision to stay at Verney's instead of entering his own home the night Taylor drove him from Hyde Park Corner.

Rolfe also possessed the professional faculty of observation, but in a different degree. He had seen Mr. Holymead talking to his wife and Miss Fewbanks, but he had noticed nothing but gentlemanly ease in the barrister's manner. What did astonish him in connection with Mr. Holymead was that after he had left the ladies and was walking in the direction of the cab-rank he spoke to one of the former occupants of the gallery. This was a man known to the police and his associates as "Kincher." His name was Kemp, and how he had obtained his nick-name was not known. He was a criminal by profession and had undergone several heavy sentences for burglary. He was a thick-set man of medium height, about fifty years of age. Apart from a rather heavy lower jaw, he gave no external indication of his professional pursuits, but looked, with his brown and weather-beaten face and rough blue reefer suit, not unlike a seafaring man. The likeness was heightened by a tattooed device which covered the back of his right hand, and a slight roll in his gait when he walked. But appearances are deceptive, for Mr. Kemp, at liberty or in gaol, had never been out of London in his life. He was born and bred a London thief, and had served all his sentences at Wormwood Scrubbs. For over a minute he and Mr. Holymead remained in conversation. Rolfe would have described it officially as familiar conversation, but that description would have overlooked the deference, the sense of inferiority, in "Kincher's" manner. For a time Rolfe was puzzled by the incident, but he eventually lighted on an explanation which satisfied himself. It was that in the earlier days before Mr. Holymead had reached such a prominent position at the bar, he had been engaged in practice in the criminal courts, and "Kincher" had been one of his clients.

With a cheerful smile Holymead brought the conversation to an end and went on his way. Kemp walked on hurriedly in the opposite direction. He had his eyes on a young man whom he had seen in the gallery, and who had seemed to avoid his eye. It was obvious to him that this young man, for whom he had been on the watch when Mr. Holymead spoke to him, had seized the opportunity to slip past him while he was talking to the eminent K.C. The young man, even from the back view, seemed to be well-dressed.

"Hallo, Fred," exclaimed Mr. Kemp, as he reached within a yard or two of his quarry.

"Hallo, Kincher," replied the young man, turning round. "I didn't notice you. Were you up at the court?"

"Yes, I looked in," said Mr. Kemp. "There wasn't much doing, was there?"

"No," said Fred.

"He won't trouble us any more," pursued Mr. Kemp.

"No." The young man seemed to have a dread of helping along the conversation, and therefore sought refuge in monosyllables.

Mr. Kemp coughed before he formed his question.

"Did you go up there that night?"

"No." The reply came instantaneously, but the young man followed it up with a look of inquiry to ascertain if his denial was believed.

"A good thing as it happened," said Mr. Kemp.

"I had nothing to do with it," said Fred, earnestly.

"I never said you had," replied Mr. Kemp.

"Nothing whatever to do with it,"
continued the young man with emphasis.
"That's not my sort of game."

"I'm not saying anything, Fred," replied the elder man. "But whoever done it might have done it by accident-like."

"Accident or no accident, I had nothing to do with it, thank God."

"That is all right, Fred. I'm not saying you know anything about it. But even if you did you'd find I could be trusted. I don't go blabbing round to everybody."

"I know you don't. But as I said before I had nothing to do with it. I didn't go there that night—I changed my mind."

"A very lucky thing then, because if they do look you up you can prove an alibi."

"Yes," said Fred, "I can prove an alibi easy enough. But what makes you talk about them looking me up? Why should they get into me—why should they look me up? I've told you I didn't go there."

"That is all right, Fred," said the other, in a soothing tone. "If that pal of yours keeps his mouth shut there is nothing to put them on your tracks. But I don't like the looks of him. He seems to me a bit nervous, and if they put him through the third degree he'll squeak. That's my impression."

"If he squeaks he'll have to settle with me," said Fred. "And he'll find there is something to pay. If he tries to put me away I'll—I'll—I'll do him in."

"Kincher" instead of being horrified at this sentiment seemed to approve of it as the right thing to be done. "I'd let him know if I was you, Fred," he said. "I didn't like the look of him. The reason I came out here to-day was to have a look at him. And when I saw him in the box I said to myself, 'Well, I'm glad I've staked nothing on you, for it seems to me that you'll crack up if the police shake their thumbscrews in your face.' I felt glad I hadn't accepted your invitation to make it a two-handed job, Fred. It was the fact that some one else I'd never seen had put up the job that kept me out of it when you asked me to go with you. A man can't be too careful—especially after he's had a long spell in 'stir,' But of course you're all right if you changed your mind and didn't go up there. But if I was you I'd have my alibi ready. It is no good leaving things until the police are at the door and making one up on the spur of the moment."

"Yes, I'll see about it," said Fred. "It's a good idea."

"Comeinandhaveadrink,Fred," said "Kincher." "Itwilldoyougood. It was dry work listening to them talking up there about the murder."

Fred accompanied Mr. Kemp into the bar of the hotel they reached, and the elder man, after an inquiring glance at his companion, ordered two whiskies. "Kincher" added water to the contents of each glass, and, lifting his glass in his right hand, waited until Fred had done the same and then said:

"Well, here's luck and long life to the man that did it—whoever he is."

Fred offered no objection to this sentiment and they drained glasses.

CHAPTER X

"And so you've had no luck, Rolfe?"

Inspector Chippenfield, glancing up from his official desk in Scotland Yard, put this question in a tone of voice which suggested that the speaker had expected nothing better.

"I've seen the heads of at least half a dozen likely West End shops," Rolfe replied, "and they tell me there is nothing to indicate where the handkerchief was bought. The scrap of lace merely shows that it was torn off a good handkerchief, but there is nothing about it to show that the handkerchief was different in any marked way from the average filmy scrap of muslin and lace which every smart woman carries as a handkerchief. I thought so myself, before I started to make inquiries."

"Well, Rolfe, we must come at it another way," said the inspector. "Undoubtedly there is a woman in the case, and it ought not to be impossible to locate her. Your theory, Rolfe, is that the murder was committed by some one who broke into the place while Sir Horace was entertaining a lady friend or waiting for the arrival of a lady he expected. Either the lady had not arrived or had left the room temporarily when the burglar broke into the house. He had spotted the place some days before and ascertained that it was empty, and when he found that Sir Horace had returned alone he decided to break in, and, covering Sir Horace with a revolver, try to extort money from him. A riskier but more profitable game than burgling an empty house—if it came off. With his revolver in his hand he made his way up to the library. Sir Horace parleyed with him until he could reach his own revolver, and then got in the first shot but missed his man. The burglar shot him and then bolted. The lady heard the shots, and, rushing in, found Sir Horace in his death agony. She was stooping over him with her handkerchief in her hand, and in his convulsive moments he caught hold of a corner of it and the handkerchief was torn. The lady left the place and on arrival home concocted that letter which was sent here telling us that Sir Horace had been murdered. Is that it?"

"Yes," assented Rolfe. "Of course, I don't lay it down that everything happened just as you've said. But that's my idea of the crime. It accounts for all the clues we've picked up, and that is something."

"It is an ingenious theory and it does you credit," said the inspector, who had not forgotten that he had proposed to Rolfe that they should help one another to the extent of taking one another fully into each other's confidence, for the purpose of getting ahead of Crewe. "But you have overlooked the fact that it is possible to account in another way for all the clues we have picked up. Suppose Sir Horace's return from Scotland was due to a message from a lady friend; suppose the lady went to see him accompanied by a friend whom Sir Horace did not like—a friend of whom Sir Horace was jealous. Suppose they asked for money—blackmail—and there was a quarrel in which Sir Horace was shot. Then we have your idea as to how the lady's handkerchief was torn—I agree with that in the main. The lady and her friend fled from the place. Later in the night the place is burgled by some one who has had his eye on it for some time, and on entering the library he is astounded to find the dead body of the owner. Suppose he went home, and on thinking things over sent the letter to Scotland Yard with the idea that if the police got on to his tracks about the burglary the fact that he had told us about the murder would show he had nothing to do with killing Sir Horace."

"That is a good theory, too," said Rolfe, in a meditative tone. "And the only person who can tell us which is the right one is Sir Horace's lady friend. The problem is to find her."

"Right," said the inspector approvingly. "And while you have been making inquiries at the shops about the handkerchief I have been down to the Law Courts branch of the Equity Bank where Sir Horace kept his account. It occurred to me that a look at Sir Horace's account might help us. You know the sort of man he was—you know his weakness for the ladies. But he was careful. I looked through his private papers out at Riversbrook expecting to get on the track of something that would show some one had been trying to blackmail him over an entanglement with a woman, but I found nothing. I couldn't even find any feminine correspondence. If Sir Horace was in the habit of getting letters from ladies he was also in the habit of destroying them. No doubt he adopted that precaution when his wife was alive, and found it such a wise one that he kept it up when there was less need for it. But a weakness for the ladies costs money, Rolfe, as you know, and that is why I had a look at his banking account. He made some payments that it would be worth while to trace—payments to West End drapers and that sort of thing. Of course, Sir Horace, being a cautious man and occupying a public position, might not care to flaunt his weakness in the eyes of West End shopkeepers, and instead of paying the accounts of his lady friend of the moment, may have given her the money and trusted to her paying the bills—a thing that women of that kind are never in a hurry to do. In that case the payments to West End shopkeepers are for goods supplied to his daughter. However, I've taken a note of the names, dates, and amounts of a number of them, and I want you to see the managers of these shops."

"We are getting close to it now," said Rolfe, approvingly.

"I think so," was the modest reply of his superior. "There is one thing about Sir Horace's account which struck me as peculiar. Every four weeks for the past eight months Sir Horace drew a cheque for £24, and every cheque of the kind was made payable to Number 365. Now, unless he wished to hide the nature of the transaction from his bankers, why not put in the cheque in the name of the person who received the money? It couldn't have been for his personal use, for in that case he would have made the cheques payable to self. Besides, a man with a banking account doesn't draw a regular £24 every four weeks for personal expenses. He draws a cheque just when he wants a few pounds, instead of carrying five-pound notes about with him. I asked the bank manager about these cheques and he looked up a couple of them and found they had been cashed over the counter. So he called up the cashier and from him I learnt that Sir Horace came in and cashed them. As far as he can remember Sir Horace cashed all these £24 cheques. I assume he did so because he realised that there was less likely to be comment in the bank than if a well-dressed good-looking young lady arrived at the bank with them. This £24 a month suggests that Sir Horace had something choice and not too expensive stowed away in a flat. That is a matter on which Hill ought to be able to throw some light. If he knows anything I'll get it out of him. It struck me as extraordinary that Sir Horace should have taken Hill into his service knowing what he was. But this, apparently, is the explanation. He knew that Hill wouldn't gossip about him for fear of being exposed, for that would mean that Hill would lose his situation and would find it impossible to get another one without a reference from him. We'll have Hill brought here—".

There was a knock at the door, and a boy in buttons entered and handed Inspector Chippenfield a card.

"Seldon from Hampstead," he explained to Rolfe. "Don't go away yet. It may be something about this case."

Police-Inspector Seldon entered the office, and held the door ajar for a man behind him. He shook hands with Inspector Chippenfield and Rolfe, and then motioned his companion to a chair.

"This is Mr. Robert Evans, the landlord of the Flowerdew Hotel, Covent Garden," he explained. He looked at Mr. Evans with the air of a police-court inspector waiting for a witness to corroborate his statement, but as that gentleman remained silent he sharply asked, "Isn't that so?"

"Quite right," said Mr. Evans, in a moist, husky voice.

He was a short fat man, with an extremely red face and bulging eyes, which watered very much and apparently required to be constantly mopped with a handkerchief which he carried in his hand. This peculiarity gave Mr. Evans the appearance of a man perpetually in mourning, and this effect was heightened by a species of incipient palsy which had seized on his lower facial muscles, and caused his lips to tremble violently. He was bald in the front of the head but not on the top. The baldness over the temples had joined hands and left isolated over the centre of the forehead a small tuft of hair, which, with the playfulness of second childhood, showed a tendency to curl.

"Yes, you're quite right," he repeated huskily, as though some one had doubted the statement. "Evans is my name and I'm not ashamed of it."

"He came to me this morning and told me that Hill gave false evidence at the inquest yesterday," Inspector Seldon explained. "So I brought him along to see you."

"False evidence—Hill?" exclaimed Inspector Chippenfield, with keen interest. "Let us hear about it."

"Well, you will remember Hill said he was at home on the night of the murder," pursued Inspector Seldon. "I looked up his depositions before I came away and what he said was this: 'I took my daughter to the Zoo in the afternoon. We left the Zoo at half past five and went home and had tea. My wife then took the child to the picture-palace and I remained at home. I did not go out that night. They returned about half-past ten, and after supper we all went to bed.' But Evans tells me he saw Hill in his bar at three o'clock on the morning of the 19th of August. He has an early license for the accommodation of the Covent Garden traffic. He can swear to Hill. A man who goes to bed at half-past ten has no right to be wandering about Covent Garden at 3 a. m. And besides, Hill told us nothing about this. So I brought Evans along to see what you make of it."

Inspector Chippenfield had taken up a pencil and was making a few notes.

"Very interesting indeed," he said. Then he turned to Evans and asked, "Are you sure you saw Hill in your bar at three a. m.? There is no possibility of a mistake?"

"He is the man who was knocked down outside by a porter running into him," said Mr. Evans, mopping his eyes. "I could bring half a dozen witnesses who will swear to him."

"You see, it's this way," interpolated Inspector Seldon, taking up the landlord's narrative. His police-court training had taught him to bring out the salient points of a story, and he was naturally of the opinion that he could tell another man's story better than the man could tell it himself. "Hill was staring about him—it was probably the first time he had been to Covent Garden in the early morning—and got knocked over. He was stunned, and some porters took him in to the bar, sat him on a form, and poured some rum into him. Some of the porters were for ringing up the ambulance; others were for carrying Hill off to the hospital, but he soon recovered. However, he sat there for about twenty minutes, and after having several drinks at his own expense he went away. Evans served him with the drinks."

"Good," said Inspector Chippenfield, who liked the circumstantial details of the story. "And you can get half a dozen porters to identify him?"

"Bill Cribb, Harry Winch, Charlie Brown, a fellow they call 'Green Violets'—I don't know his real name—"

Mr. Evans was calling on his memory for further names but was stopped by Inspector Chippenfield.

"That will do very well. And how did you happen to be at the inquest at Hampstead? That is a bit out of your way."

Mr. Evans mopped his eyes, and Inspector Seldon took upon himself to reply for him. "He has a brother-in-law in the trade at Hampstead—keeps the *Three Jugs* in Coulter Street. Evans had to go out to see his brother-in-law on business, and his brother-in-law took him along to the court out of curiosity."

Inspector Chippenfield nodded.

"Rolfe," he said, "take down Mr. Evans's statement outside and get him to sign it. Don't go away when you've finished. I want you."

Mr. Evans, even if he felt that full justice had been done to his story by Inspector Seldon, was disappointed at the police officer's failure to do justice to his manly scruples in coming forward to give evidence against a man who had never done him any harm. Addressing Inspector Chippenfield he said:

"I don't altogether like mixing myself up in this business. That isn't my way. If I have a thing to say to a man I like to say it to his face. I don't like a man to say things behind a man's back, that is, if he calls himself a man. But I thought over this thing after leaving the court and hearing this chap Hill say he hadn't left home that night, and I talked it over with my wife—"

"You did the right thing," said Inspector Chippenfield, with the emphasis of a man who had profited by the triumph of right.

Mr. Evans was under the impression that the inspector's approval referred chiefly to the part he had played as a husband in talking over his perplexity with his wife, rather than the part he had played as a man in revealing that Hill had lied in his evidence.

"I always do," he said. "My wife's one of the sensible sort, and when a man takes her advice he don't go far wrong. She advised me to go straight to the police-station and tell them all I know. 'It is a cruel murder,' she said, 'and who knows but it might be our turn next?'"

This example of the imaginative element in feminine logic made no impression on the practical official who listened to the admiring husband.

"That is all right," said Inspector Chippenfield soothingly. "I understand your scruples. They do you credit. But an honest man like you doesn't want to shield a criminal from justice—least of all a cold-blooded murderer."

When Rolfe returned to his superior with Evans's signed statement in his hand, he found the inspector preparing to leave the office.

"Put on your hat and come with me," said the inspector. "We will go out and see Mrs. Hill. I'll frighten the truth out of her and then tackle Hill. He is sure to be up at Riversbrook, and we can go on there from Camden Town."

While on the way to Camden Town by Tube, Inspector Chippenfield arranged his plans with the object of saving time. He would interview Mrs. Hill and while he was doing so Rolfe could make inquiries at the neighbouring hotels about Hill. It was the inspector's conviction that a man who had anything to do with a murder would require a steady supply of stimulants next day.

Mrs. Hill kept a small confectionery shop adjoining a cinema theatre to supplement her husband's wages by a little earnings of her own in order to support her child. Although the shop was an unpretentious one, and catered mainly for the ha'p'orths of the juvenile patrons of the picture house next door, it was called "The Camden Town Confectionery Emporium," and the title was printed over the little shop in large letters. Inspector Chippenfield walked into the empty shop, and rapped sharply on the counter.

A little thin woman, with prematurely grey hair, and a depressed expression, appeared from the back in response to the summons. She started nervously as her eye encountered the police uniform, but she waited to be spoken to.

"Is your name Hill?" asked the inspector sternly. "Mrs. Emily Hill?"

The woman nodded feebly, her frightened eyes fixed on the inspector's face.

"Then I want to have a word with you," continued the inspector, walking through the shop into the parlour. "Come in here and answer my questions."

Mrs. Hill followed him timidly into the room he had entered. It was a small, shabbily-furnished apartment, and the inspector's massive proportions made it look smaller still. He took up a commanding position on the strip of drugget which did duty as a hearth-rug, and staring fiercely at her, suddenly commenced:

"Mrs. Hill, where was your husband on the night of the 18th of August, when his employer, Sir Horace Fewbanks, was murdered?"

Mrs. Hill shrank before that fierce gaze, and said, in a low tone:

"Please, sir, he was at home."

"At home, was he? I'm not so sure of that. Tell me all about your husband's movements on that day and night. What time did he come home, to begin with?"

"He came home early in the afternoon to take our little girl to the Zoo—which was a treat she had been looking forward to for a long while. I couldn't go myself, there being the shop to look after. So Mr. Hill and Daphne went to the Zoo, and after they came home and had tea I took her to the pictures while Mr. Hill minded the shop. It was not the picture-palace next door, but the big one in High Street, where they were showing 'East Lynne,' Then when we come home about ten o'clock we all had supper and went to bed."

"And your husband didn't go out again?"

"No, sir. When I got up in the morning to bring him a cup of tea he was still sound asleep."

"But might he not have gone out in the night while you were asleep?"

"No, sir. I'm a very light sleeper, and I wake at the least stir."

Mrs. Hill's story seemed to ring true enough, although she kept her eyes fixed on her interrogator with a kind of frightened brightness. Inspector Chippenfield looked at her in silence for a few seconds.

"So that's the whole truth, is it?" he said at length.

"Yes, sir," the woman earnestly assured him. "You can ask Mr. Hill and he'll tell you the same thing."

Something reminiscent in Inspector Chippenfield's mind responded to this sentence. He pondered over it for a moment, and then remembered that Hill had applied the same phrase to his wife. Evidently there had been collusion, a comparing of tales beforehand.

The woman had been tutored by her cunning scoundrel of a husband, but undoubtedly her tale was false.

"The whole truth?" said the inspector, again.

"Yes, sir," answered Mrs. Hill.

"Now, look here," said the police officer, in his sternest tones, as he shook a warning finger at the little woman, "I know you are lying. I know Hill didn't sleep in the house, that night. He was seen near Riversbrook in the early part of the night and he was seen wandering about Covent Garden after the murder had been committed. It is no use lying to me, Mrs. Hill. If you want to save your husband from being arrested for this murder you'll tell the truth. What time did he leave here that night?"

"I've already told you the truth, sir," replied the little woman. "He didn't leave the place after he came back from the Zoo."

Inspector Chippenfield was puzzled. It seemed to him that Mrs. Hill was a woman of weak character, and yet she stuck firmly to her story. Perhaps Evans had made a mistake in identifying Hill as the man who had been carried into his bar after being knocked down. Nothing was more common than mistakes of identification. His glance wandered round the room, as though in search of some inspiration for his next question. His eye took mechanical note of the trumpery articles of rickety furniture; wandered over the cheap almanac prints which adorned the walls; but became riveted in the cheap overmantel which surmounted the fire-place. For, in the slip of mirror which formed the centre of that ornament, Inspector Chippenfield caught sight of the features of Mrs. Hill frowning and shaking her head at somebody invisible. He turned his head warily, but she was too quick for him, and her features were impassive again when he looked at her. Following the direction indicated by the mirror, Inspector Chippenfield saw Mrs. Hill had been signalling through a window which looked into the back yard. He reached it in a step and threw open the window. A small and not over-clean little girl was just leaving the yard by the gate.

Inspector Chippenfield called to her pleasantly, and she retraced her steps with a frightened face.

"Come in, my dear, I want you," said the inspector, wreathing his red face into a smile. "I'm fond of little girls."

The little girl smiled, nodded her head, and presently appeared in response to the inspector's invitation. He glanced at Mrs. Hill, noticed that her face was grey and drawn with sudden terror. She opened her mouth as though to speak, but no words came.

The inspector lifted the child on to his knee. She nestled to him confidingly enough, and looked up into his face with an artless glance.

"What is your name, my dear?"

"Daphne, sir—Daphne Hill."

"How old are you, Daphne?"

"Please, sir, I'm eight next birthday."

"Why, you're quite a big girl, Daphne! Do you go to school?"

"Oh, yes, sir. I'm in the second form."

"Do you like going to school, Daphne?"

"Yes, sir."

"I suppose you like going to the Zoo better? Did you like going with father the other day?"

The child's eyes sparkled with retrospective pleasure.

"Oh, yes," she said, delightedly. "We saw all kinds of things: lions and tigers, and elephants. I had a ride on a elephant"—her eyes grew big with the memory—"an' 'e took a bun with his long nose out of my hand."

"That was splendid, Daphne! Which did you like best—the Zoo or the pictures?"

"I liked them both," she replied.

"Was Father at home when you came home from the pictures?"

"No," said the little girl innocently. "He was out."

Mrs. Hill, standing a little way off with fear on her face, uttered an inarticulate noise, and took a step towards the inspector and her daughter.

"Better not interfere, Mrs. Hill, unless you want to make matters worse," said the inspector meaningly. "Now, tell me, Daphne, dear, when did your father come home?"

"Not till morning," replied the little girl, with a timid glance at her mother.

"How do you know that?"

"Because I slept in Mother's bed that night with Mother, like I always do when Father is away, but Father came home in the morning and lifted me into my own bed, because he said he wanted to go to bed."

"What time was that, Daphne?"

"I don't know, sir."

"It was light, Daphne? You could see?"

"Oh, yes, sir."

Inspector Chippenfield told the child she was a good girl, and gave her sixpence. The little one slipped off his knee and ran across to her mother with delight, to show the coin; all unconscious that she had betrayed her father. The mother pushed the child from her with a heart-broken gesture.

A heavy step was heard in the shop, and the inspector, looking through the window, saw Rolfe. He opened the door leading from the shop and beckoned his subordinate in.

Rolfe was excited, and looked like a man burdened with weighty news. He whispered a word in Inspector Chippenfield's ear.

"Let's go into the shop," said Inspector Chippenfield promptly. "But, first, I'll make things safe here." He locked the door leading to the kitchen, put the key into his pocket, and followed his colleague into the shop. "Now, Rolfe, what is it?"

"I've found out that Hill put in nearly the whole day after the murder drinking in a wine tavern. He sat there like a man in a dream and spoke to nobody. The only thing he took any interest in was the evening papers. He bought about a dozen of them during the afternoon."

"Where was this?" asked the inspector.

"At a little wine tavern in High Street, where he's never been seen before. The man who keeps the place gave me a good description of him, though. Hill went there about ten o'clock in the morning, and started drinking port wine, and as fast as the evening papers came out he sent the boy out for them, glanced through them, and then crumpled them up. He stayed there till after five o'clock. By that time the 6.30 editions would reach Camden Town, and if you remember it was the six-thirty editions which had the first news of the murder. The tavern-keeper declares that Hill drank nearly two bottles of Tarragona port, in threepenny glasses, during the day."

"I should have credited Hill with a better taste in port, with his opportunities as Sir Horace Fewbanks's butler," said Inspector Chippenfield drily. "What you have found out, Rolfe, only goes to bear out my own discovery that Hill is deeply implicated in this affair. I have found out, for my part, that Hill did not spend the night of the murder at home here."

There was a ring of triumph in Inspector Chippenfield's voice as he announced this discovery, but before Rolfe could make any comment upon it there was a quick step behind them, and both men turned, to see Hill. The butler was astonished at finding the two police officers in his wife's shop. He hesitated, and apparently his first impulse was to turn into the street again; but, realising the futility of such a course, he came forward with an attempt to smooth his worried face into a conciliatory smile.

"Hill!" said Inspector Chippenfield sternly. "Once and for all, will you own up where you were on the night of the murder?"

Hill started slightly, then, with admirable self-command, he recovered himself and became as tight-lipped and reticent as ever.

"I've already told you, sir," he replied smoothly. "I spent it in my own home. If you ask my wife, sir, she'll tell you I never stirred out of the house after I came back from taking my little girl to the Zoo."

"I know she will, you scoundrel!" burst out the choleric inspector. "She's been well tutored by you, and she tells the tale very well. But it's no good, Hill. You forgot to tutor your little daughter, and she's innocently put you away. What's more, you were seen in London before daybreak the night after the murder. The game's up, my man."

Inspector Chippenfield produced a pair of handcuffs as he spoke. Hill passed his tongue over his dry lips before he was able to speak.

"Don't put them on me," he said imploringly, as Inspector Chippenfield advanced towards him. "I'll—I'll confess!"

CHAPTER XI

Inspector Chippenfield's first words were a warning.

"You know what you are saying, Hill?" he asked. "You know what this means? Any statement you make may be used in evidence against you at your trial."

"I'll tell you everything," faltered Hill. The impassive mask of the well-trained English servant had dropped from him, and he stood revealed as a trembling elderly man with furtive eyes, and a painfully shaken manner. "I'll be glad to tell you everything," he declared, laying a twitching hand on the inspector's coat. "I've not had a minute's peace or rest since—since it happened."

The dry official manner in which Inspector Chippenfield produced a note-book was in striking contrast to the trapped man's attitude.

"Go ahead," he commanded, wetting his pencil between his lips.

Before Hill could respond a small boy entered the shop—a ragged, shock-headed dirty urchin, bareheaded and barefooted. He tapped loudly on the counter with a halfpenny.

"What do you want, boy?" roughly asked the inspector.

"A 'a'porth of blackboys," responded the child, in the confident tone of a regular customer.

"If you'll permit me, sir, I'll serve him," said Hill and he glided behind the little counter, took some black sticky sweetmeats from one of the glass jars on the shelf and gave them to the boy, who popped one in his mouth and scurried off.

"I think we had better go inside and hear what Hill has to say, Inspector, while Mrs. Hill minds the shop," said Rolfe. He had caught a glimpse of Mrs. Hill's white frightened face peering through the dirty little glass pane in the parlour door.

Inspector Chippenfield approved of the idea.

"We don't want to spoil your wife's business, Hill—she's likely to need it," he said, with cruel official banter. "Come here, Mrs. Hill," he said, raising his voice.

The faded little woman appeared in response to the summons, bringing the child with her. She shot a frightened glance at her husband, which Inspector Chippenfield intercepted.

"Never mind looking at your husband, Mrs. Hill," he said roughly. "You've done your best for him, and the only thing to be told now is the truth. Now you and your daughter can stay in the shop. We want your husband inside."

Mrs. Hill clasped her hands quickly.

"Oh, what is it, Henry?" she said. "Tell me what has happened? What have they found out?"

"Keep your mouth shut," commanded her husband harshly. "This way, sir, if you please."

Inspector Chippenfield and Rolfe followed him into the parlour.

"Now, Hill," impatiently said Inspector Chippenfield.

The butler raised his head wearily.

"I suppose I may as well begin at the beginning and tell you everything," he said.

"Yes," replied the inspector, "it's not much use keeping anything back now."

"Oh, it's not a case of keeping anything back," replied Hill. "You're too clever for me, and I've made up my mind to tell you everything, but I thought I might be able to cut the first part short, so as to save your time. But so that you'll understand everything I've got to go a long way back—shortly after I entered Sir Horace Fewbanks's service. In fact, I hadn't been long with him before I began to see he was leading a strange life—a double life, if I may say so. A servant in a gentleman's house—particularly one in my position—sees a good deal he is not meant to see; in fact, he couldn't close his eyes to it if he wanted to, as no doubt you, from your experience, sir, know very well. A confidential servant sees and hears a lot of things, sir."

Inspector Chippenfield nodded his head sharply, but he did not speak.

"I think Sir Horace trusted me, too," continued Hill humbly, "more than he would have trusted most servants, on account of my—my past. I fancy, if I may say so, that he counted on my gratitude because he had given me a fresh start in life. And he was quite right—at first." Hill dropped his voice and looked down as he uttered the last two words. "I'd have done anything for him. But as I was saying, sir, I hadn't been long in his house before I found out that he had a—a weakness—" Hill timidly bowed his head as though apologising to the dead judge for assailing his character—"a weakness for—for the ladies. Sometimes Sir Horace went off for the week-end without saying where he was going and sometimes he went out late at night and didn't return till after breakfast. Then he had ladies visiting him at Riversbrook—not real ladies, if you understand, sir. Sometimes there was a small party of them, and then they made a noise singing music-hall songs and drinking wine, but generally they came alone. Towards the end there was one who came a lot oftener than the others. I found out afterwards that her name was Fanning—Doris Fanning. She was a very pretty young woman, and Sir Horace seemed very fond of her. I knew that because I've heard him talking to her in the library. Sir Horace had rather a loud voice, and I couldn't help overhearing him sometimes, when I took things to his rooms.

"One night,—it was before Sir Horace left for Scotland—a rainy gusty night, this young woman came. I forgot to mention that when Sir Horace expected visitors he used to tell me to send the servants to bed early. He told me to do so this night, saying as usual, 'You understand, Hill?' and I replied, 'Yes, Sir Horace,' The young woman came about half-past ten o'clock, and I let her in the side door and showed her up to the library on the first floor, where he used to sit and work and read. Half an hour afterwards I took up some refreshments—some sandwiches and a small bottle of champagne for the young lady—and then went back downstairs till Sir Horace rang for me to let the lady out, which was generally about midnight. But this night, I'd hardly been downstairs more than a quarter of an hour, when I heard a loud crash, followed by a sort of scream. Before I could get out of my chair to go upstairs I heard the study door open, and Sir Horace called out, 'Hill, come here!'

"I went upstairs as quick as I could, and the door of the study being wide open, I could see inside. Sir Horace and the young lady had evidently been having a quarrel. They were standing up facing each other, and the table at which they had been sitting was knocked over, and the refreshments I had taken up had been scattered all about. The young woman had been crying—I could see that at a glance—but Sir Horace looked dignified and the perfect gentleman—like he always was. He turned to me when he saw me, and said, 'Hill, kindly show this young lady out,' I bowed and waited for her to follow me, which she did, after giving Sir Horace an angry look. I let her out the same way as I let her in, and took her through the plantation to the front gate, which I locked after her. When I got inside the house again, and was beginning to bolt up things for the night Sir Horace called me again and I went upstairs. 'Hill,' he said, in the same calm and collected voice, 'if that young lady calls again you're to deny her admittance. That is all, Hill,' And he turned back into his room again.

"I didn't see her again until the morning after Sir Horace left for Scotland. I had arranged for the female servants to go to Sir Horace's estate in the country during his absence, as he instructed before his departure, and they and I were very busy on this morning getting the house in order to be closed up—putting covers on the furniture and locking up the valuables.

"It was Sir Horace's custom to have this done when he was away every year instead of keeping the servants idling about the house on board wages, and the house was then left in my charge, as I told you, sir, and after the servants went to the country it was my custom to live at home till Sir Horace returned, coming over two or three times a week to look over the place and make sure that everything was all right. On this morning, sir, after superintending the servants clearing up things, I went outside the house to have a final look round, and to see that the locks of the front and back gates were in good working order. I was going to the back first, sir, but happening to glance about me as I walked round the house, I saw the young woman that Sir Horace had ordered me to show out of the house the night before he went to Scotland, peering out from behind one of the fir trees of the plantation in front of the house. As soon as she saw that I saw her she beckoned to me.

"I would not have taken any notice of her, only I didn't want the women servants to see her. Sir Horace, I knew, would not have liked that. So I went across to her. I asked her what she wanted, and I told her it was no use her wanting to see Sir Horace, for he had gone to Scotland. 'I don't want to see him,' she said, as impudent as brass. 'It's you I want to see, Field or Hill or whatever you call yourself now.' It gave me quite a turn, I assure you, to find that this young woman knew my secret, and I turned round apprehensive-like, to make sure that none of the servants had heard her. She noticed me and she laughed. 'It's all right, Hill,' she said. 'I'm not going to tell on you. I've just brought you a message from an old friend—Fred Birchill—he wants to see you to-night at this address.' And with that she put a bit of paper into my hand. I was so upset and excited that I said I'd be there, and she went away.

"This Fred Birchill was a man I'd met in prison, and he was in the cell next to me. How he'd got on my tracks I had no idea, but I seemed to see all my new life falling to pieces now he knew. I'd tried to run straight since I served my sentence, and I knew Sir Horace would stand to me, but he couldn't afford to have any scandal about it, and I knew that if there was any possibility of my past becoming known I should have to leave his employ. And then there was my poor wife and child, and this little business, sir. Nothing was known about my past here. So I determined to go and see this Birchill, sir. The address she had given me was in Westminster, and, as my time was practically my own when Sir Horace wasn't home, I went down that same evening, and when I got up the flight of stairs and knocked at the door it was a woman's voice that said 'Come in,' I thought I recognised the voice. When I opened the door, you can imagine my surprise when I saw the young woman to be Doris Fanning, who had had the quarrel with Sir Horace that night and had brought me the note that morning. Birchill was sitting in a corner of the room, with his feet on another chair, smoking a pipe. 'Come in, No. 21,' he says, with an unpleasant smile, 'come in and see an old friend. Put a chair for him, Doris, and leave the room.'

"The girl did so, and as soon as the door was closed behind her Birchill turned round to me and burst out, 'Hill, that damned employer of yours has served me a nasty trick, but I'm going to get even with him, and you're going to help me!' I was taken back at his words, but I wanted to hear more before I spoke. Then he told me that the young woman I had seen had been brutally treated by Sir Horace. She had been living in a little flat in Westminster on a monthly allowance which Sir Horace made her, but he'd suddenly cut off her allowance and she'd have to be turned out in the street to starve because she couldn't pay her rent. 'A nice thing,' said Birchill fiercely, 'for this high-placed loose liver to carry on like this with a poor innocent girl whose only fault was that she loved him too well. If I could show him up and pull him down, I would. But I've done time, like you, Hill. He was the judge who sentenced me, and if I tried to injure him that way my word would carry no weight; but I'll put up a job on him that'll make him sorry the longest day he lives, and you'll help me. Sir Horace is in Scotland, Hill, and you're in charge of his place. Get rid of the servants, Hill, and we'll burgle his house. We can easily do it between us.'"

At this stage of his narrative, Hill stopped and looked anxiously at his audience as though to gather some idea of their feelings before he proceeded further. But Inspector Chippenfield, with a fierce stare, merely remarked:

"And you consented?"

"I didn't at first," Hill retorted earnestly, "but when I refused he threatened me—threatened that he'd expose me and drag me and my wife and child down to poverty. I pleaded with him, but it was of no use, and at last I had to consent. I had some hope that in doing so I might find an opportunity to warn Sir Horace, but Birchill did not give me a chance. He insisted that the burglary should take place without delay. All I was to do was to give him a plan of the house, explain where to find the most valuable articles that had been left there, and wait for him at the flat while he committed the burglary. His idea in making me wait for him at the flat was to make sure that I didn't play him false—put the double on him, as he called it—and he told the girl not to let me out of her sight till he came back, if anything went wrong I should have to pay for it when he came back.

"In accordance with Sir Horace's instructions, I sent the servants off to his country estate. It had been arranged that Birchill was to wait for me to come over to the flat on the 18th of August, the night fixed for the burglary. But about 7 o'clock, while I was at Riversbrook, I heard the noise of wheels outside, and looking out, I saw to my dismay Sir Horace getting out of a taxi-cab with a suit-case in his hand. My first impulse was to tell him everything—indeed, I think that if I had had a chance I would have—but he came in looking very severe, and without saying a word about why he had returned from Scotland, said very sharply, 'Hill, have the servants been sent down to the country, as I directed?' I told him that they had. 'Very good,' he said, 'then you go away at once, I won't want you any more. I want the house to myself to-night.' 'Sir Horace,' I began, trembling a little, but he stopped me. 'Go immediately,' he said; 'don't stand there,' And he said it in such a tone that I was glad to go. There was something in his look that frightened me that night. I got across to Birchill's place and found him and the girl waiting for me. I told him what had happened, and begged him to give up the idea of the burglary. But he'd been drinking heavily, and was in a nasty mood. First he said I'd been playing him false and had warned Sir Horace, but when I assured him that I hadn't he insisted on going to commit the burglary just the same. With that he pulled out a revolver from his pocket, and swore with an oath that he'd put a bullet through me when he came back if I'd played him false and put Sir Horace on his guard, and that he'd put a bullet in the old scoundrel—meaning Sir Horace—if he interrupted him while he was robbing the house.

"He sat there, cursing and drinking, till he fell asleep with his head on the table, snoring. I sat there not daring to breathe, hoping he'd sleep till morning, but Miss Fanning woke him up about nine, and he staggered to his feet to get out, with his revolver stuck in his coat pocket. He was away over three hours and the girl and I sat there without saying a word, just looking at each other and waiting for a clock on the mantelpiece to chime the quarters. It was a cuckoo clock, and it had just chimed twelve when we heard a quick step coming upstairs to the flat. The girl fixed her big dark eyes inquiringly on me, and then we heard a hoarse whisper through the keyhole telling us to open the door.

"The girl ran to the door and let him in, but she shrieked at the sight of him when she saw him in the light. For he looked ghastly, and there was a spot of blood on his face, and his hands were smeared with it. He was shaking all over, and he went to the whisky bottle and drained the drop of spirit he'd left in it. Then he turned to us and said, 'Sir Horace Fewbanks is dead—murdered!' I suppose he read what he saw in our eyes, for he burst out angrily, 'Don't stand staring at me like a pair of damned fools. You don't think I did it? As God's my judge, I never did it. He was dead and stiff when I got there.'

"Then he told us his story of what had happened. He said that when he got to Riversbrook there was a light in the library and he got over the fence and hid himself in the garden. Then he noticed that there was a light in the hall and that the hall door was open. He thought Sir Horace had left it open by mistake, and he was going to creep into the house and hide himself there till after Sir Horace went to bed. But suddenly the light in the library went out and Birchill again hid behind a tree, for he thought Sir Horace was retiring for the night. Then the light in the hall went out and immediately after Birchill heard the hall door being closed. Then he heard a step on the gravel path and saw a woman walking quickly down the path to the gate. She was a well-dressed woman, and Birchill naturally thought that she was one of Sir Horace's lady friends. But he thought it odd that Sir Horace, who was always a very polite gentleman to the ladies, should not have shown her off the premises. He waited in the garden about half an hour, and as everything in the house seemed quite still, he made his way to a side window and forced it open. He had an electric torch with him, and he used this to find his way about the house. First of all, he wanted to find out in which room Sir Horace was sleeping, and he knew from the plan he'd made me draw for him which was Sir Horace's bedroom, so he went there and opened the door quietly and listened. But he could not hear anyone breathing. Then he tried some of the other rooms and turned on his torch, but could see no one. He thought that perhaps Sir Horace had fallen asleep in a chair in the library, and he went there. He listened at the door but could hear no sound. Then he turned on his torch and by its light he saw a dreadful sight. Sir Horace was lying huddled up near the desk—dead—just dead, he thought, because there were little bubbles of blood on his lips as if they had been blown there when breathing his last. He didn't wait to see any more, but he turned and ran out of the house.

"I didn't believe his story, though Miss Fanning did, but he stuck to it and seemed so frightened that I thought there might be something in it till he brought out that he'd lost his revolver somewhere. Then I remembered the horrid threats he'd used against Sir Horace, and I was convinced that he had committed the murder. But of course I dared not let him think I suspected him, and I pretended to console him. But the feeling that kept running through my head was that both of us would be suspected of the murder.

"I told this to Birchill, and that frightened him still more. 'What are we to do?' he kept saying. 'We shall both be hanged.' Then, after a while, we recovered ourselves a bit and began to look at it from a more common-sense point of view. Nobody knew about Birchill's visit to the house except our two selves and the girl, and there was no reason why anybody should suspect us as long as we kept that knowledge to ourselves. Birchill's idea, after we'd talked this over, was that I should go quietly home to bed, and pay a visit to Riversbrook on Friday as usual, discover Sir Horace Fewbanks's body, and then tell the police. But I didn't like to do that for two reasons. I didn't think that my nerves would be in a fit state to tell the police how I found the body without betraying to them that I knew something about it; and I couldn't bear to think of Sir Horace's body lying neglected all alone in that empty house till the following day—though I kept that reason to myself.

"It was the girl who hit on the idea of sending a letter to the police. She said that it would be the best thing to do, because if they were informed and went to the house and discovered the body it wouldn't be so difficult for me to face them afterwards. I agreed to that, and so did Birchill, who was very frightened in case I might give anything away, and consented on that account. The girl showed us how to write the letter, too—she said she'd often heard of anonymous letters being written that way—and she brought out three different pens and a bottle of ink and a writing pad. After we'd agreed what to write, she showed us how to do it, each one printing a letter on the paper in turn, and using a different pen each time."

"You took care to leave no finger-prints," said Inspector Chippenfield.

"We used a handkerchief to wrap our hands in," said Hill. "Birchill got tired of passing the paper from one to another and wrote all his letters, leaving spaces for the girl and me to write in ours. When the letter was written we wrote the address on the envelope the same way, and stamped it. Then I went out and posted the letter in a pillar-box."

"At Covent Garden?" suggested Inspector Chippenfield.

"Yes, at Covent Garden," said Hill.

"When I got home my wife was awake and in a terrible fright. She wanted to know where I'd been, but I didn't tell her. I told her, though, that my very life depended on nobody knowing I'd been out of my own home that night, and I made her swear that no matter who questioned her she'd stick to the story that I'd been at home all night, and in bed. She begged me to tell her why, and as I knew that she'd have to be told the next day, I told her that Sir Horace Fewbanks had been murdered. She buried her face in her pillow with a moan, but when I took an oath that I had had no hand in it she recovered, and promised not to tell a living soul that I had been out of the house and I knew I could depend on her.

"Next morning, as soon as I got up, I hurried off to a little wine tavern and asked to see the morning papers. It was a foolish thing to do, because I might have known that nothing could have been discovered in time to get into the morning papers, for I hadn't posted the letter until nearly four o'clock. But I was all nervous and upset, and as I couldn't face my wife or settle to anything until I knew the police had got the letter and found the body, I—though a strictly temperate man in the ordinary course of life, sir—sat down in one of the little compartments of the place and ordered a glass of wine to pass the time till the first editions of the evening papers came out—they are usually out here about noon. But there was no news in the first editions, and so I stayed there, drinking port wine and buying the papers as fast as they came out. But it was not till the 6.30 editions came out, late in the afternoon, that the papers had the news. I hurried home and then went up to Riversbrook and reported myself to you, sir."

As Hill finished his story he buried his face in his hands, and bowed his head on the table in an attitude of utter dejection. Rolfe, looking at him, wondered if he were acting a part, or if he had really told the truth. He looked at Inspector Chippenfield to see how he regarded the confession, but his superior officer was busily writing in his note-book. In a few moments, however, he put the pocket-book down on the table and turned to the butler.

"Sit up, man," he commanded sternly. "I want to ask you some questions."

Hill raised a haggard face.

"Yes, sir," he said, with what seemed to be a painful effort.

"What is this girl Fanning like?"

"Rather a showy piece of goods, if I may say so, sir. She has big black eyes, and black hair and small, regular teeth."

"And Sir Horace had been keeping her?"

"I think so, sir."

"And a fortnight before Sir Horace left for Scotland there was a quarrel—Sir Horace cast her off?"

"That is what it looked like to me," said the butler.

"What was the cause of the quarrel?"

"That I don't know, sir."

"Didn't Birchill tell you?"

"Well, not in so many words. But I gathered from things he dropped that Sir Horace had found out that he was a friend of Miss Fanning's and didn't like it."

"Naturally," said the philosophic police official. "Is Birchill still at this flat and is the girl still there?"

"The last I heard of them they were, sir. Of course they had been talking of moving after Sir Horace stopped the allowance."

"Well, Hill, I'll investigate this story of yours," said the inspector, as he rose to his feet and placed his note-book in his pocket. "If it is true—if you have given us all the assistance in your power and have kept nothing back, I'll do my best for you. Of course you realise that you are in a very serious position. I don't want to arrest you unless I have to, but I must detain you while I investigate what you have told us. You will come up with us to the Camden Town Station and then your statement will be taken down fully. I'll give you three minutes in which to explain things to your wife."

CHAPTER XII

"Do you think Hill's story is true?" Rolfe asked Inspector Chippenfield, as they left the Camden Town Police Station and turned in the direction of the Tube station.

"We'll soon find out," replied the inspector. "Of course, there is something in it, but there is no doubt Hill will not stick at a lie to save his own skin. But we are more likely to get at the truth by threatening to arrest him than by arresting him. If he were arrested he would probably shut up and say no more."

"And are you going to arrest Birchill?"

"Yes."

"For the murder?" asked Rolfe.

"No; for burglary. It would be a mistake to charge him with murder until we get more evidence. The papers would jeer at us if we charged him with murder and then dropped the charge.'"

"Do you think Birchill will squeak?"

"On Hill?" said the inspector. "When he knows that Hill has been trying to fit him for the murder he'll try and do as much for Hill. And between them we'll come at the truth. We are on the right track at last, my boy. And, thank God, we have beaten our friend Crewe."

Inspector Chippenfield's satisfaction in his impending triumph over Crewe was increased by a chance meeting with the detective. As the two police officials came out of Leicester Square Station on their way to Scotland Yard to obtain a warrant for Birchill's arrest, they saw Crewe in a taxi-cab. Crewe also saw them, and telling the driver to pull up leaned out of the window and looked back at the two detectives. When they came up with the taxi-cab they saw that Crewe had on a light overcoat and that there was a suit-case beside the driver. Crewe was going on a journey of some kind.

"Anything fresh about the Riversbrook case?" he asked.

"No; nothing fresh," replied Inspector Chippenfield, looking Crewe straight in the face.

"You are a long time in making an arrest," said Crewe, in a bantering tone.

"We want to arrest the right man," was the reply. "There's nothing like getting the right man to start with; it saves such a lot of time and trouble. Where are you off to?"

"I'm taking a run down to Scotland."

The inspector glanced at Crewe rather enviously.

"You are fortunate in being able to enjoy yourself just now," he said meaningly.

"I won't drop work altogether," remarked Crewe. "I'll make a few inquiries there."

"About the Riversbrook affair?"

"Yes."

With the murderer practically arrested, Inspector Chippenfield permitted himself the luxury of smiling at the way in which Crewe was following up a false scent.

"I thought the murder was committed in London—not in Scotland," he said.

"Wrong, Chippenfield," said Crewe, with a smile. "Sir Horace was murdered in Scotland and his body was brought up to London by train and placed in his own house in order to mislead the police. Good-bye."

As the taxi-cab drove off, Inspector Chippenfield turned to his subordinate and said, "We'll rub it into him when he comes back and finds that we have got our man under lock and key. He's on some wild-goose chase. Scotland! He might as well go to Siberia while's he's about it."

With a warrant in his pocket Inspector Chippenfield, accompanied by Rolfe, set out for Macauley Mansions, Westminster. They found the Mansions to be situated in a quiet and superior part of Westminster, not far from Victoria Station, and consisting of a large block of flats overlooking a square—a pocket-handkerchief patch of green which was supposed to serve as breathing-space for the flats which surrounded it.

Macauley Mansions had no lift, and Number 43, the scene of the events of Hill's confession, was on the top floor. Inspector Chippenfield and Rolfe mounted the stairs steadily, and finally found themselves standing on a neat cocoanut door-mat outside the door of No. 43. The door was closed.

"Well, well," said the inspector, as he paused, panting, on the door-mat and rang the bell. "Snug quarters these—very snug. Strange that these sort of women never know enough to run straight when they are well off."

The door opened, and a young woman confronted them. She was hardly more than a girl, pretty and refined-looking, with large dark eyes, a pathetic drooping mouth, and a wistful expression. She wore a well-made indoor dress of soft satin, without ornaments, and her luxuriant dark hair was simply and becomingly coiled at the back of her head. She held a book in her left hand, with one finger between the leaves, as though the summons to the door had interrupted her reading, and glanced inquiringly at the visitors, waiting for them to intimate their business. She was so different from the type of girl they had expected to see that Inspector Chippenfield had some difficulty in announcing it.

"Are you Miss Fanning?" he asked.

"Yes," she replied.

"Then you are the young woman we wish to see, and, with your permission, we'll come inside," said Inspector Chippenfield, recovering from his first surprise and speaking briskly.

They followed the girl into the hall, and into a room off the hall to which she led the way. A small Pomeranian dog which lay on an easy chair, sprang up barking shrilly at their entrance, but at the command of the girl it settled down on its silk cushion again. The apartment was a small sitting-room, daintily furnished in excellent feminine taste. Both police officers took in the contents of the room with the glance of trained observers, and both noticed that, prominent among the ornaments on the mantelpiece, stood a photograph of the late Sir Horace Fewbanks in a handsome silver frame.

The photograph made it easy for Inspector Chippenfield to enter upon the object of the visit of himself and his subordinate to the flat.

"I see you have a photograph of Sir Horace Fewbanks there," he said, in what he intended to be an easy conversational tone, waving his hand towards the mantelpiece.

The wistful expression of the girl's face deepened as she followed his glance.

"Yes," she said simply. "It is so terrible about him."

"Was he a—a relative of yours?" asked the inspector.

She had come to the conclusion they were police officers and that they were aware of the position she occupied.

"He was very kind to me," she replied.

"When did you see him last? How long before he—before he died?"

"Are you detectives?" she asked.

"From Scotland Yard," replied Inspector Chippenfield with a bow.

"Why have you come here? Do you think that I—that I know anything about the murder?"

"Not in the least." The inspector's tone was reassuring. "We merely want information about Sir Horace's movements prior to his departure for Scotland. When did you see him last?"

"I don't remember," she said, after a pause.

"You must try," said the inspector, in a tone which contained a suggestion of command.

"Oh, a few days before he went away."

"A few days," repeated the inspector. "And you parted on good terms?"

"Yes, on very good terms." She met his glance frankly.

Inspector Chippenfield was silent for a moment. Then, fixing his fiercest stare on the girl, he remarked abruptly:

"Where's Birchill?"

"Birchill?" She endeavoured to appear surprised, but her sudden pallor betrayed her inward anxiety at the question. "I—I don't know who you mean."

"I mean the man you've been keeping with Sir Horace Fewbanks's money," said the inspector brutally.

"I've been keeping nobody with Sir Horace Fewbanks's money," protested the girl feebly. "It's cruel of you to insult me."

"That'll about do to go on with," said Inspector Chippenfield, with a sudden change of tone, rising to his feet as he spoke. "Rolfe, keep an eye on her while I search the flat."

Rolfe crossed over from where he had been sitting and stood beside the girl. She glanced up at him wildly, with terror dawning in the depths of her dark eyes.

"What do you mean? How dare you?" she cried, in an effort to be indignant.

"Now, don't try your tragedy airs on us," said the inspector. "We've no time for them. If you won't tell the truth you had better say nothing at all." He plunged his hand into a *jardinière* and withdrew a briar-wood pipe. «This looks to me like Birchill›s property. Keep that dog back, Rolfe."

The little dog had sprung off his cushion and was eagerly following the inspector out of the room. Rolfe caught up the animal in his arms, and returned to where the girl was sitting. Her face was white and strained, and her big dark eyes followed Inspector Chippenfield, but she did not speak. The inspector tramped noisily into the little hall, leaving the door of the room wide open. Rolfe and the girl saw him fling open the door of another room—a bedroom—and stride into it. He came out again shortly, and went down the hall to the rear of the flat. A few minutes later he came back to the room where he had left Rolfe and the girl. His knees were dusty, and some feathers were adhering to his jacket, as though he had been plunging in odd nooks and corners, and beneath beds. He was hot, flurried, and out of temper.

"The bird's flown!" were his first words, addressed to Rolfe. "I've hunted high and low, but I cannot find a sign of him. It beats me how he's managed it. He couldn't have gone out the front way without my seeing him go past the door, and the back windows are four stories high from the ground."

"Perhaps he wasn't here when we came in," suggested Rolfe.

"Oh, yes, he was. Why, he'd been smoking that pipe in this very room. She was clever enough to open the window to let out the tobacco smoke before she let us in, but she didn't hide the pipe properly, for I saw the smoke from it coming out of the *jardinière*, and when I put my hand on the bowl it was hot. Feel it now."

Rolfe placed his hand on the pipe, which Inspector Chippenfield had deposited on the table. The bowl was still warm, indicating that the pipe had recently been alight.

"He must have been smoking the pipe when we knocked at the door, and dashed away to hide before she let us in," grumbled the inspector. "But the question is—where can he have got to? I've hunted everywhere, and there's no way out except by the front door, so far as I can see. Go and have a look yourself, Rolfe, and see if you can find a trace of him. I'll watch the girl."

Rolfe put down the little dog he had been holding, and went out into the hall. The dog accompanied him, frisking about him in friendly fashion. Rolfe first examined the bedroom that he had seen Inspector Chippenfield enter. It was a small room, containing a double bed. It was prettily furnished in white, with white curtains, and toilet-table articles in ivory to match. A glance round the room convinced Rolfe that it was impossible for a man to secrete himself in it. The door of the wardrobe had been flung open by the inspector, and the dresses and other articles of feminine apparel it contained flung out on the floor. There was no other hiding-place possible, except beneath the bed, and the ruthless hand of the inspector had torn off the white muslin bed hangings, revealing emptiness underneath. Rolfe went out into the hall again, and entered the room next the bedroom. This apartment was apparently used as a dining-room, for it contained a large table, a few chairs, a small sideboard, a spirit-stand, a case of books and ornaments, and two small oak presses. Plainly, there was no place in it where a man could hide himself. The next room was the bathroom, which was also empty. Opposite the bathroom was a small bedroom, very barely furnished, offering no possibility of concealment. Then the passage opened into a large roomy kitchen, the full width of the rooms on both sides of the hall, and the kitchen completed the flat.

Rolfe glanced keenly around the kitchen. There were no cooking appliances visible, or pots or pans, but there was much lumber and odds and ends, as though the place were used as a store-room. Presumably Miss Fanning obtained her meals from the restaurant on the ground floor of the mansions and had no use for a kitchen. The room was dirty and dusty and crowded with all kinds of rubbish. But the miscellaneous rubbish stored in the room offered no hiding-place for a man. Rolfe nevertheless made a conscientious search, shifting the lumber about and ferreting into dark corners, without result. Finally he crossed the room to look out of the window, which had been left open, no doubt by Inspector Chippenfield.

The mansions in which the flat was situated formed part of a large building, with back windows overlooking a small piece of ground. The flat was on the fourth story. Rolfe looked around the neighbouring roofs and down onto the ground fifty feet below, but could see nothing.

He withdrew his head and was turning to leave the room when his attention was attracted by the peculiar behaviour of the dog, which had followed him throughout on his search. The little animal, after sniffing about the floor, ran to the open window and started whining and jumping up at it. Rolfe quickly returned to the window and looked out.

"Why, of course!" he muttered. "How could I have overlooked it? Inspector," he called aloud, "come here!"

Inspector Chippenfield appeared in the kitchen in a state of some excitement at the summons. He carried the key of the front room in his hand, having taken the precaution to lock Miss Fanning in before he responded to the call of his colleague.

"What is it, Rolfe?" he asked eagerly.

"This dog has tracked him to the window, so he's evidently escaped that way," explained Rolfe briefly. "He's climbed along the window-ledge."

Inspector Chippenfield approached the window and looked out. A broad window-ledge immediately beneath the window ran the whole length of the building beneath the windows on the fourth floor, and, so far as could be seen, continued round the side of the house. It was a dizzy, but not a difficult feat for a man of cool head to walk along the ledge to the corner of the house.

"I wonder where that infernal ledge goes to?" said Inspector Chippenfield, vainly twisting his neck and protruding his body through the window to a dangerous extent to see round the corner of the building. "I daresay it leads to the water-pipe, and the scoundrel, knowing that, has been able to get round, shin down, and get clear away."

"I'll soon find out," said Rolfe. "I'll walk along to the corner and see."

"Do you think you can do it, Rolfe?" asked the inspector nervously. "If you fell—" he glanced down to the ground far below with a shudder.

"Nonsense!" laughed Rolfe. "I won't fall. Why, the ledge is a foot broad, and I've got a steady head. He may not have got very far, after all, and I may be able to see him from the corner."

He got out of the window as he spoke, and started to walk carefully along the ledge towards the corner of the building. He reached it safely, peered round, screwed himself round sharply, and came back to the open window almost at a run.

"You're right!" he gasped, as he sprang through. "I saw him. He is climbing down the spouting, using the chimney brickwork as a brace for his feet. If we get downstairs we may catch him."

He was out of the kitchen in an instant, up the passage, and racing down three steps at a time before the inspector had recovered from his surprise. Then he followed as quickly as he could, but Rolfe had a long start of him. When Inspector Chippenfield reached the ground floor Rolfe was nowhere in sight. The inspector looked up and down the street, wondering what had become of him.

At that instant a tall young man, bareheaded and coat-less, came running out of an alley-way, pursued by Rolfe.

"Stop him!" cried Rolfe, to his superior officer.

Inspector Chippenfield stepped quickly out into the street in front of the fugitive. The young man cannoned into the burly officer before he could stop himself, and the inspector clutched him fast. He attempted to wrench himself free, but Rolfe had rushed to his superior's assistance, and drew the baton with which he had provided himself when he set out from Scotland Yard.

"You needn't bother about using that thing," said the young man contemptuously. "I'm not a fool; I realise you've got me."

"We'll not give you another chance." Inspector Chippenfield dexterously snapped a pair of handcuffs on the young man's wrists.

"What are these for?" said the captive, regarding them sullenly.

"You'll know soon enough when we get you upstairs," replied the inspector. "Now then, up you go."

They reascended the stairs in silence, Inspector Chippenfield and Rolfe walking on each side of their prisoner holding him by the arms, in case he tried to make another bolt. They reached the flat and found the front door open as they had left it. The inspector entered the hall and unlocked the drawing-room door.

The girl was sitting on the chair where they had left her, with her head bowed down in an attitude of the deepest dejection. She straightened herself suddenly as they entered, and launched a terrified glance at the young man.

"Oh, Fred!" she gasped.

"They were too good for me, Doris," he responded, as though in reply to her unspoken query. "I would have got away from this chap" —he indicated Rolfe with a nod of his head—"but I ran into the other one."

He stooped as he spoke to brush with his manacled hands some of the dirt from his clothes, which he had doubtless gained in his perilous climb down the side of the house, and then straightened himself to look loweringly at his captors. He was a tall, slender young fellow of about twenty-five or twenty-six, clean-shaven, with a fresh complexion and a rather effeminate air. He was well dressed in a grey lounge suit, a soft shirt, with a high double collar and silk necktie. He looked, as he stood there, more like a dandified city clerk than the desperate criminal suggested by Hill's confession.

"Come on, what's the charge?" he demanded insolently, with a slight glance at his manacled hands.

"Is your name Frederick Birchill?" asked Inspector Chippenfield.

The young man nodded.

"Then, Frederick Birchill, you're charged with burglariously entering the house of Sir Horace Fewbanks, at Hampstead, on the night of the 18th of August."

"Burglary?" said Birchill "Anything else?"

"That will do for the present," replied the inspector. "We may find it necessary to charge you with a more serious crime later."

"Well, all I can say is that you've got the wrong man. But that is nothing new for you chaps," he added with a sneer.

"Surely you are not going to charge him with the murder?" said the girl imploringly.

The inspector's reply was merely to warn the prisoner that anything he said might be used in evidence against him at his trial.

"He had nothing whatever to do with it—he knows nothing about it," protested the girl. "If you let him go I'll tell you who murdered Sir Horace."

"Who murdered him?" asked the inspector.

"Hill," was the reply.

CHAPTER XIII

Doris Fanning got off a Holborn tram at King's Cross, and with a hasty glance round her as if to make sure she was not followed, walked at a rapid pace across the street in the direction of Caledonian Road. She walked up that busy thoroughfare at the same quick gait for some minutes, then turned into a narrow street and, with another suspicious look around her, stopped at the doorway of a small shop a short distance down.

The shop sold those nondescript goods which seem to afford a living to a not inconsiderable class of London's small shopkeepers. The windows and the shelves were full of dusty old books and magazines, trumpery curios and cheap china, second-hand furniture and a collection of miscellaneous odds and ends. A thick dust lay over the whole collection, and the shop and its contents presented a deserted and dirty appearance. Moreover, the door was closed as though customers were not expected. The girl tried the door and found it locked—a fact which seemed to indicate that customers were not even desired. After another hasty look up and down the street she tapped sharply on the door in a peculiar way.

The door was opened after the lapse of a few minutes by a short thickset man of over fifty, whose heavy face displayed none of the suavity and desire to please which is part of the stock-in-trade of the small shopkeeper of London. A look of annoyance crossed his face at the sight of the girl, and his first remark to her was one which no well-regulated shopkeeper would have addressed to a prospective customer.

"You!" he exclaimed. "What in God's name has brought you here? I told you on no account to come to the shop. How do you know somebody hasn't followed you?"

"I could not help it, Kincher," the girl responded piteously. "I'm distracted about Fred, and I had to come over to ask your advice."

"You women are all fools," the man retorted. "You might have known that I would read all about the case in the papers, and that I'd let you hear from me."

"Yes, Kincher," she replied humbly, "but they let me see Fred for a few minutes yesterday at the police court and he told me to come over and see you. Oh, if you only knew what I've suffered since he was arrested. Yesterday he was committed for trial. I haven't closed my eyes for over a week."

"So you attended the police-court proceedings?" said Kemp. And when the girl nodded her head he went on, "The more fool you. I suppose it would be too much to expect a woman to keep away even though she knew she could do no good."

"I knew that, Kincher, but I simply had to go. I should have died if I had stayed in that dreadful flat alone. I tried to, but I couldn't. I got so nervous that I had to put my handkerchief into my mouth to prevent myself from screaming aloud."

"Well, since you are here you had better come inside instead of standing there and giving yourself and me away to every passing policeman."

He led the way inside, and the girl followed him to a dirty, cheerless room behind the shop which was furnished with a sofa-bedstead, a table, and a chair. It was evident that Kemp lived alone and attended to his own wants. The remains of an unappetising meal were on a corner of the table, and a kettle and a teapot stood by the fireplace in which a fire had recently been made with a few sticks for the purpose of boiling a kettle. Bedclothes were heaped on the sofa-bedstead in a disordered state, and in the midst of them nestled a large tortoise-shell cat.

"Sit down," said Kemp. There was an old chair near the fireplace and he pushed it towards her with his foot. "What's brought you over here?"

The girl sank into the chair and began to cry.

"I can't help it, Kincher," she said. "I don't know what to say or do. Fancy Fred being charged with murder! Oh, it's too dreadful to think about. And yet I can think of nothing else."

"Crying your eyes out won't help matters much," replied the unsympathetic Kemp.

The girl did not reply, but rocked herself backwards and forwards on the chair. She sobbed so violently that she appeared to be threatened with an attack of hysteria. Kemp watched her silently. The cat on the sofa-bedstead, as if awakened by the noise, got up, yawned, looked inquiringly round, and then with a measured leap sprang into the girl's lap. She was startled by his act and then she smiled through her sobs as she stroked the animal's coat.

"Poor old Peter!" she exclaimed. "He wants to console me! don't you, Peter? I say, Kincher, I wish you'd give me Peter; you don't want him. Oh, look at the dear!" The cat had perched himself on one of her knees to beg, and he sawed the air appealingly with his forepaws. "I must give him a tit-bit for that." She eyed the remains of the meal on the table disdainfully. "No, Peter, there is nothing fit for you to eat — positively nothing. Why, he understands me like a human being," she continued in amazement as the huge cat dropped on all fours and deliberately sprang back to the sofa-bedstead. "I say, Kincher, you really want a woman in this place to look after you. It's in a most shocking state — it's like a pigsty."

Kemp made no reply but continued to watch her. Her tears had vanished and she sat forward with her dark eyes sparkling, one hand supporting her pretty face as she glanced round the room.

"Have you a cigarette?" she asked suddenly.

Kemp went into the shop and came back with a packet of cheap cigarettes. The girl pushed them away petulantly.

"I don't like that brand," she said; "haven't you anything better?"

The man shook his head.

"No? Then here goes — I must have a smoke of some sort." She stuck one of the cheap cigarettes daintily into her mouth. "A match, Kincher! Why, the box is filthy! You must have a woman in to look after you, even if I have to find you one myself."

"I don't want any woman in the place," retorted Kemp. "There is no peace for a man when a woman is about. But let us have no more of this idle chatter. What's brought you over here? I suppose it's about Fred."

"Poor Fred!" The girl looked downcast for a moment, then she tossed her head, puffed out some smoke, and exclaimed energetically, "But he's not guilty, Kincher, and we'll get him off, won't we?"

"Not merely by saying so," replied Kemp. "But you'd better tell me how it came about that he was arrested for the murder. The police gave away nothing at the police court. Bill Dobbs was down there and he told me they let out nothing, except that their principal witness against Fred is that fellow Hill. I always knew he'd squeak. I told Fred to have nothing to do with the job."

The girl's eyes flashed viciously. She tossed the cigarette into the fire-place and straightened herself.

"That's the low, dirty scoundrel who committed the murder," she exclaimed. "He ought to be in the dock—not Fred."

"Was Fred up there that night?" asked Kemp.

"Up where?"

"At Riversbrook, or whatever they call it."

"Yes."

"He told me he didn't go."

"It's because he was up there that the police have arrested him," said the girl. "Hill gave him away. Oh, he's a double-dyed villain, is Hill. And so quiet and respectable looking with it all! He used to let me in when I went to Riversbrook, and let me out again, and pocket the half-crowns I gave him. And I like a fool never suspected him once, or thought that he knew anything about Fred coming to the flat. He didn't let it out till the night Sir Horace quarrelled with me. Sir Horace found out about—about Fred—and when I went up to see him as usual, he told me that he had finished with me and he called Hill up to show me out. 'Show this young lady out,' he said in that cold haughty voice of his, and the wily old villain Hill just bowed and held the door open. He followed me down stairs and let me out at the side door. There he said, 'I'll escort you to the front gate, if you will permit me, miss. I usually lock the gate about this time.' I thought nothing of this because he had come with me to the front gate before. He followed me down the garden path through the plantation till we reached the front gate. He opened the gate for me and I said 'Good night, Hill,' but instead of his replying 'Good night, Miss Fanning,' as he usually did, he hissed out like a serpent, 'You tell Birchill I want to see him to-morrow, and I'll come to the flat about 9 o'clock. Tell him an old friend named Field wants to see him. Don't forget the name—

Field!' Then he locked the gate and was gone before I could speak a word.

"I gave Fred his message next morning—I wish to God that I hadn't," she continued. "I asked Fred not to keep the appointment, but he insisted on doing so. He said that he and Field had been good friends in the gaol, and that Field had told him that if he ever got on to anything he would let him know. He seemed quite pleased at the idea of meeting Field again. I told him to beware that Field wasn't laying a trap for him, but he wouldn't listen to me.

"Sure enough, Field—or Hill as he calls himself now—did come over that evening and I let him in myself. I took him into the sitting-room where Fred was, and I sat down in a corner of the room pretending to read a book so that I could hear what our visitor had to say. But the cunning old devil whispered something to Fred, and Fred came over to me and asked if I'd mind leaving them alone for half an hour. I didn't mind so much because I knew I could get it all out of Fred after Hill had gone.

"He remained shut up with Fred for nearly two hours and then I heard Fred letting him out of the front door. Fred came in to me, and I soon got the strength of it all from him. What do you think Hill had come for? To get Fred to burgle Sir Horace's house! And Fred had agreed to do it. I cried and I stormed and went into hysterics, but he wouldn't budge—you know how obstinate he can be when he likes. He said that Hill had told him there was a good haul to be picked up. Sir Horace was going to Scotland for the shooting, and the servants were to be sent to his country house, so the coast would be clear. Hill was to leave everything right at Riversbrook on the afternoon of the 18th of August, and he was to come across to the flat and let Fred know.

"Hill came, as he promised, but as soon as he came in I could see that something had happened. The first words he said were that Sir Horace had returned unexpectedly from Scotland. I was glad to hear it, for I thought that meant that there would be no burglary. I said as much to Fred, and he would have agreed with me, but that devil Hill was too full of cunning. 'Of course, if you're frightened, we'd better call it off,' he said. Fred had been drinking during the day, and you know what he's like when he's had a little too much. 'I was never frightened of any job yet,' he said, 'and I'd do this job to-night if the house was full of rozzers,' Hill pretended that he wasn't particular whether the thing came off or not that night, but all the while he kept egging Fred on to do it. Oh, I can see now what his game was. In spite of all I could do or say, it was arranged that Fred should go over, and see if it was quite safe to carry out the job. Hill said he thought Sir Horace was going out that night, and wouldn't be home until the early morning. About 9 o'clock Fred went off, leaving Hill and me alone in the flat together. How I wish now that I had killed him when I had such a good chance.

"We sat there scarcely speaking, and heard the clock strike the hours. After midnight I began to get restless, for I thought something must have happened to Fred. Hill said in a low voice: 'It's time Fred was back.' The words were scarcely out of his mouth when I heard Fred's step outside, and I ran to let him in. He came in as white as a sheet. 'Fred,' I cried as soon as I saw him, 'there's some blood on your face.'

"He didn't answer a word until he had taken a big drink of whisky out of the decanter. Then he said in a whisper: 'Sir Horace Fewbanks has been murdered!' 'Murdered!' cried Hill, leaping up from his chair—he can act well, I can tell you—'My God, Fred, you don't mean it!' 'He's dead, I tell you,' replied Fred fiercely. I thought, and at the time I suppose Hill thought, that Fred had shot him either accidentally or in order to escape capture. He seemed to guess what we were thinking, for he swore that he had had nothing to do with it—Sir Horace was dead on the floor when he got there.

"He told us all that had happened. When he got to Riversbrook he found lights burning on the ground floor. He jumped over the fence at the side and hid in the garden. He was there only a few minutes when he saw the lights go out. Then the front door was slammed and a woman walked down the garden path to the gate."

"A woman!" exclaimed Kemp.

"Yes, a woman. Why not? She had been to see Sir Horace. One of his Society mistresses. I'll bet it was on her account that he came back from Scotland."

"What time was this?" he asked with interest.

"About half-past ten," replied the girl.

"And this woman—this lady—turned out the lights and closed the front door?"

"So Fred says. Of course he thought Sir Horace had done it, but he found out later that Sir Horace was dead."

"I can't understand it," said Kemp. "What was she doing there? If she found the man dead, why didn't she inform the police? No, wait a minute! She'd be afraid to do that if she was a Society woman."

"It might be her who killed him," said the girl.

"Does Fred think that?" asked Kemp, looking at her closely.

"Fred doesn't know what to think," she replied. "But it must have been this woman or Hill who killed him. I feel sure myself that it was Hill."

"This woman puzzles me," said Kemp thoughtfully. "She must have been a cool hand if she went round turning out the lights after finding his dead body. About half-past ten, you said?"

"That is as near as Fred can make it."

"Go on with your story," he said. "I'm interested in this. You were saying that Fred saw the lights go out, and then this woman came out of the house and walked away."

"Well, Fred got into the house through one of the windows at the side—the one Hill had told him to try," continued the girl. "But first of all he waited about half an hour in the garden, so as to give Sir Horace time to go to sleep. He was able to find his way about the house as Hill had given him a plan. He felt his way upstairs and finding a door open he went into the room and flashed his electric torch. By its light he saw Sir Horace Fewbanks lying huddled up in a corner with a big pool of blood beside him on the floor. He felt him to see if he was dead. The body was quite warm, but it was limp. Sir Horace was dead. Fred says he lost his nerve and ran for it as hard as he could. He rushed down stairs and out of the house and got back to the flat as fast as he could.

"The three of us sat there shaking with fear and wondering what to do. Hill was the first to recover himself. In his cunning plausible way, he pointed out that it was altogether unlikely that suspicion would fall on Fred or him. All we had to do was to keep quiet and say nothing; then we'd have no awkward questions put to us. It was his suggestion that we should send an anonymous letter to Scotland Yard telling them Sir Horace had been murdered. That would be much better, he said, than leaving the body there until he went over and found it when he had to go over to Riversbrook to take a look round, in accordance with the instructions that had been given him when Sir Horace went to Scotland. Knowing what he did, he was afraid that if he was allowed to discover the body and inform the police, he would let something slip when the police came at him with their hundreds of questions. We printed the letter to Scotland Yard, each one doing a letter at a time. Hill took it with him, saying he would post it on his way home.

"When he left, Fred and I sat there thinking. Suddenly it came to me as clear as daylight that Hill had committed the murder, and had fixed up things so as to throw suspicion on Fred. He must have known Sir Horace was coming back from Scotland that night, and he had laid in wait for him and shot him. Then he had come over to my flat in order to persuade Fred to carry out the burglary, and direct suspicion to Fred for the murder, if the police worried him. I told Fred what I thought, but he only laughed at me and said I was talking nonsense. But I was right, for a week afterwards the police came and arrested Fred at the flat."

"How did they get him?" asked Kemp.

"I saw them coming along the street from the window, and I pointed them out to Fred. He tried to get away through the kitchen window along the ledge and down the spouting. He almost got away, but one of the detectives saw him before he reached the ground, and they dashed down stairs and got him in the street. Next day I saw in the papers that Hill had made an important statement to the police, and this had led to Fred's arrest. Hill is the murderer, Kincher. The cunning, wicked, treacherous villain told the police about Fred being up there. He wants to see Fred hang in order to save his own neck." The girl's voice rose to a shriek, and she sprang to her feet with blazing eyes. "Kincher," she cried, "you've got to help me put the rope round this wretch's neck. Do you hear me?"

Kemp's impassivity was in marked contrast to the girl's hysterical excitement.

"What do you want me to do?" he asked.

"Fred wants you to get up an alibi for him. He sent me over to ask you to arrange it without delay. He wants you and two or three others to swear that he was over here on the night of the murder. That will be sufficient to get him off."

"Not me," said Kemp, shaking his head decidedly. "I won't do it; it's too risky. The police have too many things against me for my word to be any good as a witness. I'd only be landing myself in trouble for perjury instead of helping Fred out of trouble. He ought to have got an alibi ready before he was arrested. I told him at the inquest that he ought to look after it, and he swore he'd not been up there on the night of the murder. It is too late to do anything in the alibi line now. I don't know anybody I could get to come forward and swear Fred was in their company that night—there is a difference between fixing up a tale for the police before a man's arrested, and going into the witness box and committing perjury on oath."

He spoke in such an uncompromising tone that the girl saw it was useless to pursue the matter further.

"Suppose I went to the police and told them that Hill is the murderer?" she suggested.

Kemp shook his head slowly.

"There is only your word for it that Hill killed him," he said. "It doesn't look to me as if he did, when he went over to your flat and told Fred that Sir Horace had come back from Scotland. If he had killed him he would have let Fred go over without saying a word about it."

"That was part of his cunning," said the girl. "If he had said nothing about Sir Horace's return, Fred would have suspected him when he found the dead body. I'm as certain that Hill committed the murder as if I had seen him do it with my own eyes."

Kemp shrugged his shoulders as though realising the uselessness of attempting to combat such a feminine form of reasoning.

"Didn't Fred say that the body was warm when he touched it?" he asked.

She meditated a moment over this evidence of Hill's innocence.

"Well, if Hill didn't kill him, the woman Fred saw leaving the house must have done so," she declared.

"There is something in that," said Kemp. "Look here, we've got to get Fred a good lawyer to defend him, and we must be guided by his advice as to what is the best thing to do. He knows more about what will go down with a jury than you do."

"I paid a solicitor to defend him at the police court," said the girl, "but the money I gave him was thrown away. He said nothing and did nothing."

"That shows he is a man who knows his business," replied Kemp. "What's the good of talking to police court beaks in a case that is bound to go to trial? It's a waste of breath. The thing is to see that Fred is properly defended when the case comes on at the Old Bailey. We want somebody who can manage the jury. I should say Holymead is the man if you can get him. I don't know as he'd be likely to take up the case, for he don't go in much for criminal courts—and yet it seems to me that he might. You ought to try to get him, at least. He used to be a friend of your friend Sir Horace, so if he took up the case it would look as if he believed Fred had nothing to do with the murder. It would be bound to make a good impression on the jury."

"Wouldn't he be very expensive?" asked the girl.

"Not so expensive as getting hanged," said Kemp grimly. "You take my advice and have him if you can get him. Never mind what he costs, if you can raise the money. You've got some money saved up, haven't you?"

"Yes, I've nearly £200. Sir Horace put £100 in the Savings Bank for me on my last birthday. And the furniture at the flat is mine. I'd sell that and everything I've got, for Fred's sake."

"That is the way to talk," said Kemp. "You go to this solicitor you had at the police court, and tell him you want Holymead to defend Fred. Tell him he must brief Holymead—have nobody else but Holymead. Tell him that Holymead was a friend of Sir Horace Fewbanks's and that if he appears for Fred the jury will never believe that Fred had anything to do with the murder. And I don't think he had, though he did lie to me and swear he hadn't been up there that night," he added after a moment's reflection.

CHAPTER XIV

"There is one link in the chain missing," said Rolfe, who was discussing with Inspector Chippenfield, in the latter's room at Scotland Yard, the strength of the case against Birchill.

"And what is that?" asked his superior.

"The piece of woman's handkerchief that I found in the dead man's hand. You remember we agreed that it showed there was a woman in the case."

"Well, what do you call this girl Fanning? Isn't she in the case? Surely, you don't want any better explanation of the murder than a quarrel between her and Sir Horace over this man Birchill?"

"Yes, I see that plain enough," replied Rolfe. "There is ample motive for the crime, but how that piece of handkerchief got into the dead man's hand is still a mystery to me. It would be easily explained if this girl was present in the room or the house when the murder was committed. But she wasn't. Hill's story is that she was at the flat with him."

"When you have had as much experience in investigating crime as I have, you won't worry over little points that at first don't seem to fit in with what we know to be facts," responded the inspector in a patronising tone. "I noticed from the first, Rolfe, that you were inclined to make too much of this handkerchief business, but I said nothing. Of course, it was your own discovery, and I have found during my career that young detectives are always inclined to make too much of their own discoveries. Perhaps I was myself, when I was young and inexperienced. Now, as to this handkerchief: what is more likely than that Birchill had it in his pocket when he went out to Riversbrook on that fatal night? He was living in the flat with this girl Fanning: what was more natural than that he should pick up a handkerchief off the floor that the girl had dropped and put it in his pocket with the intention of giving it to her when she returned to the room? Instead of doing so he forgot all about it. When he shot Sir Horace Fewbanks he put his hand into his pocket for a handkerchief to wipe his forehead or his hands—it was a hot night, and I take it that a man who has killed another doesn't feel as cool as a cucumber. While stooping over his victim with the handkerchief still in his hand, the dying man made a convulsive movement and caught hold of a corner of the handkerchief, which was torn off." Inspector Chippenfield looked across at his subordinate with a smile of triumphant superiority.

"Yes," said Rolfe meditatively. "There is nothing wrong about that as far as I can see. But I would like to know for certain how it got there."

Inspector Chippenfield was satisfied with his subordinate's testimony to his perspicacity.

"That is all right, Rolfe," he said in a tone of kindly banter. "But don't make the mistake of regarding your idle curiosity as a virtue. After the trial, if you are still curious on the point, I have no doubt Birchill will tell you. He is sure to make a confession before he is hanged."

But it was more a spirit of idle curiosity than anything else that brought Rolfe to Crewe's chambers in Holborn an hour later. Having secured the murderer, he felt curious as to what Crewe's feelings were on his defeat. It was the first occasion that he had been on a case which Crewe had been commissioned to investigate, and he was naturally pleased that Inspector Chippenfield and he had arrested the author of the crime while Crewe was all at sea. It was plain from the fact that the latter had thought it necessary to visit Scotland that he had got on a false scent. It was not Scotland, but Scotland Yard that Crewe should have visited, Rolfe said to himself with a smile.

Crewe, in pursuance of his policy of keeping on the best of terms with the police, gave Rolfe a very friendly welcome. He produced from a cupboard two glasses, a decanter of whisky, a siphon of soda, and a box of cigars. Rolfe quickly discovered that the cigars were of a quality that seldom came his way, and he leaned back in his chair and puffed with steady enjoyment.

"Then you are determined to hang Birchill?" said Crewe, as with a cigar in his fingers he faced his visitor with a smile.

"We'll hang him right enough," said Rolfe. He pulled the cigar out of his mouth and looked at it approvingly. Though the talk was of hanging, he had never felt more thoroughly at peace with the world.

"It will be a pity if you do," said Crewe.

"Why?"

"Because he's the wrong man."

"It would take a lot to make me believe that," said Rolfe stoutly. "We've got a strong case against him—there is not a weak point in it. I admit that Hill is a tainted witness, but they'll find it pretty hard to break down his story. We've tested it in every way and find it stands. Then there are the bootmarks outside the window. Birchill's boots fit them to the smallest fraction of an inch. The jemmy found in the flat fits the mark made in the window at Riversbrook, and we've got something more—another witness who saw him in Tanton Gardens about the time of the murder. If Birchill can get his neck out of the noose, he's cleverer than I take him for."

Crewe did not reply directly to Rolfe's summary of the case.

"I see that they've briefed Holymead for the defence," he said after a pause.

"A waste of good money," said the police officer. Something appealed to his sense of humour, for he broke out into a laugh.

"What are you laughing at?" asked Crewe.

"I was wondering how Sir Horace feels when he sees the money he gave this girl Fanning being used to defend his murderer."

"You are a hardened scamp, Rolfe, with a very perverse sense of humour," said Crewe.

"It was a cunning move of them to get Holymead," said Rolfe. "They think it will weigh with the jury because he was such a close friend of Sir Horace—that he wouldn't have taken up the case unless he felt that Birchill was innocent. But you and I know better than that, Mr. Crewe. A lawyer will prove that black is white if he is paid for it. In fact, I understand that, according to the etiquette of the bar, they have got to do it. A barrister has to abide by his brief and leave his personal feelings out of account."

"That's so. Theoretically he is an officer of the Court, and his services are supposed to be at the call of any man who is in want of him and can afford to pay for them. Of course, a leading barrister, such as Holymead, often declines a brief because he has so much to do, but he is not supposed to decline it for personal reasons."

"His heart will not be in the case," said Rolfe philosophically.

"On the contrary, I think it will," said Crewe. "My own opinion is that, if necessary, he will exert his powers to the utmost in order to get Birchill off, and that he will succeed."

"Not he," said Rolfe confidently. "Our case is too strong."

"You've got a lot of circumstantial evidence, but a clever lawyer will pull it to pieces. Circumstantial evidence has hung many a man, and it will hang many more. But a jury will hesitate to convict on circumstantial evidence when it can be shown that the conduct of the prisoner is at variance with what the conduct of a guilty man would be. I don't bet, but I'll wager you a box of cigars to nothing that Holymead gets Birchill off."

"It's a one-sided wager, but I'll take the cigars because I could do with a box of these," said Rolfe. "You might as well give them to me now, Mr. Crewe."

"No, no," said Crewe with a smile. "Put a couple in your pocket now, because you won't win the box."

"Of course, I understand, Mr. Crewe, why you say Birchill is the wrong man. You feel a bit sore because we have beaten you. I would feel sore myself in your place, and I don't deny that we got information that put us on Birchill's track, and therefore it was easier for us to solve the mystery than it was for you."

"I'm not a bit sore," said Crewe. "I can take a beating, especially when the men who beat me are good sportsmen." He bowed towards Rolfe, and that officer blushed as he recalled how Inspector Chippenfield and he had agreed to withhold information from Crewe and try to put him on a false scent.

"I wish you'd tell me what you consider the weak points of our case against Birchill," asked Rolfe.

"Your case is based on Hill's confession, and that to my mind is false in many details," said Crewe. "Take, for instance, his account of how he came into contact with Birchill again. This girl Fanning, after a quarrel with Sir Horace, came over to Riversbrook with a message for

Hill which was virtually a threat. Now does that seem probable? The girl who had been in the habit of visiting Sir Horace goes over to see Hill. No woman in the circumstances would do anything of the sort. She had too good an opinion of herself to take a message to a servant at a house from which she had been expelled by the owner, who had been keeping her. How would she have felt if she had run into Sir Horace? It is true that Sir Horace left for Scotland the day before, but it is improbable that the girl who had quarrelled with Sir Horace a fortnight before knew the exact date on which he intended to leave. And how did Hill behave when he got the message? According to his story, he consented to go and see Birchill under threat of exposure, and he consented to become an accomplice in the burglary for the same reason. Sir Horace knew all about Hill's past, so why should he fear a threat of exposure?"

"Hill explained that," interposed Rolfe. "He pointed out that, though Sir Horace knew his past, he couldn't afford to have any scandal about it."

"Quite so. But could Birchill afford to threaten a man who was under the protection of Sir Horace Fewbanks? Would Birchill pit himself against Sir Horace? I think that Sir Horace, knowing the law pretty thoroughly, would soon have found a way to deal with Birchill. If Hill was threatened by Birchill, his first impulse, knowing what a powerful protector he had in Sir Horace Fewbanks, would have been to go to him and seek his protection against this dangerous old associate of his convict days. According to Hill's own story, he was something in the nature of a confidential servant, trusted to some extent with the secrets of Sir Horace's double life. What more likely than such a man, threatened as he describes, should turn to his master who had shielded him and trusted him?"

"I confess that is a point which never struck me," said Rolfe thoughtfully.

"Now, let us go on to the meeting between Hill and Birchill," continued Crewe. "This girl Fanning, discarded by Sir Horace, because he'd discovered she was playing him false with Birchill, is made the ostensible reason for Birchill's wishing to commit a burglary at Riversbrook, because Birchill wants, as he says, to get even with Sir Horace Fewbanks. Is it likely that Birchill would confide his desire for revenge so frankly to Sir Horace's confidential servant, the trusted custodian of his master's valuables, who could rely on his master's protection—the protection of a highly-placed man of whom Birchill stood admittedly in fear, and whom he knew, according to Hill's story, was unassailable from his slander? What had Hill to fear, from the threats of a man like Birchill, when he was living under Sir Horace Fewbanks's protection? All that Hill had to do when Birchill tried to induce him, by threats of exposure of his past, to help in a burglary at his master's house, was to threaten to tell everything to Sir Horace. Birchill told Hill that he was frightened of Sir Horace Fewbanks, the judge who had sentenced him.

"Then Birchill's confidence in Hill is remarkable, any way you look at it. He sends for Hill, whom he had known in gaol, and whom he hadn't seen since, to confide in him that it is his intention to burgle his employer's house. He rashly assumes that Hill will do all that he wishes, and he proceeds to lay his cards on the table. But even supposing that Birchill was foolish enough to do this—to trust a chance gaol acquaintance so implicitly—there is a far more puzzling action on his part. Why did he want Hill's assistance to burgle a practically unprotected house? I confess I have great difficulty in understanding why such an accomplished flash burglar as Birchill, one of the best men at the game in London at the present time, should want the assistance of an amateur like Hill in such a simple job."

Rolfe looked startled.

"Hill says he wanted a plan of the house and to know what valuables it contained."

Crewe smiled.

"And has it been your experience among criminals, Rolfe, that a burglar must have a plan of the place he intends to burgle, and that to get this plan he will give himself away to any man who can supply it? A plan has its uses, but it is indispensable only when a very difficult job is being undertaken, such as breaking through a wall or a ceiling to get at a room which contains a safe. This job was as simple as A B C. And besides, as far as I can make out, Birchill knew—the girl Fanning must have known—that Sir Horace would be going away some time in August and that the house would be empty. Did he want a plan of an empty house? He would be free to roam all over it when he had forced a window."

"He wanted to know what valuables were there," said Rolfe.

"And therefore took Hill into his confidence. If Hill had told his master—even Birchill would realise the risk of that—there would be no valuables to get. Next, we come to Sir Horace Fewbanks's unexpected return. According to Hill's story, he made some tentative efforts to commence a confession as soon as he saw his employer, but Sir Horace was upset about something and was too impatient to listen to a word. Is such a story reasonable or likely? Hill says that Sir Horace had always treated him well; and according to his earlier statement, when he permitted himself to be terrorised into agreeing to this burglary, he told himself that chance would throw in his way some opportunity of informing his master. And he told you that Birchill, mistrusting his unwilling accomplice, hurried on the date of the burglary so as to give him no such opportunity. Well, chance throws in Hill's way the very opportunity he has been seeking, but he is too frightened to use it because Sir Horace happens to return in an angry or impatient mood.

"Let us take Birchill's attitude when Hill tells him that Sir Horace has unexpectedly returned from Scotland. Birchill is suspicious that Hill has played him false, and naturally so, but Hill, instead of letting him think so, and thus preventing the burglary from taking place, does all he can to reassure him, while at the same time begging him to postpone the burglary. That was hardly the best way to go about it. Let us charitably assume that Hill was too frightened to let Birchill remain under the impression that he'd played him false, and let us look at Birchill's attitude. It is inconceivable that Birchill should have permitted himself to be reassured, when right through the negotiations between himself and Hill he showed the most marked distrust of the latter. Yet, according to Hill, he suddenly abandons this attitude for one of trusting credulity, meekly accepting the assurance of the man he distrusts that Sir Horace Fewbanks's unexpected return from Scotland on the very night the burglary is to be committed is not a trap to catch him, but a coincidence. Then, after drinking himself nearly blind, he sets forth with a revolver to commit a burglary on the house of the judge who tried him, on Hill's bare word that everything is all right. Guileless, trusting, simple-minded Birchill!

"Hill is left locked up in the flat with the girl; for Birchill, who has just trusted him implicitly in a far more important matter affecting his own liberty, has a belated sense of caution about trusting his unworthy accomplice while he is away committing the burglary. The time goes on; the couple in the flat hear the clock strike twelve before Birchill's returning footsteps are heard. He enters, and immediately announces to Hill and the girl, with every symptom of strongly marked terror, that while on his burglarious mission, he has come across the dead body of Sir Horace Fewbanks—murdered in his own house. Mark that! he tells them freely and openly—tells Hill—as soon as he gets in the flat. Allowing for possible defects in my previous reasoning against Hill's story, admitting that an adroit prosecuting counsel may be able to buttress up some of the weak points, allowing that you may have other circumstantial evidence supporting your case, that is the fatal flaw in your chain: because of Birchill's statement on his return to the flat no jury in the world ought to convict him."

"I don't see why," said Rolfe.

Crewe fixed his deep eyes intently on Rolfe as he replied:

"Because, if Birchill had committed this murder, he would never have admitted immediately on his returning, least of all to Hill, anything about the dead body."

"But he told Hill that he didn't commit the murder," protested Rolfe.

"But you say that he did commit the murder," retorted the detective. "You cannot use that piece of evidence both ways. Your case is that this man Birchill, while visiting Riversbrook to commit a burglary which he and Hill arranged, encountered Sir Horace Fewbanks and murdered him. I say that his admission to Hill on his return to the flat that he had come across the body of Sir Horace Fewbanks, is proof that Birchill did not commit the murder. No murderer would make such a damning admission, least of all to a man he didn't trust—to a man who he believed was capable of entrapping him. Next you have Birchill consenting to a message being sent to Scotland Yard conveying the information that Sir Horace had been murdered. Is that the action of a guilty man? Wouldn't it have been more to his interest to leave the dead man's body undiscovered in the empty house and bolt from the country? It might have remained a week or more before being discovered. True, he would have had to find some way of silencing Hill while he got away from the country.

He might have had to resort to the crude method of tying Hill up, gagging him, and leaving him in the flat. But even that would have been better than to inform the police immediately of the murder and place his life at the mercy of Hill, whom he distrusted."

"Looked at your way, I admit that there are some weak points in our case," said Rolfe. "But you'll find that our Counsel will be able to answer most of them in his address to the jury. If Birchill didn't commit the murder, who did? Do you deny that he went up to Riversbrook that night?"

"The letter sent to Scotland Yard shows that some one was there besides the murderer. If Birchill was there and helped to write the letter—and so much is part of your case—he wasn't the murderer. In short, I believe Birchill went up there to commit a burglary and found the murdered body of Sir Horace."

"Do you think that Hill did it?" asked Rolfe.

"That is more than I'd like to say. As a matter of fact I have been so obtuse as to neglect Hill somewhat in my investigations. In fact, I didn't know until I got hold of a copy of his statement to the police that he was an ex-convict. Inspector Chippenfield omitted to inform me of the fact."

"I didn't know that," said Rolfe, without a blush, as he rose to go. "He ought to have told you."

CHAPTER XV

When Rolfe left Crewe's office he went back to Scotland Yard. He found Inspector Chippenfield still in his office, and related to him the substance of his interview with Crewe. The inspector listened to the recital in growing anger.

"Birchill not the right man?" he spluttered. "Why, of course he is. The case against him is purely circumstantial, but it's as clear as daylight."

"Then you don't think there's anything in Crewe's points?" asked Rolfe.

"I think so little of them that I look upon Birchill as good as hanged! That for Crewe's points!" Inspector Chippenfield snapped his fingers contemptuously. "And I'm surprised to think that you, Rolfe, whose loyalty to your superior officer is a thing I would have staked my life on, should have sat there and listened to such rubbish. I wouldn't have listened to him for two minutes—no, not for half a minute. He was trying to pick our case to pieces out of blind spite and jealousy, because we've got ahead of him in the biggest murder case London's had for many a long day. A man who jaunts off to Scotland looking for clues to a murder committed in London is a fool, Rolfe—that's what I call him. We have beaten him—beaten him badly, and he doesn't like it. But it is not the first time Scotland Yard has beaten him, and it won't be the last."

"I suppose you're right," said Rolfe. "But there's one point he made which rather struck me, I must say—that about Birchill telling Hill he'd found the dead body. Would Birchill have told Hill that, if he'd committed the murder?"

"Nothing more likely," exclaimed the inspector. "My theory is that Birchill, while committing the burglary at Riversbrook, was surprised by Sir Horace Fewbanks. It is possible that the judge tried to capture Birchill to hand him over to the police, and Birchill shot him. I believe that Birchill fired both shots—that he had two revolvers. But whatever took place, a dangerous criminal like Birchill would not require much provocation to silence a man who interrupted him while he was on business bent, and a man, moreover, against whom he nursed a bitter grudge. In this case it is possible there was no provocation at all. Sir Horace Fewbanks may have simply heard a noise, entered the room where Birchill was, and been shot down without mercy. Birchill heard him coming and was ready for him with a revolver in each hand. You've got to bear in mind that Birchill went to the house in a dangerous mood, half mad with drink, and furious with anger against Sir Horace Fewbanks for cutting off the allowance of the girl he was living with. He threatened before he left the flat to commit the burglary that he'd do for the judge if he interfered with him."

"That's according to Hill's statement," said Rolfe.

Inspector Chippenfield glanced at his subordinate in some surprise.

"Of course it's Hill's statement," he said. "Isn't he our principal witness, and doesn't his statement fit in with all the facts we have been able to gather? Well, the murder of Sir Horace, no matter how it was committed, was committed in cold blood. But immediately Birchill had done it the fact that he had committed a murder would have a sobering effect on him. Although he bragged before he left the flat for Riversbrook about killing the judge if he came across him, he had no intention of jeopardising his neck unnecessarily, and after he had shot down the judge in a moment of drunken passion he would be anxious to keep Hill—whom he mistrusted—from knowing that he had committed the murder. But he was fully aware that Hill would be the person who'd discover the body next day, and that if he wasn't put on his guard he would bring in the police and probably give away everything that Birchill had said and done. So, to obviate this risk and prepare Hill, Birchill hit on the plan of telling him that he'd found the judge's dead body while burgling the place. It was a bold idea, and not without its advantages when you consider what an awkward fix Birchill was in. Not only did it keep Hill quiet, but it forced him into the position of becoming a kind of silent accomplice in the crime. You remember Hill did not give the show away until he was trapped, and then he only confessed to save his own skin. He's a dangerous and deep scoundrel, this Birchill, but he'll swing this time, and you'll find that his confession of finding the body will do more than anything else to hang him—properly put to the jury, and I'll see that it is properly put."

Rolfe pondered much over these two conflicting points of view—Crewe's and Inspector Chippenfield's—for the rest of the day. He inclined to Inspector Chippenfield's conclusions regarding Birchill's admission about the body. The idea that he had assisted in arresting the wrong man and had helped to build up a case against him was too unpalatable for him to accept it. But he was forced to admit that Crewe's theory was distinctly a plausible one. Though it was impossible for him to give up the conviction that Birchill was the murderer, he felt that Crewe's analysis of the case for the prosecution contained several telling points which might be used with some effect on a jury in the hands of an experienced counsel. Rolfe had no doubt that Holymead would make the most of those points, and he also knew that the famous barrister was at his best in attacking circumstantial evidence.

That night, while walking home, the idea occurred to Rolfe of going over to Camden Town after supper to see if by questioning Hill again he could throw a little more light on what had taken place at Doris Tanning's flat the night Sir Horace Fewbanks was murdered. Hill had been questioned and cross-questioned at Scotland Yard by Inspector Chippenfield concerning the events of that night, and professed to have confessed to everything that had happened, but Rolfe thought it possible he might be able to extract something more which might assist in strengthening what Crewe regarded as the weak points in the police case against Birchill. Rolfe had every justification for such a visit, for, though Hill had not been arrested, he had been ordered by Inspector Chippenfield to report himself daily to the Camden Town Police Station, and the police of that district had been instructed to keep a strict eye on his movements. Inspector Chippenfield did not regard his principal witness in the forthcoming murder trial as the sort of man likely to bolt, but if he permitted him for politic reasons to retain his liberty, he took every precaution to ensure that Hill should not abuse his privilege.

Rolfe lived in lodgings at King's Cross, and, as the evening was fine and he was fond of exercise, he decided to walk across to Hill's place.

As he walked along his thoughts revolved round the murder of Sir Horace Fewbanks, and the baffling perplexities which had surrounded its elucidation. Had they got hold of the right man—the real murderer—in Fred Birchill? Rolfe kept asking himself that question again and again. A few hours ago he had not the slightest doubt on the point; he had looked upon the great murder case as satisfactorily solved, and he had thought with increasing satisfaction of his own share in bringing the murderer to justice. He had anticipated newspaper praise on his sharpness: judicial commendation, a favourable official entry in the departmental records of Scotland Yard, with perhaps promotion for the good work he had accomplished in this celebrated case. These rosy visions had been temporarily dissipated by the conversation he had had with Crewe that morning. If Crewe had not succeeded in destroying Rolfe's conviction that the murderer of Sir Horace Fewbanks had been caught, he had pointed out sufficient flaws in the police case to shake Rolfe's previous assurance of the legal conviction of Birchill for the crime. The way in which Crewe had pulled the police case to pieces had shown Rolfe that the conviction of Birchill was by no means a foregone conclusion, and had left him a prey to doubts and anxiety which Inspector Chippenfield's subsequent depreciation of the detective's views had not altogether removed.

The little shop kept by the Hills was empty when Rolfe entered it, but Mrs. Hill appeared from the inner room in answer to his knock. The faded little woman did not recognise the police officer at first, but when he spoke she looked into his face with a start. She timidly said, in reply to his inquiry for her husband, that he had just "stepped out" down the street.

"Then you had better send your little girl after him," said Rolfe, seating himself on the one rickety chair on the outside of the counter. "I want to see him."

Mrs. Hill seemed at a loss to reply for a moment. Then she answered, nervously plucking at her apron the while: "I don't think it'd be much use doing that, sir. You see, Mr. Hill doesn't always tell me where he's going and I don't really know where he is."

"Then why did you tell me that he had just stepped out down the street?" asked Rolfe sharply.

"Because I thought he mightn't be far away."

"Then, as a matter of fact, you don't know where he is or when he'll be back?"

"No, sir."

Her prompt and uncompromising reply indicated that she did not want him to wait for her husband.

"I think I'll wait," said Rolfe, looking at her steadily.

"Yes, sir."

Daphne appeared at the door of the parlour which led into the shop and her mother waved her back angrily.

"Go to bed this instant, miss; it's long past your bedtime," she said.

It was obvious that Mrs. Hill retained a vivid recollection of how disastrous had been Daphne's appearance during Inspector Chippenfield's first visit to the shop.

"Perhaps your little girl knows where her father is," said Rolfe maliciously.

"No, she doesn't," replied Mrs. Hill with some spirit. "You can ask her if you like."

Rolfe was suddenly struck with an idea and he decided to test it.

"I won't wait—I've changed my mind. But if your husband comes in tell him not to go to bed until I've seen him. I'll be back."

"Yes, sir," she replied.

"Do you think he was going to Riversbrook?" he asked.

The woman flushed suddenly and then went pale. She knew as well as Rolfe that her husband was strictly forbidden, pending the trial, to go near the place of his former employment, and that the police had relieved him of his keys and taken possession of the silent house and locked everything up.

"No, sir," she replied, with trembling lips, "Mr. Hill hasn't gone over there."

"How can you be certain, if he didn't tell you where he was going?" asked Rolfe.

"Because it's the last place in the world he'd think of going to," gasped Mrs. Hill. "Such a thought would never enter his head. I do assure you, sir, Mr. Hill would never dream of going over there, sir, you can take my word for it."

Rolfe walked thoughtfully up High Street. Was it possible that Hill had gone to his late master's residence in defiance of the orders of the police? If so, only some very powerful motive, and probably one which affected the crime, could have induced him to risk his liberty by making such a visit after he had been commanded to keep away from the place. And how would he get into the house? Rolfe had himself locked up the house and had locked the gates, and the bunch of keys was at that moment hanging up in Inspector Chippenfield's room in Scotland Yard. But even as he asked that question, Rolfe found himself smiling at himself for his simplicity. Nothing could be easier for a man like Hill—an ex-criminal—to have obtained a duplicate key, before handing over possession of the keys. Rolfe had noticed with surprise when he was locking up the house that the French windows of the morning room were locked from the outside by a small key as well as being bolted from the inside. Hill had explained that the late Sir Horace Fewbanks had generally used this French window for gaining access to his room after a nocturnal excursion.

Rolfe looked at his watch. It was nine o'clock. He decided to go to Hampstead and put his suspicions to the test. It was quite possible he was mistaken, but if, on the other hand, Hill was paying a nocturnal visit to Riversbrook and he had the luck to capture him, he might extract from him some valuable evidence for the forthcoming trial that Hill had kept back. And Rolfe was above all things interested at that moment in making the case for the prosecution as strong as possible.

Rolfe walked to the Camden Town Underground station, bought a ticket for Hampstead, and took his seat in the tube in that state of exhilarated excitement which comes to the detective when he feels that he is on the road to a disclosure. The speed of the train seemed all too slow for the police officer, and he looked at his watch at least a dozen times during the short journey from Camden Town to Hampstead.

When Rolfe arrived at Hampstead he set out at a rapid walk for Riversbrook. It was quite dark when he reached Tanton Gardens. He turned into the rustling avenue of chestnut trees, and strode swiftly down till he reached the deserted house of the murdered man.

The gate was locked as he had left it, but Rolfe climbed over it. A late moon was already throwing a refulgent light through the evening mists, silvering the tops of the fir trees in front of the house. Rolfe walked through the plantation, his footsteps falling noiselessly on the pine needles which strewed the path. He quickly reached the other side of the little wood, and the Italian garden lay before him, stretching in silver glory to the dark old house beyond.

Rolfe stood still at the edge of the wood, and glanced across the moonlit garden to the house. It seemed dark, deserted and desolate. There was no sign of a light in any of the windows facing the plantation.

The moon, rising above the fringe of trees in the woodland which skirted the meadows of the east side of the house, cast a sudden ray athwart the upper portion of the house. But the windows of the retreating first story still remained in shadow. Rolfe scrutinised these windows closely. There were three of them—he knew that two of them opened out from the bedroom the dead man used to occupy, and the third one belonged to the library adjoining—the room where the murder had been committed. The moonlight, gradually stealing over the house, revealed the windows of the bedroom closed and the blinds down, but the library was still in shadow, for a large chestnut-tree which grew in front of the house was directly in the line of Rolfe's vision.

Rolfe remained watching the house for some time, but no sign or sound of life could he detect in its silent desolation. "I must have been mistaken," he muttered, with a final glance at the windows of the first story. "There's nobody in the house."

He turned to go, and had taken a few steps through the pinewood when suddenly he started and stood still. His quick ear had caught a faint sound—a kind of rattle—coming from the direction of the house. What was that noise which sounded so strangely familiar to his ears? He had it! It was the fall of a Venetian blind. Instantaneously there came to Rolfe the remembrance that Inspector Chippenfield had ordered the library blind to be left up, so that when the sun was high in the heavens its rays, striking in through the window over the top of the chestnut-tree, might dry up the stain of blood on the floor, which washing had failed to efface. Somebody was in the library and had dropped the blind.

Rolfe hurriedly retraced his steps to the edge of the plantation, and raced across the Italian garden, feeling for his revolver as he ran. Some instinct told him that he would find entrance through the French windows on the west side of the morning room, and thither he directed his steps. He pulled out his electric torch and tried the windows. They were shut, and the first one was locked. The second one yielded to his hand. He pulled it open, and stepped into the room. Making his way by the light of his torch to the stairs, he swiftly but silently crept up them and turned to the library on the left of the first landing. The door was closed but not locked, and a faint light came through the keyhole. Rolfe pushed the door open, and looked into the room. A man was leaning over the dead judge's writing-desk, examining its contents by the light of a candle which he had set down on the desk. He was so engrossed in his occupation that he did not hear the door open.

"What are you doing there?" demanded Rolfe sternly. His voice sounded hollow and menacing as it reverberated through the room.

The man at the desk started up, and turned round. It was Hill. When he saw Rolfe he looked as though he would fall. He made as if to step forward. Then he stood quite still, looking at the officer with ashen face.

"Hill," said Rolfe quietly, "what does this mean?"

The butler had regained his self-composure with wonderful quickness. The mask of reticence dropped over his face again, and it was in the smooth deferential tones of a well-trained servant that he replied:

"Nothing, sir, I just slipped over from the shop to see if everything was all right."

"How did you get into the house?"

"By the French window, sir. I had a duplicate key which Sir Horace had made."

"And I see you also have a duplicate key of the desk. Why didn't you give these keys up with the others to Inspector Chippenfield?"

"I forgot about them at the time, sir. I found them in an old pocket this evening, and I was so uneasy about the house shut up with a lot of valuable things in it and nobody to give an eye to them that I just slipped across to see everything was all right."

"You came here after dark, and let yourself in with a private key after you had been strictly ordered not to come near the place? You have the audacity to admit you have done this?"

"Well, it's this way, sir. I was a trusted servant of Sir Horace's. I knew a great deal about his private life, if I may say so. I know he kept a lot of private papers in this room, and I wanted to make sure they were safe—I didn't like them being in this empty house, sir. I couldn't sleep in my bed of nights for thinking of them, sir. I felt last night as if my poor dead master was standing at my bedside, urging me to go over. I am very sorry I disobeyed the police orders, Mr. Rolfe, but I acted for the best."

"Hill, you are lying, you are keeping something back. Unless you immediately tell me the real reason of your visit to this house tonight I will take you down to the Hampstead Police Station and have you locked up. This visit of yours will take a lot of explaining away after your previous confession, Hill. It's enough to put you in the dock with Birchill."

Hill's eyes, which had been fixed on Rolfe's face, wavered towards the doorway, as though he were meditating a rush for freedom. But he merely remarked:

"I've told you the truth, sir, though perhaps not all of it. I came across to see if I could find some of Sir Horace's private papers which are missing."

"How do you know there are any papers missing?"

"As I said before, Mr. Rolfe, Sir Horace trusted me and he didn't take the trouble to hide things from me."

"You mean that he often left his desk open with important papers scattered about it?"

"Yes, sir."

"And you made a practice of going through them?"

"I didn't make a practice of it," protested Hill. "But sometimes I glanced at one or two of them. I thought there was no harm in it, knowing that Sir Horace trusted me."

"And some papers that you knew were there are now missing. Do you mean stolen?"

"Yes, sir."

"When did you see them last?"

"Just before Inspector Chippenfield came—the morning after the body was discovered. You remember, sir, that he came straight up here while you stayed downstairs talking to Constable Flack."

"Do you mean to suggest that Inspector Chippenfield stole them?"

"Oh, no, sir, I don't think he saw them. Sir Horace kept them in this little place at the back of the desk. Look at it, sir. It's a sort of secret drawer."

Rolfe went over to the desk, and Hill explained to him how the hiding place could be closed and opened. It was at the back of the desk under the pigeonholes, and the fact that the pigeonholes came close down to the desk hid the secret drawer and the spring which controlled it.

"What was the nature of these papers?" asked Rolfe.

"Well, sir, I never read them. Sir Horace set such store by them that I never dared to open them for fear he would find out. They were mostly letters and they were tied up with a piece of silk ribbon."

"A lady's letters, of course," said Rolfe.

"Judging from the writing on the envelopes they were sent by a lady," said Hill.

Rolfe breathed quickly, for he felt that he was on the verge of a discovery. Here was evidence of a lady in the case, which might lead to a startling development. Perhaps Crewe was right in declaring that Birchill was the wrong man, he said to himself. Perhaps the murderer was not a man, but a woman.

"And who do you think stole them?" he asked Hill.

"That is more than I would like to say," replied the butler.

"Are you sure they were in this hiding place when Inspector Chippenfield took charge of everything?"

"Yes, sir. I dusted out the room the morning you and he came to Riversbrook together, and the papers were there then, because I happened to touch the spring as I was dusting the desk, and it flew open and I saw the bundle there."

"Why didn't you tell Inspector Chippenfield about the papers and the secret drawer?"

"That is what I intended to do, sir, if he didn't find them himself. But when I had found they had gone I didn't like to say anything to him, because, as you may say, I had no right to know anything about them."

"When did they go: when did you find they were missing?"

"When Inspector Chippenfield went out for his lunch. I looked in the desk and found they had gone."

"Who could have taken them? Who had access to the room?"

"Well, sir, Mr. Chippenfield had some visitors that morning."

"Yes. There were about a dozen newspaper reporters during the day at various times. There were Dr. Slingsby and his assistant, who came out to make the post-mortem: Inspector Seldon, who came to arrange about the inquest, and there was that man from the undertakers who came to inquire about the funeral arrangements. But none of these men were likely to take the papers, and still less to know where they were hidden. In any case, no visitor could get at the desk while Mr. Chippenfield was in the room. And he is too careful to have left any visitor alone in this room—it was here that the murder was committed."

"He left one of his visitors alone here for a few minutes," said Hill in a voice which was little more than a whisper.

"Which one?" asked Rolfe eagerly.

"A lady."

"Who was she?"

"Mrs. Holymead."

"Oh!" Rolfe's exclamation was one of disappointment. "She is a friend of the family. She came out to see Miss Fewbanks—it was a visit of condolence."

"Yes, sir," said the obsequious butler. "She was a friend of the family, as you say. She was a friend of Sir Horace's. I have heard that Sir Horace paid her considerable attention before she married Mr. Holymead—it was a toss up which of them she married, so I've been told."

Rolfe saw that he had made a mistake in dismissing the idea of Mrs. Holymead having anything to do with the missing papers. "Do you think that she stole these letters—these papers?" he asked. "Do you think she knew where they were?"

"While she was in the room, Inspector Chippenfield came rushing downstairs for a glass of water. He said she had fainted."

"Whew!" Rolfe gave a low prolonged whistle. "And after she left you took the first opportunity of looking to see if the papers were still there, and you found they were gone?"

"Yes, sir."

"What made you suspect Mrs. Holymead would take them?"

"Well, sir, I didn't suspect her at the time. I just looked to see if Inspector Chippenfield had found them. I saw they had gone, and as I couldn't see any sign of them about anywhere else I concluded they must have been taken without Inspector Chippenfield knowing anything about it. The reason I came over here to-night was to have another careful look round for them."

Rolfe was silent for a moment.

"What would you have done with the papers if you had found them?" he asked suddenly.

"I would have handed them over to the police, sir," said the butler, who obviously had been prepared for a question of the kind.

"And what explanation would you have given for having found them—for having come over here in defiance of your orders from Inspector Chippenfield?"

"The true explanation, sir," said the butler, with a mild note of protest in his voice. "I would have told Inspector Chippenfield what I have already told you. And it is the simple truth."

Rolfe was plainly taken back at this rebuke, but he did not reply to it.

"In your statement of what took place when Birchill returned to the flat after committing the murder, he said something about having seen a woman leave the house by the front door as he was hiding in the garden—a fashionably dressed woman I think he said."

"Yes, sir, that was it."

"Do you believe that part of his story was true?"

"Well, sir, with a man like Birchill it is impossible to say when he is telling the truth, and when he isn't."

"There was no lady with Sir Horace when you left him that night when he returned from Scotland?"

"No, sir."

"I think you said he was in a hurry to get you out of the house, and told you not to come back?"

"That is what I thought at the time, sir."

"Well, Hill," said Rolfe, resuming his severe official tone; "all this does not excuse in any way your conduct in coming over here and forcing your way into the house in defiance of the police; opening this desk, and prying about for private papers that don't concern you. The proper course for you to adopt was to come to Scotland Yard and tell your story about these missing papers to Inspector Chippenfield or myself. However, I don't propose to take any action against you at present. Only there is to be no more of it. If you come hanging about here again on your own account, you'll find yourself in the dock beside Birchill. Hand me over the duplicate key of the door by which you came in, and also the key of the desk which you had still less right to have in your possession. Say nothing to anyone about those papers until I give you permission to do so."

CHAPTER XVI

The day fixed for the trial of Frederick Birchill was wet, dismal, and dreary. The rain pelted intermittently through a hazy, chilly atmosphere, filling the gutters and splashing heavily on the slippery pavements. But in spite of the rain a long queue, principally of women, assembled outside the portals of the Old Bailey long before the time fixed for the opening of the court. At the private entrance to the courthouse arrived fashionably-dressed ladies accompanied by well-groomed men. They had received cards of admission and had seats reserved for them in the body of the court. Many of them had personally known the late Sir Horace Fewbanks, and their interest in the trial of the man accused of his murder was intensified by the rumours afloat that there were to be some spicy revelations concerning the dead judge's private life.

The arrival of Mr. Justice Hodson, who was to preside at the trial, caused a stir among some of the spectators, many of whom belonged to the criminal class. Sir Henry Hodson had presided at so many murder trials that he was known among them as "the Hanging Judge." Among the spectators were some whom Sir Henry had put into mourning at one time or another; there were others whom he had deprived of their bread-winners for specified periods. These spectators looked at him with curiosity, fear, and hatred. Mr. Holymead, K.C., drove up in a taxi-cab a few minutes later, and his arrival created an impression akin to admiration. In the eyes of the criminal class he was an heroic figure who had assumed the responsibility of saving the life of one of their fraternity. The eminent counsel's success in the few criminal cases in which he had consented to appear had gained him the respectful esteem of those who considered themselves oppressed by the law, and the spectators on the pavement might have raised a cheer for him if their exuberance had not been restrained by the proximity of the policeman guarding the entrance.

When the court was opened Inspector Chippenfield took a seat in the body of the court behind the barrister's bench. He ranged his eye over the closely-packed spectators in the gallery, and shook his head with manifest disapproval. It seemed to him that the worst criminals in London had managed to elude the vigilance of the sergeant outside in order to see the trial of their notorious colleague, Fred Birchill. He pointed out their presence to Rolfe, who was seated alongside him.

"There's that scoundrel Bob Rogers, who slipped through our hands over the Ealing case, and his pal, Breaker Jim, who's just done seven years, looking down and grinning at us," he angrily whispered. "I'll give them something to grin about before they're much older. You'd think Breaker would have had enough of the Old Bailey to last him a lifetime. And look at that row alongside of them—there's Morris, Hart, Harry the Hooker, and that chap Willis who murdered the pawnbroker in Commercial Road last year, only we could never sheet it home to him. And two rows behind them is old Charlie, the Covent Garden 'drop,' with Holder Jack and Kemp, Birchill's mate. Why, they're everywhere. The inquest was nothing to this, Rolfe."

"Kemp must be thanking his lucky stars he wasn't in that Riversbrook job with Fred Birchill," said Rolfe, "for they usually work together. And there's Crewe, up in the gallery."

"Where?" exclaimed Inspector Chippenfield, with an indignant start.

"Up there behind that pillar there—no, the next one. See, he's looking down at you."

Crewe caught the inspector's eye, and nodded and smiled in a friendly fashion, but Inspector Chippenfield returned the salutation with a haughty glare.

"The impudence of that chap is beyond belief," he said to his subordinate. "One would have thought he'd have kept away from court after his wild-goose chase to Scotland and piling up expenses, but not him! Brazen impudence is the stock-in-trade of the private detective. If Scotland Yard had a little more of the impudence of the private detective, Rolfe, we should be better appreciated."

"I suppose he's come in the hopes of seeing the jury acquit Birchill," said Rolfe.

"No doubt," replied Inspector Chippenfield. "But he's come to the wrong shop. A good jury should convict without leaving the box if the case is properly put before them by the prosecution. Crewe would like to triumph over us, but it is our turn to win."

But Inspector Chippenfield was wrong in thinking that Crewe's presence in court was due to a desire for the humiliation of his rivals. Crewe had spent most of the previous night reading and revising his summaries and notes of the Riversbrook case, and in minutely reviewing his investigations of it. Over several pipes in the early morning hours he pondered long and deeply on the secret of Sir Horace Fewbanks's murder, without finding a solution which satisfactorily accounted for all the strange features of the case. But one thing he felt sure of was that Birchill had not committed the murder. He based that belief partly on the butler's confession, and partly on his own discoveries. He believed Hill to be a cunning scoundrel who had overreached the police for some purpose of his own by accusing Birchill, and who, to make his story more probable, had even implicated himself in the supposed burglary as a terrorised accomplice. And Crewe had been unable to test the butler's story, or find out what game he was playing, because of the assiduity with which the principal witness for the prosecution had been "nursed" by the police from the moment he made his confession. Crewe bit hard into his amber mouthpiece in vexation as he recalled the ostrich-like tactics of Inspector Chippenfield, who, having accepted Hill's story as genuine, had officially baulked all his efforts to see the man and question him about it.

He had come to court with the object of witnessing Birchill's behaviour in the dock and the efforts of any of his criminal friends to communicate with him. As a man who had had considerable experience in criminal trials he knew the irresistible desire of the criminal in the gallery of the court to encourage the man in the dock to keep up his courage. Communications of the kind had to be made by signs. It was Crewe's impression that by watching Birchill in the dock and Birchill's friends in the gallery he might pick up a valuable hint or two. It was also his intention to study closely the defence which Counsel for the prisoner intended to put forward.

It was therefore with a feeling of mingled annoyance and surprise that Crewe, looking down from his point of vantage at the bevy of fashionably-dressed ladies in the body of the court, recognised Mrs. Holymead, Mademoiselle Chiron and Miss Fewbanks seated side by side, engaged in earnest conversation. Before he could withdraw from their view behind the pillar in front of him, Miss Fewbanks looked up and saw him. She bowed to him in friendly recognition, and Crewe saw her whisper to Mrs. Holymead, who glanced quickly in his direction and then as quickly averted her gaze. But in that fleeting glance of her beautiful dark eyes Crewe detected an expression of fear, as though she dreaded his presence, and he noticed that she shivered slightly as she turned to resume her conversation with Miss Fewbanks.

His Honour Mr. Justice Hodson entered, and the persons in the court scrambled hurriedly to their feet to pay their tribute of respect to British law, as exemplified in the person of a stout red-faced old gentleman wearing a scarlet gown and black sash, and attended by four of the Sheriffs of London in their fur-trimmed robes. The judge bowed in response and took his seat. The spectators resumed theirs, craning their necks eagerly to look at the accused man, Birchill, who was brought into the dock by two warders. The work of empanelling a jury commenced, and when it was completed Mr. Walters, K.C., opened the case for the prosecution.

Mr. Walters was a long-winded Counsel who had detested the late Mr. Justice Fewbanks because of the latter's habit of interrupting the addresses of Counsel with the object of inducing them to curtail their remarks. This practice was not only annoying to Counsel, who necessarily knew better than the judge what the jury ought to be told, but it also tended to hold Counsel up to ridicule in the eyes of ignorant jurymen as a man who could not do his work properly without the watchful correction of the judge. But Mr. Walters, whose legal training had imbued in him a respect for Latin tags, subscribed to the adage, *de mortuis nil nisi bonum*. Therefore he began his address to the jury with a glowing reference to the loss, he might almost say the irreparable loss, which the judiciary had sustained, he would go so far as to say the loss which the nation had sustained by the death, the violent death, in short, the murder, of an eminent judge of the High Court Bench, whose clear and vigorous intellect, whose marvellous mastery of the legal principles laid down by the judicial giants of the past, whose inexhaustible knowledge drawn from the storehouses of British law, whose virile interpretations of the principles of British justice, whose unfailing courtesy and consideration to Counsel, the memory of which would long be cherished by those who had had the privilege of pleading before him, had made him an acquisition and an ornament to a Bench which in the eyes of the nation had always represented, and at no time more than the present—at this point Mr. Walters bowed to the presiding judge—the embodiment of legal knowledge, legal experience, and legal wisdom.

After this tribute to the murdered man and the presiding judge, Mr. Walters proceeded to lay the facts of the crime before the jury, who had read all about them in the newspapers.

With methodical care he built up the case against the accused man, classifying the points of evidence against him in categorical order for the benefit of the jury. The most important witness for the prosecution was a man known as James Hill, who had been in Sir Horace Fewbanks's employ as a butler. Hill's connection with the prisoner was in some aspects unfortunate, for himself, and no doubt counsel for the defense would endeavour to discredit his evidence on that account, but the jury, when they heard the butler tell his story in the witness box, would have little difficulty in coming to the conclusion that the man Hill was the victim of circumstances and his own weakness of temperament. However much they might be disposed to blame him for the course he had pursued, he was innocent of all complicity in his master's death, and had done his best to help the ends of justice by coming forward with a voluntary confession to the police.

Mr. Walters made no attempt to conceal or extenuate the black page in Hill's past, but he asked the jury to believe that Hill had bitterly repented of his former crime, and would have continued to lead an honest life as Sir Horace Fewbanks's butler, if ill fate had not forged a cruel chain of circumstances to link him to his past life and drag him down by bringing him in contact with the accused man Birchill, whom he had met in prison. Sir Horace Fewbanks was the self-appointed guardian of a young woman named Doris Fanning, the daughter of a former employee on his country estate, who had died leaving her penniless. Sir Horace had deemed it his duty to bring up the girl and give her a start in life. After educating her in a style suitable to her station, he sent her to London and paid for music lessons for her in order to fit her for a musical career, for which she showed some aptitude. Unfortunately the young woman had a self-willed and unbalanced temperament, and she gave her benefactor much trouble. Sir Horace bore patiently with her until she made the chance acquaintance of Birchill, and became instantly fascinated by him. The acquaintance speedily drifted into intimacy, and the girl became the pliant tool of Birchill, who acquired an almost magnetic influence over her. As the intimacy progressed she seemed to have become a willing partner in his criminal schemes.

When Sir Horace Fewbanks heard that the girl had drifted into an association with a criminal like Birchill he endeavoured to save her from her folly by remonstrating with her, and the girl promised to give up Birchill, but did not do so. When Sir Horace found out that he was being deceived he was compelled to renounce her. Birchill, who had been living on the girl, was furious with anger when he learnt that Sir Horace had cut off the monetary allowance he had been making her, and, on discovering by some means that his former prison associate Hill was now the butler at Sir Horace Fewbanks's house, he planned his revenge. He sent the girl Fanning to Riversbrook with a message to Hill, directing him, under threat of exposure, to see him at the Westminster flat.

Hill, who dreaded nothing so much as an exposure of that past life of his which he hoped was a secret between his master and himself, kept the appointment. Birchill told him he intended to rob the judge's house in order to revenge himself on Sir Horace for cutting off the girl's allowance, and he asked Hill to assist him in carrying out the burglary. Hill strenuously demurred at first, but weakly allowed himself to be terrorised into compliance under Birchill's threats of exposure. Hill's participation in the crime was to be confined to preparing a plan of Riversbrook as a guide for Birchill. Birchill said nothing about murder at this time, but there is no doubt he contemplated violence when he first spoke to Hill. When Hill, alarmed by his master's return on the actual night for which the burglary had been arranged, hurried across to the flat to urge Birchill to abandon the contemplated burglary, Birchill obstinately decided to carry out the crime, and left the flat with a revolver in his hand, threatening to murder Sir Horace if he found him, because of his harsh treatment—as he termed it—of the girl Fanning.

"Birchill left the flat at nine o'clock," continued Mr. Walters, who had now reached the vital facts of the night of the murder. "I ask the jury to take careful note of the time and the subsequent times mentioned, for they have an important bearing on the circumstantial evidence against the accused man. He returned, according to Hill's evidence, shortly after midnight. Evidence will be called to show that Birchill, or a man answering his description, boarded a tramcar at Euston Road at 9.30 p.m., and journeyed in it to Hampstead. He was observed both at Euston Road and the Hampstead terminus by the conductor, because of his obvious desire to avoid attention. There were only two other passengers on the top of the car when it left Euston Road. The conductor directed the attention of the driver to his movements, and they both watched him till he disappeared in the direction of the Heath. In fairness to the prisoner, it was necessary to point out, however, that neither the conductor nor the driver can identify him positively as the man they had seen on their car that night, but both will swear that to the best of their belief Birchill is the man. Assuming that it was the prisoner who travelled to Hampstead by the Euston Road tram—a route he would probably prefer because it took him to Hampstead by the most unfrequented way—he would have a distance of nearly a mile to walk across Hampstead Heath to Tanton Gardens, where Sir Horace Fewbanks's house was situated. The evidence of the tram-men is that he set off across the Heath at a very rapid rate. The tram reached Hampstead at four minutes past ten, so that, by walking fast, it would be possible for a young energetic man to reach Riversbrook before a quarter to eleven. Another five minutes would see an experienced housebreaker like Birchill inside the house. At twenty minutes past eleven a young man named Ryder, who had wandered into Tanton Gardens while endeavouring to take a short cut home, heard the sound of a report, which at the time he took to be the noise of a door violently slammed, coming from the direction of Riversbrook. A few moments afterwards he saw a man climb over the front fence of Riversbrook to the street. He drew back cautiously into the shade of one of the chestnut trees of the street avenue, and saw the man plainly as he ran past him. Ryder will swear that the man he saw was Birchill."

"It's a lie! It's a lie! You're trying to hang him, you wicked man. Oh, Fred, Fred!"

The cry proceeded from the girl Doris Fanning. Her unbalanced temperament had been unable to bear the strain of sitting there and listening to Mr. Walters' cold inexorable construction of a legal chain of evidence against her lover. She rose to her feet, shrieking wildly, and gesticulating menacingly at Mr. Walters. The Society ladies turned eagerly in their seats to take in through their *lorgnons* every detail of the interruption.

"Remove that woman," the judge sternly commanded.

Several policemen hastened to her, and the girl was partly hustled and partly carried out of court, shrieking as she went. When the commotion caused by the scene subsided, the judge irritably requested to be informed who the woman was.

"I don't know, my lord," replied Mr. Walters. "Perhaps—" He stopped and bent over to Detective Rolfe, who was pulling at his gown. "Er—yes, I'm informed by Detective Rolfe of Scotland Yard, my lord, that the young woman is a witness in the case."

"Then why was she permitted to remain in court?" asked Sir Henry Hodson angrily. "It is a piece of gross carelessness."

"I do not know, my lord. I was unaware she was a witness until this moment," returned Mr. Walters, with a discreet glance in the direction of Detective Rolfe, as an indication to His Honour that the judicial storm might safely veer in that direction. Sir Henry took the hint and administered such a stinging rebuke to Detective Rolfe that that officer's face took on a much redder tint before it was concluded. Then the judge motioned to Mr. Walters to resume the case.

Counsel, with his index finger still in the place in his brief where he had been interrupted, rose to his feet again and turned to the jury.

"Birchill returned to the flat at Westminster shortly after midnight," he continued. "Hill had been compelled by Birchill's threats to remain at the flat with the girl while Birchill visited Riversbrook, and the first thing Birchill told him on his return was that he had found Sir Horace Fewbanks dead in his house when he entered it. On his way back from committing the crime belated caution had probably dictated to Birchill the wisdom of endeavouring to counteract his previous threat to murder Sir Horace Fewbanks. He probably remembered that Hill, who had heard the threat, was an unwilling participator in the plan for the burglary, and might therefore denounce him to the police for the greater crime if he (Birchill) admitted that he had committed it. In order to guard against this contingency still further Birchill forced Hill to join in writing a letter to Scotland Yard, acquainting them with the murder, and the fact that the body was lying in the empty house. Birchill's object in acting thus was a twofold one. He dared not trust Hill to pretend to discover the body the next day and give information to the police, for fear he should not be able to retain sufficient control of himself to convince the detectives that he was wholly ignorant of the crime, and he also thought that if Hill had a share in writing the letter he would feel an additional complicity in the crime, and keep silence for his own sake. Birchill was right in his calculations—up to a point. Hill was at first too frightened to disclose what he knew, but as time went on his affection for his murdered master, and his desire to bring the murderer to justice, overcame his feelings of fear for his own share in bringing about the crime, and he went and confessed everything to the police, regardless of the consequences that might recoil upon his own head. The case against Birchill depends largely on Hill's evidence, and the jury, when they have heard his story in the witness-box, and bearing in mind the extenuating circumstances of his connection with the crime, will have little hesitation in coming to the conclusion that the prisoner in the dock murdered Sir Horace Fewbanks."

The first witness called was Inspector Seldon, who gave evidence as to his visit to Riversbrook shortly before 1 p. m. on the 19th of August as the result of information received, and his discovery of the dead body of Sir Horace Fewbanks. He described the room in which the body was found; the position of the body; and he identified the blood-stained clothes produced by the prosecution as being those in which the dead man was dressed when the body was discovered. In cross-examination by Holymead he stated that Sir Horace Fewbanks was fully dressed when the body was found. The witness also stated in cross-examination that none of the electric lights in the house were burning when the body was discovered.

The next witness was Dr. Slingsby, the pathological expert from the Home Office who had made the post mortem examination, and who was much too great a man to be kept waiting while other witnesses of more importance to the case but of less personal consequence went into the box. Dr. Slingsby stated that his examinations had revealed that death had been caused by a bullet wound which had penetrated the left lung, causing internal hemorrhage.

Mr. Finnis, the junior counsel for the defence, suggested to the witness that the wound might have been self-inflicted, but Dr. Slingsby permitted himself to be positive that such was not the case. With professional caution he assured Mr. Finnis, who briefly cross-examined him, that it was impossible for him to state how long Sir Horace Fewbanks had been dead. *Rigor mortis*, in the case of the human body, set in from eight to ten hours after death, and it was between three and four o'clock in the afternoon of the day the crime was discovered that he first saw the corpse. The body was quite stiff and cold then.

"Is it not possible for death to have taken place nineteen or twenty hours before you saw the body?" asked Mr. Finnis, eagerly.

"Quite possible," replied Dr. Slingsby.

"Is it not also possible, from the state of the body when you examined it, that death took place within sixteen hours of your examination of the body?" asked Mr. Walters, as Mr. Finnis sat down with the air of a man who had elicited an important point.

"Quite possible," replied Dr. Slingsby, with the prim air of a professional man who valued his reputation too highly to risk it by committing himself to anything definite.

Dr. Slingsby was allowed to leave the box, and Inspector Chippenfield took his place. Inspector Chippenfield did not display any professional reticence about giving his evidence—at least, not on the surface, though he by no means took the court completely into his confidence as to all that had passed between him and Hill. On the other hand he told the judge and jury everything that his professional experience prompted him as necessary and proper for them to know in order to bring about a conviction. In the course of his evidence he made several attempts to introduce damaging facts as to Birchill's past, but Mr. Holymead protested to the judge. Counsel for the defence protested that he had allowed his learned friend in opening the case a great deal of latitude as to the relations which had previously existed between the witness Hill and the prisoner, because the defence did not intend to attempt to hide the fact that the prisoner had a criminal record, but he had no intention of allowing a police witness to introduce irrelevant matter in order to prejudice the jury against the prisoner. His Honour told the witness to confine himself to answering the questions put to him, and not to volunteer information.

After this rebuke Inspector Chippenfield resumed giving evidence. He related what Birchill had said when arrested, and declared that he was positive that the footprints found outside the kitchen window were made by the boots produced in court which Birchill had been wearing at the time he was arrested. He produced a jemmy which he had found at Fanning's flat, and said that it fitted the marks on the window at Riversbrook which had been forced on the night of the 18th of August.

Inspector Chippenfield's evidence was followed by that of the two tramway employees, who declared that to the best of their belief Birchill was the man who boarded their tram at half-past nine on the night of the 18th of August, and rode to the terminus at Hampstead, which they reached at 10.4 p. m. Both the witnesses showed a very proper respect for the law, and were obviously relieved when the brief cross-examination was over and they were free to go back to their tram-car.

CHAPTER XVII

"James Hill!" called the court crier.

The butler stepped forward, mounted the witness-stand, and bowed his head deferentially towards the judge. He was neatly dressed in black, and his sandy-grey hair was carefully brushed. His face was as expressionless as ever, but a slight oscillation of the Court Bible in his right hand as he was sworn indicated that his nerves were not so calm as he strove to appear. He looked neither to the right nor left, but kept his glance downcast. Only once, as he stood there waiting to be questioned, did he cast a furtive look towards the man whose life hung on his evidence, but the malevolent vindictive gaze Birchill shot back at him caused him to lower his eyelids instantly.

Hill commenced his evidence in a voice so low that Mr. Walters stopped him at the outset and asked him to speak in a louder tone. It soon became apparent that his evidence was making a deep impression on the court. Sir Henry Hodson listened to him intently, and watched him keenly, as Hill, with impassive countenance and smooth even tones, told his strange story of the night of the murder. When he had drawn to a conclusion he gave another furtive glance at the dock, but Birchill was seated with his head bowed down, as though tired, and with one hand supporting his face.

Mr. Walters methodically folded up his brief and sat down, with a sidelong glance in the direction of Mr. Holymead as he did so. Every eye in court was turned on Holymead as the great K.C. settled his gown on his shoulders and got up to cross-examine the principal Crown witness.

His cross-examination was the admiration of those spectators whose sympathies were on the side of the man in the dock as one of themselves. Hill was cross-examined as to the lapse from honesty which had sent him to gaol, and he was reluctantly forced to admit, that so far from the theft being the result of an impulse to save his wife and child from starvation, as the Counsel for the prosecution had indicated, it was the result of the impulse of cupidity. He had robbed a master who had trusted him and had treated him with kindness. Having extracted this fact, in spite of Hill's evasions and twistings, Holymead straightened himself to his full height, and, shaking a warning finger at the witness, said:

"I put it to you, witness, that the reason Sir Horace Fewbanks engaged you as butler in his household at Riversbrook was because he knew you to be a man of few scruples, who would be willing to do things that a more upright honest man would have objected to?"

"That is not true," replied Hill.

"Is it not true that your late master frequently entertained women of doubtful character at Riversbrook?" thundered the K.C.

Hill gasped at the question. When he had first heard that his late master's old friend, Mr. Holymead, was to appear for Birchill, he had immediately come to the conclusion that Mr. Holymead was taking up the case in order to save Sir Horace's name from exposure by dealing carefully with his private life at Riversbrook. But here he was ruthlessly tearing aside the veil of secrecy. Hill hesitated. He glanced round the curious crowded court and saw the eager glances of the women as they impatiently awaited his reply. He hesitated so long that Holymead repeated the question.

"Women of doubtful character?" faltered the witness. "I do not understand you."

"You understand me perfectly well, Hill. I do not mean women off the streets, but women who have no moral reputation to maintain— women who do not mind letting confidential servants see that they have no regard for the conventional standards of life. I mean, witness, that your late master frequently entertained at Riversbrook, women—I will not call them ladies—who were not particular at what hour they went home. Sometimes one or more of them stayed all night, and you were entrusted with the confidential task of smuggling them out of the house without other servants knowing of their presence. Is not that so?"

"I—I—"

"Answer the question without equivocation, witness."

"Y-es, sir."

There was a slight stir in the body of the court due to the fact that Miss Fewbanks and Mrs. Holymead had risen and were making their way to the door. The fashionably-dressed women in the court stared with much interest at the daughter of the murdered man, whom most of them knew, in order to see how she was taking the disclosures about her dead father's private life.

"And sometimes there were quarrels between your late master and these visitors, were there not?" continued Holymead.

"Quarrels, sir?"

"Surely you know that under the influence of wine some people become quarrelsome?"

"Yes, sir."

"Well, did your late master's nocturnal visitors ever become quarrelsome?"

"Sometimes, sir."

"In the exercise of your confidential duties did you sometimes see quarrelsome ladies off the premises?"

"Sometimes, sir."

"And it was no uncommon thing for them to say things to you about your master, eh?"

"Sometimes they didn't care what they said."

"Quite so," commented Counsel drily. "They indulged in threats?"

"Not all of them," replied Hill, who at length saw where the cross-examination was tending.

"I do not suggest that all of them did—only that the more violent of them did so."

"Quite so, sir."

"So we may take it that the quarrel between your late master and Miss Fanning was not the only quarrel of the kind which came under your notice?"

"There were not many others," said Hill.

"It was not the only one?" persisted Counsel.

"No, sir."

"In your evidence-in-chief you said nothing about Miss Fanning using threats against your master when you were showing her out?"

"No, sir."

"She did not use any?"

"Not in my hearing, sir."

There was a pause at this stage while Mr. Holymead consulted the notes he had made of Mr. Walters's cross-examination of the witness.

"What o'clock was it when you left Riversbrook on the 18th of August after your master's return from Scotland?"

"About half-past seven, sir."

"And what time did Sir Horace arrive home?"

"About seven o'clock, sir."

"What were you doing between seven and seven-thirty?"

"I unpacked his bags and got his bedroom ready. I took him some refreshment up to the library."

"And he told you he wouldn't want you again until the following night about eight o'clock?"

"Yes, sir. He said he thought he would be going back to Scotland by the night express, and I was to get his bag packed and lock up the house."

"You told Counsel for the prosecution in the course of your evidence that you were afraid of Birchill," continued Holymead.

"Yes, sir."

"Were you afraid of physical violence from him, or only that he would expose your past to the other servants?"

"I was afraid of him both ways," said Hill.

"Was it because of this fear that you made out for him a plan of Riversbrook to assist him in the burglary?"

"Yes, sir."

"When did you make out this plan?"

"The day after Sir Horace left for Scotland."

"Was that on your first visit to Miss Fanning's flat in Westminster after the prisoner had sent her to Riversbrook to tell you he wanted to see you?"

"Yes, sir."

"Did Birchill stand over you while you made out this plan?"

"Yes, sir."

"Would you know the plan again if you saw it?"

"Yes, sir."

Mr. Finnis, who had been hiding the plan under the papers before him, handed a document up to his chief.

Mr. Holymead unfolded it, and with a brief glance at it handed it up to the witness.

"Is that the plan?" he asked.

Hill was somewhat taken aback at the production of the plan. It was drawn in ink on a white sheet of paper of foolscap size, with a slightly bluish tint. The paper was by no means clean, for Birchill had carried it about in his pocket. The witness reluctantly admitted that the plan was the one he had given to Birchill. To his manifest relief Counsel asked no further questions about it. In a low tone Mr. Holymead formally expressed his intention to put the plan in as evidence. He handed it to Mr. Walters, who, after a close inspection of it, passed it along to the judge's Associate for His Honour's inspection.

The rest of Hill's cross-examination concerned what happened at the flat on the night of the burglary. He adhered to the story he had told, and could not be shaken in the main points of it. But Mr. Holymead made some effective use of the discrepancy between the witness's evidence at the inquest as to his movements on the night of the murder and his evidence in court. He elicited the fact that the police had discovered his evidence at the inquest was false and had forced him to make a confession by threatening to arrest him for the murder.

Mr. Holymead signified that he had nothing further to ask the witness, and Mr. Walters called his last witness, a young man named Charles Ryder, a resident of Liverpool, who had spent a week's holiday in London from the 14th to the 21st of August. Ryder had stayed with some friends at Hampstead, and when making his way home on the night of the 18th of August had walked down Tanton Gardens in the belief that he was taking a short cut. The time was about 11.20. He saw a man running towards him along the footpath from the direction of Riversbrook. He caught a good glimpse of the man, who seemed to be very excited. He was sure the prisoner was the man he had seen. In cross-examination by Mr. Holymead he was far less positive in his identification of the prisoner, and finally admitted that the man he saw that night might be somebody else who resembled the prisoner in build.

CHAPTER XVIII

The second day of the trial began promptly when Mr. Justice Hodson took his seat. Mr. Holymead's opening statement to the jury was brief. He reminded them that the life of a fellow creature rested on their verdict. If there was any doubt in their minds whether the prisoner had fired the shot which killed Sir Horace Fewbanks the prisoner was entitled to a verdict of "not guilty." It was obligatory on the prosecution to prove guilt beyond all reasonable doubt.

He submitted that the prosecution had not established their case. After hearing the case for the prosecution the jury must have grave doubts as to the guilt of the prisoner, and it was his duty as Counsel for the prisoner to put before the jury facts which would not only increase their doubts but bring them to the positive conclusion that the prisoner was not guilty. He was not going to attempt to deny that the prisoner went to Riversbrook on the night of the murder. He went there to commit a burglary. But so far from Hill being terrorised into complicity in that crime it was he who had first suggested it to Birchill and had arranged it. Material evidence on that point would be submitted to the jury.

Hill was a man who was incapable of gratitude. His disposition was to bite the hand that fed him. After being well treated by Sir Horace Fewbanks he had made up his mind to rob him as he had robbed his former master Lord Melhurst. He knew that Sir Horace had quarrelled with this girl Fanning because of her association with Birchill, and he went to Birchill and put before him a proposal to rob Riversbrook. Birchill consented to the plan, and when on the night of the 18th August he broke into the house he found the murdered body of Sir Horace in the library. That was the full extent of the prisoner's connection with the crime. To the superficial and suspicious mind it might seem an improbable story, but to an earnest mind it was a story that carried conviction because of its simple straightforwardness—

its crudity, if the jury liked to call it that. It lacked the subtlety and the finish of a concocted story. The murder took place before Birchill reached Riversbrook on his burglarious errand.

"It is my place," added Mr. Holymead, in concluding his address, "to convince you that my client is not guilty, or, in other words, to convince you that the murder was committed before he reached the house. It is only with the greatest reluctance that I take upon myself the responsibility of pointing an accusing finger at another man. In crimes of this kind you cannot expect to get anything but circumstantial evidence. But there are degrees of circumstantial evidence, and my duty to my client lays upon me the obligation of pointing out to you that there is one person against whom the existing circumstantial evidence is stronger than it is against my client."

Crewe, who had secured his former place in the gallery of the court, looked down on the speaker. He had carefully followed every word of Holymead's address, but the concluding portion almost electrified him. He flattered himself that he was the only person in court who understood the full significance of the sonorous sentences with which the famous K.C. concluded his address to the jury.

As his eyes wandered over the body of the court below, Crewe saw that Mrs. Holymead and Mademoiselle Chiron were sitting in one of the back seats, but that they were not accompanied by Miss Fewbanks. It was evident to him by the way in which Mrs. Holymead followed the proceedings that her interest in the case was something far deeper than wifely interest in her husband's connection with it as counsel for the defence. Leaning forward in her seat, with her hands clasped in her lap, she listened eagerly to every word. During the day his gaze went back to her at intervals, and on several occasions he became aware that she had been watching him while he watched her husband.

The first witness for the defence was Doris Fanning. The drift of her evidence was to exonerate the prisoner at the expense of Hill. She declared that she had not gone to Riversbrook to see Hill after the final quarrel with Sir Horace. Hill had come to her flat in Westminster of his own accord and had asked for Birchill. She went out of the room while they discussed their business, but after Hill had gone Birchill told her that Hill had put up a job for him at Riversbrook. Birchill showed her the plan of Riversbrook that Hill had made, and asked her if it was correct as far as she knew. Yes, she was sure she would know the plan again if she saw it.

The judge's Associate handed it to Mr. Holymead, who passed it to the witness.

"Is this it?" he asked.

"Yes," she replied emphatically, almost without inspecting it.

"I want you to look at it closely," said Counsel. "When Birchill showed you the plan immediately after Hill's departure, what impression did you get regarding it?"

She looked at him blankly.

"I don't understand you," she said.

"You can tell the difference between ink that has been newly used and ink that has been on the paper some days. Was the ink fresh?"

"No, it was old ink," she said.

"How do you know that?"

"Because ink doesn't go black till a long while after it is written. At least, the letters I write don›t." She shot a veiled coquettish glance at the big K.C. from under her long eyelashes.

The K.C. returned the glance with a genial smile.

"What do you write your letters on, Miss Fanning?"

She almost giggled at the question.

"I use a writing tablet," she replied.

"Ruled or unruled?"

"Ruled. I couldn't write straight if there weren't lines." She smiled again.

"And what colour do you affect—grey, rose-pink or white paper?"

"Always white."

"Is that all the paper you have at your flat for writing purposes?"

"Yes."

"Then what did Birchill write on when he wanted to write a letter?"

"He used mine."

"Are you sure of that?"

"Yes. When he wanted to write a letter he used to ask me for my tablet and an envelope. And generally he used to borrow a stamp as well." She pouted slightly, with another coquettish glance.

"Look at that plan again," said the K.C. "Have you ever had paper like it at your flat?"

She shook her head.

"Never."

"Have you ever seen paper of that kind in Birchill's possession before he showed you the plan?"

"Never."

"When he showed you the plan had the paper been folded?"

"Yes."

The K.C. took the witness, now very much at her ease, to the night of the murder. She denied strenuously that Hill tried to dissuade Birchill from carrying out the burglary because Sir Horace Fewbanks had returned unexpectedly from Scotland. It was Birchill who suggested postponing the burglary until Sir Horace left, but Hill urged that the original plan should be adhered to. He declared that Sir Horace would remain at home at least a fortnight, and perhaps longer. His master was a sound sleeper, he said, and if Birchill waited until he went to bed there would be no danger of awakening him. She contradicted many details of Hill's evidence as to what took place when the prisoner returned from breaking into Riversbrook. It was untrue, she said, that there was a spot of blood on Birchill's face or that his hands were smeared with blood. He was a little bit excited when he returned, but after one glass of whisky he spoke quite calmly of what had happened.

The next witness was a representative of the firm of Holmes and Jackson, papermakers, who was handed the plan of Riversbrook which Hill had drawn. He stated that the paper on which the plan was drawn was manufactured by his firm, and supplied to His Majesty's Stationery Office. He identified it by the quality of the paper and the watermark. In reply to Mr. Walters the witness was sure that the paper he held in his hand had been manufactured by his firm for the Government. It was impossible for him to be mistaken. Other firms might manufacture paper of a somewhat similar quality and tint, but it would not be exactly similar. Besides, he identified it by his firm's watermark, and he held the plan up to the light and pointed it out to the court.

Counsel for the defence called two more witnesses on this point—one to prove that supplies of the paper on which the plan was drawn were issued to legal departments of the Government, and an elderly man named Cobb, Sir Horace Fewbanks's former tipstaff, who stated that he took some of the paper in question to Riversbrook on Sir Horace's instructions. And then, to the astonishment of junior members of the bar who were in court watching his conduct of the case in order to see if they could pick up a few hints, he intimated that his case was closed. It seemed to them that the great K.C. had put up a very flimsy case for the defence, and that in spite of the fact that the prosecutor's case rested mainly on the evidence of a tainted witness Holymead would be very hard put to it to get his man off.

"Isn't my learned friend going to call the prisoner?" suggested Mr. Walters, with the cunning design of giving the jury something to think of when they were listening to his learned friend's address.

"It's scarcely necessary," said Mr. Holymead, who saw the trap, and replied in a tone which indicated that the matter was not worth a moment's consideration.

He began his address to the jury by emphasising the fact that a fellow creature's life depended on the result of their deliberations. The duty that rested upon them of saying whether the prosecution had established beyond all reasonable doubt that the prisoner shot Sir Horace Fewbanks was a solemn and impressive one. He asked them to consider the case carefully in all its bearings. He could not claim for his client that he was a man of spotless reputation. The prisoner belonged to a class who earned their living by warring against society. But that fact did not make him a murderer. On what did the case for the prosecution rest? On the evidence of Hill and three other witnesses who, on the night of the murder, had seen a man somewhat resembling the prisoner in the vicinity of Riversbrook, or making towards the vicinity of that house. But so far from wishing to emphasise the weakness of identification he admitted that the prisoner went to Riversbrook with the intention of committing a burglary.

"We admit that he went there the night Sir Horace Fewbanks returned from Scotland," he continued. "Counsel for the prosecution will make the most of those admissions in the course of his address to you, but the point to which I wish to direct your attention is that we make this damaging admission so that you may decide between the prisoner and the man who led him into a trap by instigating the burglary. Now we come to the evidence of Hill. I know you will not convict a man of murder on the unsupported evidence of a fellow criminal. But I want to point out to you that even if Hill's evidence were true in every detail, even if Hill had not swerved one iota from the truth, there is nothing in his evidence to lead to the positive conclusion that the prisoner murdered Hill's master, Sir Horace Fewbanks. What does Hill's evidence against the prisoner amount to? Let us accept it for the moment as absolutely true. Later on I will show you plainly that the man is a liar, that he is a cunning scoundrel, and that his evidence is utterly unreliable. But accepting for the moment his evidence as true the case against the prisoner amounts to this: by threats of exposure Birchill compelled Hill to consent to Riversbrook being robbed while the owner was in Scotland.

"Hill's complicity, according to his own story, extended only to supplying a plan of the house and giving Birchill some information as to where various articles of value would be found. On the 18th of August Hill went to Riversbrook to see that everything was in order for the burglary that night. While he was there his master returned unexpectedly. Hill then went to the flat in Westminster and told Birchill that Sir Horace had returned. His own story is that he tried to get Birchill to abandon the idea of the burglary, but that Birchill, who had been drinking, swore that he would carry out the plan, and that if he came across Sir Horace he would shoot him. What grudge had Birchill against Sir Horace Fewbanks? The fact that Sir Horace had discarded the woman Fanning because of her association with Birchill. Gentlemen, does a man commit a murder for a thing of that kind?

"Let us test the credibility of the man who has tried to swear away the life of the prisoner. You saw him in the witness-box, and I have no doubt formed your own conclusions as to the type of man he is. Did he strike you as a man who would stand by the truth above all things, or a man who would lie persistently in order to save his own skin? That the man cannot be believed even when on his oath has been publicly demonstrated in the courts of the land. The story he told the court yesterday in the witness-box of his movements on the day of the murder is quite different to the story he told on his oath at the inquest on the body of Sir Horace Fewbanks. Let me read to you the evidence he gave at the inquest."

Mr. Finnis handed to his leader a copy of Hill's evidence at the inquest, and Mr. Holymead read it out to the jury. He then read out a shorthand writer's account of Hill's evidence on the previous day.

"Which of these accounts are we to believe?" he said, turning to the jury. "The latter one, the prosecution says. But why, I ask? Because it tallies with the statement extorted from Hill by the police under the threat of charging him with the murder. Does that make it more credible? Is a man like Hill, who is placed in that position, likely to tell the truth, the whole truth, and nothing but the truth? It is an insult to the jury as men of intelligence to ask you to believe Hill's evidence. I do not ask you to believe the story he told at the inquest in preference to the story he told here in the witness-box yesterday. I ask you to regard both stories as the evidence of a man who is too deeply implicated in this crime to be able to speak the truth.

"I will prove to you, gentlemen of the jury, that the man is a criminal by instinct and a liar by necessity—the necessity of saving his own skin. He robbed his former master, Lord Melhurst, and he planned to rob his late master, Sir Horace Fewbanks. But knowing that his former crime would be brought against him when the police came to investigate a robbery at Riversbrook he was too cunning to rob Riversbrook himself. He looked about him for an accomplice and he selected Birchill. You heard him say in the witness-box that he drew Birchill a plan of Riversbrook—the plan I now hold in my hand. I will ask you to inspect the plan closely. Hill told us that Birchill terrorised him into drawing this plan by threats of exposure. Exposure of what? His master, Sir Horace Fewbanks, knew he had been in gaol, so what had he to fear from exposure? His proper course, if he were an honest man, would have been to tell his master that Birchill was planning to rob the house and had endeavoured to draw him into the crime. But he did nothing of the kind, for the simple reason that the plan to rob Riversbrook was his own, and not Birchill's.

"Now, gentlemen, you have all seen the plan which this tainted witness declares was drawn by him because Birchill terrorised him and stood over him while he drew it. Is there anything in that plan to suggest that it was drawn by a man in a state of nervous terror? Why, the lines are as firmly drawn as if they had been made by an architect working at his leisure in his office. Was this plan drawn by a man in a state of nervous terror with his tormentor standing threateningly over him, or was it drawn up by a man working at leisure, free not only from terror but from interruption? The answer to that question is supplied in the evidence given by three witnesses as to the paper used. Hill says the plan was drawn at the flat. Two other witnesses swore that it was paper supplied exclusively for Government Departments, and another witness swore that he had taken such paper to Riversbrook for the use of Sir Horace Fewbanks, who, like every one of His Majesty's judges, found it necessary to do some of his judicial work at home. What is the inevitable inference? I ask you if you can have any doubt, after looking at that plan and after hearing the evidence given to-day about the paper, that the proposal to rob Riversbrook was Hill's own proposal, that Hill drew a plan of the house on paper he abstracted from his master's desk—paper which this confidential servant was apparently in the habit of using for private purposes—and that he gave it to Birchill when he asked Birchill to join him in the crime?

"When one of the main features of Hill's story is proved to be false, how can you believe any of the rest? In the light in which we now see him, with his cunning exposed, what significance is to be attached to his statement that Birchill in his presence threatened to shoot Sir Horace Fewbanks if the master of Riversbrook interfered with him? Such a threat was not made, but why should Hill say it was made? For the same reason that he lied about the plan—to save his own skin. I submit to you, gentlemen, that when Hill went to see Birchill at the Westminster flat on the night arranged for the burglary Sir Horace Fewbanks was dead—murdered—and that Hill knew he was murdered. His own story is that he tried to persuade Birchill to abandon the proposed burglary, but, according to the witness Fanning, he did all in his power to induce Birchill to carry out the original plan when he saw that Birchill was disposed to postpone the burglary in view of the return of the master of Riversbrook. Why did he want Birchill to carry out the burglary? Because he knew that his master's murdered body was lying in the house, and he wanted to be in the position to produce evidence against Birchill as the murderer if he found himself in a tight corner as the result of the subsequent investigations of the police. Remember that the body of the victim was fully dressed when it was discovered by the police, and that none of the electric lights were burning. Does not that prove conclusively that the murder was not committed by Birchill, that Sir Horace Fewbanks was dead when Birchill broke into the house?

"Birchill, an experienced criminal, would not break into the house while there was anybody moving about. He would wait until the house was in darkness and the inmates asleep. To do otherwise would increase enormously the risks of capture. But the fact that the police found the body of the murdered man fully dressed shows that Sir Horace was murdered before he went to bed—before Birchill broke into the house. It shows conclusively that the murder was committed before dusk. Your only alternatives to that conclusion are that the murdered man went to bed with his clothes on, or that the murderer broke into the house before Sir Horace had gone to bed and after killing Sir Horace went coolly round the house turning out the lights instead of fleeing in terror at his deed without even waiting to collect any booty. I am sure that as reasonable men you will reject both these alternatives as absurd. No evidence has been produced to show that anything has been stolen from the place. It was evidently the theory of the prosecution that the prisoner, after shooting Sir Horace, had fled. The evidence of Hill was that he arrived at Fanning's flat in a state of great excitement. His excitement would be consistent with his story of having discovered the body of a murdered man, but not consistent with the conduct of a cold-blooded calculating murderer who had broken into the house before Sir Horace had undressed for bed, had shot him, and had then gone round the house turning out the lights without having any apparent object in doing so.

"Gentlemen, I think you will admit that the crime must have been committed before dusk; before any lights were turned on. I do not ask you to say that Hill is guilty. The responsibility of saying what man other than the prisoner shot Sir Horace Fewbanks does not rest with you. But I do urge you to ask yourselves whether, as between Hill and the prisoner, the probability of guilt is not on the side of this witness who lied to the coroner's court about his movements on the night of the murder, and who lied to this court about the plan for the robbery of Riversbrook. I have shown you that Hill was the master mind in planning the burglary, and, that being so, would not Birchill have consented to the postponement of the burglary if Hill had urged him to do so when he visited the flat after the unexpected return of the master of Riversbrook? Is not the evidence of the witness Fanning, that Hill urged Birchill to carry out the burglary after Sir Horace had gone to sleep, more credible than Hill's statement that he endeavoured to induce Birchill to abandon the proposed crime? Knowing what you know of Hill's past as a man who will rob his master, knowing that he attempted to deceive you with regard to this plan of Riversbrook in order that you might play your part in his cunning scheme, I urge you to ask yourselves whether it is not more probable that Hill fired the shot which killed Sir Horace Fewbanks than that the prisoner did so. Is it not extremely probable that the unexpected return of Sir Horace upset Hill, who was giving a final look round the house before the burglary took place? That, instead of answering his master with the suave obsequious humility of the well-trained servant, he revealed the baffled ferocity of a criminal whose carefully arranged plan seemed to have miscarried; that his master angrily rebuked him, and Hill, losing control of himself, sprang at Sir Horace, and the struggle ended with Hill drawing a revolver and shooting his master?

"The rest of the story from that point can be constructed without difficulty. The murderer's first thought was to divert suspicion from himself, and the best way to do that was to divert suspicion elsewhere. He locked up the house and went to see Birchill. He urged Birchill to break into Riversbrook, in which the dead body of the murdered man lay. It is true that he need not have told Birchill that Sir Horace had returned unexpectedly; but his object in doing so was to make Birchill search about the house until he inadvertently stumbled across the dead body. Had Birchill been under the impression that he had broken into an entirely empty house he would have collected the valuables and might not have entered the library in which the dead body lay. It was necessary for Hill's purpose that Birchill should come across the corpse; then he would be vitally interested in diverting suspicion from himself (Birchill) and that is why he cunningly revealed to Birchill that Sir Horace had returned. I put it to the jury that such is a more probable explanation of how Sir Horace met his death than that he was shot down by Birchill. I ask you again to remember that the body was fully dressed when it was found by the police. I put it to you that in this matter the prisoner walked into a trap prepared by his more cunning fellow criminal. And I urge you, with all the earnestness it is possible for a man to use when the life of a fellow creature is at stake, not to be led into a trap—not to play the part this cunning criminal Hill has designed for you—in the sacrifice of the life of an innocent man for the purpose of saving himself from his just deserts. Looking at the whole case—as you will not fail to do—with the breadth of view of experienced men of the world, with some knowledge of the workings of human nature, with a natural horror of the depths of cunning of which some natures are capable, with a deep sense of the solemn responsibility for a human life upon you, I confidently appeal to you to say that the prisoner was not the man who shot Sir Horace Fewbanks, and to bring in a verdict of 'not guilty.'"

A short discussion arose between the bench and bar on the question of adjourning the court or continuing the case in the hope of finishing it in a few hours. Sir Henry Hodson wanted to finish the case that night, but Counsel for the prosecution intimated that his address to the jury would take nearly two hours. As it was then nearly five o'clock, and His Honour had to sum up before the jury could retire, it was hardly to be hoped that the case could be finished that night, as the jury might be some time in arriving at a verdict. His Honour decided to adjourn the court and finish the case next day.

CHAPTER XIX

Mr. Walters began his address to the jury on orthodox lines. He referred to the fact that his learned friend had warned them that the life of a fellow creature rested on their verdict. It was right that they should keep that in mind; it was right that they should fully realise the responsible nature of the duty they were called upon to perform, but it would be wrong for them to over-estimate their responsibility, or to feel weighed down by it. It would be wrong for them to be influenced by sentimental considerations of the fact that a fellow creature's life was at stake. Strictly speaking, that had nothing whatever to do with them. Their responsibility ended with their verdict. If their verdict was "guilty" the responsibility of taking the prisoner's life would rest upon the law—not on the jury, not on His Honour who passed the sentence of death, not on the prison officials who carried out the execution. The jury would do well to keep in mind the fact that their responsibility in this trial, impressive and important as every one must acknowledge it to be, was nevertheless strictly limited as far as the taking of the life of the prisoner was concerned.

He then went over the evidence in detail, building up again the case for the prosecution where Mr. Holymead had made breaches in it, and attempting to demolish the case for the defence. Hill, he declared, was an honest witness. The man had made one false step but he had done his best to retrieve it, and with the help he had received from his late master, Sir Horace Fewbanks, he would have buried the past effectively if it had not been for the fact that the prisoner, who was a confirmed criminal, had determined to drag him down. There was no doubt that Hill's association with Birchill had been unfortunate for him. It had dragged his past into the light of day, and he stood before them a ruined man. He had tried to live down the past, and but for Birchill he would have succeeded in doing so. But now no one would employ him as a house servant after the revelations that had been made in this court. They had seen Hill in the witness-box, and he would ask the jury whether he looked like the masterful cunning scoundrel which the defence had described, or a weak creature who would be easily led by a man of strong will, such as the prisoner was.

As to what took place at the flat, they had a choice between the evidence of Hill and the evidence of the girl Fanning. Hill had told them that he had tried to dissuade the prisoner from going to Riversbrook to burgle the premises, because his master had returned unexpectedly; Fanning had told them that the prisoner was in favour of postponing the crime, but that Hill had urged him to carry it out. Which story was the more probable? What reliance could they place on the evidence of Fanning? He did not wish to say that the witness was utterly vicious and incapable of telling the truth—a description that the defence had applied to Hill—but they must take into consideration the fact that Fanning was the prisoner's mistress. Was it likely that a woman, knowing her lover's life was at stake, would come here and speak the truth, if she knew the truth would hang him? He was sure that the jury, as men who knew the world thoroughly, would not hesitate between the evidence of Hill and that of Fanning.

The case for the defence depended to a great extent on the plan of Riversbrook which Hill candidly admitted he had drawn. His learned friend had called evidence to show that the paper on which the plan was drawn was of a quality which was not procurable by the general public. That might be so, but what his learned friend had not succeeded in doing, and could not possibly have hoped to succeed in doing, was to show that Birchill could not have obtained possession in any other way of paper of that kind. Yet it was necessary for the defence to prove that, in order to prove that the plan was not drawn at Fanning's flat by Hill under threats from Birchill, but that Hill had drawn it at Riversbrook, and that he gave it to Birchill in order to induce him to consent to the proposal to break into the house. There were dozens of ways in which paper of this particular quality might have got to the flat. Might not Birchill have a friend in His Majesty's Stationery Office? Was it impossible that the witness Fanning had a friend in that Office, or in one of the Government Departments to which the paper was supplied? Was it impossible in view of her relations with the victim of this crime for Fanning to have obtained some of the paper at Riversbrook and to have taken it home to her flat? She had sworn in the witness-box that she had not had paper of that kind in her possession, but with her lover's life at stake was she likely to stick at a lie if it would help to get him off?

Counsel for the defence had endeavoured to make much of the fact that the dead body of Sir Horace Fewbanks was fully dressed when the police discovered it. He endeavoured to persuade them that such a fact established the complete innocence of the prisoner and that because of it they must bring in a verdict of "not guilty." He asked them to accept it as evidence not only that Sir Horace Fewbanks was dead when the prisoner broke into the house, but that he was dead when Hill left Riversbrook at 7.30 p. m. to meet Birchill at Fanning's flat. With an ingenuity which did credit to his imagination, he put before them as his theory of the crime that a quarrel took place between Sir Horace Fewbanks and Hill at Riversbrook, that Hill shot his master and then went to Fanning's flat so as to see that Birchill carried out the burglary as arranged, and at the same time found Sir Horace's dead body, and thus directed suspicion to himself. The only support for this, far-fetched theory was that the body when discovered by the police was fully dressed, and that none of the electric lights were burning. Counsel for the defence contended that these two facts established his theory that the murder was committed before dusk. They established nothing of the kind. There were half a dozen more credible explanations of these things than the one he asked the jury to accept. What mystery was there in a man being fully dressed in his own house at midnight? The defence had been at great pains to show that Sir Horace Fewbanks was a man of somewhat irregular habits in his private life. Did not that suggest that he might have turned off the lights and gone to sleep in an arm-chair in the library with the intention of going out in an hour or two to keep an appointment? If he had an appointment—and his sudden and unexpected return from Scotland would suggest that he had a secret and important appointment—he would be more likely to take a short nap in his chair than to undress and go to bed. Might not the prisoner, who was a bold and reckless man, have broken into the house when the lights were burning and his victim was awake and fully dressed? In that case what was to prevent his turning off the lights before leaving the house instead of leaving them burning to attract attention? What was to prevent the prisoner turning off the lights in order to convey the impression that the crime had been committed in daylight?

"I want you to keep in mind, when arriving at your verdict, that there are certain material facts which have been admitted by the defence," said Mr. Walters in concluding his address to the jury. "It has been admitted that the prisoner was a party to a proposal to break into Riversbrook. As far as that goes, there is no suggestion that he walked into a trap. Whether he arranged the burglary and compelled Hill to help him, or whether Hill arranged it and sought out the prisoner's assistance is, after all, not very material. What is admitted is that the prisoner went to Riversbrook with the intention of committing a crime. It is admitted that he knew Sir Horace Fewbanks had returned home. In that case is it not reasonable to suppose that the prisoner would arm himself, I do not say with the definite intention of committing murder, but for the purpose of threatening Sir Horace if necessary in order to make good his escape? What is more likely than that Sir Horace heard the burglar in the house, crept upon him, and then tried to capture him? There was a struggle, and the prisoner, determined to free himself, drew his revolver and shot Sir Horace. Is not such a theory of the crime—that Sir Horace was shot while trying to capture the prisoner—more probable than the theory of the defence that Hill, the weak-willed, frightened-looking man you saw in the witness-box, was a masterful, cunning criminal who for some inexplicable reason had turned ferociously on the master who had befriended him and given him a fresh start in life, had killed him and left the body in the house, and had then managed to direct suspicion to the prisoner? The theory of the defence does great credit to my learned friend's imagination, but it is one which I am sure the jury will reject as too highly coloured. Looking at the plain facts of the case and dismissing from your minds the attempt to make them fit into a purely imaginative theory, I am sure that you will come to the conclusion that Sir Horace Fewbanks met his death at the hands of the prisoner."

The junior bar agreed that the case was one which might go either way. If they had possessed any money the betting market would have shown scarcely a shade of odds. Everything depended on the way the jury looked at the case, on the particular bits of evidence to which they attached most weight, on the view the most argumentative positive-minded members of the jury adopted, for they would be able to carry the others with them. In the opinion of the junior bar the summing up of Mr. Justice Hodson would not help the jury very much in arriving at a verdict. There were some judges who summed up for or against a prisoner according to the view they had formed as to the prisoner's guilt or innocence. There were other judges who summed up so impartially and gave such even-balanced weight to the points against the prisoner and to the points in his favour, as to make on the minds of the jurymen the impression that the only way to arrive at a well-considered verdict was to toss a coin. Another type of judge conveyed to the jury that the prosecution had established an unanswerable case, but the defence had shown equal skill in shattering it, and therefore he did not know on which side to make up his mind, and fortunately English legal procedure did not render it necessary for him to do so. The prisoner might be guilty and he might be innocent. Some of the jury might think one thing and the rest of the jury might think another. But it was the duty of the jury to come to an unanimous verdict. It did not matter if they looked at some things in different ways, but their final decision must be the same.

Mr. Justice Hodson belonged to the impartial, impersonal type of judge. He had no personal feelings or conviction as to the guilt or innocence of the prisoner. It was for the jury to settle that point and it was his duty to assist them to the best of his ability. He went over his notes carefully and dealt with the evidence of each of the witnesses. It was for the jury to say what evidence they believed and what they disbelieved. There was a pronounced conflict of evidence between Hill and Fanning. They were the chief witnesses in the case, but the guilt or innocence of the prisoner did not rest entirely upon the evidence of either of these witnesses. Hill might be speaking the truth and the prisoner might be innocent though the presumption would be, if Hill's evidence were truthful in every detail, that the prisoner was guilty. Fanning's evidence might be true as far as it went, but it would not in itself prove that the prisoner was innocent. Hill had admitted that he had drawn the plan of Riversbrook to assist Birchill to commit burglary. It was for the jury to determine for themselves whether he had been terrorised into drawing the plan for Birchill or whether he was the instigator of the burglary.

The defence had contended that Hill had drawn the plan at his leisure at a time when he had access to a special quality of paper supplied to his master. If that were so, Hill's version of how he came to draw the plan was deliberately false and had been concocted for the purpose of exculpating himself. But they would not be justified in dismissing Hill's evidence entirely from their minds because they were satisfied he had perjured himself with regard to the plan. They would be justified, however, in viewing the rest of his evidence with some degree of distrust. Counsel for the defence had made an ingenious use of the facts that the body of the victim was fully dressed when discovered and that none of the electric lights in the house were burning. These facts lent support to the idea that the murder was committed in daylight, but they by no means established the theory as unassailable. They did not establish the innocence of the prisoner, although to some extent they told in his favour. Counsel for the prosecution had put before them several theories to account for these two facts consistent with his contention that the murder had been committed by the prisoner. The jury must give full consideration to these theories as well as to the theory of the defence. They were not called upon to say which theory was true except in so far as their opinions might be implied in the verdict they gave.

The defence, continued His Honour, was that Hill had committed the murder and had then decided to direct suspicion to the prisoner. If the jury acquitted the prisoner, their verdict would not necessarily mean that they endorsed the theory of the defence. It might mean that, but it might mean only that they were not satisfied that the prisoner had committed the murder. If the jury were convinced beyond all reasonable doubt that the prisoner had committed the murder, they must bring in a verdict of "guilty," and if they were not satisfied they must bring in a verdict of acquittal.

The jury filed out of their apartment, and as they retired to consider their verdict the judge retired to his own room. The prisoner was removed from the dock and taken down the stairs out of sight. There was an immediate hum of voices in the court. Inspector Chippenfield approached the table and whispered to Mr. Walters. The latter nodded affirmatively and left the court room in company with Mr. Holymead. The sibilant sound of whispering voices died down after a few minutes and then began the long tedious wait for the return of the jury.

The occupants of the gallery, who had no difficulty in coming to an immediate decision on the guilt or innocence of the prisoner, could not understand what was keeping the jury away so long. They failed to understand the jury's point of view. These gentlemen had sat in court for three days listening intently to proceedings concerning a matter in which their degree of personal interest was only a form of curiosity. And now the end of the case had been reached, except for the climax, which was in their control. To arrive at an immediate decision in a case that had occupied the court for three days would indicate they had no proper realisation of the responsibilities of their position. A verdict was a thing that had to be nicely balanced in relation to the evidence. Where the case against the prisoner was weak or overwhelmingly strong, the jury might arrive at a verdict with great speed as an indication that too much of their valuable time had already been wasted on the case. But where the evidence for and against the prisoner was fairly equal it behoved the jury to indicate by the time they took in arriving at their verdict that they had given the case the most careful consideration.

Two hours and twenty minutes after the jury had retired, the prisoner was brought back into the dock. This was an indication that the jury had arrived at their verdict and were ready to deliver it. The prisoner looked worn and anxious, but he received encouraging smiles from his friends in the gallery. A minute later the judge entered the court and resumed his seat. The jury filed into court and entered the jury-box. Amid the noise of barristers resuming their seats and court officials gliding about, the judge's Associate called over the names of the jurymen. The suspense reached its climax as the Associate put the formal questions to the foreman whether the jury had agreed on their verdict.

"What say you: guilty or not guilty?" asked the Associate in a hard metallic voice in which there was no trace of interest in the answer.

"Not guilty," replied the foreman.

There was a muffled cheer from the gallery, which was suppressed by the stentorian cry of the ushers, "Silence in the court!"

"A pack of damned fools," said the exasperated Inspector Chippenfield.

Rolfe understood that his chief referred to the jury, and he nodded the assent of a subordinate.

CHAPTER XX

"Hill has bolted!"

Rolfe flung the words at Inspector Chippenfield in a tone which he was unable to divest entirely of satisfaction. "Fancy his being the guilty party after all," he added, with the tone of satisfaction still more evident in his voice. "I often thought that he was our man, and that he was playing with you—I mean with us."

Inspector Chippenfield had betrayed surprise at the news by dropping his pen on the official report he was preparing. But it was in his usual tone of cold official superiority that he replied:

"Do you mean that Hill, the principal witness in the Riversbrook murder trial, has disappeared from London?"

"Disappeared from London? He's bolted clean out of the country by this time, I tell you! Cleared out for good and left his unfortunate wife and child to starve."

"How have you learnt this, Rolfe?"

"His wife told me herself. I went to the shop this afternoon to have a few words with Hill and see how he felt after the way Holymead had gone for him at the trial. His wife burst out crying when she saw me, and she told me that her husband had cleared out last night after he came home from court. The hardened scoundrel took with him the few pounds of her savings which she kept in her bedroom, and had even emptied the contents of the till of the few shillings and coppers it contained. All he left were the half-pennies in the child's money-box. He cleared out in the middle of the night after his wife had gone to bed. He left her a note telling her she must get along without him. I have the note here—his wife gave it to me."

Rolfe took a dirty scrap of paper out of his pocket-book and laid it before Inspector Chippenfield. The paper was a half sheet torn from an exercise-book, and its contents were written in faint lead pencil. They read:

"Dear Mary:

"I have got to leave you. I have thought it out and this is the only thing to do. I am too frightened to stay after what took place in the court to-day. I'll make a fresh start in some place where I am not known, and as soon as I can send a little money I will send for you and Daphne. Keep your heart up and it will be all right.

"Keep on the shop.

"YOUR LOVING HUSBAND."

"The poor little woman is heartbroken," continued Rolfe, when his superior officer had finished reading the note. "She wants to know if we cannot get her husband back for her. She says the shop won't keep her and the child. Unless she can find her husband she'll be turned into the streets, because she's behind with the rent, and Hill's taken every penny she'd put by."

"Then she'd better go to the workhouse," retorted Inspector Chippenfield brutally. "We'd have something to do if Scotland Yard undertook to trace all the absconding husbands in London. We can do nothing in the matter, and you'd better tell her so."

Inspector Chippenfield handed back Hill's note as he spoke. Rolfe eyed him in some surprise.

"But surely you're going to take out a warrant for Hill's arrest?" he said.

"Certainly not," responded Inspector Chippenfield impatiently. "I've already said that Scotland Yard has something more to do than trace absconding husbands. There's nothing to prevent your giving a little of your private time to looking for him, Rolfe, if you feel so tender-hearted about the matter. But officially—no. I'm astonished at your suggesting such a thing."

"It isn't that," replied Rolfe, flushing a little, and speaking with slight embarrassment. "But surely after Hill's flight you'll apply for a warrant for his arrest on—the other ground."

"On what other ground?" asked his chief coldly.

"Why, on a charge of murdering Sir Horace Fewbanks," Rolfe burst out indignantly. "Doesn't this flight point to his guilt?"

"Not in my opinion." Inspector Chippenfield's voice was purely official.

"Why, surely it does!" Rolfe's glance at his chief indicated that there was such a thing as carrying official obstinacy too far. "This letter he left behind suggests his guilt, clearly enough."

"I didn't notice that," replied Inspector Chippenfield impassively. "Perhaps you'll point out the passage to me, Rolfe."

Rolfe hastily produced the note again.

"Look here!"—his finger indicated the place—"'I'm frightened to stay after what took place in the court to-day,' Doesn't that mean, clearly enough, that Hill realised the acquittal pointed to him as the murderer, and he determined to abscond before he could be arrested?"

"So that's your way of looking at it, eh, Rolfe?" said Inspector Chippenfield quizzically.

"Certainly it is," responded Rolfe, not a little nettled by his chief's contemptuous tone. "It's as plain as a pikestaff that the jury acquitted Birchill because they believed Hill was guilty. Holymead made out too strong a case for them to get away from—Hill's lies about the plan and the fact that the body was fully dressed when discovered."

"You're a young man, Rolfe," responded Inspector Chippenfield in a tolerant tone, "but you'll have to shed this habit of jumping impulsively to conclusions—and generally wrong conclusions— if you want to succeed in Scotland Yard. This letter of Hill's only strengthens my previous opinion that a damned muddle-headed jury let a cold-blooded murderer loose on the world when they acquitted Fred Birchill of the charge of shooting Sir Horace Fewbanks. Why, man alive, Holymead no more believes Hill is guilty than I do. He set himself to bamboozle the jury and he succeeded. If he had to defend Hill to-morrow he would show the jury that Hill couldn't have committed the murder and that it must have been committed by Birchill and no one else. He's a clever man, far cleverer than Walters, and that is why I lost the case."

"He led Hill into a trap about the plan of Riversbrook," said Rolfe. "When I saw that Hill had been trapped on that point I felt we had lost the jury."

"Only because the jury were a pack of fools who knew nothing about evidence. Granted that Hill lied about the plan—that he drew it up voluntarily in his spare time to assist Birchill—it proves nothing. It doesn't prove that Hill committed the murder. It only proves that Hill was going to share in the proceeds of the burglary; that he was a willing party to it. The one big outstanding fact in all the evidence, the fact that towered over all the others, is that Birchill broke into the house on the night Sir Horace Fewbanks was murdered. The defence made no attempt to get away from that fact because they could not do so. But Holymead vamped up all sorts of surmises and suppositions for the purpose of befogging the jury and getting their minds away from the outstanding feature of the case for the prosecution. We proved that Birchill was in the house on a criminal errand. What more could they expect us to prove? They couldn't expect us to have a man looking through the window or hiding behind the door when the murder was committed. If we could get evidence of that kind we could do without juries. We could hang our man first and try him afterwards. I don't think a verdict of acquittal from a befogged jury would do so much harm in such a case."

"You are still convinced that Birchill did it?" said Rolfe questioningly.

"I have never wavered from that opinion," said his superior. "If I had, this note of Hill's would restore my conviction in Birchill's guilt."

"Why, how do you make out that?" replied Rolfe blankly.

"Hill says he's clearing out of the country because he's frightened. What's he frightened of? His own guilty conscience and the long arm of the law? Not a bit of it! Hill's an innocent man. If he had been guilty he'd never have stood the ordeal of the witness-box and the cross-examination. Hill's cleared out because he was frightened of Birchill."

"Of Birchill?"

"Yes. Didn't Birchill tell Hill, just before he set out for Riversbrook on the night of the murder, that if Hill played him false he'd murder him? Hill *did* play him false, not then, but afterwards, when he made his confession and Birchill was arrested for the murder in consequence. When Birchill was acquitted at the trial his first thought would be to wreak vengeance on Hill. A man with one murder on his soul would not be likely to hesitate about committing another. Hill knew this, and fled to save his life when Birchill was acquitted. That's the explanation of his letter, Rolfe."

"So that's the way you look at it?" said Rolfe.

"Of course I do! It's the only way Hill's flight can be looked at in the light of all that's happened. The theory dovetails in every part. I'm more used than you to putting these things together, Rolfe. Hill's as innocent of the murder as you are."

"And where do you think Hill's gone to?"

"Certainly not out of London. He's too much of a Cockney for that. Besides, he's a man who is fond of his wife and child. He's hiding somewhere close at hand, and I shouldn't wonder if the whole thing's a plant between him and his wife. Have you forgotten how she tried to hoodwink us before? I'll go to the shop to-morrow and see if I can't frighten the truth out of her. Meanwhile, you'd better put the Camden Town police on to watching the shop. If he's hiding in London he's bound to visit his wife sooner or later, or she'll visit him, so we ought not to have much difficulty in getting on to his tracks again."

Rolfe departed, to do his chief's bidding, a little crestfallen. He was at first inclined to think that he had made a bit of a fool of himself in his desire to prove to Inspector Chippenfield that he had been hoodwinked by Hill into arresting Birchill. But that night, as he sat in his bedroom smoking a quiet pipe, and reviewing this latest phase of the puzzling case, the earlier doubts which had assailed him on first learning of Hill's flight recurred to him with increasing force. If Hill were innocent he would have been more likely to seek police protection before flight. Hill's flight was hardly the action of an innocent man. It pointed more to a guilty fear of his own skin, now that the man he had accused of the murder was free to seek vengeance. Chippenfield's theory seemed plausible enough at first sight, but Rolfe now recalled that he knew nothing of the missing letters and Hill's midnight visit to Riversbrook to recover them. Rolfe had concealed that episode from his superior officer because he lacked the courage to reveal to him how he had been hoodwinked by Mrs. Holymead's fainting fit the morning he was conducting his official inquiry at Riversbrook into the murder.

"It's an infernally baffling case," muttered Rolfe, refilling his pipe from a tin of tobacco on the mantelpiece, and walking up and down the cheap lodging-house drugget with rapid strides. "If Birchill is not the murderer who is? Is it Hill?"

He lit his pipe, closed the window, opened his pocket-book and sat down to peruse the notes he had taken during his investigation of Sir Horace Fewbanks's murder. He read and re-read them, earnestly searching for a fresh clue in the pencilled pages. After spending some time in this occupation he took a clean sheet of paper and a pencil, and copied afresh the following entries from his notebook:

August 19. Went Riversbrook. Saw Sir H.F.'s body. Discovered fragment of lady's handkerchief clenched in right hand.

August 22. Made inquiries handkerchief. Unable find where purchased.

September 8. Found Hill at Riversbrook searching Sir H.F.'s papers. Told me about bundle of lady's letters tied up with pink ribbon which had been taken from secret drawer. Says they disappeared morning after murder when investigation was taking place. C.'s visitors that day: Dr. Slingsby / Seldon to arrange inquest / newspaper men / undertaker's representatives / Crewe. C. saw one visitor alone, Hill says. Mrs. H——, who fainted. C. fetched glass of water, leaving her alone in room. Hill suggests her letters indicate friendly relations between her and Sir H.F. Sir H.F. expected visit, probably from lady, night of murder. Hurried Hill off when he returned from Scotland. Mem: Inadvisable disclose this to C.

Underneath his entries of the case Rolfe had written finally:

Points to be remembered:

(1) Crewe said before the trial that Birchill was not the murderer and would be acquitted. Birchill was acquitted.

(2) Crewe suggested we had not got the whole truth out of Hill. Hill disappears the night after the trial. Is Hill the murderer?

(3) The handkerchief and the letters point to a woman in the case, although this was not brought out at the trial. Is it possible that woman is Mrs. H.?

Rolfe realised that the chief pieces of the puzzle were before him, but the difficulty was to put them together. He felt sure there was a connection between these facts, which, if brought to light, would solve the Riversbrook mystery. Without knowing it, he had been so influenced by Crewe's analysis of the case that he had practically given up the idea that Birchill had anything to do with the murder. His real reason for going to Hill's shop that morning was to try and extract something from Hill which might put him on the track of the actual murderer. He believed Hill knew more than he had divulged. Hill, before his disappearance, had placed in his hands an important clue, if he only knew how to follow it up. That incident of the missing letters must have some bearing on the case, if he could only elucidate it.

Should he disclose to Chippenfield Hill's story of the missing letters? Rolfe dismissed the idea as soon as it crossed his mind. He knew his superior officer sufficiently well to understand that he would be very angry to learn that he had been deceived by Mrs. Holymead, and, as she was outside the range of his anger, he would bear a grudge against his junior officer for discovering the deception which had been practised on him, and do all he could to block his promotion in Scotland Yard in consequence. Apart from that, he could offer Chippenfield no excuse for not having told him before.

Should he consult Crewe?

Rolfe dismissed that thought also, but more reluctantly. Hang it all, it was too humiliating for an accredited officer of Scotland Yard to consult a private detective! Rolfe had acquired an unwilling respect for Crewe's abilities during the course of the investigations into the Riversbrook case, but he retained all the intolerance which regular members of the detective force feel for the private detectives who poach on their preserves. Rolfe's professional jealousy was intensified in Crewe's case because of the brilliant successes Crewe had achieved during his career at the expense of the reputation of Scotland Yard. Rolfe had an instinctive feeling that Crewe's mind was of finer quality than his own, and would see light where he only groped in darkness. If Crewe had been his superior officer in Scotland Yard, Rolfe would have gone to him unhesitatingly and profited by his keener vision, but he could not do so in their existing relative positions. He ransacked his brain for some other course.

After long consideration, Rolfe decided to go and see Mrs. Holymead and question her about the packet of letters which Hill declared she had removed from Riversbrook after the murder. He realised that this was rather a risky course to pursue, for Mrs. Holymead was highly placed and could do him much harm if she got her husband to use his influence at the Home Office, for then he would have to admit that he had gone to her without the knowledge of his superior officer, on the statement of a discredited servant who had arranged a burglary in his master's house the night he was murdered. Nevertheless, Rolfe decided to take the risk. The chance of getting somewhere nearer the solution of the Riversbrook mystery was worth it, and what a feather in his cap it would be if he solved the mystery! He was convinced that Chippenfield had shut out important light on the mystery by doggedly insisting, in order to buttress up his case against Birchill, that the piece of handkerchief which had been found in the dead man's hand was a portion of a handkerchief which had belonged to the girl Fanning, and had been brought by Birchill from the Westminster flat on the night of the murder. It was more likely, in view of Hill's story of the letters, that the handkerchief belonged to Mrs. Holymead. Rolfe had not made up his mind that Mrs. Holymead had committed the murder, but he was convinced that she and her letters had some connection with the baffling crime, and he determined to try and pierce the mystery by questioning her. Having arrived at this decision, he replaced his notebook in his coat pocket, knocked the ashes out of his pipe, and went to bed.

CHAPTER XXI

Rolfe went to Hyde Park next day and walked from the Tube station to Holymead's house at Princes Gate. The servant who answered his ring informed him, in reply to his question, that Mrs. Holymead was "Not at home."

"Do you know when she will be home?" persisted Rolfe, forestalling an evident desire on the servant's part to shut the door in his face.

The man looked at Rolfe doubtfully. Well-trained English servant though he was, and used to summing up strangers at a glance, he could not quite make out who Rolfe might be. But before he could come to a decision on the point a feminine voice behind him said:

"What is it, Trappon?"

The servant turned quickly in the direction of the voice. "It's a er—er—party who wants to see Madam, mademoiselle," he replied.

"*Parti?* What mean you by *parti?* Explain yourself, Trappon."

"A person—a gentleman, mademoiselle," replied Trappon, determined to be on the safe side.

"Open the door, Trappon, that I may see this gentleman."

Trappon somewhat reluctantly complied, and a young lady stepped forward. She was tall and dark, with charming eyes which were also shrewd; she had a fine figure which a tight-fitting dress displayed rather too boldly for good taste, and she was sufficiently young to be able to appear quite girlish in the half light.

"You wish to see Madame Holymead?" she said to Rolfe. Her manner was engagingly pleasant and French.

Rolfe felt it incumbent upon him to be gallant in the presence of the fair representative of a nation whom he vaguely understood placed gallantry in the forefront of the virtues. He took off his hat with a courtly bow.

"I do, mademoiselle," he replied, "and my business is important."

"Then, monsieur, step inside if you will be so good, and I will see you."

She led Rolfe to a small, prettily-furnished room at the end of the hall, and carefully shut the door. Then she invited Rolfe to be seated, and asked him to state his business.

But this was precisely what Rolfe was not anxious to do except to Mrs. Holymead herself.

"My business is private, and must be placed before Mrs. Holymead," he said firmly. "I wish to see her."

"I regret, monsieur, but Madame Holymead is out of town. She went last week. If you had only come before she went"—Mademoiselle Chiron looked genuinely sorry.

Rolfe was a little taken aback at this intelligence, and showed it.

"Out of town!" he repeated. "Where has she gone to?"

She looked at him almost timidly.

"But, monsieur, I do not know if I ought to tell you without knowing who you are. Are you a friend of Madame's?"

"My name is Detective Rolfe—I come from Scotland Yard," replied Rolfe, in the authoritative tone of a man who knew that the disclosure was sure to command respect, if not a welcome.

"Scotland? You come from Scotland? Madame will regret much that she has missed you."

"Scotland Yard, I said," corrected Rolfe, "not Scotland."

"Is it not the same?" Mademoiselle Chiron looked at him helplessly. "Scotland Yard—is it not in Scotland? What is the difference?"

Rolfe, with a Londoner's tolerance for foreign ignorance, painstakingly explained the difference. She looked so puzzled that he felt sure she did not understand him. But that, he reflected, was not his fault.

"So you see, mademoiselle, my business with Mrs. Holymead is important, therefore I'll be obliged if you will tell me where I can find her," he said. "In what part of the country is she?"

Mademoiselle Chiron looked distressed. "Really, monsieur, I cannot tell you. She is motoring, and I should have been with her but that I have *un gros rhume*"—she produced a tiny scrap of lace handkerchief and held it to her nose as though in support of her statement—"and she rings me on the telephone from different places and tells me the things she does need, and I do send them on to her."

"Where does she ring you up from?" asked Rolfe, eyeing Mademoiselle Chiron's handkerchief intently.

"From Brighton—from Eastbourne—wherever she stops."

"What place was she stopping at when you heard from her last?"

"Eastbourne, monsieur."

"And when will she return here?"

"That, monsieur, I do not know. To-night—to-morrow—next week—she does not tell me. If Monsieur will leave me a message I will see that she gets it, for it is always me she wants, and it is always me that talks to her. What shall I tell her when next she rings the telephone? If Monsieur will state his business I will tell Madame what he tells me. I am Madame's cousin by marriage—in me she has confidence."

She spoke in a tone which invited confidence, but Rolfe was not prepared to go to the length of trusting the young woman he saw before him, despite her assurance that she was in the confidence of Mrs. Holymead. He rose to his feet with a keen glance at Mademoiselle Chiron's handkerchief, which she had rolled into a little ball in her hand.

"I cannot disclose my business to you, mademoiselle," he said courteously. "I must see Mrs. Holymead personally, so I shall call again when she has returned."

"But, monsieur, why will you not tell me?" she asked coaxingly. "You are a police agent? Have you therefore come to see Madame about the case?"

Rolfe showed that he was taken aback by the direct question.

"The case!" he stammered. "What case?"

"Why, monsieur, what case should it be but that of which I have so often heard Madame speak? Le judge—the good friend of Monsieur and Madame Holymead, who was killed by the base assassin!

Madame is disconsolate about his terrible end!" Mademoiselle Chiron here applied the handkerchief to her eyes on her own account. "Have you come to tell her that you have caught the wicked man who did assassinate him? Madame will be overjoyed!"

"Why, hardly that," replied Rolfe, completely off his guard. "But we're on the track, mademoiselle—we're on the track."

"And is it that you wanted me to tell Madame?" persisted Mademoiselle Chiron.

"I wanted to ask her a question or two about several things," said Rolfe, who had determined to disclose his hand sufficiently to bring Mrs. Holymead back to London if she had anything to do with the crime. "I want to ask her about some letters that were stolen—no, I won't say stolen—letters that were removed from Riversbrook. I have been informed that even if these letters are no longer in existence she can give the police a good idea of what was in them."

The telephone bell in the corner of the room rang suddenly. Mademoiselle Chiron ran to answer it, and accidentally dropped her handkerchief on the floor in picking up the receiver.

Mademoiselle Chiron began speaking on the telephone, but she stopped suddenly, staring with frightened eyes into the mirror at the other side of the room. The glass reflected the actions of Rolfe at the table. Seated with his back towards her, he had taken advantage of her being called to the telephone to examine her handkerchief, which he had picked up from the floor. He had produced from his pocketbook the scrap of lace and muslin which he had found in the murdered man's hand. He had the two on the table side by side comparing them, and Mademoiselle Chiron noticed a smile of satisfaction flit across his face as he did so. While she looked he restored the scrap to his pocket-book, and the pocket-book to his pocket. Hastily she turned to the telephone again and continued, in a voice which a quick ear would have detected was slightly hysterical.

Then she hung up the receiver and turned to Rolfe.

"But, monsieur, you were saying—"

Rolfe handed the handkerchief to its owner with a courtly bow which he flattered himself was equal to the best French school.

"I picked this up off the floor, mademoiselle. It is yours, I think?"

"This?" Mademoiselle Chiron touched the handkerchief with a dainty forefinger. "It is my handkerchief. I dropped it."

"It is very pretty," said Rolfe, with simulated indifference. "I suppose you bought that in Paris. It does not look English,"

"But no, monsieur, it is quite Engleesh. I bought it in the shop."

"Indeed! A London shop?" inquired Rolfe, with equal indifference.

"The *lingerie* shop in Oxford Street—what do you call it—Hobson›s?"

"I'm sure I don't know—these ladies' things are a bit out of my line," said Rolfe, rising as he spoke with a smile, in which there was more than a trace of self-satisfaction.

He felt that he had acquitted himself with an adroitness which Crewe himself might have envied. He had made an important discovery and extracted the name of the shop where the handkerchief had been bought without—so he flattered himself—arousing any suspicions on the part of the lady. Rolfe knew from his inquiries in West End shops that handkerchiefs of that pattern and quality were stocked by many of the good shops, but the fact that he had found a handkerchief of this kind in the house of a lady who had abstracted secret letters from the murdered man's desk, and had, moreover, discovered the name of the shop where she bought her handkerchiefs, convinced him that he had struck a path which must lead to an important discovery.

Mademoiselle Chiron followed Rolfe into the hall and watched his departure from a front window. When she saw his retreating figure turn the corner of the street she left the window, ran upstairs quickly, and knocked lightly at the closed door.

The door was opened by Mrs. Holymead, who appeared to be in a state of nervous agitation. Her large brown eyes were swollen and dim with weeping, her hair had become partly unloosened, her face was white and her dress disordered. She caught the Frenchwoman by the wrist and drew her into the bedroom, closing the door after her.

"What did he want, Gabrielle?" she gasped. "What did he say? Has he come about—*that*?"

Gabrielle nodded her head.

"Gabrielle!" Mrs. Holymead's voice rose almost to a cry. "Oh, what are we to do? Did he come to arrest—"

"No, no! He was not so bad. He did not come to do dreadful things, but just to have a little talk."

"A little talk? What about?"

"He wanted to see you, and ask you one or two little questions. I put him off. He was like wax in my hands. Pouf! He has gone, so why trouble?"

"But he will come again! He is sure to come again!"

"No doubt. He says he will come again—in a week—when you return."

Mrs. Holymead wrung her hands helplessly.

"What are we to do then?" she wailed.

"We will look the tragedy in the face when it comes. *Ma foi!* What have you been doing to yourself? For nothing is it worth to look like *that*." With deft and loving fingers Gabrielle began to arrange Mrs. Holymead's hair. "We will have everything right before this little police agent returns. We will show him he is the complete fool for suspecting you know about the murder."

"But what can you do, Gabrielle?" asked Mrs. Holymead.

She looked at Gabrielle with her large brown eyes, as though she were utterly dependent on the other's stronger will for support and assistance. Mademoiselle Chiron stopped in her arrangement of Mrs. Holymead's hair and, bending over, kissed her affectionately.

"*Ma petite,*" she said, "do not worry. I have thought of a plan—oh, a most excellent plan—which I will myself execute to-morrow, and then shall all your troubles be finished, and you will be happy again."

CHAPTER XXII

"A lady to see you, sir."

"What sort of a lady, Joe?"

"Furren, I should say, sir, by the way she speaks. I arskt her if she had an appointment, and she said no, but she said she wanted to see you on very urgent and particular business. I told her most people says that wot comes to see you, but she says hers was *reely* important. Arskt me to tell you, sir, that it was about the Riversbrook case."

"The Riversbrook case? I'll see her, Joe. Has not Stork returned yet?"

"No, sir."

"Tell him to go to his dinner when he comes back. Show the lady in, Joe."

Crewe regarded his caller keenly as Joe ushered her in, placed a chair for her, and went out, closing the door noiselessly behind him. She was a tall, well-dressed, graceful woman, fairly young, with dark hair and eyes. She looked quickly at the detective as she entered, and Crewe was struck by the shrewd penetration of her glance.

"You are Monsieur Crewe, the great detective—is it not so?" she asked, as she sat down. The glance she now gave the detective at closer range from her large dark eyes was innocent and ingenuous, with a touch of admiration. The contrast between it and her former look was not lost on Crewe, and he realised that his visitor was no ordinary woman.

"My name is Crewe," he said, ignoring the compliment. "What do you wish to see me for?"

The visitor did not immediately reply. She nervously unfastened a bag she carried, and taking out a singularly unfeminine-looking handkerchief—a large cambric square almost masculine in its proportions, and guiltless of lace or perfume—held it to her face for a moment. But Crewe noticed that her eyes were dry when she removed it to remark:

"What I say to you, monsieur, is in strictest confidence—as sacred as the confession."

"Anything you say to me will be in strict confidence," said Crewe a little grimly.

"And the boy? Can he not hear through the keyhole?" Crewe's visitor glanced expressively at the door by which she had entered.

"You are quite safe here, madame—mademoiselle, I should say," he added, with a quick glance at her left hand, from which she slowly removed the glove as she spoke.

"Mademoiselle Chiron, monsieur," said Gabrielle, flashing another smile at him. "I am Madame Holymead's relative—her cousin. I come to see you about the dreadful murder of the judge, Madame's friend."

"You come from Mrs. Holymead?" said Crewe quickly. "Then, Mademoiselle Chiron, before—"

"No, no, monsieur, no!" Her agitation was unmistakably genuine. "I do not come *from* Madame Holymead. I am her relative, it is true, but I come—how shall I say it?—from myself. I mean she does not know of my visit to you, monsieur."

"I quite understand," replied Crewe.

"Monsieur Crewe," said Gabrielle hurriedly, "although I have not come from Madame Holymead, it is for her sake that I come to see you—to save her from the persecution of one of your police agents who wants to ask her questions about this so sordid—so terrible a crime! He has come once, this agent—last night he came—and he told me he wanted to question Madame Holymead about the murder of her dear friend the judge. I do not want Madame worried with these questions, so I told him Madame was away in the motor in the country; but he says he will come again and again till he sees her. Madame is distracted when she learns of his visit; it opens up her bleeding heart afresh, for she and her husband were *intime* with the dead judge, and deeply, terribly, they deplore his so dreadful end. I see Madame cry, and I say to myself I will not let this little police agent spoil her beauty and give her the migraine: his visits must be, shall be, prevented. I have heard of the so great and good Monsieur Crewe, and I will go and see him. We will—as you say in your English way—put our heads together, this famous detective and I, and we will find some way of—how do you call it?—circumventing this police agent so that my dear Madame shall cry no more. Monsieur Crewe, I am here, and I beg of you to help me."

Crewe listened to this outburst with inward surprise but impassive features. Apparently the police had come to the conclusion that they had blundered in arresting Birchill for the murder of Sir Horace Fewbanks, and had recommenced inquiries with a view to bringing the crime home to somebody else. He did not know whether their suspicions were now directed against Mrs. Holymead, but they had conducted their preliminary inquiries so clumsily as to arouse her fears that they did. So much was apparent from Mademoiselle Chiron's remarks, despite the interpretation she sought to place on Mrs. Holymead's fears. He wondered if the "police agent" was Rolfe or Chippenfield. It was obvious that the cool proposal that he should help to shield Mrs. Holymead against unwelcome police attentions covered some deeper move, and he shaped his conversation in the endeavour to extract more from the Frenchwoman.

"I am very sorry to hear that Mrs. Holymead has been subjected to this annoyance," he said warily. "This police agent, did he come by himself?"

"But yes, monsieur, I have already said it."

"I know, but I thought he might have had a companion waiting for him in a taxi-cab outside. Scotland Yard men frequently travel in pairs."

"He had no taxi-cab," declared Mademoiselle Chiron, positively. "He walked away on foot by himself. I watched him from the window."

Crewe registered a mental note of this admission. If she had watched the detective's departure from the window she evidently had some reason for wanting to see the last of him. Aloud he said:

"I expect I know him. What was he like?"

"Tall, as tall as you, only bigger—much bigger. And he had the great moustache which he caressed again and again with his fingers." Gabrielle daintily imitated the action on her own short upper lip.

"I know him," declared Crewe with a smile. "His name is Rolfe. There should be nothing about him to alarm you, mademoiselle. Why, he is quite a ladies' man."

Gabrielle shrugged her shoulders disdainfully.

"That may be," she replied; "but I like him not, and I do not wish him to worry Madame Holymead."

"But why not let him see Mrs. Holymead?" suggested Crewe, after a short pause. "As he only wants to ask her a few short questions, it seems to me that would be the quickest way out of the difficulty, and would save you all the trouble and worry you speak of."

"I tell you I will not," declared Gabrielle vehemently. "I will not have Madame Holymead worried and made ill with the terrible ordeal. Bah! What do you men—so clumsy—know of the delicate feelings of a lady like Madame Holymead? The least soupçon of excitement and she is disturbed, distraite, for days. After last night—after the visit of the police agent—she was quite hysterical."

"Why should she be when she had nothing to be afraid of?" rejoined Crewe.

He spoke in a tone of simple wonder, but Gabrielle shot a quick glance at him from under her veiled lashes as she replied:

"Bah! What has that to do with it? I repeat: Monsieur Crewe, you men cannot understand the feelings of a lady like Madame Holymead in a matter like this. She and her husband were, as I have said before, *intime* with the great judge. They visited his house, they dined with him, they met him in Society. Behold, he is brutally, horribly killed. Madame, when she hears the terrible news, is ill for days; she cannot eat, she cannot sleep; she can interest herself in nothing. She is forgetting a little when the police agents they catch a man and say he is the murderer. Then comes the trial of this man at the court with so queer a name—Old Bailee. The papers are full of the terrible story again; of the dead man; how he looked killed; how he lay in a pool of blood; how they cut him open! Madame Holymead cannot pick up a paper without seeing these things, and she falls ill again. Then the jury say the man the police agents caught is not the murderer. He goes free, and once more the talk dies away. Madame Holymead once more begins to forget, when this police agent comes to her house to remind her once more all about it. It is too cruel, monsieur, it is too cruel!"

Gabrielle's voice vibrated with indignation as she concluded, and Crewe regarded her closely. He decided that her affection for Mrs. Holymead was not simulated, and that it would be best to handle her from that point of view.

"I am sorry," he said coldly, "but I do not see how I can help you."

"Monsieur," said the Frenchwoman, clasping her hands, "I entreat you not to say so. It would be so easy for you to help—not me, but Madame."

"How?"

"You know this police agent. You also are a police agent, though so much greater. Therefore you whisper just one little word in the ear of your friend the police agent, and he will not bother Madame Holymead again. I think you could do this. And if you need money to give to the police agent, why, I have brought some." She fumbled nervously at her hand-bag.

"Stay," said Crewe. "What you ask is impossible. I have nothing whatever to do with Scotland Yard. I could not interfere in their inquiries, even if I wished to. They would only laugh at me."

Gabrielle's dark eyes showed her disappointment, but she made one more effort to gain her end. She leant nearer to Crewe, and laid a persuasive hand on his arm.

"If you would only make the effort," she said coaxingly, "my beautiful Madame Holymead would be for ever grateful."

"Mademoiselle, once more I repeat that what you ask is impossible," returned Crewe decisively. "I repeat, I cannot see why Mrs. Holymead should object to answering a few questions the police wish to ask her. She is too sensitive about such a trifle."

Gabrielle shrugged her shoulders slightly in tacit recognition of the fact that the man in front of her was too shrewd to be deceived by subterfuge.

"There is another reason, monsieur," she whispered.

"You had better tell it to me."

"If you had been a woman you would have guessed. The great judge who was killed was in his spare moments what you call a gallant—he did love my sex. In France this would not matter, but in England they think much of it—so very much. Madame Holymead is frightened for fear the least breath of scandal should attach to her name, if the world knew that the police agent had visited her house on such an errand. Madame is innocent—it is not necessary to assure you of that; but the prudish dames of England are censorious."

"The Scotland Yard people are not likely to disclose anything about it," said Crewe.

"That may be so, but these things come out," retorted Gabrielle.

"Monsieur," she added, after a pause, and speaking in a low tone, "I know that you can do much—very much—if you will, and can stop Madame Holymead from being worried. Would you do so if you were told who the murderer was—I mean he who did really kill the great judge?" Crewe was genuinely surprised, but his control over his features was so complete that he did not betray it. "Do you know who Sir Horace Fewbanks's murderer is?" he asked, in quiet even tones. "Monsieur, I do. I will tell you the whole story in secret—how do you say?—in confidence, if you promise me you will help Madame Holymead as I have asked you." "I cannot enter into a bargain like that," rejoined Crewe. "I do not know whether Mrs. Holymead may not be implicated—concerned—in what you say."

"Monsieur, she is not!" flashed Gabrielle indignantly. "She knows nothing about it. What I have to tell you concerns myself alone."

"In that case," rejoined Crewe, "I think you had better speak to me frankly and freely, and if I can I will help you."

"You are perhaps right," she replied. "I will tell you everything, provided you give me your word of honour that you will not inform the police of what I will tell you."

"If you bind me to that promise I do not see how I can help you in the direction you indicate," said Crewe, after a moment's thought. "If the police are asked to abandon their inquiries about Mrs. Holymead, they will naturally wish to know the reason."

"You are quite right," said Gabrielle. "I did not think of that. But if I tell you everything, and you have to tell the police agents so as to help Madame, will you promise that the police agents do not come and arrest *me*?"

"Provided you have not committed murder or been in any way accessory to it, I think I can promise you that," rejoined Crewe.

"Monsieur, I do not understand you, but I can almost divine your meaning. Your promise is what you call a guarded one. Nevertheless, I like your face, and I will trust you."

Gabrielle relapsed into silence for some moments, looking at Crewe earnestly.

"Monsieur," she said at length, "it is a terrible story I have to relate, and it is difficult for me to tell a stranger what I know. Nevertheless, I will begin. I knew the great judge well."

"You knew Sir Horace Fewbanks?" exclaimed Crewe.

"He was—my lover, monsieur."

She brought the last two words out defiantly, with a quick glance at Crewe to see how he took the avowal. She seemed to find something reassuring in his answering glance, and she continued, in more even tones:

"I had often seen him at the house of Madame Holymead when I came to London to visit her. I admired Sir Horace when I saw him— often he used to call and dine, for he was the friend of Monsieur Holymead. But Madame told me that the great judge was what in England you call a lover of the ladies—that he was dangerous— so I must be careful of him. I used to look at him when he called, and thought he was handsome in the English way, and sometimes he looked at me when he was unobserved, and smiled at me. But Madame did not like me looking at him; she said I was foolish; she warned me to be careful."

Gabrielle shrugged her shoulders expressively.

"Of what use was Madame's warning? It did but make me wish to know more of this great lover of my sex. He saw that, and made the opportunity, and made love to me. He was so ardent, so fervid a lover that I was conquered.

"After we had been lovers I told him my secret—that I was married. Pierre Simon, my husband, was a bad man, and so I left him. But Madame must not know that I was married, for that is my secret. It does not do to tell everything—besides, it would have distressed her.

"Monsieur, I was happy with my lover, the great judge. He was charming. He had that charm of manner which you English lack. Faithful? I do not know. Often we were together, and often we wrote letters when to meet was impossible. He kept my letters—they amused him so, he said—they were so French, so piquant, so different to English ladies' letters. Alas, monsieur, there had been others— many others there must have been, for he understood my sex so well.

"One afternoon I was out for a walk looking in the great shops in Regent Street, when I felt a hand placed on my shoulder, and looking round I saw Pierre, my husband. He was pleased at the meeting, but I was not pleased. He took me to a café where we could talk. It was what he always did talk about—money, money, money. He always wanted money. He said I must find him some, and when I told him I had none he said I must find some way of getting it, or he would come to the house and expose my secret. I walked away out of the café and left him there. But I soon saw him again, and again. He followed me and talked to me against my will.

"Monsieur, I was very much distressed, and for a long time I tried to think of a way to get rid of Pierre, for I was afraid that he would come to the house and tell Madame Holymead I was married. Then I thought of the great judge, my lover. He would know how to send Pierre away, for Pierre would be frightened of him. But Sir Horace was in Scotland, shooting the poor birds. But I wrote to him and asked him for my sake to come at once, because I was in distress and needed help. Monsieur, he came—but he came to his death. He sent me a letter to meet him at Riversbrook at half-past ten o'clock. He was sorry it was so late, but he thought it would be safer not to come to the house till after dark in the long summer evening, for people were so censorious. I was to tell Madame Holymead that I was going to the theatre with a friend.

"I was so pleased to think that I would get rid of Pierre, that on the morning, when he stopped me to ask me again about the money, I showed him the letter of the great judge, and told him I would make the judge put him in prison if he did not go away and leave me alone. 'He is your lover,' said Pierre. 'I will kill him.' But I laughed, for I knew Pierre did not care if I had many lovers. I said to him, 'Pierre, you would extort the money'—blackmail, the English call it, do they not, Monsieur Crewe?—'but you would not kill. Sir Horace is not afraid of you. If you go near him he would have you taken off to gaol,' But Pierre he was deep in thought. Several times he said, 'I want money,' Each time I said to him, 'Then you must work for it,' 'That is no way to get money,' he answered. 'This great judge, he has much money, is it not so?'

"I left him, monsieur, thinking of money. But I did not know how bad his thoughts were. I returned home, and I told Madame Holymead I would go to the theatre that night. I left the house at eight o'clock, and after walking along Piccadilly and Regent Street took the train to Hampstead. Then I walked up to the house of Sir Horace so as not to be too early. The gate was open and I thought that strange, but I had no thought of murder. As I walked up the garden I heard a shot—two shots—and then a cry, and the sound of something falling on the floor. The door of the house was open, and the light was burning in the hall. Upstairs I heard the noise of footsteps—quick footsteps—and then I heard them coming down the staircase. I was afraid, and I hid myself behind the curtains in the hall. The footsteps came down, and nearer and nearer, and when they passed me I looked out to see. Monsieur, it was Pierre. I called to him softly, 'Pierre, Pierre!' He looked round, and his face, it was so different—so dreadful. He did not know my voice, and he ran away from me with a cry.

"Monsieur, my heart is a brave one. I have not what you call nerves, but when I knew I was alone in the great house with I knew not what, a great fear clutched me. I stood still in the hall with my eyes fixed on the stairs above. At first all was silent, then I heard a dreadful sound—a groan. I wanted to run away then, monsieur, but the good God commanded me to go up and into the room, where a fellow creature needed me. I went upstairs, and along to the door of a room which was half open. I pushed it wide open and went in.

"*Mon Dieu!* the judge was alone there, dying. Pierre had shot him. He lay along the floor, gasping, groaning, and the blood dripping from his breast. When I saw this I ran forward and took his poor head on my knee, and tried to stop the blood with my handkerchief. But as I did this the judge groaned once more. He knew me not, though I called him by name. In terrible agony he writhed his head off my breast. His hand clutched at the hole in his breast, closing on my handkerchief. And so he died.

"Monsieur, strange it may seem, but I do assure you that I became calm again when he was dead. I rose to my feet and looked round me in the room. On the floor near him I saw a revolver. I picked it up and hid it in my bag. The tube of it was warm. Then I sat down in a chair and thought what I must do. The police must not know I was there. They must not know he was my lover. I thought of my letters that I wrote to him. He had them hidden in a little drawer at the back of his desk—a secret drawer. Often had he showed me my letters there, and once he had showed me where to find the spring that opened the drawer. So I searched for the spring and I found it. The drawer opened and there were my letters tied together. I took them all and hid them in my bag, and then I closed the hiding place. There remained but the handkerchief which my lover held in his hand. I tried to get it out, but I could not. In my hurry I dragged it out—it came away then, but left a little bit in his hand. It did not show. I dared not wait longer. I turned out the light, and hurried out of the room and downstairs. Again I turned out the light, and closed the door, and hurried away.

"That, monsieur, is my story."

CHAPTER XXIII

As Gabrielle finished her story, she cast a quick glance at Crewe's face as though seeking to divine his decision. But apparently she could read nothing there, and with an imperious gesture she exclaimed:

"You will do what I ask now that I have exposed my secret—my shame to you—and told everything? You will save Madame Holymead from being persecuted by these police agents?"

"I must ask you a few questions first."

The contrast between the detective's quiet English tones and the Frenchwoman's impetuous appeal was accentuated by the methodical way in which Crewe slowly jotted down an entry in his open notebook. Her dark eyes sparkled in an agony of impatience as she watched him.

"Ask them quick, monsieur, for I burn in the suspense."

"In the first place, then, have you any—"

"Hold, monsieur! I know what you would ask! You would say if I have any proofs? Stupid that I am to forget things so important. I have brought you the proofs."

She fumbled at the clasp of her hand-bag, as she spoke, and before she had finished speaking she had torn it open and emptied its contents on the table in front of Crewe—a dainty handkerchief and a revolver.

"See, monsieur!" she cried; "here is the handkerchief of which I told you. It is that which the judge seized when I tried to stop the blood flowing in his breast—look at the corner and you will see that a little bit has been torn off by his almost dead hand. And the revolver—it is that which I picked up on the floor near him. I have had it locked up ever since."

Crewe examined both articles closely. The revolver was a small, nickel-plated weapon with silver chasing, with the murdered man's initials engraved in the handle. It had five chambers, and one of the cartridges had been discharged. The other four chambers were still loaded. Crewe carefully extracted the cartridges, and examined them closely. One of them he held up to the light in order to inspect it more minutely.

"Did you do this?" he asked: "Have you been trying to fire off the revolver?"

"No, no, monsieur," she exclaimed quickly. "I would not fire it, I do not understand it. I have been careful not to touch the little thing that sets it going."

"The trigger," said Crewe. He again studied the cartridge that had attracted his attention. It had missed fire, for on the cap was a dint where the hammer had struck it. He placed the four cartridges on the table and turning his attention to the handkerchief examined it minutely. It was one of those filmy scraps of muslin and lace which ladies call a handkerchief—an article whose cost is out of all proportion to its usefulness. Gabrielle, who was watching him keenly as he examined it, exclaimed:

"The handkerchief—a box of them—were given me by Sir Horace because he knew I love pretty things."

She laid a finger on the missing corner, which might indeed have been torn off in the manner described. A scrap of the lace was missing, and it was evident that it had been removed with violence, for the lace around the gap was loosened, and the muslin slightly frayed.

"You say that the corner was torn off when you wrenched the handkerchief from the dead man's hold?" said Crewe. "But it was not found in his hand by the police or anyone else. And he was not buried with it, for I examined the body carefully. What became of it?"

Gabrielle looked at him quickly as though she suspected some trap.

"You would play with me," she said at length. "What became of it? Why, you must surely know that the police of Scot—Scotland Yard have it. The police agent who called on Madame had it. What is his name—Rudolf?"

"Rolfe?" exclaimed Crewe. "Has he got it?"

"Yes," she replied. "He did not show it to me, but I saw it nevertheless. I dropped my handkerchief when I spoke at the telephone and Monsieur Rolfe picked it up. Quickly he studied my handkerchief—not this one, monsieur, but one of the same kind—and from his pocket-book he took out the missing piece that was in the dead man's hand and he studied them side by side. He thought I did not see—that my back was turned—but I saw in the mirror which hung on the wall. Then, when I finished my telephone, he bowed and said, 'Your handkerchief, mademoiselle.' It was not so badly done—for a clumsy police agent."

She was not able to recognise how keen was Crewe's interest in her statement, but she saw that she had pleased him.

"It is because of this that he will come again," she continued. "It is because of this that he would question Madame Holymead. And then what will happen? I do not know. The police make so many mistakes—blunders you English call them. Would they arrest her with their blunders? That is why I come to you to ask you to save her."

"May I have the revolver and the handkerchief?" asked Crewe. "I will take great care of them."

"They are at your disposal, for you will use them to confront the police agent."

Crewe again examined the articles in silence before taking them to his secrétaire and locking them up in one of the pigeon-holes. Then he turned to Gabrielle, whose large luminous eyes met his unhesitatingly. She even smiled slightly—a frank engaging smile, as she remarked:

"And now, monsieur, any more questions?"

Crewe smiled back at her.

"You have told a remarkable story, mademoiselle, and corroborated it with two important pieces of evidence, which are in themselves almost sufficient to carry conviction," he said. "But the Scotland Yard police are a suspicious lot, and it is necessary for me to have further information in order to convince them—if I am to help you as you wish."

Gabrielle flashed a look of gratitude at Crewe. She understood from his words that he believed her story and was disposed to help her, although the police of Scotland Yard might prove harder to convince than him.

"Bah! those police agents—they are the same everywhere," she exclaimed. "They deal so much with crime that their minds get the taint, and between the false and true they cannot tell the difference. *Que voulez-vous?* They are but small in brains. With you, the case is different. You have it here—and there." She touched her temples lightly with a finger of each hand. «Proceed, monsieur: ask me what questions you will. I shall endeavour to answer them."

"You said that as you were hiding behind the curtains on the stairway landing, Pierre, your husband, rushed down past you. You are quite sure it was he?"

"Of that, monsieur, unfortunately there is no doubt. I saw his face quite distinctly when he passed me, and when he turned round."

"The light would be shining from behind, and would not reveal his face very closely," suggested Crewe.

"Nevertheless, monsieur, it was quite sufficient for me to see Pierre clearly. His head was half-turned as he ran, as though he was looking back expecting to see the judge rise up and punish him for his dreadful deed, and I saw him *en silhouette,* oh, most distinctly— impossible him to mistake. I called softly—'Pierre!' just like that, and he turned his face right round, and then with a cry he disappeared along the path."

"About what time was this?"

"The time—it was half-past ten, for that was the time I was to be there according to the letter the judge sent me."

"But are you sure it was half-past ten? Weren't you early? Wasn't it just about ten o'clock?"

"No, monsieur," she replied sadly. "If it had been ten o'clock I would have been in time to save the life of my lover—to prevent this great tragedy which brings grief to so many."

Crewe looked at her sharply, and then nodded his head in acquiescence of the fact that much misery would have been averted if she had been in time to save the life of Sir Horace Fewbanks.

"When you went into the room, Sir Horace Fewbanks, you say, was lying on the floor, dying. Whereabouts in the room was he?"

"If he had been in this room he would have been lying just behind you, with his head to the wall and his feet pointing towards that window. He struggled and groaned after I went in, and altered his position a little, but not much. He died so."

Crewe rapidly reviewed his recollection of the room in which the judge had been killed. Once again Gabrielle's statement tallied with his own reconstruction of the crime and the manner of its perpetration. If the murder had been committed in his office the second bullet would have gone through the window instead of imbedding itself in the wall, and the judge would have fallen in the spot where she indicated.

"And where was the writing-desk from where you got your letters?" was Crewe's next question.

"It was over there—almost by that—your little bookcase there."

She pointed to a small oaken bookstand which stood slightly in advance of the more imposing shelves in which reposed the portentous volumes of newspaper clippings and photographs which constituted Crewe's "Rogues' Library."

"Now we come to the letters. You took them from the secret drawer in the desk. Why did you remove them?"

"Because I would not have the police agents find them, for then they would want to know so much."

"And what did you do with them?"

"Monsieur Crewe, I destroyed them. When I got home I burnt them all—I was so frightened."

"You mean you were frightened to keep them in your possession after the judge was killed?"

"Yes. What place had I to keep them safe from prying eyes? So, monsieur, I burnt them all—one by one—and the charred fragments I kept and took into the Park next day, where I scattered them unobserved."

"And what became of the letter you wrote to Sir Horace Fewbanks at Craigleith Hall, asking him to come to London and save you from your husband's persecutions?"

She looked at him earnestly in the endeavour to ascertain if he had laid a trap for her.

"Sir Horace destroyed it in Scotland, I suppose, if the police did not find it."

"Strange that he should have kept all your other letters so carefully and destroyed that one. Perhaps it was in his pocket-book that was stolen."

"I do not know. What does it matter? It has gone." She shrugged her shoulders lightly and indifferently.

"Do you know who stole the pocket-book?"

"No, monsieur. I thought it was stolen in the train."

"That is the police theory," replied Crewe. "But let that go. Have you, since the night of the murder, seen anything of Pierre?"

"Monsieur, I have not. It is as though the earth has him swallowed. He keeps silent with the silence of the grave."

"He is wise to do so," responded Crewe. "Now, mademoiselle, I have no more questions to ask you. Your confidence is safe; you need be under no apprehensions on that score."

"I care not for myself, Monsieur Crewe, so long as Madame Holymead is freed from the persecutions of the police agents," replied Gabrielle, rising from her seat as she spoke. "If, after hearing my story, you could but give me the assurance—"

"I think I can safely promise you that Mrs. Holymead will not be troubled with any further police attentions," said Crewe, after a moment's pause.

Gabrielle broke into profuse expressions of gratitude as she turned to go.

"For the rest then, I care not what happens. I am—how do you say it—I am overjoyed. *Je vous remercie*, monsieur, I beg you not, I can find my way out unattended."

But Crewe showed her to the stairs, where again he had to listen to her profuse thanks before she finally departed. He watched her graceful figure till it was lost to sight in the winding staircase, and then he turned back to his office. In the outer office he stopped to speak to Joe, who, perched on an office-footstool, was tapping quickly on the office-table with his pen-knife, swaying backwards and forwards dangerously on his perch in the intensity of his emotions as he played the hero's part in the drama of saving the runaway engine from dashing into the 4.40 express by calling up the Red Gulch station on the wire.

"Joe," said Crewe, "I'll see nobody for an hour at least—nobody. You understand?"

Joe came out of the cinema world long enough to nod his head in emphatic understanding of the instructions. In his own room Crewe pulled out his notebook and once more gave himself up to the study of the baffling Riversbrook mystery, in the new light of Gabrielle's confession.

Part of her story, he reflected, must be true. She had produced Sir Horace's revolver, and, still more important, a handkerchief which he had clutched in his dying struggles. It was obvious that she or some other woman had been at Riversbrook the night of the murder, and in the room with the murdered man before he died. That tallied with Birchill's statement to Hill that he had seen a woman close the front door and walk along the garden path while he was hiding in the garden. Crewe, recalling Gabrielle's description of the room, came to the conclusion that it was probably she who had been with the judge in his dying moments. No one but a person who had actually seen it could have described the room with such minuteness.

She had been in the room, then. For what object? For the reasons stated in her confession? Crewe shook his head doubtfully.

"She evaded the trap about the pocket-book, but she made one bad mistake," he mused. "The letters in the secret drawer were taken away, and I have no doubt were burnt as she says. But were they her letters? Was Sir Horace her lover? At any rate, she did not get hold of them in the way she said. They were not taken away on the night Sir Horace was murdered, for the simple reason that they were not in the secret drawer at the time."

CHAPTER XXIV

Rolfe was spending a quiet evening in his room after a trying day's inquiries into a confidence trick case; inquiries so fruitless that they had brought down on his head an official reproof from Inspector Chippenfield.

Rolfe had left Scotland Yard that evening in a somewhat despondent frame of mind in consequence, but a brisk walk home and a good supper had done him so much good, that with a tranquil mind and his pipe in his mouth, he was able to devote himself to the hobby of his leisure hours with keen enjoyment.

This hobby would have excited the wondering contempt of Joe Leaver, whose frequent attendance at cinema theatres had led him to the conclusion that police detectives—who, unlike his master, had to take the rough with the smooth—spent their spare time practising revolver shooting, and throwing daggers at an ace of hearts on the wall. Rolfe's hobby was nothing more exciting than stamp collecting. He was deeply versed in the lore of stamps, and his private ambition was to become the possessor of a "blue Mauritius." His collection, though extensive, was by no means of fabulous value, being made up chiefly of modest purchases from the stamp collecting shops, and finds in the waste-paper-baskets at Scotland Yard after the arrival of the foreign mails.

That day he had made a particularly good haul from the waste-paper-baskets, for his "catch" included several comparatively good specimens from Japan and Fiji. He sat gloating over these treasures, examining them carefully and holding each one up to the light as he separated it from the piece of paper to which it had been affixed. He pasted them one by one in his stamp album with loving, lingering fingers, adjusting each stamp in its little square in the book with meticulous care. He was so absorbed in this occupation that he did not hear the ascending footsteps drawing nearer to his door, and did not see a visitor at the door when the footsteps ceased. It was Crewe's voice that recalled him back from the stamp collector's imaginary world.

"Why, Mr. Crewe," said Rolfe, with evident pleasure, "who'd have thought of seeing you?"

"Your landlady asked me if I'd come up myself," said Crewe, in explaining his intrusion. "She's 'too much worried and put about, to say nothing of having a bad back,' to show me upstairs."

"I've never known her to be well," said Rolfe, with a laugh. "Every morning when she brings up my breakfast I've got to hear details of her bad back which should be kept for the confidential ear of the doctor. But she regards me as a son, I think—I've been here so long. But now you are here, Mr. Crewe—" Rolfe waited in polite expectation that his visitor would disclose the object of his visit.

But Crewe seemed in no hurry to do so. He produced his cigar case and offered Rolfe a cigar, which the latter accepted with a pleasant recollection of the excellent flavour of the cigars the private detective kept. When each of them had his cigar well alight, Crewe glanced at the open stamp album and commenced talking about stamps. It was a subject which Rolfe was always willing to discuss. Crewe declared that he was an ignorant outsider as far as stamps were concerned, but he professed to have a respectful admiration for those who immersed themselves in such a fascinating subject. Rolfe, with the fervid egoism of the collector, talked about stamps for half an hour without recalling that his visitor must have come to talk about something else.

"I've got a small stamp collection in my office," said Crewe, when Rolfe paused for a moment. "It belonged to that Jewish diamond merchant who was shot in Hatton Gardens two years ago. You remember his case?"

"Rather! That was a smart bit of work of yours, Mr. Crewe, in laying your hands on the woman who did it and getting back the diamond."

Crewe smiled in response.

"The Jew was very grateful, poor fellow. He died in the hospital after the trial, so she was lucky to escape with twelve years. He left me a diamond ring and a stamp album that had come into his possession."

"I should like to see it," said Rolfe eagerly. "It is more than likely that there are some good specimens in it. The Jews are keen collectors. If you let me have a look at it, I'll tell you what the collection is worth."

"You can have it altogether," said Crewe. "I'll send my boy Joe round with it in the morning."

"Oh, Mr. Crewe, it's very good of you," said Rolfe, with the covetousness of the collector shining in his eyes.

"Nonsense! Why shouldn't you have it? But I didn't come round here solely to talk about stamps, Rolfe. I came to have a little chat about the Riversbrook case. How are you getting on with it?"

"Why, really," said Rolfe, "I've not done much with it since, since—"

"Since Birchill was acquitted, eh! But you are not letting it drop altogether, are you? That would be a pity—such an interesting case. Whom have you your eye on now as the right man?"

Rolfe, who thought he detected a suspicion of banter in Crewe's remarks, evaded the latter question by answering the first part of Crewe's inquiry.

"Why hardly that, Mr. Crewe. But the chief is not very keen on the case. Birchill's acquittal was too much of a blow to him. He reckons that nowadays juries are too soft-hearted to convict on a capital charge."

"It's just as well that they are too soft-hearted to convict the wrong man," said Crewe.

"Yes; you told me from the first that we were on the wrong track," was the reply. "I haven't forgotten that and the chief is not allowed to forget it, either. All the men at the Yard know that you held the opinion that we had got hold of the wrong man when we arrested Birchill, and he has had to stand so much chaff in the office, that he's pretty raw about it." Rolfe spoke in the detached tone of a junior who had no share in his chief's mistakes or their attendant humiliation, and he added, "That's once more that you've scored over Scotland Yard, Mr. Crewe, and you ought to be proud of it." He glanced covertly at Crewe to see how he took the flattery.

"So you've done very little about the case since Birchill was acquitted?" was his only remark.

"I've been so busy," replied Rolfe, again evading the question, and avoiding meeting Crewe's glance by turning over the leaves of his stamp album. "You see, there has been a rush of work at Scotland Yard lately. There is that big burglary at Lord Emden's, and the case of the woman whose body was found in the river lock at Peyton, and half a dozen other cases, all important in their way. There has been quite an epidemic of crime lately, as you know, Mr. Crewe. I don't seem to get a minute to myself these times."

"Rolfe," said Crewe drily, "you protest too much. You don't suppose that after coming over here to see you that I can be deceived by such talk?"

Rolfe flushed at these uncompromising words, but before he could speak Crewe proceeded in a milder tone.

"I don't blame you a bit for trying to put me off. It's all part of the game. We're rivals, in a sense, and you are quite right not to lose sight of that fact. But as a detective, Rolfe, your methods lack polish. Really, I blush for them. You might have known that I came over here to see you to-night because I had an important object in view, and you should have tried to find out what it was before playing your own cards,—and such cards, too! You're sadly lacking in finesse, Rolfe. You'd never make a chess player; your concealed intentions are too easily discovered. You must try not to be so transparent if you want to succeed in your profession."

Crewe delivered his reproof with such good humour that Rolfe stared at him, as if unable to make out what his visitor was driving at.

"I don't know what you are talking about, Mr. Crewe," he said at length.

"Oh, yes, you do. You know I'm speaking about your latest move in the Riversbrook case, which you've been so busy with of late. And I've come to tell you in a friendly way that once more you're on the wrong track."

"What do you mean?" asked Rolfe quickly.

"Why, Princes Gate, of course," replied Crewe cheerily. "You don't suppose that a fine-looking young man like yourself could be seen in the neighbourhood of Princes Gate without causing a flutter among feminine hearts there, do you?"

"So the servants have been talking, have they?" muttered Rolfe.

"They have and they haven't. But that's beside the point. What I want to say is that you're on the wrong track in suspecting Mrs. Holymead, and I strongly advise you to drop your inquiries if you don't want to get yourself into hot water. She's as innocent of the murder of Sir Horace Fewbanks as Birchill is, but you cannot afford to make a false shot in the case of a lady of her social standing, as you did with a criminal like Birchill."

At this rebuke Rolfe gave way to irritation.

"Look here, Mr. Crewe, I'll thank you to mind your own business," he said. "It's got nothing to do with you where I make inquiries. I'll have you remember that! I don't interfere with you, and I won't have you interfering with me."

"But I'm interfering only for your own good, man! What do you suppose I'm doing it for? I tell you you're riding for a very bad fall in suspecting Mrs. Holymead and shadowing her."

Crewe's plain words were an echo of a secret fear which Rolfe had entertained from the time his suspicions were directed towards Mrs. Holymead. But he was not going to allow Crewe to think he was alarmed.

"If I'm making inquiries about Mrs. Holymead, it's because I have ample justification for doing so," he said stiffly.

"And I tell you that you have not."

"Prove it!" exclaimed Rolfe defiantly.

Crewe produced from his pocket a revolver and a lady's handkerchief, and handed them to Rolfe without speaking.

Rolfe's embarrassment was almost equal to his astonishment as he examined the articles. In the handkerchief with its missing corner, he speedily recognised something for which he had searched in vain. He had never confided to Crewe the discovery of the missing corner in the dead man's hand, and therefore the production of the handkerchief by Crewe considerably embarrassed him. He longed to ask Crewe how he had obtained possession of the handkerchief, but he could not trust his voice to frame the question without betraying his feelings, so he picked up the revolver and examined it closely. Then he put it down and again gave his attention to the handkerchief, bending his head over it so that Crewe should not see his face.

"You do not seem very astonished at my finds, Rolfe," said Crewe quizzically. "Perhaps you've seen these articles before?"

"No, I haven't," said Rolfe, still avoiding his visitor's eye.

"Well, the torn handkerchief is not exactly new to you," said Crewe. "You've got the missing part; you found it in Sir Horace's hand after he was murdered."

"You're too clever for me, and that's the simple truth, Mr. Crewe," said Rolfe, in a mortified tone. "I did find a small piece of a lady's handkerchief in his hand, and here it is." He produced his pocket-book and took out the piece. "How you found out I had it, is more than I know."

"Mere guess-work," said Crewe.

Rolfe shook his head slowly.

"I know better than that," he said. "You're deep. You don't miss much. I wish now that I had told you about that bit of handkerchief at the first. But Chippenfield and I wanted to have all the credit of elucidating the Riversbrook mystery. I hunted high and low to get trace of this handkerchief, but I couldn't. And now you've beaten me, although you couldn't have known at first that there was such a thing as a missing handkerchief in the case. I hope you bear me no malice, Mr. Crewe."

"What for, Rolfe?"

"For not telling you about the handkerchief, after I found this piece in Sir Horace's hand."

"Not in the least," said Crewe. "Why should you have told me? I don't tell you everything that I find out. It's all part of the game. That piece of the handkerchief was a good find, Rolfe, and I congratulate you on getting it. How did you come to discover it?"

"I was trying to force open the murdered man's hand, and I found it clenched between the little finger and the next. Of course it was not visible with his hand closed. Chippenfield, who missed it, didn't half like my discovery, and all along he underestimated the value of it as a clue."

"Well, he has had to pay for his folly."

"He has, and serves him right," replied Rolfe viciously. "He's the most pig-headed, obstinate, vain, narrow-minded man you could come across." It occurred to Rolfe that it was not exactly good form on his part to condemn his superior officer so vigorously in the presence of a rival, so he broke off abruptly and asked Crewe how he came into possession of the revolver and handkerchief.

Crewe's reply was that he had obtained these articles under a promise of secrecy from some one who had assured him that Mrs. Holymead had no connection with the crime. When he was at liberty to tell the story as it had been told to him, Rolfe would be the first to hear it.

"Mrs. Holymead had no connection with the crime?" exclaimed Rolfe impatiently. "Perhaps you don't know that the morning after the murder was discovered she went out to Riversbrook and removed some secret papers from the murdered man's desk—papers that he had been in the habit of hiding in a secret drawer?"

"Yes, I know that," said Crewe.

"Well, doesn't that look as if she knew something about the crime?"

"Not necessarily."

"Well, to me it does. What were these secret papers? They were letters, I am told."

"I believe so. And you, Rolfe, as a man of the world, know that a married woman would not like the police to get possession of letters she had written to a man of the reputation of Sir Horace Fewbanks."

"I admit that her action is capable of a comparatively innocent interpretation, but taken in conjunction with other things it looks to me mighty suspicious. In Hill's statement to us he told us that on the night of the murder, Birchill when hiding in the garden waiting for the lights to go out before breaking into the house, heard the front door slam and saw a stylish sort of woman walk down the path to the gate."

"That was not Mrs. Holymead," said Crewe.

"How do you know? If it was not her, who was it? Do you know?"

"I think I know, and when I am at liberty to speak I will tell you."

"Then there is a third point," continued Rolfe. "Look at this handkerchief you brought. I saw a handkerchief of exactly similar pattern at Mrs. Holymead's house when I called there."

"Wasn't that the property of her French cousin, Mademoiselle Chiron?"

"Yes, she dropped it on the floor while I was there. But it is probable the handkerchief was one of a set given her by Mrs. Holymead."

"Quite probably, Rolfe. But scores of ladies who are fond of expensive things have handkerchiefs of a similar pattern. You will find if you inquire among the West End shops, that although it is a dainty, expensive article from the man's point of view, there is nothing singular about the quality or the pattern."

"Perhaps so," said Rolfe, "but the possession of handkerchiefs of this kind is surely suspicious when taken in conjunction with her removal of the letters. I wish I could get hold of that infernal scoundrel Hill again. I am convinced that he knows a great deal more about this murder than he has yet told us, and a great deal more about Mrs. Holymead and her letters. I've had his shop watched day and night since he disappeared, but he keeps close to his burrow, and I've not been able to get on his track."

"I'd give up watching for him if I were you," said Crewe, as he flicked the ash of his cigar into the fireplace. "You're not likely to find him now. As a matter of fact, he has left the country."

"Hill left the country?" echoed Rolfe. "I think you are mistaken there, Mr. Crewe. He had no money; how could he get away?"

Crewe selected another cigar from his case and lighted it before answering.

"The fact is, I advanced him the money," he said. "Technically it's a loan, but I do not think any of it will be paid back."

Rolfe stared hard at Crewe to see if he was joking.

"What on earth made you do that?" he demanded at length. "Hill may be the actual murderer for all we know."

"Not at all," was the reply. "Before I helped him to leave England I satisfied myself that he had absolutely nothing to do with the murder. He does not know who shot Sir Horace Fewbanks, though, of course, he still half believes that it was Birchill. When I got in touch with him after his disappearance he was in a pitiable state of fright—waking or sleeping, he couldn't get his mind off the gallows. There were two or three points on which I wanted his assistance in clearing up the

Riversbrook case, and I promised to get him out of the country if he would make a clean breast of things and tell me the truth as far as he knew it. He made a confession—a true one this time. I took it down and I'll let you have a copy. There are a few interesting points on which it differs materially from the statement he made to the police when you and Chippenfield cornered him."

"What are they?" asked Rolfe.

"In the first place the burglary was his idea, and not Birchill's," replied Crewe. "After the quarrel between Sir Horace and the girl Fanning, he went out to her flat and suggested to Birchill that he should rob Riversbrook. Hill's real object in arranging this burglary was to get possession of the letters which Mrs. Holymead subsequently removed, but he did not tell Birchill this. His plan was to go to Riversbrook the morning after the burglary and then break open Sir Horace's desk and open the secret drawer before informing the police of the burglary. To the police and Sir Horace it would look as though the burglar had accidentally found the spring of the secret drawer. With these letters in his possession Hill intended to blackmail Sir Horace, or Mrs. Holymead, without disclosing himself in the transaction.

"When Sir Horace returned unexpectedly from Scotland on the 18th of August, Hill had just removed the letters from the desk, being afraid that when Birchill broke into the house he might find them accidentally. He was naturally in a state of alarm at Sir Horace's return. He tried to get an opportunity to put the letters back as Sir Horace might discover they had been removed, but Sir Horace dismissed him for the night before he could get such an opportunity. Then he went to Fanning's flat and told Birchill that Sir Horace had returned. Birchill was in favour of postponing the burglary, but Hill, who had possession of the letters, and did not know when he would get an opportunity to put them back, urged Birchill to carry out the burglary. He assured Birchill that Sir Horace was a very sound sleeper and that there would be no risk. In order to arouse Birchill's cupidity and to protect himself from the suspicions of Sir Horace regarding the letters, he told Birchill that he had seen a large sum of money in his possession when he returned, and that this money would probably be hidden in the secret drawer of the desk, until Sir Horace had an opportunity of banking it. He told Birchill to break open the desk, and explained to him how to find the spring of the secret drawer."

"What a damned cunning scoundrel he is," exclaimed Rolfe, in unwilling admiration of the completeness of Hill's scheme. "Don't you think, Mr. Crewe, that, after all, he may be the actual murderer—that he told you a lot of lies just as he did to us? Holymead in his address to the jury made out a pretty strong case against him."

"No one knows better than Holymead that Hill did not commit the murder," said Crewe. "Hill is an incorrigible liar, but he has no nerve for murder."

"Did he put the letters back?" asked Rolfe. "He told me that Mrs. Holymead stole them the day after the murder was discovered. But he is such a liar—"

"I believe he spoke the truth in that case," said Crewe. "He told me he put the letters back in the secret drawer the night after the murder, when he went to Riversbrook to report himself to Chippenfield. He put them back because he was afraid that if the police found them in his possession, they would think he had a hand in the murder. His idea was to remove them from the secret drawer after the excitement about the murder died down, and then blackmail Mrs. Holymead, but she acted with a skill and decision that robbed him of his chance to blackmail her."

"How did you get hold of the cunning scoundrel?" asked Rolfe. "I've had his wife's shop watched day and night, as I've said. I made sure he would try to communicate with her sooner or later, but he didn't."

"It was Joe who found him," said Crewe. "I knew you were watching Mrs. Hill's shop, so it was superfluous for me to set anybody to watch it. Besides, I didn't think Hill would visit his wife or attempt to communicate with her, for he would think that the police, if they wanted him, would be sure to watch the shop. I tried to consider what a man like Hill would do in the circumstances. He had no money—I knew that—and, so far as I was able to ascertain, he had no friends who were likely to hide him. Without friends or money he could not go very far. Finally it occurred to me that he might be hiding somewhere in Riversbrook—either in that unfinished portion of the third floor, or in one of the outbuildings. He knew the run of the rambling old place so well. Have you ever been over it carefully? No. Well, there are several good places in the upper stories where a man might conceal himself. I put Joe on the job, and after watching for several nights Joe got him. Hill had made a hiding place in the loft above the garage. It appears that he subsisted on the stores that had been left in the house; he was able to make his way into the main building through one of the kitchen windows. He was on one of these foraging expeditions when Joe discovered him—emaciated, dirty, and half demented through terror of the gallows."

"So that is how you got him!" said Rolfe. "I never thought of looking for him at Riversbrook. Sometimes I am inclined to agree with you that he had no nerve for murder. But an unpremeditated murder doesn't want much nerve. He might have done it in a moment of passion." Rolfe was endeavouring to take advantage of Crewe's communicative mood and to arrive by a process of elimination at the person against whom Crewe had accumulated his evidence.

"It was not Hill," said Crewe. "The murder was committed in a moment of passion, and yet it was far from being unpremeditated."

"You are trying to mystify me," said Rolfe despairingly.

"No; it is the case itself which has mystified you," replied Crewe.

"It has," was Rolfe's candid confession. "The more thought I give it, the more impossible it seems to see through it. Was Sir Horace killed before dusk—before the lights were turned on? If he was killed after dark, who turned out the lights?"

"He was killed between 10 and 10.30 at night," said Crewe. "The lights were turned out by the woman Birchill saw leaving the house about 10.30. But she was not the murderer, and she was not present in the room, or even in the house, when Sir Horace was shot. She arrived a few minutes too late to prevent the tragedy. Turning out the lights was an instinctive act due to her desire to hide the crime, or rather to hide the murderer."

"How do you know all this?" asked Rolfe, who had been staring at Crewe with open-mouthed astonishment.

"That woman was not Mrs. Holymead," continued Crewe. "I had a visit to-day from the woman who did these things, and as evidence of the truth of her story she brought me the revolver and the handkerchief."

"What did she come to you for?" asked Rolfe, with breathless interest. "What did she want?"

"She came to me to make a full confession," said Crewe, in even tones.

"A confession!" exclaimed Rolfe. "She ought to have come to the police. Why didn't she come to us?"

Crewe smiled at the puzzled, indignant detective.

"I think she came to me because she wanted to mislead me," he said.

CHAPTER XXV

Joe Leaver, worn out after nearly a week's work of watching the movements of Mr. Holymead, had fallen asleep in an empty loft above a garage which overlooked Verney's Hotel in Mayfair. He had seen Mr. Holymead disappear into the hotel, and he knew from the experience gained in his watch that the K.C. would spend the next couple of hours in dressing for dinner, sitting down to that meal, and smoking a cigar in the lounge. So Joe had relaxed, for the time being, the new task which his master had set him, and had flung himself on some straw in the loft to rest. He did not intend to go to sleep, but he was very tired, and in a few minutes he was in a profound slumber.

In his sleep Joe dreamed that he had attained the summit of his ambition, and was being paid a huge salary by an American film company to display himself in emotional dramas for the educational improvement of the British working classes. In his dream he had to rescue the heroine from the clutches of the villains who had carried her off. They had imprisoned her at the top of a "skyscraper" building and locked the lift, but Joe climbed the fire escape and caught the beautiful girl in his arms. The villains, who were on the watch, set fire to the building, and when Joe attempted to climb out of the window with the heroine clinging round his neck, the flames drove him back. As he stood there the wind swept a sheet of flame towards Joe until it scorched his face. The pain was so real that Joe opened his eyes and sprang up with a cry.

A man was standing over him, a man past middle age, short and broad in figure, whose clean-shaven face directed attention to his protruding jaw. He was wearing a blue serge suit which had seen much use.

"You are a sound sleeper, sonny," said the man, grinning at Joe's alarm. "But when you wake—why you wake up properly; I'll say that for you. You nearly broke my pipe, you woke up that sudden."

He made this remark with such a malicious grin that Joe, whose face was still smarting, had no hesitation in connecting his sudden awakening with the hot bowl of the man's pipe. It was a joke Joe had often seen played on drunken men in Islington public-houses in his young days.

"You just leave me alone, will you?" he said, rubbing his cheek ruefully. "It's nothing to do with you whether I'm a sound sleeper or not."

"That's just where you're wrong, young fellow," was the reply. "It's a lot to do with me. Ain't your name Joe Leaver?"

Joe nodded his head.

"How did you find out?" he asked.

"Perhaps a friend of mine pointed you out to me."

"Perhaps he did, and perhaps he didn't," said Joe. "Anyway, what is your name?"

"Mr. Kemp is my name, my boy. And unless you're pretty civil I'll give you cause to remember it."

"What have you got to do with me?" asked the boy in an injured tone. "I've never done nothing to you."

"You mind your P's and Q's and me and you'll get along all right," said Mr. Kemp, in a somewhat softer tone. "When you ask me what I've got to do with you, my answer is I've got a lot to do with you, for I'm your guardian, so to speak."

Joe looked at Mr. Kemp with a gleam of comprehension in his amazement. He had had some experience in his Islington days of the strange phenomena produced by drink.

"Rats!" he retorted rudely. "I've never had a guardian and I don't want none. What made you a guardian, I'd like to know?"

"Your father did," was the reply.

"Oh, him!" said Joe, in a tone which indicated pronounced antipathy to his parent. "Do you know him? Are you one of his sort?"

"Now don't try to be insulting, my boy, or I'll take you across my knee. We won't say nothing about where your father is, because in high society Wormwood Scrubbs isn't mentioned. All we'll say is that he has been unfortunate like many another man before him, and that for the present he can't come and go as he likes. But he has still got a father's heart, Joe, and there are times when he worries about his family and about there being no one with them to keep an eye on them and see they grow up a credit to him. He has been particularly worried about you, Joe. So when I was coming away he asked me to look you up if I had time, and let him know how you was getting on, seeing that none of his family has gone near him for a matter of three years or so, though there is one regular visiting day each week."

"I don't want to see him no more," said Joe. "He's no good."

"That's a nice way for a boy to talk about his own father," said Mr. Kemp, in a reproving tone. "I don't know what the young generation is coming to."

"If you want to send him word about me, you can tell him that I'm not going to be a thief," said Joe defiantly.

"No," said Mr. Kemp tauntingly, "you'd sooner be a nark."

"Yes, I would," said the boy.

"And that's what you are now," declared the man wrathfully. "You're a nark for that fellow Crewe. I know all about you."

"I'm earning an honest living," said Joe.

"As a nark," said Mr. Kemp, with a sneer.

"I'm earning an honest living," said the boy doggedly. So much of his youth had been spent among the criminal classes that he still retained the feeling that there was an indelible stigma attached to those individuals described as narks.

"How can any one earn a respectable honest living by being a nark?" asked Mr. Kemp contemptuously. "And more than that, it's one of the best men that ever breathed that you are a-spying on. I'll have you know that he's a friend of mine. That is to say he's done things for me that I ain't likely to forget. There's nothing I won't do for him, if the chance comes my way. I'll see that no harm happens to him through you and your Mr. Crewe. You've got to stop this here spying. Stop it at once, do you understand? For if you don't, by God, I'll deal with you so that you'll do no more spying in this world! And I'd have you and your master know that I'm a man what means what he says." Mr. Kemp shook his fist angrily at Joe as he moved away to the door of the loft after having delivered his menacing warning.

"My last words to you is, Stop it!" he said, as he turned to go down the stairs.

Half an hour later Mr. Kemp entered the lounge of Verney's Hotel as though in quest of some one. Most of the hotel guests had finished their after-dinner coffee and liqueurs, and the hall was comparatively empty, but a few who remained raised their eyes in well-bred protest at the intrusion of a member of the lower orders into the corridor of an exclusive hotel. Mr. Kemp felt somewhat out of place, and he stared about the luxuriously furnished lounge with a look in which awe mingled with admiration. Before he could advance further, a liveried porter of massive proportions came up to him and barred the way.

"Now, now, my man," said the porter haughtily, "what do you think you are doing here? This ain't your place, you know. You've made a mistake. Out you go."

"I want to see Mr. Holymead," said Mr. Kemp in a gruff voice.

Verney's was such a high-class hotel that seedy-looking persons seldom dared to put a foot within the palatial entrance. The porter, unused to dealing with the obtrusive impecunious type to which he believed Mr. Kemp to belong, made the mistake of trying to argue with him.

"Want to see Mr. Holymead?" he repeated. "How do you know he's here? Who told you? What do you want to see him for?"

"What's that got to do with you?" retorted Mr. Kemp. "You don't think Mr. Holymead would like me to discuss his business with the likes of you? That ain't what you're here for. You go and tell Mr. Holymead that some one wants to see him. Tell him Mr. Kemp wants to see him." Mr. Kemp drew himself up and buttoned the coat of his faded serge suit.

The porter, uncertain how to deal with the situation, looked around for help. The manager of the hotel emerged from the booking office at that moment, and the porter's appealing look was seen by him. The manager approached. He was faultlessly attired, suave in demeanour, and walked with a noiseless step, despite his tendency to corpulence. It was his daily task to wrestle with some of the manifold difficulties arising out of the eccentricities of human nature as exhibited by a constant stream of arriving and departing guests. But though he approached the distressed porter with full confidence in his ability to deal with any situation, his eyebrows arched in astonishment as he took in the full details of the intruder's attire.

"What does this mean, Hawkins?" he exclaimed, in a tone of disapproval.

The porter trembled at the implication that he had grievously failed in his duty by allowing such an individual as Mr. Kemp to get so far within the exclusive portals of Verney's, and in his nervousness he relaxed from the polish of the hotel porter to his native cockney.

"This 'ere party says 'e wants to see Mr. Holymead, Sir."

The manager went through the motion of washing a spotlessly clean pair of hands, and then brought the palms together in a gentle clap. He smiled pityingly at Hawkins and then looked condescendingly at Mr. Kemp.

"Wants to see Mr. Holymead, does he?" he said, transferring his glance to the worried porter. "And didn't you tell him that Mr. Holymead has gone to the theatre and won't be back for some considerable time?"

"That's a lie!" said Mr. Kemp, who had acquired none of the art of dealing with his fellow men, and was too uneducated to appreciate art in any form. "I've been watching over the other side of the street, and I saw him passing a window not ten minutes ago. I'm going to see him if I wait here all night. I'll soon make meself comfortable on one of them big chairs." He pointed to an empty chair beside a man in evening dress, who was holding a conversation with a haughty looking matron. "You tell Mr. Holymead Mr. Kemp wants to see him," he said to the manager.

"What name did you say?" asked the manager in a tone which seemed to express astonishment that the lower orders had names.

"Mr. Kemp. You tell him Mr. Kemp wants to see him on important business." He walked towards the vacant chair and seated himself on it. He dug his toes into the velvet pile carpet with the air of a man who was trying to take anchor. Fortunately the man on the adjoining chair, and the haughty matron, were so engrossed in their conversation that they did not notice that the air in their immediate vicinity was being polluted by the presence of a man in shabby clothes and heavy boots.

The manager despatched the porter in search of Mr. Holymead and then went in pursuit of Mr. Kemp.

"Will you come this way, if you please, Mr. Kemp?" he said, with a low bow.

He saw that Mr. Kemp was following him and led the way into an unfrequented corner of the smoking room, where, with the information that Mr. Holymead would come to him in a few moments, he asked Mr. Kemp to be seated.

The manager withdrew a few yards, and then took up a position which enabled him to guard the hotel guests from having their digestions interfered with by the contaminating spectacle of a seedy man. To the manager's great relief, Mr. Holymead appeared, having been informed by the hall porter that a party who said his name was Kemp had asked to see him. The manager hurried towards Mr. Holymead and endeavoured to explain and apologise, but the K.C. assured him that there was nothing to apologise for. He went over to the corner of the smoking room, where the visitor who had caused so much perturbation was waiting for him.

"Well, Kemp, what do you want?" There was nothing in his manner to indicate that he was put out by Mr. Kemp's appearance. He spoke in quiet even tones such as would seem to suggest that he was well acquainted with his visitor.

"Can I speak to you on the quiet for a moment, sir?" whispered Kemp hoarsely.

Holymead looked round the room. The manager had gone back to the booking office and Hawkins had vanished. The few people who were in the room seemed occupied with their own affairs.

"No one will overhear us if we speak quietly," he said as he took a seat close to Kemp. "What is it?"

"You're watched and followed, sir," said Kemp in a whisper. "Somebody has been watching this place for days past and whenever you go out you're followed."

"By whom?" asked Holymead.

"By a varmint of a boy—a slippery young imp whose father's in gaol for a long stretch. I got hold of him this afternoon and told him what I'd do to him if he kept on with his game. He's living in an old loft at the back of the hotel garage, and he keeps a watch on you day and night. I thought I'd better come here and tell you, as you mightn't know about him."

"You did quite right, Kemp. What's this boy like?"

"An undersized putty-faced brat with a big head. He's about fourteen or fifteen, I should say."

"Who is he? Do you know him?"

"Leaver is the name, sir. To tell you the truth, I don't know him as well as I know his father. His father is a 'lifer' for manslaughter. I've known him both in and out of gaol. And when I was coming out four months ago Bob Leaver, this here boy's father, asked me to look up his family and send him word about them. I went to the address Bob told me, in Islington, but I found they had all gone. The mother was dead and the kids—a girl and this here boy—had cleared out. The old Jew who had the second-hand clothes shop Mrs. Leaver used to keep told me that the boy had gone off with that private detective, Crewe, more than two years ago. So it looks to me as if he has turned nark and Crewe has put him on to watch you."

"Can you describe this boy more closely?"

"Well, sir, I don't know if I can say anything more about him except that he has red hair and big bright eyes that are too large for his face."

"I thought so," said Holymead as if speaking to himself. "It's the same boy."

"What did you say, sir?" asked Kemp.

"Nothing, Kemp, except that I think I've seen a boy of this description hanging about the street near the hotel."

Holymead rose to his feet as he spoke, as an indication that the interview was at an end. Kemp got up and looked at him anxiously.

"I beg your pardon, sir, for coming here," he said, fumbling with the rim of his hat as he spoke. "I didn't know how you'd take it, but I hope I've done right. They didn't want to let me see you."

"You did quite right, Kemp. I am very much obliged to you." He was feeling in his pocket for silver, but Kemp stopped him.

"No, no, sir. I don't want to be paid anything. I wanted to oblige you like; I wanted to do you a good turn. I'd do anything for you, sir—you know I would."

"I believe you would, Kemp. Good night."

"Good night, sir."

As Kemp passed down the hall he met the manager, who was obviously pleased to see such an unwelcome visitor making his departure. Kemp scowled at the manager as if he were a valued patron of the hotel and said, "It seems to me that you don't know how to treat people properly when they come here."

CHAPTER XXVI

It was the first occasion on which Mrs. Holymead had visited her husband's chambers in the Middle Temple. Mr. Mattingford, who had been Mr. Holymead's clerk for nearly twenty years, seemed to realise that the visit was important, though as a married man he knew that a meeting between husband and wife in town was usually so commonplace as to verge on boredom for the husband. There were occasions when he had to meet Mrs. Mattingford, but these meetings were generally for the purpose of handing over to the lady her weekly dress allowance of ten shillings out of his salary, so that she might attend the sales at the big drapery shops in the West End and inspect the windows containing expensive articles that she could not hope to buy. Mr. Mattingford was an exceedingly thrifty man, and his wife possessed some of the qualities of a spendthrift. Thus it came about that Mr. Mattingford kept up the fiction that he had no savings and that each week's salary must see him through till the next week. Mrs. Mattingford knew that her husband had saved money, and theoretically she would have given a great deal to know how much. She repeatedly accused him of being a miser, but this is a wifely denunciation which in all classes of life is lightly made when the purchase of feminine finery is under discussion. There are some men who resent it, but Mr. Mattingford was not one of these. Protests and prayers, abuse and cajolery, were alike powerless to win his consent to his wife's perpetual proposal that she should be allowed to draw her dress allowance for some months, or even some weeks ahead. Mr. Mattingford had a horror of bad debts. He endeavoured to show his wife that the transaction she proposed was unsound from a business point of view and reckless from a legal point of view. She had no security to offer for the repayment of the advance—even if he were in a financial position to make the advance—and he stoutly declared that he was not. She might die at any moment, and then he would be left with no means of redress against her estate because she had no estate. Of course, if she first insured her life out of her dress allowance and handed the policy to him it would constitute protection for the repayment of the advance, in the event of her death, but it was not any real protection in the event of her continuing to live, for a newly-executed policy had no surrender value. As his own legal adviser, Mr. Mattingford strongly urged himself not to consider his wife's proposal, and such was his respect for the law and for those who had been brought up in a legal atmosphere that he had no hesitation in accepting the advice.

He was a little man of nearly fifty years, with a very bald head and an extremely long moustache, which when waxed at the ends made him look as fierce as a clipped poodle. He knew Mrs. Holymead from his having called frequently at his chief's house in Princes Gate on business matters, and he admired her for her good looks, but still more for her good taste in staying away from her husband's chambers. There were some ladies, the wives of barristers, who almost haunted their husbands' chambers—a practice of which Mr. Mattingford strongly disapproved. It seemed to him an insidious attempt on the part of an insidious sex to force the legal profession to throw open its doors to women. As a man who lived in the mouldy atmosphere of precedent, Mr. Mattingford hated the idea of change, and to him the thought of a lady in wig and gown pleading in the law courts indicated not merely change but a revolution which might well usher in the end of the world. So strict was he in keeping the precincts of the law sacred from the violating tread of women that he never allowed his wife to set foot in the Middle Temple. Their meetings on those urgent occasions when Mrs. Mattingford came to town for her dress allowance in order to go bargain-hunting took place at one of the cheap tearooms in Fleet Street.

Although Mr. Mattingford was somewhat flustered by the unexpected appearance of Mrs. Holymead, he did not depart from precedent to the extent of regarding her as entitled to any other treatment than that accorded to clients who called on business. He asked her if she wanted to see Mr. Holymead, placed a chair for her, then knocked deferentially at his chief's door, went inside to announce Mrs. Holymead to her husband, and came out with the information that Mr. Holymead would see her. He held open the door leading into his chief's private room, and after Mrs. Holymead had entered closed it softly and firmly.

But the formal business manner of Mr. Mattingford to his chief's wife seemed to her friendly and cordial compared with the strained greetings she received from her husband. He motioned her to a chair and then got up from his own.

"I wrote to you to come and see me here instead of going to the house to see you," he said, "because I thought it would be better for both. It would have given the servants something to talk about. I hope you don't mind?"

She looked at him with her large dark eyes in which there was more than a suggestion of tears. What she had read into his note, when she received it, was his determination not to go to his home to see her for fear she would interpret that as a first step towards reconciliation.

"What I wanted to speak to you about is this detective Crewe whom Miss Fewbanks has employed in connection with her father's death," he continued.

Her breath came quickly at this unwelcome information. She noted that he had spoken of Sir Horace's death and not his murder.

He began pacing backwards and forwards across the room as if with the purpose of avoiding looking at her.

"This man Crewe is a nuisance—I might even say a danger. I don't know what he has found out, but I object to his ferreting into my affairs. He must be stopped."

She nodded her assent, for she could not trust herself to speak. Each time he turned his back on her as he crossed the room her eyes followed him, but as he faced her she turned her gaze on the floor.

"There is no legal redress—no legal means of dealing with his impertinent curiosity," he went on. "He is within his rights in trying to find out all he can. But if he is allowed to go on unchecked the thing may reach a disastrous stage. I have no doubt that he knows that I was at Riversbrook the night that man was killed. He was not long in getting on the track of that. And the more mysterious my visit seems to him—and the fact that I have not disclosed to the police that I went up to Riversbrook and saw Sir Horace on the night of the tragedy is to his way of thinking very significant—the more reason is there for suspecting me of complicity in the crime."

When he turned to cross the room her eyes lingered on him and she glanced quickly at his face.

"I don't want to dwell on matters that must pain you—that must pain us both," he said slowly, "but it is necessary that you should be made acquainted with the danger that threatens me from this man. I am anxious to avoid anything in the nature of a public scandal—I am anxious quite as much if not more on your account than my own. But if this wretched man is allowed to go on trying to build up a case against me—and I must admit that he would probably obtain circumstantial evidence of a kind which would make some sort of a case for the prosecution—there is grave danger of everything coming out. If he went to the length of having me arrested and charged with the crime, there are bound to be some disclosures and the newspapers would make the most of them. It is impossible to foresee the exact nature of them, but I do not see how I could adopt any line of defence which would not hint at things that are best unrevealed. You yourself might be so ill-advised as to tell the whole story in the end. Of course, I would try to prevent you, and as far as the trial is concerned, I think I could use means to prevent you. But if the result was unfavourable— and knowing what eccentric things juries do, we must recognise the possibility of an unfavourable verdict—you might consider it advisable to disclose everything in the hope of having the conviction quashed by an appeal."

For the first time since she had sat down he looked at her, and as he caught her upward gaze he flushed.

"I would tell everything if you were arrested," she said, in a low voice.

"Ah, so I thought," he said, in a tone of disapproval. "The question now is what means can be adopted to prevent a catastrophe. I have thought earnestly about it, and as you are almost as much concerned in preventing public disclosures as I am, I desired to consult you before taking any definite course. It is this man Crewe who is the danger, and the question is how are we to stop him proceeding to extremes. One way is for me to see him and take him into my confidence—to explain fully to him what happened. He would not be satisfied with less than the full story. If I kept anything back his suspicions would remain; in fact, they would be strengthened. I would have to explain to him why and how I induced Sir Horace to return unexpectedly from Scotland on that fatal night, and what took place at Riversbrook. You will understand why I have hesitated to adopt that course. I would not suggest it to you now except that I see it would save you from the danger of something a great deal worse. Of course it would save me from the annoyance of being suspected of knowing something about the actual murder, but it is your interests that come first in the matter. It would be effective in putting an end to all our fears—all my fears. I would bind him to secrecy, of course. I do not ask you to come to a decision immediately, but I do ask you to think it over and let me know. I have been extremely reluctant to put this proposal before you, because I should hate carrying it out, because I should hate telling this man of things which are really no concern of anyone but ourselves. But I cannot disguise from myself that it would remove a greater danger. I believe the secret would be safe with him. I understand that in private life he is a gentleman, and that I would be safe in taking his word of honour. It would not be necessary for him to tell the police—still less to tell Miss Fewbanks."

"Is there no other way?" she asked. "Have you thought of any other way?"

"Yes. The only other way out that I have been able to find is for me to see Miss Fewbanks and ask her to withdraw the case from Crewe. I would not tell her everything—I would not bring you into it at all. But I could tell her that I had had an urgent matter to discuss with her father; that he came from Scotland to discuss it with me, and that after I left him he was murdered. I would tell her that it was quite impossible for me to disclose what the business was about, but that Crewe, having learnt that I had seen her father that night, was extremely suspicious. I would ask her to accept my word of honour that I had no knowledge of who killed her father, and to relieve me of the annoyance of the attentions of this man Crewe. I think she would agree to that proposal. That is the other way out, and from something which has happened this morning I am inclined to think that it is the better and quicker course to pursue."

She was thinking so deeply that she did not reply. At length she became conscious of a long silence.

"It is very good of you to ask my opinion—to consult with me at all. It is you that have everything at stake. I would like to do my best, but I think if you gave me time—Is there any great urgency? Two days at most is all I want."

"I cannot give you two days," he replied, with a sombre smile. "You must decide to-day—at once—otherwise it will be too late."

She looked at him with parted lips and alarm in her eyes.

"What do you mean?" she breathed. "What have you hidden? Is the danger immediate?"

"I think so. For some days past my movements have been dogged by a boy in Crewe's employ. Nearly a week ago I decided, after the worry and anxiety of this—this unhappy affair, to go away for a short trip. I thought a sea-voyage to America and back might do me good and fit me for my work again." He sighed unconsciously, and went on: "Crewe has become acquainted with my intended departure and has placed his own interpretation on it. He assumes that I am seeking safety in flight—that I have no intention of coming back to England. The result has been that the boy Crewe had set to watch my movements has been replaced by two men from Scotland Yard—one watching these chambers from the front, and the other from the rear." He walked across to the window and glanced quickly through the curtain. "Yes, they are still here."

She sprang from her seat and followed him to the window.

"Where are they?" she gasped. "Show them to me."

"There. Do not move the curtain or they will suspect we are watching them. Look a little to the left, by the lamp-post. The other you can catch a glimpse of if you look between those two trees."

"What does it mean? Why are they waiting?" she burst out. Her face had gone very pale, and her big dark eyes glared affrightedly from the window to her husband.

"Hush! I beg you not to lose your self-control; it is essential neither of us should lose our heads," he said, warningly.

She regained command of herself with an effort, and whispered, rather than spoke, with twitching lips;

"What does the presence of these men mean?"

"It means that Crewe has already communicated with Scotland Yard."

"And that you will be arrested for *his* murder?" Her trembling lips could hardly frame the words.

"I think so—it's almost certain. But apparently the warrant is not yet issued, or those men would come here and arrest me. But they are watching to prevent my escape—if I thought of escaping. We may yet have a few hours to arrange something, but you must come to a prompt decision."

"Tell me what to do, and I will do it. Oh, let me help you if I can. What is the best thing to do? To see Crewe?"

"No. I forbid you to see Crewe," he said harshly. "If we decide on that course I will see him myself."

"And you may be arrested the moment you go out of these chambers," she returned. "Oh, no, no; that is not a good plan—we have not the time. I will go to Mabel Fewbanks at once, and beg her, for all our sakes, not to allow this to go any further."

He shook his head.

"You must not sacrifice yourself," he said. "That would be foolish."

"I will not sacrifice myself. I would tell her just what you have told me—that her father came from Scotland to discuss an urgent matter with you, and that he was murdered after you left. I feel certain this man Crewe is going to extremes without her knowledge or consent, and that she will be the first to bury this awful thing when she learns that you have been implicated. Is not this the best thing to do?"

"It is," he reluctantly admitted. "But I do not wish you to be mixed up in it at all."

"I am not mixing myself up in it—I am too selfish for that. But I swear to you if you do not let me do this I will confess everything. I know Mabel Fewbanks, and I repeat, she is not aware of what this man Crewe has done. She would not—will not, permit it. I shall go down to Dellmere at once." Her face was pale, and her eyes glittered as she looked at her husband, but she spoke with unnatural self-possession. With feverish energy she pulled on a glove she had taken off when she entered, and buttoned it. "I will—I shall—arrive in time. In two hours—in three at most—you will hear from me."

She passed out into the outer office before her husband could reply, and closed the door behind her. Mr. Mattingford dashed to open the outer door of his room leading into the main staircase. He thought Mrs. Holymead looked strange as she passed him and descended the stairs, and he rubbed his hands gleefully. He came to the conclusion that she had come in for a cheque for £50 as an advance of her dress allowance, and that her request had been refused.

CHAPTER XXVII

She left her husband's chambers with her brain in a whirl, hardly knowing where she was going until she found herself held up with a stream of pedestrians at the island intersection of Waterloo Bridge and the Strand. She thought the policeman who was regulating the traffic eyed her curiously, and, more with the object of evading his eye than with any set plan in her mind, she stepped into an empty taxi-cab which was waiting to cross the street.

"Where to, ma'am?" asked the driver.

"Where to?" she repeated vacantly. With an effort of will she concentrated her thoughts on the task in front of her, and hastily added, "To Victoria, as quick as you can. No—wait—driver, first take me to the nearest bookstall."

The taxi-cab took her to a bookstall in the Strand, where she got out and purchased a railway guide. As the taxi-cab proceeded towards Victoria she hastily turned the pages to the trains for Dellmere. She had never been to Dellmere, but she had heard from Miss Fewbanks that her father's place was reached from a station called Horleydene, on the main line to Wennesden, and that though there were many through trains, comparatively few stopped at Horleydene. But she was unused to time-tables, and found it difficult to grasp the information she required. There was such a bewildering diversity of letters at the head of the lists of trains for that line, and so many reference notes on different pages to be looked up before it was possible to ascertain with any degree of certainty what trains stopped at Horleydene on week-days, that, in her shaken frame of mind, with the necessity for hurry haunting her, she became confused, and failed to comprehend the perplexing figures. She signalled to the driver to stop, and handed him the book.

"I cannot understand this time-table," she said, in an agitated way. "Would you find out for me, please, when the next train leaves Victoria for Horleydene?"

The driver consulted the time-table with a businesslike air.

"The next train leaves at 12.40," he informed her. "After that there isn't another one stopping there till 4.5."

Mrs. Holymead consulted her watch anxiously.

"It's almost half-past twelve now. Can you catch the 12.40?" she asked.

The driver looked dubious.

"I'll try, ma'am, but it'll take some doing. It depends whether I get a clear run at Trafalgar Square."

"Try, try!" she cried. "Catch it, and I will double your fare."

She caught the train with a few seconds to spare. She had a first-class compartment to herself, and as the train rushed out of London, and the grimy environs of the metropolis gradually gave place to green fields, she endeavoured to compose her mind and collect her thoughts for her coming interview with the daughter of the murdered man. But her mind was in such a distraught condition that she could think of no plan but to sacrifice herself in order to save her husband. With cold hands pressed against her hot forehead, she muttered again and again, as if offering up an invocation that gained force by repetition:

"I must save him. I will tell her everything."

The train ran into Horleydene shortly after two, and Mrs. Holymead was the only passenger who alighted at the lonely little wayside station which stood in a small wood in a solitude as profound as though it had been in the American prairie, instead of the heart of an English county. The only sign of life was a dilapidated vehicle with an elderly man in charge, which stood outside the station yard all day waiting for chance visitors.

"Cab, ma'am?" exclaimed the driver of this vehicle in an ingratiating voice, touching his hat.

"No, thank you," replied Mrs. Holymead. "I'll walk."

Miss Fewbanks was astonished when the parlourmaid announced the arrival of Mrs. Holymead. She hurried to the drawing-room to meet her visitor, but the warm greeting she offered her was checked by her astonishment at the ill and worn appearance of her beautiful friend.

"Please, don't," said the visitor, as she held up a warning hand to keep away a sisterly kiss. She looked at Miss Fewbanks with the air of a woman nerving herself for a desperate task, and said quickly: "I have dreadful things to tell you. You can never think of me again except with loathing—with horror."

The impression Miss Fewbanks received was that her visitor had taken leave of her senses. This impression was deepened by Mrs. Holymead's next remark.

"I want you to save my husband."

There was an awkward pause while Mrs. Holymead waited for a reply and Miss Fewbanks wondered what was the best thing to do.

"Say you will save him!" exclaimed Mrs. Holymead. "Do what you like with me, but save him."

"Don't you think, dear, you would be better if you had a rest and a little sleep?" said Miss Fewbanks. "I am sure you could sleep if you tried. Come upstairs and I'll make you so comfortable."

"You think I am mad," said the elder woman. "Would to God that I was."

"Come, dear," said Miss Fewbanks coaxingly. She turned to the door and prepared to lead the way upstairs.

"Sleep!" exclaimed Mrs. Holymead bitterly. "I have not had a peaceful sleep since your father was killed. I have been haunted day and night. I cannot sleep."

"I know it was a dreadful shock to you, but you must not take it so much to heart. You must see your doctor and do what he tells you. Mr. Holymead should send you away."

At the mention of her husband's name Mrs. Holymead came back to the thought that had been foremost in her mind.

"Will you save him?" she exclaimed.

"You know I will do anything I can for him," answered the girl gently. Her intention was to humour her visitor, for she was quite sure that Mr. Holymead was in no danger.

"Will you stop Mr. Crewe?"

"Stop Mr. Crewe?" Miss Fewbanks repeated the words in a tone that showed her interest had been awakened. "Stop him from what?"

"Stop him from arresting my husband."

"Do you mean to say that Mr. Crewe thinks Mr. Holymead had anything to do with the murder of my father?"

"If I tell you everything will you stop him? Oh, Mabel, darling, for the sake of the past—before I came on the scene to mar the lives of both of them—will you save him? It is I—not he—who should pay the penalty of this awful tragedy. Will you save him?"

"Tell me everything," said the girl firmly.

To the stricken wife there was a promise in the demand for light, and in broken phrases she poured out her story of shame and sorrow. With a feeling that everything was falling away from her the girl learnt from her visitor's disconnected story that there had been a liaison between her murdered father and her friend. Mr. Holymead had discovered it after Sir Horace had gone to Scotland and husband and wife were away in the country. He was at first distracted at finding that his lifelong friend had seduced his wife, then he made her promise not to see or communicate with Sir Horace until he made up his mind what course of action to take. Three days later he caught an evening train to London and told her he was not returning, but would write to her.

It crossed her mind that he had gone up to London to meet Sir Horace, and in her distress at the thought of what might happen when they met she consulted her cousin Gabrielle, who had always been in her confidence. Gabrielle had offered to go to Riversbrook to see if Sir Horace had returned from Scotland, or was expected back. Her train was delayed by an accident, and when she arrived at Riversbrook it was after half-past ten. She arrived a few minutes too late to prevent the tragedy. She found the front door open and the electric light burning in the hall. She went up the staircase and in the library she found Sir Horace, who was lying on the floor at the point of death. She tried to lift him to a sitting position, but with a convulsive gasp he died in her arms.

She laid him down and then looked hurriedly around the room with the object of removing any evidence of how or why the crime had been committed, her main thought being to save her friend from the shame of a public scandal. She picked up a revolver which was lying on the floor near Sir Horace, turned out the lights in the library and in the hall so that the house was in darkness, and then closed the hall door after her as she went out. But Mr. Crewe had discovered in some way that Mr. Holymead had visited Sir Horace that night. Only a week ago Gabrielle had gone to him and tried to put him off the track, but it was no use.

The wretched woman made a pathetic appeal for her husband's life. She deplored the sinfulness which had resulted in the tragedy. She took on herself the blame for it all. She had sent one man to his death, and her husband stood in peril of a shameful death on the gallows. But it was in the power of Mabel to save him. On her knees she pleaded for his life; she pleaded to be saved from the horror of sending her husband to the gallows. If Mabel's father could make his wishes known he too would plead for the life of the friend he had betrayed.

The door opened and the parlourmaid entered. Miss Fewbanks stepped quickly across the room so that she should not witness the distress of Mrs. Holymead. The servant handed her a card and waited for instructions. Miss Fewbanks looked at the card in an agony of indecision. Then she made up her mind firmly.

"Show him into my study," she whispered to the girl.

She returned to her visitor, who was sitting with her face buried in her hands.

"Mr. Crewe has just motored down," she said. "I will save your husband if I can."

CHAPTER XXVIII

She was conscious that the revelation that her father had been killed by Mr. Holymead was a less shock than the revelation that her father had dishonoured the great friendship of his life by seducing his friend's wife. Her father had been dead three months, and her grief had run its course. The shock caused by the discovery that he had been murdered had passed away, and she had begun to accept his violent death as part of her own experience of life. But the discovery that he had betrayed his best friend, in a way that a pure-minded woman regards as the most dishonourable way possible, was a fresh revelation to her of human infamy.

The knowledge that her father had been a man of immoral habits was not new to her. His predilection for fast women had long ago made it impossible for her to live in the same house with him for more than a week at a time. But that he had trampled in the mire the lifelong friendship of an honourable man for the sake of an ignoble passion revealed an unexpected depth of shame. That Mr. Holymead had killed him seemed almost a natural result of the situation. It was not that she felt that a just retribution had overtaken her father, but rather that she was glad his shameful conduct had come to an end. As she thought of her dead father—dead these three months—she gave a sigh of relief. The wretched guilty woman, who had shared with him the shame of his ignoble intrigue, had said that if her father could make his wishes known he would plead for the life of the friend he had dishonoured. But it was not her father's plea for the life of his friend that would have impressed her so much as a plea to bury the whole unsavoury scandal from the light. She had promised to save Mr. Holymead if she could, but that promise had sprung less from the spirit of mercy than from the desire to save her father's name from a scandal, which would hold him up to public obloquy.

She greeted Crewe with friendly warmth in spite of the feeling of oppression caused by the consciousness of the situation in front of her. He did not sit down again after greeting her, but stood with one hand resting on an inlaid chess table, with wonderful carved red and white Japanese chessmen ranged on each side, which he had been examining when she entered the room.

"I came down to make my report to you because I think my work is finished," he said.

"You have found out who killed my father?" she asked quietly.

Crewe had sufficient personal pride to feel a little hurt when he saw the calm way in which she accepted the result of his investigations, instead of congratulating him on his success in a difficult task.

"I think so," he said. "Before I tell you who it is you must prepare yourself for a great shock."

"I know who it is" she said—"Mr. Holymead."

There was no pretence about his astonishment.

"How on earth did you find out?"

She smiled a little at such a revelation of his appreciation of his own cleverness in having probed the mystery.

"I did not find it out," she said. "I had to be told."

"And who told you, Miss Fewbanks?" he asked. "Has he confessed to you? How long have you known it?"

"I have known it only a few minutes," she said. "Will you tell me how you got on the track and all you have done? I am greatly interested. You have been wonderfully clever to find out. I should never have guessed Mr. Holymead had anything to do with it—I should never have thought it possible. When you have finished I will tell you how I came to know. The story is extremely simple—and sordid."

The fact that the key of the mystery had been in her hands only a few minutes was a solace to Crewe, as it detracted but little from the story he had to tell of patient investigations extending over weeks.

He pieced together the story of the tragedy as he had unravelled it. Hill, he said, had conceived the idea of blackmailing her father after he had discovered the existence of some letters in a secret drawer of Sir Horace's desk. The fact that Sir Horace had kept these letters instead of destroying them as he had destroyed other letters of a somewhat similar kind showed that he was very much infatuated with the lady who wrote them. That lady, as doubtless Miss Fewbanks had guessed, was Mrs. Holymead—a lady with whom Sir Horace had been on very friendly terms before she married Mr. Holymead.

"What became of the letters?" asked Miss Fewbanks. "Have you got them?"

"I think they are destroyed," he said. "Mrs. Holymead removed them from the secret drawer the day after the discovery of the murder. She removed them when the police had charge of the house, and almost from under the eyes of Inspector Chippenfield. It was a daring plan and well carried out."

Miss Fewbanks heaved a sigh of relief on learning the fate of the letters. It had been her intention to endeavour to obtain them if they were in Crewe's possession, and destroy them.

Crewe explained that Hill was afraid to take the letters and then boldly blackmail Sir Horace. The butler conceived the plan of getting Birchill to break into the house. He did not take Birchill into his confidence with regard to the blackmailing scheme, but in order to induce Sir Horace to believe the burglar had stolen the letters he told Birchill to force open the desk, as he would probably find money or papers of value there. But in order to prevent Birchill getting the letters if he should happen to stumble across the secret drawer, Hill removed them the day before. His plan was to go to Riversbrook in the morning after the burglary, and after leaving open the secret drawer which had contained the letters, to report the burglary to the police. When Sir Horace came home unexpectedly Hill had just removed the letters and had them in his possession. Hill was greatly perturbed at his master's unexpected return, and had to get an opportunity to replace the letters in the secret drawer, but Sir Horace told him to go home, as he was not wanted till the morning. Hill went to that girl's flat in Westminster, and there saw Birchill. He told Birchill that Sir Horace had returned unexpectedly, but he urged Birchill to carry out the burglary as arranged, and assured him that as Sir Horace was a heavy sleeper there would be no risk if he waited until Sir Horace went to bed. Hill's position was that if the burglary was postponed Sir Horace might make the discovery that the letters had been stolen from the secret drawer. In that case Sir Horace would immediately suspect Hill, who, he knew, was an ex-convict. It was just possible that Sir Horace, before going to bed, would discover that the letters had been stolen—that is, if he went to bed before Birchill got into the place—but Hill had to take that risk.

It was the fact that the burglary Hill had arranged with Birchill took place on the night Sir Horace was killed that had given rise to the false clues which had misled the police. Crewe, as he himself modestly put it, was so fortunate as to get on the right track from the start. His suspicions were directed to Holymead when he saw the latter carrying away a walking-stick from Riversbrook after his visit of condolence to Miss Fewbanks. Crewe explained what tactics he had adopted to obtain a brief inspection of the stick in order to ascertain for his own satisfaction if it had belonged to Holymead. His suspicions against Holymead were strengthened when he discovered that the latter, when driving to his hotel on the night of the tragedy, had thrown away a glove which was the fellow of the one found by the police in Sir Horace's library.

"The next point to settle was whether Holymead had had anything to do with your father's sudden return from Scotland," said Crewe, continuing his story. "If that proved to be the case, and if evidence could be obtained on which to justify the conclusion that these two old friends had had a deadly quarrel, the circumstantial evidence against Holymead as the man who killed your father was very strong. I may say that before I went to Scotland I came across evidence of the estrangement of Holymead and his wife. Do you remember when you and Mrs. Holymead were leaving the court after the inquest that Mr. Holymead came up and spoke to you? He shook hands with you and was on the point of shaking hands with his wife as if she were a lady he had met casually. Then, on the night of the murder, the taxi-cab driver at Hyde Park Corner drove him to his house at Princes Gate, but was ordered to drive back and take him to Verney's Hotel. All this was interesting to me—doubly interesting in the light of the fact that Sir Horace had known Mrs. Holymead before her second marriage, and had paid her every attention.

"I went to Scotland and made inquiries at Craigleith Hall, where Sir Horace had been shooting. My object was to endeavour to obtain a clue to the reason for his sudden journey to London. The local police had made inquiries on this point on behalf of Scotland Yard, and had been unable to obtain any clue. No telegram had been received by Sir Horace, and he had sent none. Of course he had received some letters.

He had told none of the other members of the shooting party the object of his departure for London, but he had declared his intention of being back with them in less than a week. It had occurred to me when the crime was discovered that his missing pocket-book might not have been stolen by his murderer, but might have been lost in Scotland. I made inquiries in that direction and eventually found that the man who had attended to Sir Horace on the moors had the pocket-book. His story was that Sir Horace had lost it the day before his departure for London. He had taken off his coat owing to the heat on the moor, and the pocket-book had dropped out. He ascertained his loss before he left for London, and told this man Sanders where he thought the pocket-book had dropped out. Sanders was to look for it, and if he found it was to keep it until Sir Horace came back. He did find it, and after learning of your father's death was tempted to keep it, as it contained four five-pound notes. Sanders is an ignorant man, and can scarcely read. He professed to know nothing of the pocket-book when I questioned him, but I became suspicious of him, and laid a trap which he fell into. Then he handed me the pocket-book, which he had hidden on the moor, under a stone. In the pocket-book I found a letter from Holymead asking your father to come to London at once as there were to be two new appointments to the Court of Appeal, and that Sir Horace had an excellent chance of obtaining one if he came to London and used his influence with the Chancellor and the Chief Justice, who were still in town. The writer indicated that he was doing all that was possible in Sir Horace's interests, and that he would meet Sir Horace at Riversbrook at 9.30 on Wednesday night and let him know the exact position. There is nothing suspicious in such a letter, but my inquiries concerning new appointments to the Court of Appeal suggest that the statements in the letter are false.

"Now let us consider the conduct of Holymead and his wife since the night of the murder. His course of action has not been that of a man anxious to assist the police in the discovery of the murderer of his old friend. We have first of all his secrecy regarding his visit to Riversbrook that night; the fact of the visit being established by the stick, and the glove he left behind. We have the estrangement of husband and wife. We have Mrs. Holymead's visit to Riversbrook on the morning that the first details of the crime appeared in the newspapers. Ostensibly she came to see you and pay her condolences, but as she knew that you had been away in the country she ought to have telephoned to learn if you had come up to London. Instead of telephoning, she went to Riversbrook direct, and when she found you were not there she was admitted to the presence of my old friend, Inspector Chippenfield. He is an excellent police officer, but I do not think he is a match for a clever woman. And Mrs. Holymead is such a fine-looking woman that I feel sure Chippenfield was so impressed by her appearance that he forgot he was a police officer and remembered only that he was a man. She managed to get him out of the room long enough to enable her to open the secret drawer in Sir Horace's desk and remove the letters. No doubt Sir Horace had shown her where he kept them, as their neat little hiding place was an indication of the value he placed upon them. She was under the impression that no one knew about the letters, and her object in removing them was to prevent the police stumbling across them and so getting on the track of her husband. But as I have already told you, Hill knew about the letters, and on the night of the murder had them in his possession. On the night after the murder, while Inspector Chippenfield was making investigations at Riversbrook, Hill had managed to obtain the opportunity to put the letters back. He naturally thought that if the police discovered some of Sir Horace's private papers in his possession they would conclude that he had had something to do with the murder.

"The next point of any consequence is Holymead's defence of Birchill and the deliberate way in which he blackened your father's name while cross-examining Hill. If we regard Holymead's conduct solely from the standpoint of a barrister doing his best for his client his defence of Birchill is not so remarkable. But we have to remember that your father and Holymead had been life-long friends. His acceptance of the brief for the defence was in itself remarkable. The fee, as I took the trouble to find out, was not large; indeed, for a man of Holymead's commanding eminence at the bar it might be called a small one, and he should have returned the brief because the fee was inadequate. We have, therefore, two things to consider—his defence of the man charged with the murder of your father, and his readiness to do the work without regard to the monetary side of it. Much was said at the time in some of the papers about a barrister being a servant of the court and compelled by the etiquette of the bar to place his services at the disposal of anyone who needs them and is prepared to pay for them.

A great deal of nonsense has been said and written on that subject. A barrister can return a brief because for private reasons he does not wish to have anything to do with the case. It was Holymead's duty to do his best to get Birchill off whether he believed his client was guilty or innocent. Could Holymead have done his best for Birchill if he had believed that Birchill was the murderer of his lifelong friend? Would he have trusted himself to do his best? No, Holymead knew that Birchill was innocent; he knew who the guilty man was, and, knowing that, knowing that his action in defending the man charged with the murder of an old friend would weigh with the jury, he took up the case because he felt there was a moral obligation on him to get Birchill off. His conduct of the defence, during which he attacked the moral character of your father, was remarkable, coming from him— the friend of the dead man. As the action of defending counsel it was perfectly legitimate. It gave rise to some discussion in purely legal circles—whether Holymead did right or wrong in violating a long friendship in order to get his man off. The academic point is whether he ought to have violated his personal feelings for an old friend, or violated his duty to his client by doing something less than his best for him.

"Apart from the circumstantial and inferential evidence against Holymead, there is the fact that his wife knows that he committed the crime. Her acts point to that; her conduct throughout springs from the desire to shield him. Even the removal of the letters from the secret drawer was prompted more by the desire to save him than to save herself. Their discovery would not have been very serious for her, but it would have put the police on her husband's track. If I remember rightly, she asked you to keep her in touch with all the developments of the investigations of the police and myself. You told me that she was greatly interested in the fact that I did not believe Birchill was guilty, and particularly anxious to know if I suspected anyone. At Birchill's trial she did me the honour of watching me very closely. I was watching both her and her husband. When she discovered through her womanly intuition that I suspected her husband; that I was accumulating evidence against him; she sent round her friend, Mademoiselle Chiron, with some interesting information for me. An extremely clever young woman that—like all her countrywomen she is wonderfully sharp and quick, with a natural aptitude for intrigue.

Of course, the information she gave me was intended to mislead me—intended to show me that Mr. Holymead had nothing to do with the crime. But some of it was extremely interesting when it dealt with actual facts, and some of the facts were quite new to me. For instance, I had not previously known that a piece of a lady's handkerchief was found clenched in your father's right hand after he was dead. The police very kindly kept that information from me. Had they told me about it I might have been inclined to suspect Mrs. Holymead and to believe that her husband was trying to shield her. His conduct would bear that interpretation if she had happened to be guilty. The police unconsciously saved me from taking up that false scent.

"I have detained you a long time in dealing with these points, Miss Fewbanks, but I wanted to make everything clear. I have all but reached the end. Let us take in chronological order what happened on the night of the tragedy. We have your father's sudden return from Scotland. Hill was at Riversbrook when he arrived, and having the secret letters in his possession, was greatly perturbed by the unexpected return of Sir Horace. He went to Doris Fanning's flat in Westminster to see Birchill. In his absence Holymead arrived. It is probable that he took the Tube from Hyde Park Corner to Hampstead and walked to Riversbrook. He rang the bell; was admitted by your father, and, leaving his hat and stick in the hall-stand as he had often done before, the two went upstairs to the library. There was an angry interview, Holymead accusing your father of having wronged him and demanding satisfaction. My own opinion is that there was an irregular sort of duel. Each of them fired one shot. It is quite conceivable that Holymead, in spite of his mission, being that of revenge, gave your father a fair chance for his life. A man in Holymead's position would probably feel indifferent whether he killed the man who had ruined his home or was killed by him. But whereas your father's shot missed by a few inches, Holymead's inflicted a fatal wound. When he saw your father fall and realised what he had done, the instinct of self-preservation asserted itself. He grabbed at the gloves he had taken off, but in his hurry dropped one on the floor. He ran downstairs, took his hat from the hall-stand, but left his stick. Then he rushed out of the house, leaving the front door open. He made his way back to Hampstead Tube station, got out at Hyde Park and took a cab to his hotel.

"Within a few minutes of Holymead's departure from Riversbrook the Frenchwoman arrived. She may have passed Holymead in Tanton Gardens, or Holymead, when he saw her approaching, may have hidden inside the gateway of a neighbouring house. She had come up from the country on learning that Holymead had come to London. She caught the next train, but unfortunately it was late on arriving at Victoria owing to a slight accident to the engine. I take it that she was sent by Mrs. Holymead to follow her husband if possible and see if he had any designs on Sir Horace. She took a cab as far as the Spaniards Inn and then got out, and walked to Riversbrook. When she arrived at the house she found the front door open and the lights burning. There was no answer to her ring and she entered the house and crept upstairs. Opening the library door, she saw your father lying on the floor. She endeavoured to raise him to a sitting posture, but it was too late to do anything for him. With a convulsive movement he grasped at the handkerchief she was holding in one hand, and a corner of it was torn off and remained in his hand. When she saw he had breathed his last she laid him down on the floor. Since she had been too late to prevent the crime, the next best thing in the interests of Mrs. Holymead was to remove traces of Holymead's guilt. She picked up the revolver, which she thought belonged to Holymead, turned off the light in the room, went downstairs, turned off the light in the hall, and closed the hall door as she went out.

"She behaved with remarkable courage and coolness, but she overlooked the glove in the room of the tragedy, and Holymead's stick in the hall-stand. Later in the night we have Birchill's entry into the house, his alarm at finding your father had been killed, and his return to the flat where Hill was waiting for him."

When Crewe had finished he looked at the girl. She had followed his statement with breathless interest.

"You have been wonderfully clever," she said. "It is perfectly marvellous."

Crewe's eyes had wandered to the inlaid chess-table and the Japanese chessmen set in prim rows on either side. Mechanically he began to arrange a problem on the board. His interest in the famous murder mystery seemed to have evaporated.

"I was very fortunate," he said absently, in reply to Miss Fewbanks. "Everything seemed to come right for me."

"You made everything come right," she replied. "I do not know how to thank you for giving so much of your time to unravelling the mystery."

"It was fascinating while it lasted," he replied, his fingers still busy with the chessmen. "Of course, I am pleased with my success, but in a way I am sorry the work has come to an end. I thought that the knowledge that Holymead was the guilty man would come as a great shock to you. But I am glad you are able to take it so well."

"A few minutes before you arrived I learned that it was Mr. Holymead. But what has been more of a shock to me, Mr. Crewe, is the discovery that my father had ruined his home. Oh, Mr. Crewe, it is terrible for me to have to hold my dead father up to judgment, but it is more terrible still to know that he was not faithful even to his lifelong friendship with Mr. Holymead."

"Your nerves are unstrung," he said. "You want rest and quiet— you want a long sea voyage."

"Yes, I want to forget," she said. "But there are others who want to forget, too. Cannot we bury the whole thing in forgetfulness?"

Crewe's growing interest in the chessboard and his problem suddenly vanished. His eyes became instantly riveted on her face in a keen, questioning look.

"What is it to me or you that Mr. Holymead should be publicly proved guilty of this terrible thing?" she went on, passionately. "Why drag into the light my father's conduct in order to make a day's sensation for the newspapers? For his sake, what better thing could I do than let his memory rest?"

"Do you mean that Holymead should be allowed to go free?" he asked, in astonishment.

"Yes."

"I'm extremely sorry," he said slowly.

"Won't you let it all drop?" she pleaded.

"I could not take upon myself the responsibility of condoning such a crime—the responsibility of judging between your father and his murderer," he said solemnly. "But even if I could it is too late to think of doing so. There is already a warrant out for Holymead's arrest"

CHAPTER XXIX

The newspapers made a sensation out of the announcement of Holymead's arrest on a charge of having murdered Sir Horace Fewbanks. They declared that the arrest of the eminent K.C. on a capital charge would come as a surprising development of the Riversbrook case. It would cause a shock to his many friends, and especially to those who knew what a close friendship had existed between the arrested man and the dead judge. The papers expatiated on the fact that Holymead had appeared for the defence when Frederick Birchill had been tried for the murder. As the public would remember, Birchill had been acquitted owing to the great ability with which his defence was conducted.

It was somewhat remarkable, said the *Daily Record*, that in his speech for the defence Holymead had attempted to throw suspicion on one of the witnesses for the prosecution. The journal hinted that it was the result of something which Counsel for the defence had let drop at this trial that Inspector Chippenfield had picked up the clue which had led to Holymead's arrest. The papers had very little information to give the public about this new development of the Fewbanks mystery, but they boldly declared that some startling revelations were expected when the case came before the court.

In the absence of interesting facts apropos of the arrest of the distinguished K.C., some of the papers published summaries of his legal career, and the more famous cases with which he had been connected. These summaries would have been equally suitable to an announcement that Mr. Holymead had been promoted to the peerage or that he had been run over by a London bus.

There were people who declared without knowing anything about the evidence the police had in their possession that in arresting the famous barrister the police had made a far worse blunder than in arresting Birchill. It was even hinted that the arrest of the man who had got Birchill off was an expression of the police desire for revenge. To these people the acquittal of Holymead was a foregone conclusion. The man who had saved Birchill's life by his brilliant forensic abilities was not likely to fail when his own life was at stake.

But when the case came before the police court and the police produced their evidence, it was seen that there was a strong case against the prisoner. The whispers as to the circumstances under which the prisoner had taken the life of a friend of many years appealed to a sentimental public. These whispers concerned the discovery by the prisoner that his friend had seduced his beautiful wife. In the police court proceedings there were no disclosures under this head, but the thing was hinted at. In view of the legal eminence of the prisoner and the fear of the police that he would prove too much for any police officer who might take charge of the prosecution, the Direction of Public Prosecutions sent Mr. Walters, K.C., to appear at the police court. The prisoner was represented by Mr. Lethbridge, K.C., an eminent barrister to whom the prisoner had been opposed in many civil cases.

Inspector Chippenfield, who realised that the important position the prisoner occupied at the bar added to the importance of the officer who had arrested him, gave evidence as to the arrest of the prisoner at his chambers in the Middle Temple. With a generous feeling, which was possibly due to the fact that he was entitled to none of the credit of collecting the evidence against the prisoner, Inspector Chippenfield allowed Detective Rolfe a subordinate share in the glory that hung round the arrest by volunteering the information in the witness-box that when making the arrest he was accompanied by that officer. He declared that the prisoner made no remark when arrested and did not seem surprised. Mr. Walters produced a left-hand glove and witness duly identified it as the glove which he found in the room in which the murder took place.

Inspector Seldon gave formal evidence of the discovery of the body of Sir Horace Fewbanks on the 19th of August. Dr. Slingsby repeated the evidence that he had given at the trial of Birchill as to the cause of death, and was again professionally indefinite as to the length of time the victim had been dead when he saw the body. Thomas Taylor, taxi-cab driver, gave evidence as to driving the prisoner from Hyde Park Corner on the night of the 18th of August and the finding of the glove.

Crewe went into the witness-box and swore that on the second day after the discovery of the murder he was present at Riversbrook when the prisoner visited the house and saw Miss Fewbanks. When the prisoner arrived he was not carrying a walking-stick, but he had one in his hand when he took his departure from the house. Witness followed the prisoner, and a boy who collided with the prisoner knocked the stick out of his hands. Witness picked up the stick and inspected it. He identified the stick produced in court as the one which the prisoner had been carrying on that day.

The most difficult, and most important witness, as far as new evidence was concerned was Alexander Saunders, a big, broad red-faced Scotchman, whose firm grasp on the tam-o'-shanter he held in his hand seemed to indicate a fear that all the pickpockets in London had designs on it. With great difficulty he was made to understand his part in the witness-box, and some of the questions had to be repeated several times before he could grasp their meaning. Mr. Lethbridge humorously suggested that his learned friend should have provided an interpreter so that his pure English might be translated into Lowland Scotch.

By slow degrees Saunders was able to explain how he had found the pocket-book which Sir Horace Fewbanks had lost while shooting at Craigleith Hall. Witness identified a letter produced as having been in the pocket-book when he found it. The letter, which had been written by the prisoner to Sir Horace Fewbanks, urged Sir Horace to return to London at once, as if he did so there was a good possibility of his obtaining promotion to the Court of Appeal. The writer promised to do all he could in the matter, and to call on Sir Horace at Riversbrook as soon as he returned from Scotland.

Percival Chambers, an elderly well-dressed man with a grey beard, and wearing glasses, who was secretary of the Master of Rolls, swore that he knew of no prospective vacancies on the Court of Appeal Bench. Were any vacancies of the kind in view he believed he would be aware of them.

This closed the case for the police, and Mr. Lethbridge immediately asked for the discharge of the prisoner on the ground that there was no case to go before a jury. The magistrate shook his head, and merely asked Mr. Lethbridge if he intended to reserve his defence.

Mr. Lethbridge replied with a nod, and the accused was formally committed for trial at the next sittings at the Old Bailey.

The newspapers reported at great length the evidence given in the police court, and their reports were eagerly read by a sensation-loving public. Even those people who, when Holymead's arrest was announced, had ridiculed the idea of a man like Holymead murdering a lifelong friend, had to admit that the police had collected some damaging evidence. Those people who at the time of the arrest had prided themselves on possessing an open mind as to the guilt of the famous barrister, confessed after reading the police court evidence that there could be little doubt of his guilt. The only thing that was missing from the police court proceedings was the production of a motive for the crime, but it was whispered that there would be some interesting revelations on this point when the prisoner was tried at the Old Bailey.

Fortunately he had not long to wait for his trial, as the next sittings of the Central Criminal Court had previously been fixed a week ahead of the date of his commitment. That week was full of anxiety for Mr. Lethbridge, for he realised that he had a poor case. What increased his anxiety was the fact that Holymead insisted on the defence being conducted on the lines he laid down. It was a new thing in Lethbridge's experience to accept such instructions from a prisoner, but Holymead had threatened to dispense with all assistance unless his instructions were carried out. He was particularly anxious that his wife's name should be kept out of court as much as possible. Lethbridge had pointed out to him that the prosecution would be sure to drag it in at the trial in suggesting a motive for the murder, and that for the purposes of the defence it was best to have a full and frank disclosure of everything so that an appeal could be made to the jury's feelings. Holymead's beautiful wife, who was almost distracted by her husband's position, implored his Counsel to allow her to go into the box and make a confession. But that course did not commend itself to Lethbridge, who realised that she would make an extremely bad witness and would but help to put the rope round her husband's neck. He put her off by declaring that there was a good prospect of her husband being acquitted, but that if the verdict unfortunately went against him her confession would have more weight in saving him, when the appeal against the verdict was heard.

It amazed Lethbridge to find that the prisoner expressed the view that Birchill had committed the murder. This view was based on his contention that Sir Horace Fewbanks was alive when he (Holymead) left him about ten o'clock. The interview between them had been an angry one, but Holymead persisted in asserting that he had not shot his former friend. He declared that he had not taken a revolver with him when he went to Riversbrook.

Lethbridge was one of those barristers who believe that a knowledge of the guilt of a client handicapped Counsel in defending him. He had his private opinion as to the result of the angry interview between Holymead and Sir Horace Fewbanks, but he preferred that Holymead should protest his innocence even to him. That made it easier for him to make a stirring appeal to the jury than it would have been if his client had fully confessed to him. His private opinion as to the author of the crime was strengthened by Holymead's admission that Birchill had not confessed to him or to his solicitor at the time of his trial that he had shot Sir Horace Fewbanks. He was astonished that Holymead had taken up Birchill's defence, but Holymead's explanation was the somewhat extraordinary one that the man who had killed the seducer of his wife had done him a service by solving a problem that had seemed insoluble without a public scandal. There was no doubt that although Sir Horace Fewbanks was in his grave, Holymead's hatred of him for his betrayal of his wife burned as strongly as when he had made the discovery that wrecked his home life. Neither death nor time could dim the impression, nor lessen his hatred for the dead man who had once been his closest friend.

Lethbridge, feeling that it was his duty as Counsel for the prisoner to try every avenue which might help to an acquittal, asked Mr. Tomlinson, the solicitor who was instructing him in the case, to find Birchill and bring him to his chambers. Birchill was found and kept an appointment. Lethbridge explained to him that he had nothing further to fear from the police with regard to the murder of Sir Horace Fewbanks. Having been acquitted on this charge he could not be tried on it again, no matter what discoveries were made. He could not even be tried for perjury, as he had not gone into the witness-box. Having allowed these facts to sink home, he delicately suggested to Birchill that he ought to come forward as a witness for the defence of

Holymead—he ought to do his best to try and save the life of the man who had saved his life.

"What do you want me to swear?" asked Birchill, in a tone which indicated that although he did not object to committing perjury, he wanted to know how far he was to go.

"Well, that Sir Horace Fewbanks was alive when you went to Riversbrook," suggested Lethbridge.

"But I tell you he was dead," protested Birchill. He seemed to think that reviving a dead man was beyond even the power of perjury.

"That was your original story, I know," agreed Lethbridge suavely. "But as you were not put into the witness-box to swear it you can alter it without fear of any consequences."

"You want me to swear that he was alive?" said Birchill, meditatively.

"If you can conscientiously do so," replied Lethbridge.

"That he was alive when I left Riversbrook?" asked Birchill.

"Well, not necessarily that," said Lethbridge.

Birchill sprang up in alarm.

"Good God, do you want me to swear that I killed him?" he demanded.

Lethbridge endeavoured to explain that he would have nothing to fear from such a confession in the witness-box, but Birchill would listen to no further explanations. He felt that he was in dangerous company, and that his safety depended on getting out of the room.

"You've made a mistake," he said, as he reached the door. "If you want a witness of that kind you ought to look for him in Colney Hatch."

CHAPTER XXX

The impending trial of Holymead produced almost as much excitement in staid legal circles as it did among the general public. It was rumoured that there was a difficulty in obtaining a judge to preside at the trial, as they all objected to being placed in the position of trying a man who was well-known to them and with whom most of them had been on friendly terms. There was a great deal of sympathy for the prisoner among the judges. Of course, they could not admit that any man had the right to take the law into his own hands, but they realised that if any wrong done to an individual could justify this course it was the wrong Sir Horace Fewbanks had done to an old friend.

When it became known that Mr. Justice Hodson was to preside at the Old Bailey during the trial of Holymead, legal rumour concerned itself with statements to the effect that there was now a difficulty in obtaining a K.C. to undertake the prosecution. When it was discovered that Mr. Walters, K.C., was to conduct the prosecution, it was whispered that he had asked to be relieved of the work and had even waited on the Attorney-General in the matter, but that the latter had told him that he must put his personal feelings aside and act in accordance with that high sense of duty he had always shown in his professional career.

In Newgate Street a long queue of people waited for admission to Old Bailey on the day the trial was to begin. They were inspected by two fat policemen to decide whether they appeared respectable enough to be entitled to a free seat at the entertainment in Number One Court. When the doors opened at 10.15 a.m. the first batch of them were admitted, but on reaching the top of the stairs, where they were inspected by a sergeant, they were informed that all the seats in the gallery of Number One Court had been filled, but that he would graciously permit them to go to Numbers Two, Three, Four, or Five

Courts. Those who were not satisfied with this generosity could get out the way they had come in and be quick about it. What the sergeant did not explain was that so many people with social influence had applied to the presiding judge for permission to be present at the trial that it had been found necessary to reserve the gallery for them as well as most of the seats in the body of the court. Fashionably-dressed ladies and well-groomed men drove up to the main entrance of the Old Bailey in motors and taxi-cabs. The scene was as busy as the scene outside a West End theatre on a first night. The services of several policemen were necessary to regulate the arrival and departure of taxi-cabs and motor-cars and to keep back the staring mob of disappointed people who had been refused admission to the court by the fat sergeant, but were determined to see as much as they could before they went away. Elderly ladies and young ladies were assisted from smart motor-cars by their escorts, and greeted their friends with feminine fervour. Some of the younger ones exchanged whispered regrets, as they swept into the court, that such a fine-looking man as Holymead should have got himself into such a terrible predicament.

The legal profession was numerously represented among the spectators in the body of the court. So many distinguished members of the profession had applied for tickets of admission that there was little room for members of the junior bar. It was many years since a trial had created so much interest in legal circles. When Mr. Justice Hodson entered the court, followed by no fewer than eight of the Sheriffs of London, those present in the court rose. The members of the profession bowed slowly in the direction of His Honour. The prisoner was brought into the dock from below, and took the seat that was given to him beside one of the two warders who remained in the dock with him. He looked a little careworn, as though with sleepless nights, but his strong, clean-shaven face was as resolute as ever, and betrayed nothing of the mental agony which he endured. His keen dark eyes glanced quietly through the court, and though many members of the bar smiled at him when they thought they had caught his eye, he gave no smile in return. As he looked at Mr. Justice Hodson, the distinguished judge inclined his head to what was almost a nod of recognition, but the prisoner looked calmly at the judge as though he had never seen him before and had never been inside a court in his life till then.

Among those persons standing in the body of the court were Crewe and Inspector Chippenfield and Detective Rolfe. Inspector Chippenfield displayed so much friendliness to Crewe as he drew his attention to the number of celebrities in court that it was evident he had buried for the time being his professional enmity. This was because Crewe had allowed him to appropriate some of the credit of unravelling Holymead's connection with the crime. As the jury were being sworn in Crewe and Chippenfield made their way out of court into the corridor. As they were to be called as witnesses they would not be allowed in court until after they had given their evidence.

Mr. Walters in his opening address paid tribute to the exceptional circumstances of the case by some slight show of nervousness. Several times he insisted that the case was what he termed unique. The prisoner in the dock was a man who by his distinguished abilities had won for himself a leading position at the bar, and had been honoured and respected by all who knew him. It was not the first occasion that a member of the legal profession had been placed on trial on a capital charge, though he was glad to say, for the honour of the profession, that cases of the kind were extremely rare. But what made the case unique was that it was not the first trial in connection with the murder of Sir Horace Fewbanks, and that at the first trial when a man named Frederick Birchill had been placed in the dock, the prisoner now before the court had appeared as defending Counsel, and by his brilliant conduct of the defence had materially contributed to the verdict of acquittal which had been brought in by the jury. Some evidence would be placed before the jury about the first trial and the conduct of the defence. He ventured to assert that the jury would find in this evidence some damaging facts against the prisoner—that they would find a clear indication that the prisoner had defended Birchill because he knew himself to be guilty of this murder, and felt an obligation on him to place his legal knowledge and forensic powers at the disposal of a man whom he knew to be innocent. At the former trial the prisoner, as Counsel for the defence, had attempted to throw suspicion on a man named Hill, who had been butler to the late Sir Horace Fewbanks, but evidence would be placed before the jury to show that in doing so the prisoner had been smitten by some pangs of conscience at casting suspicion on a man who he knew was not guilty.

It was not incumbent on the prosecution to prove a motive for the murder, continued Mr. Walters, though where the motive was plainly proved the case against the prisoner was naturally strengthened. In this case there was no doubt about the motive, but the extent of the evidence to be placed before the jury under that head would depend upon the defence. The prosecution would submit some evidence on the point, but the full story could only be told if the defence placed the wife of the prisoner in the witness-box. It was impossible for the prosecution to call her as a witness, as English law prevented a wife giving evidence against her husband. She could, however, give evidence in favour of her husband, and doubtless the defence would take full advantage of the privilege of calling her.

The evidence which he intended to call would show that for years past very friendly relations had existed between the prisoner and the murdered man. They had been at Cambridge together and had studied law together in chambers. Their friendship continued after their marriages. The prisoner had married a second time, and at that time Sir Horace Fewbanks was a widower. Sir Horace Fewbanks was what was known as a ladies' man, and at the previous trial prisoner, as defending Counsel, had tried to bring out that Sir Horace was a man of immoral reputation among women. There was no doubt that the prisoner, during Sir Horace's absence in Scotland, became convinced that Sir Horace had been paying attention to his wife. There was no doubt that, being a man of a jealous disposition, his suspicions went beyond that. At any rate he wrote a letter to Sir Horace at Craigleith Hall, where the latter was shooting, asking him to come to London at once. In order to induce Sir Horace to return, and in order not to arouse suspicion as to his real object, he concocted a story about a vacancy in the Court of Appeal Bench to which, it appeared, Sir Horace Fewbanks desired to be appointed. In this letter, which would be produced in evidence, the prisoner pretended to be working in Sir Horace's interests, and offered to meet him on the night of his return at Riversbrook and let him know fully how matters stood. Sir Horace apparently wrote to the prisoner making an appointment with him for the night of the 18th of August. The prisoner kept that appointment, charged Sir Horace with carrying on an intrigue with his wife, and then shot him.

"That is the case for the prosecution which I will endeavour to establish to the satisfaction of the jury," said Mr. Walters, in concluding his speech, "Of course it is impossible to produce direct evidence of the actual shooting. But I will produce a silent but indisputable witness in the form of a glove which belonged to the prisoner, that he was present in the room in which the murder took place. I will produce evidence to show that the prisoner left his stick behind in the hat-stand in the hall on the night of the murder. These things prove conclusively that he left Riversbrook in a state of considerable excitement. The fact that after the murder was discovered he kept hidden in his own breast the knowledge that he had been there on that night, instead of going to the police and, in the endeavour to assist them to detect the murderer of his lifelong friend, informing them that he had called on Sir Horace, shows conclusively that he went there on a mission on which he dared not throw the light of day."

Those witnesses who had given evidence at the police court were called and repeated their statements. Inspector Seldon was closely cross-examined by Mr. Lethbridge as to the way in which the dead body was dressed when he discovered it. He declared that Sir Horace had been wearing a light lounge suit of grey colour, a silk shirt, wing collar and black bow tie. Dr. Slingsby's cross-examination was directed to ascertaining as near as possible the time when the murder was committed, but this was a point on which the witness allowed himself to be irritatingly indefinite. The murder might have taken place three or four hours before midnight on the 18th of August, and on the other hand it might have taken place any time up to three or four hours after midnight.

Hill, who had not been available as a witness at the police court—being then on the way back from America in response to a cablegram from Crewe—reappeared as a witness. He looked much more at ease in the witness-box than on the occasion when he gave evidence against Birchill. He had fully recovered from his terror of being arrested for the murder, and obviously had much satisfaction in giving evidence against the man who, according to his impression, had tried to bring the crime home to him.

He gave evidence as to the unexpected return of his master from Scotland on the 18th of August, and also in regard to the relations between his master and Mrs. Holymead. On several occasions he had seen his master kiss Mrs. Holymead, and once he had heard the door of the room in which they were together being locked.

Two new witnesses were called to testify to the suggestion of the prosecution that illicit relations had existed between Sir Horace Fewbanks and Mrs. Holymead. These were Philip Williams, who had been the dead man's chauffeur, and Dorothy Mason, who had been housemaid at Riversbrook. The chauffeur gave evidence as to meeting Mrs. Holymead's car at various places in the country. He formed the opinion from the first that these meetings between Sir Horace and the lady were not accidental.

The last of the prosecution's witnesses was the legal shorthand writer who had taken the official report of the trial of Birchill. In response to the request of Mr. Walters, he read from his notebook the final passage in the opening address delivered by the prisoner at that trial as defending Counsel: "'It is my duty to convince you that my client is not guilty, or, in other words, to convince you that the murder was committed before he reached the house. It is only with the greatest reluctance that I take upon myself the responsibility of pointing an accusing finger at another man. In crimes of this kind you cannot expect to get anything but circumstantial evidence. But there are degrees of circumstantial evidence, and my duty to my client lays upon me the obligation of pointing out to you that there is one person against whom the existing circumstantial evidence is stronger than it is against my client.'"

Mr. Lethbridge was unexpectedly brief in his opening address. He ridiculed the idea that a man like the prisoner, trained in the atmosphere of the law, would take the law into his own hands in seeking revenge for a wrong that had been done to him. According to the prosecution the prisoner had calmly and deliberately carried out this murder. He had sent a letter to Sir Horace Fewbanks with the object of inducing him to return to London, and had subsequently gone to Riversbrook and shot the man who had been his lifelong friend. Could anything be more improbable than to suppose that a man of the accused's training, intellect, and force of character, would be swayed by a gust of passion into committing such a dreadful crime like an immature ignorant youth of unbalanced temperament? The discovery that his wife and his friend were carrying on an intrigue would be more likely to fill him with disgust than inspire him with murderous rage. He would not deny that accused had gone up to Riversbrook a few hours after Sir Horace Fewbanks returned from Scotland; he would admit that when the accused sought this interview he knew that his quondam friend had done him the greatest wrong one man could do another; but he emphatically denied that the prisoner killed Sir Horace Fewbanks or threatened to take his life.

His learned friend had asked why had not the prisoner gone to the police after the murder was discovered and told them that he had seen Sir Horace at Riversbrook that night. The answer to that was clear and emphatic. He did not want to take the police into his confidence with regard to the relations that had existed between his wife and the dead man. He wanted to save his wife's name from scandal. Was not that a natural impulse for a high-minded man? The prisoner had believed that in due course the police would discover the actual murderer, and that in the meantime the scandal which threatened his wife's name would be buried with the man who had wronged her. If the prisoner could have prevented it his wife's name would not have been dragged into this case even for the purpose of saving himself from injustice. But the prosecution, in order to establish a motive for the crime, had dragged this scandal into light. He did not blame the prosecution in the least for that. In fact he was grateful to his learned friend for doing so, for it had released him from a promise extracted from him by the prisoner not to make any use of the matter in his conduct of the case. The defence was that, although the accused man had gone to Riversbrook on the night of the 18th of August to accuse Sir Horace Fewbanks of base treachery, he went there unarmed, and with no intention of committing violence. No threats were used and no shot was fired during the interview. And in proof of the latter contention he intended to call witnesses to prove that Sir Horace Fewbanks was alive after the prisoner had left the house.

The name of Daniel Kemp was loudly called by the ushers, and when Kemp crossed the court on the way to the witness-box, Chippenfield and Crewe, who had returned to the court after giving their evidence, looked at one another.

"He's a dead man," whispered Chippenfield, nodding his head towards the prisoner, "if this is a sample of their witnesses."

Kemp had brushed himself up for his appearance in the witness-box. He wore a new ready-made tweed suit; his thick neck was encased in a white linen collar which he kept fingering with one hand as though trying to loosen it for his greater comfort; and his hair had been plastered flat on his head with plenty of cold water. His red and scratched chin further indicated that he had taken considerable pains with a razor to improve his personal appearance in keeping with his unwonted part of a respectable witness in a place which knew a more sinister side of him. As he stood in the witness-box, awkwardly avoiding the significant glances that the Scotland Yard men and the police cast at him, he appeared to be more nervous and anxious than he usually was when in the dock. But Crewe, who was watching him closely, was struck by the look of dog-like devotion he hurriedly cast at the weary face of the man in the dock before he commenced to give his evidence.

He told the court a remarkable story. He declared that Birchill had told him on the 16th of August that he had a job on at Riversbrook, and had asked him to join him in it. When Birchill explained the details witness declined to have a hand in it. He did not like these put-up jobs.

Mr. Lethbridge interposed to explain to any particularly unsophisticated jurymen that "a put-up job" meant a burglary that had been arranged with the connivance of a servant in the house to be broken into.

Kemp declared that the reason he had declined to have anything to do with the project to burgle Riversbrook was that he felt sure Hill would squeak if the police threatened him when they came to investigate the burglary. He happened to be at Hampstead on the evening of the 18th of August and he took a walk along Tanton Gardens to have another look at the place which Birchill was to break into. It had occurred to him that things might not be square, and that Hill might have laid a trap for Birchill. That was about 9.30 p.m. He was just able to catch a glimpse of the house through the plantation in front of it. The mansion appeared all in darkness, but while he looked he was surprised to see a light appear in the upper portion of the house which was visible from the road. He went through the carriage gates with the intention of getting a closer view of the house. As he walked along he heard a quick footstep on the gravel walk behind him, and he slipped into the plantation. Looking out from behind a tree he could discern the figure of a man walking quickly towards the house. As he drew near him the man paused, struck a match and looked at his watch, and he saw that it was Mr. Holymead. Witness's suspicions in regard to a trap having been laid for Birchill were strengthened, and he decided to ascertain what was in the wind. He crept through the plantation to the edge of the garden in front of the house. From there he could hear voices in a room upstairs. He tried to make out what was being said, but he was too far away for that. In about half an hour the voices stopped, and a minute later a man came out of the house and walked down the path through the garden, and entered the carriage drive close to where witness was concealed in the plantation. As he passed him witness saw that it was Mr. Holymead.

About five minutes afterwards the window upstairs in the room where the voices had come from was opened, and Sir Horace Fewbanks leaned out and looked at the sky as if to ascertain what sort of a night it was. He was quite certain that it was Sir Horace Fewbanks. He was well acquainted with that gentleman's features, having been sentenced by him three years ago. Sir Horace seemed quite calm and collected. Witness was so surprised to see him, after having been told by Birchill that he was in Scotland, that he did not take his eyes off him during the two or three minutes that he remained at the window, breathing the night air. Sir Horace was fully dressed. He had on a light tweed suit, and he was wearing a soft shirt of a light colour, with a stiff collar, and a small black bow tie. When Sir Horace closed the window witness jumped over the fence back into the wood and made his way to the Hampstead Tube station with the intention of warning Birchill that Sir Horace Fewbanks was at home. He waited at the station over an hour, and as he did not see Birchill he then made his way home. During the time he was in the garden at Riversbrook listening to the voices, he heard no sound of a shot. He was certain that no shot had been fired inside the house from the time the prisoner entered the house until he left. Had a shot been fired witness could not have failed to hear it.

There could be no doubt that the effect produced in court by the evidence of the witness was extremely favourable to the prisoner. Kemp had told a plain, straightforward story. The fact that he had shown no reluctance in disclosing in his evidence that he was a criminal and the associate of criminals seemed to add to the credibility of his evidence. It was felt that he would not have come to court to swear falsely on behalf of a man who was so far removed from the class to which he belonged.

While Kemp was giving his evidence, Crewe had despatched a messenger to his chambers in Holborn for Joe. When the boy returned with the messenger Kemp was still in the witness-box, undergoing an examination at the hands of the judge. Sir Henry Hodson seemed to have been impressed by the witness's story, for he asked Kemp a number of questions, and entered his answers in his notebook.

"Joe," whispered Crewe, as the boy stole noiselessly behind him, "look at that man in the witness-box. Have you ever seen him before?"

"Rayther, guv'nor!" whispered the boy in reply. "Why, it's 'im who tried to frighten me in the loft if I didn't promise to give up watching Mr. Holymead."

"You are quite certain, Joe?"

"Certain sure, guv'nor. There ain't no charnst of me mistaking a man like that."

Crewe listened intently to Kemp's evidence, and he watched the man's face as he swore that he had seen Sir Horace Fewbanks leaning out of the window after Holymead had left the house. He hastily took out a notebook, scribbled a few lines on one of the leaves, tore it out, and beckoned to a court usher.

"Take that to Mr. Walters," he whispered.

The man did so. Mr. Walters opened the note, adjusted his glasses and read it. He started with surprise, read the note through again, then turned round as though in search of the writer. When he saw Crewe he raised his eyebrows interrogatively, and the detective nodded emphatically.

Mr. Lethbridge sat down, having finished his examination of Kemp. Mr. Walters, with another glance at Crewe's note, rose slowly in his place.

"I ask Your Honour that I may be allowed to defer until the morning my cross-examination of this witness," he said. "I am, of course, in Your Honour's hands in this matter, but I can assure Your Honour that it is desirable—highly desirable—in the interests of justice that the cross-examination of the witness should be postponed."

"I protest, Your Honour, against the cross-examination of the witness being deferred," said Mr. Lethbridge. "There is no justification of it."

"I would urge Your Honour to accede to my request," said Mr. Walters. "It is a matter of the utmost importance."

"Is your next witness available, Mr. Lethbridge?" asked the judge.

"Surely, Your Honour, you're not going to allow the cross-examination of this witness to be postponed?" protested Mr. Lethbridge. "My learned friend has given no reason for such a course."

Sir Henry Hodson looked at the court clock.

"It is now within a quarter of an hour of the ordinary time for adjournment," he began. "I think the fairest way out of the difficulty will be to adjourn the court now until to-morrow morning."

There was a loud buzz of conversation when the court adjourned. After asking Chippenfield and Rolfe to wait for him, Crewe made his way to Mr. Walters, and, after a few whispered words with that gentleman, Mr. Mathers, his junior, and Mr. Salter, the instructing solicitor, he returned to Chippenfield and Rolfe and asked them to accompany him in a taxi-cab to Riversbrook.

"What do you want to go out there for?" asked Inspector Chippenfield. "You don't expect to discover anything there this late in the day, do you?"

"I want to find out whether this man Kemp is lying or telling the truth."

"Of course he is lying," replied the positive police official. "When you've had as much experience with criminals as I have had, Mr. Crewe, you won't expect a word of truth from any of them."

"Well, let us go to Riversbrook and prove that he is lying," said Crewe.

"We'll go with you," said Inspector Chippenfield, speaking for Rolfe and himself. He did not understand how Crewe expected to obtain any evidence at Riversbrook about the truth or falsity of Kemp's story, but he did not intend to admit that. "But you can set your mind at rest. No jury will believe Kemp after we've given them his record in cross-examination."

Rolfe, whose association with Crewe in the case had awakened in him a keen admiration for the private detective's methods and abilities, permitted himself to defy his superior officer to the extent of saying that "the best way to prove Kemp a liar is to prove that his story is false."

During the drive to Hampstead from the Old Bailey the three men discussed Kemp and his past record. It was recalled that less than twelve months ago, while he was serving three years for burglary, his daughter had provided the newspapers with a sensation by dying in the dock while sentence was being passed on her. According to Inspector Chippenfield, who had been in charge of the case against her, she was a stylish, good-looking girl, and when dressed up might easily have been mistaken for a lady.

"She got in touch with a flash gang of railway thieves from America," said Inspector Chippenfield, helping himself to a cigar from Crewe's proffered case. "They used to work the express trains, robbing the passengers in the sleeping berths. She was neatly caught at Victoria Station in calling for a dressing-case that had been left at the cloak room by one of the gang. Inside the dressing-case was Lady Sinclair's jewel case, which had been stolen on the journey up from Brighton. The thief, being afraid that he might be stopped at Victoria Station when the loss of the jewel case was discovered, had placed it inside his dressing-case, and had left the dressing-case at the cloak room. He sent Dora Kemp for it a few days later, as he believed he had outwitted the police. But I'd got on to the track of the jewels, and after removing them from the dressing-case in the cloak room I had the cloak room watched. When Dora Kemp called for the dressing-case and handed in the cloakroom ticket, the attendant gave my men the signal and she was arrested."

"She died of heart disease while on trial, didn't she?" asked Crewe.

"Yes," replied Inspector Chippenfield. "Sir Horace Fewbanks was the judge. He gave her five years. And no sooner were the words out of his mouth than she threw up her hands and fell forward in the dock. She was dead when they picked her up."

"She was as game as they make them," put in Rolfe. "We tried to get her to give the others away, but she wouldn't, though she would have got off with a few months if she had. The gang got frightened and cleared out. They left her in the lurch, but she wouldn't give one of them away."

"It was Holymead who defended her," said Chippenfield. "It was a strange thing for him to do—leading barristers don't like touching criminal cases, because, as a rule, there is little money and less credit to be got out of them. But Holymead did some queer things at times, as you know. He must have taken up the case out of interest in the girl herself, for I'm certain she hadn't the money to brief him. And I did hear afterwards that Holymead undertook to see that she was decently buried."

"Why, that explains it!" exclaims Crewe, in the voice of a man who had solved a difficulty.

"Explains what?" asked Inspector Chippenfield.

"Explains why her father has taken the risk of coming forward in this case to give evidence for Holymead. Gratitude for what Holymead had done for his girl while he was in prison. My experience of criminals is that they frequently show more real gratitude to those who do them a good turn than people in a respectable walk of life. Besides, you know what a sentimental value people of his class attach to seeing their kin buried decently. If Holymead hadn't come forward the girl would have been buried as a pauper, in all probability."

"But I don't see that old Kemp is taking much risk," said Inspector Chippenfield. "He is only perjuring himself, and he is too used to that to regard it as a risk."

"Don't you think he will be in an awkward position if the jury were to acquit Holymead?" asked Crewe. "One jury has already said that Sir Horace Fewbanks was dead when Birchill broke into the house, and if this jury believes Kemp's story and says Sir Horace was alive when Holymead left it, don't you think Kemp will conclude that it will be best for him to disappear? Some one must have killed Sir Horace after Holymead left, and before Birchill arrived."

"Whew! I never thought of that," said Rolfe candidly.

"Kemp is a liar from first to last," said Inspector Chippenfield decisively.

CHAPTER XXXI

When they reached Riversbrook they entered the carriage drive and traversed the plantation until they stood on the edge of the Italian garden facing the house. The gaunt, irregular mansion stood empty and deserted, for Miss Fewbanks had left the place after her father's funeral, with the determination not to return to it. The wind whistled drearily through the nooks and crannies of the unfinished brickwork of the upper story, and a faint evening mist rose from the soddened garden and floated in a thin cloud past the library window, as though the ghost of the dead judge were revisiting the house in search of his murderer. The garden had lost its summer beauty and was littered with dead leaves from the trees. The gathering greyness of an autumn twilight added to the dreariness of the scene.

"Kemp didn't say how far he stood from the house," said Crewe, "but we'll assume he stood at the edge of the plantation—about where we are standing now—to begin with. How far are we from that library window, Chippenfield?"

"About fifty yards, I should say," said the inspector, measuring it with his eye.

"I should say seventy," said Rolfe.

"And I say somewhere midway between the two," said Crewe, with a smile. "But we will soon see. Just hold down the end of this measuring tape, one of you." He produced a measuring tape as he spoke, and started to unwind it, walking rapidly towards the house as he did so. "Sixty-two yards!" he said, as he returned. He made a note of the distance in his pocket-book. "So much for that," he said, "but that's not enough. I want you to stand under the library window, Rolfe, by that chestnut-tree in front of it, and act as pivot for the measuring tape while I look at that window from various angles. My idea is to go in a semicircle right round the garden, starting at the garage by the edge of the wood, so as to see the library window and measure the distance at every possible point at which Kemp could have stood."

"You're going to a lot of trouble for nothing, if your object is to try and prove that he couldn't have seen into the window," grunted Inspector Chippenfield, in a mystified voice. "Why, I can see plainly into the window from here."

Crewe smiled, but did not reply. Followed by Rolfe, he went back to the tree by the library window, where he posted Rolfe with the end of the tape in his hand. Then he walked slowly back across the garden in the direction of the garage, keeping his eye on the library window on the first floor from which Kemp, according to his evidence, had seen Sir Horace leaning out after Holymead had left the house. He returned to the tree, noting the measurement in his book as he did so, and then repeated the process, walking backwards with his eye fixed on the window, but this time taking a line more to the left. Again and again he repeated the process, until finally he had walked backwards from the tree in narrow segments of a big semicircle, finishing up on the boundary of the Italian garden on the other side of the grounds, and almost directly opposite to the garage from which he had started.

"There's no use going further back than that," he said, turning to Inspector Chippenfield, who had followed him round, smoking one of Crewe's cigars, and very much mystified by the whole proceedings, though he would not have admitted it on any account. "At this point we practically lose sight of the window altogether, except for an oblique glimpse. Certainly Kemp would not come as far back as this—he would have no object in doing so."

"I quite agree with you," said Inspector Chippenfield. "He would stand more in the front of the house. The tree in front of the house doesn't obstruct the view of the window to any extent."

The tree to which Inspector Chippenfield referred was a solitary chestnut-tree, which grew close to the house a little distance from the main entrance, and reached to a height of about forty feet. Its branches were entirely bare of leaves, for the autumn frosts and winds had swept the foliage away.

Rolfe, who had been watching Crewe's manoeuvres curiously, walked up to them with the tape in his hand. He glanced at the library window on the first floor as he reached them.

"Kemp could have seen the library window if he had stood here," he said. "I should say that if the blind were up it would be possible to see right into the room."

"What do you say, Chippenfield?" asked Crewe, turning to that officer.

Inspector Chippenfield had taken his stand stolidly on the centre path of the Italian garden, directly in front of the window of the library.

"I say Kemp is a liar," he replied, knocking the ash off his cigar. "A d——d liar," he added emphatically. "I don't believe he was here at all that night."

"But if he was here, do you think he saw Sir Horace leaning out of the window?"

"I don't see what was to prevent him," was the reply. "But my point is that he was a liar and that he wasn't here at all."

"And you, Rolfe—do you think Kemp could have seen Sir Horace leaning out of the window if he had been here?"

"I should say so," remarked Rolfe, in a somewhat puzzled tone.

"I am sorry I cannot agree with either of you," said Crewe. "I think Kemp was here, but I am sure he couldn't have seen Sir Horace from the window. Kemp has been up here during the past few days in order to prepare his evidence, and he's been led astray by a very simple mistake. If a man were to lean outside the library window now there would not be much difficulty in identifying him, but when the murder took place it would have been impossible to see him from any part of the garden or grounds."

"Why?" demanded Inspector Chippenfield.

"Because it was the middle of summer when Sir Horace Fewbanks was murdered. At that time that chestnut-tree would be in full leaf, and the foliage would hide the window completely. Look at the number of branches the tree has! They stretch all over the window and even round the corners of that unfinished brickwork on the first floor by the side of the library window. A man could no more see through that tree in summer time than he could see through a stone wall."

"What did I tell you?" exclaimed Inspector Chippenfield in the voice of a man whose case had been fully proved. "Didn't I say Kemp was a liar? We'll call evidence in rebuttal to prove that he is a liar—that he couldn't have seen the window. And after Holymead is convicted I'll see if I cannot get a warrant out for Kemp for perjury."

"And yet Kemp did see Sir Horace that night," said Crewe quietly.

"How do you know? What makes you say that?" The inspector was unpleasantly startled by Crewe's contention.

"He was able to describe accurately how Sir Horace was dressed—for one thing," responded Crewe.

"He might have got that from Seldon's evidence," said Inspector Chippenfield thoughtfully. "He may have had some one in court to tell him what Seldon said."

"You do not think Lethbridge would be a party to such tactics?" said Crewe. "No, no. One could tell from the way he examined Seldon and Kemp on the point that it was in his brief."

"But the fact that Kemp knew how Sir Horace was dressed doesn't prove that he saw Sir Horace after Holymead left the house," said Rolfe. "Kemp may have seen Sir Horace before Holymead arrived."

"Quite true, Rolfe," said Crewe. "I haven't lost sight of that point. I think you will agree with me that there is a bit of a mystery here which wants clearing up."

They drove back to town, and, in accordance with the arrangement Crewe had made with Mr. Walters before leaving the court, they waited on that gentleman at his chambers in Lincoln's Inn. There Crewe told him of the result of their investigations at Riversbrook. Mr. Walters was professionally pleased at the prospect of destroying the evidence of Kemp. He was not a hard-hearted man, and personally he would have preferred to see Holymead acquitted, if that were possible, but as the prosecuting Counsel he felt a professional satisfaction in being placed in the position to expose perjured evidence.

"Excellent! excellent!" he exclaimed, rubbing his hands with gratification as he spoke. "Knowing what we know now, it will be a comparatively easy task to expose the witness Kemp under cross-examination, and show his evidence to be false." Mr. Walters looked as though he relished the prospect.

It was arranged that Inspector Chippenfield should be called to give evidence in rebuttal as to the impossibility of seeing the library window through the tree, and that an arboriculturist should also be called. Mr. Walters agreed to have the expert in attendance at the court in the morning.

But Crewe had something more on his mind, and he waited until Chippenfield and Rolfe had taken their departure in order to put his views before the prosecuting counsel. Then he pointed out to him that to prove that Kemp's evidence was false was merely to obtain a negative result. What he wanted was a positive result. In other words, he wanted Kemp's true story.

"You do not think, then, that Kemp is merely committing perjury in order to get Holymead off?" asked Walters meditatively. "You think he is hiding something?"

Crewe replied, with his faint, inscrutable smile, that he had no doubt whatever that such was the case. He thought Kemp's true story might be obtained if Walters directed his cross-examination to obtaining the truth instead of merely to exposing falsehood. It was evident to him that Kemp had come forward in order to save the prisoner. How far was he prepared to go in carrying out that object? When he was made to realise that his perjury, instead of helping Holymead, had helped to convince the jury of the prisoner's guilt, would he tell the true story of how much he knew?

"My own opinion is that he will," continued Crewe. "I studied his face very closely while he was in the box to-day, and I am convinced he would go far—even to telling the truth—in order to save the only man who was ever kind to him."

Walters was slow in coming round to Crewe's point of view. He had a high opinion of Crewe, for in his association with the case he had realised how skilfully Crewe had worked out the solution of the Riversbrook mystery. But he took the view that now the case was before the court it was entirely a matter for the legal profession to deal with. He pointed out to Crewe the professional view that his own duty did not extend beyond the exposure of Kemp's perjury. It was not his duty to give Kemp a second chance—an opportunity to qualify his evidence. He believed the defence had called Kemp in the belief that his evidence was true, but the defence must take the consequences if they built up their case on perjured evidence which they had not taken the trouble to sift.

Crewe entered into the professional view sympathetically, but he was not to be turned from his purpose. He felt that too much was at stake, and he lifted the discussion out of the atmosphere of professional procedure into that of their common manhood.

"Walters, I know you are not a vain man," he said, earnestly. "A personal triumph in this case means even less to you than it does to me. I have built up what I regard as an overwhelming case against Holymead. But it is based on circumstantial evidence, and I would willingly see the whole thing toppled over if by that means we could get the final truth. This man Kemp knows the truth, and you are in a position in which you can get the truth from him. It may be the last chance anyone will have of getting it. Apart from all questions of professional procedure, isn't there an obligation upon you to get at the truth?"

"If you put it that way, I believe there is," replied Walters slowly and meditatively. There was a pause, and then he spoke with a sudden impulse. "Yes, Crewe; you can depend on me. I'll do my best."

CHAPTER XXXII

The public interest in the Holymead trial on the second day was even greater than on the first. It was realised that Kemp's evidence had given an unexpected turn to the proceedings, and that if it could be substantiated the jury's verdict would be "not guilty." There were confident persons who insisted that Kemp's evidence was sufficient to acquit the prisoner. But every one grasped the fact that the Counsel for the prosecution, by his action in applying for an adjournment of the cross-examination of Kemp, clearly realised that his case was in danger if the evidence of the first witness for the defence could not be broken down.

The public appetite for sensation having been whetted by sensational newspaper reports of the latest phase of the Riversbrook mystery, there was a great rush of people to the Old Bailey early on the morning of the second day to witness the final stages of the trial. The queue in Newgate Street commenced to assemble at daybreak, and grew longer and longer as the day wore on, but it was composed of persons who did not know that there was not the slightest possibility of their gaining admittance to Number One Court. The policeman who was invested with the duty of keeping the queue close to the wall of the building forbore to break this sad news to them. Being faithful to the limitations of the official mind, he believed that the right thing to do was to let the people in the queue receive this important information from the sergeant inside. How was he to know without authority from his superior officer that any of these people wanted to be admitted to Number One Court? So the policeman pared his nails, gallantly "minding" the places of pretty girls in the queue who, worn out by hours of waiting in the cold, desired to slip away to a neighbouring tea-shop to get a cup of tea before the court opened, and sternly rebuking enterprising youths who endeavoured to wedge themselves in ahead of their proper place.

The body of the court was packed before the proceedings commenced. The number of ladies present was even greater than on the first day, and the resources of the ushers were severely taxed to find accommodation for them all. In the back row Crewe noticed Mrs. Holymead, accompanied by Mademoiselle Chiron. They had not been in court on the previous day. Mrs. Holymead seemed anxious to escape notice, but Crewe could see that although she looked anxious and distressed, she was buoyed up by a new hope, which doubtless had come to her since Kemp had given his evidence.

There was an expectant silence in the court when Mr. Justice Hodson took his seat and the names of the jurymen were called over. Kemp entered the witness-box with a more confident air than he had worn the previous day. Mr. Walters rose to begin his cross-examination, and the witness faced the barrister with the air of an old hand who knew the game, and was not to be caught by any legal tricks or traps.

"You said yesterday, witness," commenced Mr. Walters, adjusting his glasses and glancing from his brief to the witness and from the witness back to the brief again, "that you saw the prisoner enter the gate at Riversbrook about 9.30 on the night of the 18th of August?"

"Yes." The monosyllable was flung out as insolently as possible. The speaker watched his interrogator with the lowering eyes of a man at war with society, and who realised that he was facing one of his natural enemies.

"Did he see you?"

"No."

"You are quite sure of that?"

"Haven't I just said so?"

"Do not be insolent, witness"—it was the judge's warning voice that broke into the cross-examination—"answer the questions."

"How long was it after the prisoner entered the carriage drive that you went to the edge of the plantation and heard voices upstairs?" continued Mr. Walters.

"I went as soon as Mr. Holymead passed me."

"How far were you from the house?"

"About sixty yards."

"And from that distance you could hear the voices?"

"Yes."

"Plainly?"

"Not very. I could hear the voices, but I couldn't hear what they were saying."

"Were they angry voices?"

"They seemed to me to be talking loudly."

"Yet you couldn't hear what they were saying?"

"No; I was sixty yards away."

"You said in your evidence in chief that the talking continued half an hour. Did you time it?"

"No."

"Then what made you swear that?"

"I said about half an hour. I smoked out a pipeful of tobacco while I was standing there, and that would be about half an hour." Kemp disclosed his broken teeth in a faint grin.

"What happened next?"

"I heard the front door slam, and I saw somebody walking across the garden, and go into the carriage drive towards the gate."

"Did you recognise who it was?"

"Yes; Mr. Holymead." Kemp looked at the prisoner as he gave the answer.

"You swear it was the prisoner?"

"I do."

"Let me recall your evidence in chief, witness. You swore that you identified Mr. Holymead as he went in because he struck a match to look at the time as he passed you, and you saw his face. Did he strike matches as he went out?"

"No."

"Then how are you able to swear so positively as to his identity in the dark?"

Kemp considered a moment before replying.

"Because I know him well and I was close to him," he said at length. "I was close enough to him almost to touch him. I knew him by his walk, and by the look of him. It was him right enough, I'll swear to that."

"I put it to you, witness," persisted Counsel, "that you could not positively identify a man in a plantation at that time of night. Do you still swear it was Mr. Holymead?"

"I do," replied Kemp doggedly.

"What did you do then?"

"I stayed where I was."

"What for?"

"I don't know. I didn't have any particular reason. I just stayed there watching."

"Did you think the prisoner might return?"

"No," replied the witness quickly. "Why should I think that?"

"How long did you stay watching the house?"

"It might be a matter of ten minutes more."

"And the prisoner didn't return during that time?"

"No," replied the witness emphatically.

"What did you do after that?"

"I went to the Tube station."

"Prisoner might have returned after you left?"

"I suppose he might," replied the witness reluctantly.

"Well, now, witness, you say you stayed ten minutes after Holymead left, and during that time Sir Horace opened the window and leaned out of it?"

"Yes."

"You saw him distinctly?"

"Yes."

"You are sure it was Sir Horace Fewbanks?"

"Yes."

"Now, witness," said Mr. Walters, suddenly changing his tone to one of more severity than he had previously used, "you have told us that you heard Sir Horace Fewbanks and the prisoner in the library while you stood in the wood by the garage, and that subsequently you saw Sir Horace leaning out of the window after the prisoner had gone. You are quite sure you were able to see and hear all this from where you stood?"

"Yes."

"Are you aware, witness, that there is a large chestnut-tree at the side of the library, in front of the window?"

Kemp considered for a moment.

"Yes," he said.

"And did not that tree obstruct your view of the library window?"

"No."

"Witness," said Mr. Walters solemnly, "listen to me. This tree did not obstruct your view when you went to Riversbrook a week or so ago to decide on the nature of the evidence you would give in this court. It is bare of leaves now, and you could see the library window and even see into the library from where you stood. But I put it to you that on the 18th of August, when this tree was covered with its summer foliage, you could no more have seen the library window behind its branches than you could have seen the inhabitants of Mars. What answer have you got to that, witness?"

There was a slight stir in court—an expression of the feeling of tension among the spectators. Kemp drew the back of his hand across his lips, then moistened his lips with his tongue.

"Come, witness, give me an answer," thundered prosecuting Counsel.

"I tell you I saw him after Mr. Holymead had left," declared Kemp defiantly. His voice had suddenly become hoarse.

To the surprise of the members of the legal profession who were in court, Mr. Walters, instead of pressing home his advantage, switched off to something else.

"I believe you have a feeling of gratitude towards the prisoner?" he asked, in a milder tone.

"I have," said Kemp. His defiant, insolent attitude had suddenly vanished, and he gave the impression of a man who feared that every question contained a trap.

"He did something for a relative of yours which at that time greatly relieved your mind?"

"He did, and I'll never forget it."

"Well, we won't go further into that at present. But it is a fact that you would like to do him a good turn?"

"Yes."

"You came here with the intention of doing him a good turn?"

Kemp considered for a moment before answering:

"Yes."

"You came here with the intention of giving evidence that would get him off?"

"Yes."

"You came here with the intention of committing perjury in order to get him off?" Mr. Walters waited, but there was no reply to the question, and he added, "You see what your perjured evidence has done for him?"

"What has it done?" asked Kemp sullenly.

"It has established the prisoner's guilt beyond all reasonable doubt in the minds of men of common sense. You did not see Sir Horace Fewbanks that night after the prisoner left him. You could not have seen him even if he had leaned out of the window. But your whole story is a lie, because Sir Horace was dead when the prisoner left him."

"He was not," shouted Kemp. "I saw him alive. I saw him as plain as I see you now."

The man in court who was most fascinated by the witness was Crewe. He had watched every movement of Kemp's face, every change in the tone of his voice.

"I wonder what the fool will say next," whispered Inspector Chippenfield to Crewe.

"He will tell us how Sir Horace Fewbanks was shot," was Crewe's reply.

Mr. Walters approached a step nearer to the witness-box. "You saw him as plainly as you see me now?" he repeated.

"Yes," declared Kemp, who, it was evident, was labouring under great excitement. "You say I came here to commit perjury if it would get him off." He pointed with a dramatic finger to the man in the dock. "I did. And I came here to get him off by telling the truth if perjury didn't do it. You say I've helped to put the rope round his neck. But I'm man enough to tell the truth. I'll get him off even if I have to swing for it myself."

This outburst from the witness-box created a sensation in court. Many of the spectators stood up in order to get a better view of the witness, and some of the ladies even jumped on their seats. Mr. Justice Hodson was momentarily taken aback. His first instinct was to check the witness and to ask him to be calm, but the witness took no notice of him. He displayed his judicial authority by an impressive descent of an uplifted hand which compelled the unruly spectators to resume their seats.

It was on Mr. Walters that Kemp concentrated his attention. It was Mr. Walters whom he set himself to convince as if he were the man who could set the prisoner free. Of the rest of the people in court Kemp in his excitement had become oblivious.

"Listen to me," said Kemp, "and I'll tell you who shot this scoundrel. He was a scoundrel, I say, and he ought to have been in gaol himself instead of sending other people there. I went up to the house that night to see if everything was clear, or whether that cur Hill had laid a trap—that part of my evidence is true. And from behind a tree in the plantation I saw Mr. Holymead pass me—he struck a match to look at the time, and I saw his face distinctly. A few minutes afterwards I heard loud, angry voices coming from somewhere upstairs in the house. I thought the best thing I could do was to find out what it was about. I said to myself that Mr. Holymead might want help. I walked across the garden and found that the hall door was wide open. I went inside and crept upstairs to the library. The light in the hall was turned on, as well as a little lamp on the turn of the staircase behind a marble figure holding some curtains, which led the way to the library. The library door was open an inch or two, and I listened.

"I could hear them quite plainly. Mr. Holymead was telling him what he thought of him. And no wonder. It made my blood boil to think of such a scoundrel sitting on the bench and sentencing better men than himself. I thought of the way in which he had killed my girl by giving her five years. It was the shock that killed her. Five years for stealing nothing, for she didn't handle the jewels. And here he had been stealing a man's wife and nothing said except what Mr. Holymead called him. I stood there listening in case they started to fight, and I might be wanted. But they didn't.

"I heard Mr. Holymead step towards the door, and I slipped away from where I had been standing. I saw the door of another room near me, and I opened it and went in quickly. I closed the door behind me, but I did not shut it. I looked through the crack and saw Mr. Holymead making his way downstairs. He walked as if he didn't see anything, and I watched him till he went through the curtains on the stairs at the bend of the staircase and I could see him no more.

"Then I heard a step, and looking through the crack I saw the judge coming out of the library. He walked to the head of the stairs and began to walk slowly down them. But when he reached the bend where the curtains and the marble figure were, he turned round and walked up the stairs again. He walked along as though he was thinking, with his hands behind his back, and nodding his head a little, and a little cruel, crafty smile on his face. He passed so close to me that I could have touched him by putting out my hand, and he went into the library again, leaving the door open behind him.

"Then suddenly, as I stood there, the thought came over me to go in to him and tell him what I thought about him. I opened the door softly so as not to frighten him, and walked out into the passage and into the library, and as I did so I took my revolver out of my pocket and carried it in my hand. I wasn't going to shoot him, but I meant to hold him up while I told him the truth.

"He was standing at the opposite side of the room with his back towards me and a book in his hand, but a board creaked as I stepped on it, and he swung round quickly. He was surprised to see me, and no mistake. 'What do you want here?' he said, in a sharp voice, and

I could see by the way he eyed the revolver that he was frightened. Then I opened out on him and told him off for the damned scoundrel he was. And he didn't like that either. He edged away to a corner, but I kept following him round the room telling him what I thought of him. And seeing him so frightened, I put the revolver back in my pocket and walked close to him while I told him all the things I could think of.

"As I thought of my poor girl that he'd killed I grew savage, and I told him that I had a good mind to break every bone in his body. He threatened to have me arrested for breaking into the place, but I only laughed and hit him across the face. He backed away from me with a wicked look in his eyes, and I followed him. He backed quickly towards the door, and before I knew what game he was up to he made a dart out of the room. But I was too quick for him. I got him at the head of the stairs and dragged him back into the room and shut the door and stood with my back against it. I told him I hadn't finished with him. I had mastered him so quickly, and was able to handle him so easily, that I didn't watch him as closely as I ought to have done. He had backed away to his desk with his hand behind him, and suddenly he brought it up with a revolver in his hand.

"'Now it's my turn,' he said to me with his cunning smile. Throw up your hands.'

"I saw then it was man for man. If I let him take me I was in for a good seven years. I'd sooner be dead than do seven years for him. 'Shoot and be damned,' I said. I ducked as I spoke, and as I ducked I made a dive with my hand for my hip pocket where I had put my revolver. He fired and missed. He fired again, but his toy revolver missed fire, for I heard the hammer click. But that was his last chance. I fired at his heart and he dropped beside the desk, I didn't wait for anything more—I bolted. I got tangled in the staircase curtains and fell down the stairs. As I was falling I thought what a nice trap I would be in if I broke my leg and had to lie there until the police came. But I wasn't much hurt and I got up and dashed out of the house and over the fence into the wood, the way I came."

He stopped, and his gaze wandered round the hushed court till it rested on the prisoner, who with his hands grasping the rail of the dock had leaned forward in order to catch every word. Kemp turned his gaze from the man in the dock to the man in the scarlet robe on the bench, and it was to the judge that he addressed his concluding words.

"You can call it murder, you can call it manslaughter, you can call it justifiable homicide, you can call it what you like, but what I say is that the man you have in the dock had nothing to do with it. It was me that killed him. Let him go, and put me in his place."

He held his hands outstretched with the wrists together as though waiting for the handcuffs to be placed on them.

CHAPTER XXXIII

An hour after the trial Crewe entered the chambers of Mr. Walters, K.C.

"I congratulate you on the way you handled him in the witness-box," said Crewe, who was warmly welcomed by the barrister. "You did splendidly to get it all out of him—and so dramatically too."

"I think it is you who deserves all the congratulations," replied Walters. "If it had not been for you there would not have been such a sensational development at the trial and in all probability Kemp's evidence would have got Holymead off."

"Yes, I'm glad to think that Holymead would have got off even if I hadn't seen through Kemp," replied Crewe thoughtfully. "I made a bad mistake in being so confident that he was the guilty man."

"The completeness of the circumstantial evidence against him was extraordinary," said Walters, to whom the legal aspects of the case appealed. "Personally I am inclined to blame Holymead himself for the predicament in which he was placed. If he had gone to the police after the murder was discovered, told them the story of his visit to Sir Horace that night, and invited investigation into the truth of it, all would have been well."

"No," said Crewe in a voice which indicated a determination not to have himself absolved at the expense of another. "The fact that he did not do what he ought to have done does not mitigate my sin of having had the wrong man arrested. The mistake I made was in not going to see him before the warrant was taken out. If I had had a quiet talk with him I think I would have been able to discover a flaw in my case against him. What made me confident it was flawless was the fact that both his wife and her French cousin believed him to be guilty. Mademoiselle Chiron followed Holymead from the country on the 18th of August with the intention of averting a tragedy. She arrived at Riversbrook too late for that, but in time to see Sir Horace expire, and naturally she thought that Holymead had shot him. When Mrs. Holymead realised that I also suspected her husband and had accumulated some evidence against him, she sent Mademoiselle Chiron to me with a concocted story of how the murder had been committed by a more or less mythical husband belonging to Mademoiselle's past. Ostensibly the reason for the visit of this extremely clever French girl was to induce me to deal with Rolfe, who had begun to suspect Mrs. Holymead of some complicity in the crime; but the real reason was to convince me that I was on the wrong track in suspecting Holymead. Of course she said nothing to me on that point. She produced evidence which convinced me that she was in the room when Sir Horace died, and, as I was quite sure that she believed Holymead to be guilty, I felt that there could be no doubt whatever of his guilt."

"It is one of the most extraordinary cases on record—one of the most extraordinary trials," said Walters. "You blame yourself for having had Holymead arrested but you have more than redeemed yourself by the final discovery when Kemp was in the witness-box that he was the guilty man. That was an inspiration."

"Hardly that," said Crewe with a smile. "I knew when he swore that he had seen Sir Horace leaning out of the library window that he was lying. After the murder was discovered I inspected the house and grounds carefully, and one of the first things of which I took a mental note was the fact that the foliage of the chestnut-tree completely hid the only window of the library."

"Ah, but there is a difference between knowing Kemp was committing perjury and knowing that he was the guilty man."

"There is at least a distinct connection between the two facts," said Crewe, who after his mistake in regard to Holymead was reluctant to accept any praise. "Kemp's description of the way in which Sir Horace was dressed showed that he had seen him. The inference that Kemp had been inside the house was irresistible. Sir Horace had arrived home at 7 o'clock and it was not likely that Kemp would hang about Riversbrook—the scene of a prospective burglary—until after dark, which at that time of the year would be about 8.30. He must have seen Sir Horace after dark, and in order to be able to say how the judge was dressed he must have seen him at close quarters. The rest was a matter of simple deduction. Kemp inside the house listening to the angry interview between Holymead and Fewbanks—Kemp with his hatred of the judge who had killed his daughter in the dock and with his desire to do Holymead a good turn—I had previously had proof of that from my boy Joe, whom you have seen. Besides Kemp fitted into my reconstruction of the tragedy on the vital question of time. How long did Sir Horace live after being shot? The medical opinions I was able to obtain on the point varied, but after sifting them I came to the conclusion that though he might have lived for half an hour, it was more probable that he had died within ten minutes of being hit."

"How is that vital?" asked Walters, who was keenly interested in understanding how Crewe had arrived at his conviction of Kemp's guilt.

"Holymead's appointment with Sir Horace at Riversbrook was for 9.30 p.m. The letter found in Sir Horace's pocket-book fixed that time. It was exactly 11 p.m. when he got into a taxi at Hyde Park Corner after his visit to Riversbrook. On that point the driver of the taxi was absolutely certain. I was so anxious for him to make it 11.30 that I went to see him twice about it. Assuming that Holymead arrived at Riversbrook at 9.30, I allowed half an hour for his angry interview with Sir Horace, half an hour for the walk from Riversbrook to Hampstead Tube station, and half an hour for the journey from Hampstead to Hyde Park Corner, which would have involved a change at Leicester Square. As I could not induce the driver of the taxi to make Holymead's appearance at Hyde Park Corner 11.30 instead of 11, I had to admit that Holymead must have left Riversbrook at 10. But it was 10.30 according to Mademoiselle Chiron when she found Sir Horace dying on the floor of the library. Therefore if Holymead did the shooting, the victim's death agonies must have lasted half an hour or more. Medically that was not impossible, but somewhat improbable. But a meeting between Kemp and Sir Horace after Holymead had gone filled in the blank in time. That came home to me yesterday when Kemp was in the witness-box committing perjury in his determination to get Holymead off. I take it that the interview between Kemp and his victim lasted about 20 minutes. Therefore Sir Horace was shot about 10.20; certainly before 10.30, for Mademoiselle heard no shots while nearing the house."

"You have worked it out very ingeniously," said Walters. "You must find the work of crime detection very fascinating. I am afraid that if I had been in your place—that is if I had known as much about the tragedy as you do—when Kemp was in the witness-box yesterday, I would not have seen anything more in his evidence than the fact that he was committing perjury in order to help Holymead."

"I think you would," said Crewe. "These discoveries come to one naturally as the result of training one's mind in a particular direction."

"They come to you, but they wouldn't come to me," said Walters with a smile. "But do you think Kemp's story of how Sir Horace was shot is literally true? Do you think Sir Horace got in the first shot and then tried to fire again? If that is so, I don't see how they can hope to convict Kemp of murder—a jury would not go beyond a verdict of manslaughter in such a case."

"You handled Kemp so well that he was too excited to tell anything but the truth," said Crewe. "Sir Horace fired first and missed—the bullet which Chippenfield removed from the wall of the library shows that—and he pulled the trigger again but the cartridge which had been in the revolver for a considerable time, probably for years, missed fire. Here is a silent witness to the truth of that part of Kemp's story."

Crewe produced from a waistcoat pocket one of the four cartridges he had removed from the revolver Mademoiselle Chiron had handed to him and he placed it on the table. On the cap of the cartridge was a mark where the hammer had struck without exploding the powder.